A COLORADO CLAIM

JOANNE ROCK

CROSSING TWO
LITTLE LINES

JOSS WOOD

MILLS & BOON

First Published in Great Britain 2022
by Mills & Boon, an imprint of HarperCollins*Publishers* Ltd
1 London Bridge Street, London, SE1 9GF

www.harpercollins.co.uk

HarperCollins*Publishers*
1st Floor, Watermarque Building,
Ringsend Road, Dublin 4, Ireland

A Colorado Claim © 2022 Joanne Rock
Crossing Two Little Lines © 2022 Joss Wood

ISBN: 978-0-263-30384-1

0722

MIX
Paper from
responsible sources
FSC™ C007454

This book is produced from independently certified FSC™ paper to ensure responsible forest management.

For more information visit: www.harpercollins.co.uk/green

Printed and Bound in Spain using 100% Renewable electricity at CPI Black Print, Barcelona

A COLORADO CLAIM

JOANNE ROCK

For my one and only, very best sister, Linda Watson.

One

Normally, Los Angeles-based child psychologist Lark Barclay wouldn't have wasted a Thursday afternoon day-dreaming about her next adult beverage.

Today wasn't any ordinary Thursday.

And not just because she'd flown halfway across the country to be seated in a Routt County, Colorado, court-room between the sisters she'd barely spoken to in the past decade. No, this afternoon was also different because she'd rescheduled all of her client appointments for a two-week stretch to be present at this all-important probate hearing. She hated rescheduling, taking great care to accommodate vulnerable patients who relied on her help. Yet she'd shuffled her schedule anyhow to show solidarity with her estranged siblings and to finally—*finally*—achieve a long overdue victory in an ongoing battle with her self-centered prick of a father.

Except her father hadn't shown up to today's hearing.

Even though *he'd* been the one to contest his mother's will to prevent his daughters from inheriting Crooked Elm Ranch. The judge had informed Lark, Jessamyn and Fleur Barclay that their dad's attorney had requested a continuance because they needed more time to build their case, and the judge had granted it.

Cue the need for day drinking.

"The bastard," Jessamyn muttered under her breath after the judge refused to delay the trial for the requested three weeks but did grant a one-week delay. Younger than Lark by four years, Jessamyn was the middle child who'd never acted like one. The peacekeeping role in the Barclay clan belonged to their baby sister, Fleur, while Jessamyn was more apt to kick ass and take names. "He couldn't have given us a heads-up that he was trying to delay the hearing?"

The judge moved on to the next case on her docket, freeing the Barclay sisters to leave the courtroom.

Lark, leading the way between the benches toward the exit, bit her tongue to prevent herself from responding to her sister's gripe. Jessamyn had been their father's protégé in his real estate development business, only recently coming around to recognizing what an underhanded tool Mateo Barclay could be. It galled Lark a little that Jessamyn had netted huge financial gains by closing her eyes to the truth of their father's character for most of their lives.

But Lark had promised Fleur that she would give Jessamyn a chance to prove she'd changed, a promise Lark took all the more seriously since Jessamyn had learned she was pregnant. How could she hassle an expectant mom? So Lark held in the damning words she would have preferred to speak, all the while hoping she'd spot a bar across the street once they left this godforsaken courthouse. Preferably one with a two-for-one happy hour special.

"It's fine that he postponed," Lark told Jessamyn, willing the words to be true. "The extra week gives us more time to prepare, too."

Even as the added days away from her practice could do harm to her patients. She made a mental note to increase her hours allotted for telehealth visits this week to cover the gap. At least the judge had listened to their attorney's objection that the sisters—namely Lark—could not remain in Catamount indefinitely. She had a life in Los Angeles to get back to once she settled her family affairs.

Then, shoving open the door to exit probate court, she entered the long, echoing corridor connecting that room to many more in the historic Routt County building. Marble floors stretched in either direction, while the ornate molding around every door gleamed. A few people milled outside other courts in session, including the men who waited for her sisters: Drake Alexander, a Catamount, Colorado, native and former bull rider who'd fallen hard for Lark's sister Fleur, and Ryder Wakefield, a search and rescue volunteer who had recently renewed a relationship with Jessamyn.

Well, more than *renewed*, since Ryder was the father of the child Jessamyn carried.

Since they were being called as witnesses, they hadn't come into the court. But clearly both Drake and Ryder were good, upstanding men. Wealthy, too. Exceedingly so. Too bad it was still tough for Lark to witness the electric emotions of new lovers as the pairs greeted one another. Her own failure in that department stung. Glancing away from the sappy reunions, Lark turned her gaze farther down the high-ceilinged corridor to where a mother entertained a toddler with a storybook. Next to her, a weather-beaten older man slumped on a wooden bench, absorbed in a racing form.

And, closer to Lark, a young couple dressed in matching suits with contrasting boutonnieres stared into one another's eyes, clearly on the verge of speaking marriage vows.

The sight of the pair, practically glowing with dreams for their future, provided one final gut-punch on a day already filled with cheap shots. Because Lark had been part of a couple like that once, standing beside a man she'd loved, ready to take on the world armed with nothing but foolish hope and romantic fantasies.

The memory of her short and ill-fated marriage to hockey star Gibson Vaughn sent a bitter pain through her breast even though they'd been divorced for just over two years. Twenty-six months and two days, if she was counting. Which, okay, maybe she was. But only because she didn't take it for granted that she'd been liberated from the sports media limelight ever since their split.

Free of stupid headlines about hockey's most eligible bachelor marrying a no-nonsense therapist. Free of insinuations that her superstar ex had tied himself to a hockey club with no playoff hopes to appease a bride who refused to relocate her therapy practice. Free of toxic social media comments about Gibson's dating life before he'd married her.

None of which would have bothered her if Gibson had spent even a quarter of the year with her. But the prolonged absences from home necessitated by his desire to prove himself the face of his team chipped away the foundations of their relationship. He hadn't been there when she'd needed him most.

"Lark?" Fleur's gentle voice broke through Lark's unhappy trip down memory lane. Her copper-haired sister turned gray eyes on her, still as lovely as when she'd won rodeo queen titles all over the West. "Did you want to go for a late lunch with us?"

Dragging her gaze from the husbands-to-be down the hall, Lark swallowed the regrets about her own marriage, determined to follow through on her solo plans for the afternoon. She hadn't hit a bar alone in years and this day had her feeling all kinds of edgy. Right now, she considered a tequila shot and beer chaser to be critical self-care.

"No, thank you." Lark flipped her heavy braid of dark hair behind one shoulder as she took in the sight of her sisters in love. Drake and Fleur had their arms around one another's waists, while Jessamyn's fingers laced securely through Ryder's. "I need to—" she hesitated, unwilling to share the sad truth that she couldn't abide being around the overload of love and hormones that oozed from every one of the four people in front of her "—check in with a client. I'll see you at Crooked Elm tonight."

Making a show of digging in her bag for her phone, Lark gave a half-hearted wave to her sisters as they departed with their respective men.

Once they were gone, Lark used her search browser to find the closest dive bar and found a likely candidate within walking distance. If she couldn't enjoy a courtroom victory over her lying cheat of a father today, she would use her rare time out of the office to indulge in something else that would bring her satisfaction.

Or maybe she needed to drink away the memories that being in a courtroom inevitably reawakened.

Like the day she'd stood in front of a judge and uttered the words, "irreconcilable differences." The death knell of her marriage to Gibson, and all the hopes and dreams that had gone with it.

Fueled with purpose, she jammed the device in her utilitarian cross-body bag. Was her purse a designer original? Not on a therapist's salary. Not with all her student loans. Was it even remotely feminine or delicate? Not for a woman who prized functionality above appearances.

Marching toward the exit with extra stomp in her step, she gave a polite nod to the security guards who worked the metal detector. Then, pushing her way out into the warm summer sunshine, she blinked at the small throng of people standing at the base of the courthouse steps.

Why did they look vaguely familiar?

She was certain she didn't recognize any of them in particular. But as a group, they stirred something in her memory.

The thought troubled her while she descended the stone steps. A moment later, vaguely registering the sound of the courtroom doors opening and closing behind her, she saw the small crowd move as one.

Coming toward her.

Lifting cameras she hadn't noticed before.

A moment's confusion faded as it occurred to her why the group looked familiar. Flashbacks to her former life scrolled through her brain as she recognized the scavenger behavior of reporters in "entertainment media."

And if they were here, it could only be to hound someone famous. Someone who, she slowly realized, must be behind her.

A sickening foreboding clamped her stomach in a fist. Catamount, Colorado only had so many celebrity residents.

Even as Lark thought it, she heard the first shout rise from the crowd of so-called journalists.

"Gibson! Over here, Gibson!" a woman's voice called from the left. "Can you tell us what you're doing at a courthouse?"

Gibson.

Lark froze in place on the stairs. Unable to take another step forward. Or backward.

Sort of like she'd been in the two years since her divorce.

Another reporter crowded closer, almost knocking Lark over as he lifted a boom mic above her head to a point behind her. "Gibson, is it true you're going to reconcile with your ex-wife?" the man shouted.

Cameras whirred, flashes popping in a strobe light effect that catapulted her back to some of the most infuriating moments of her life. Being caught on film at the grocery store at midnight when she'd needed supplies to help a scared mother and her daughter to escape a dangerous partner. Being hounded about Gibson's activities on a team road trip while Lark was in Los Angeles at a homeless shelter to advocate for one of her young patients.

But she couldn't think about that now when—impossibly—her ex-husband obviously stood behind her. She should pull a legger, dart away before anyone with a camera realized that the same "ex-wife" they were asking about stood just a few feet away.

For once, she was grateful her unmemorable looks had failed to draw attention since no one seemed to have made the connection. Yet.

Her sense of self-preservation kicking in, Lark ducked her head and shifted left, sidestepping the throng while all eyes were trained somewhere else. Their raised voices drowned out every other sound, even the thudding of her heart and—thankfully—the sound of her ex's voice if he bothered to respond to the questions. Even his voice was sexy, damn him. She pounded down the stairs, skirting the group, never looking back as she headed for the parking area. Screw the bar. She needed her car to escape.

Except, *crap*.

She'd left her rented vehicle on the other side of the building, only walking out the front entrance because her map app had pointed her this way toward the dive bar. Halting beside an extended cab pickup truck, she resisted the urge to look over her shoulder to possibly catch a glimpse of Gibson.

Think, think, think.

Squeezing her temples between her thumb and forefinger, she tried to settle her racing pulse. Told herself the reporters wouldn't have seen her. That, more importantly, Gibson Vaughn hadn't seen her. Had he?

A sudden clamor rose near the courthouse again. Lark glanced around to see the mob shifting in the opposite direction from her, like a swarm in pursuit of a new hive. Gibson must have moved away.

Lucky for her, he'd taken the mob with him.

Steadying herself with one hand on the gray fender of the big pickup truck, she wondered if she'd really escaped the media mayhem. Since when was she that fortunate?

Better yet, she'd dodged seeing her ex.

Shoulders slumping with relief, she debated returning to her car now. Would the path be paparazzi-free?

Adjusting the strap of her cross-body bag, she stepped out of the shadows of the pickup just as a low-slung sports car spun into view. Lark didn't need to see through the heavily tinted windows to know who would be behind the wheel of a Porsche 911 in a shade she happened to know was called Adriatic Blue.

Her gut sank to her feet as the driver's side window lowered.

Gibson Vaughn, in all his sexy glory, appeared in the driver's seat. From his dark, shoulder length hair that begged a woman's fingers to come through it to the kissable dent centered in his chin, the man had been the face of US hockey for nearly a decade for a reason. He not only played the game with a vengeance, but he was undeniably handsome. The scar through one eyebrow and the slight crook in his nose didn't begin to detract from those chiseled good looks.

"We've got about twenty seconds before they catch up." Gibson nodded toward the mob of reporters at the courthouse steps, all still looking in the wrong direction. "Hop in if you want to stay a step ahead of them."

She wished that her heartbeat skipped because she was panicked about being caught in the limelight again. But she knew perfectly well the erratic pulse and humming in her veins was all owing to the man who'd once vowed to love her forever. The man whose kisses had turned her inside out.

No way could she risk being close to him again.

"What will it be, Lark?" His voice broke through her scattered memories, terse and deep, while the engine of his high performance car purred with the promise of a fast getaway. "They're coming."

Why, in that moment, she chose to peer backward like Orpheus turning to see Eurydice, Lark couldn't have said. But the sight of the small group running with their microphones and recording equipment finally got her in motion. Especially when someone shouted, "Lark! Lark Barclay, have you reconciled with Gibson?"

She'd been recognized.

Another, deeper voice called, "Will you convince him to return to hockey?"

Her throat dried up. And this time, her speeding pulse had everything to do with panic.

Better to risk the emotional fallout of spending time with Gibson than to be surrounded by her old enemy the sports press.

Launching forward, she rounded the vehicle and flung open the passenger door before heaving herself inside the air-conditioned interior.

A second later, Gibson punched the gas, hurtling them out of the parking lot and away from the cameras. Her relief lasted for about a nanosecond before Gibson's silky baritone filled the coupe.

"It's good to see you again, Lark."

Judging by how fast her head whipped around, her forest-green eyes narrowing at him, Gibson would have thought he'd insulted Lark.

But then, hadn't that always been the way between them? He'd continually been a step behind his razor-sharp ex-wife, too consumed with his career to give her the time she deserved, and too slow to understand her moods and needs.

Except, of course, for one sort of need. They'd been remarkably in tune sexually no matter how much the rest of their relationship fell apart. And how was it he'd wound up thinking about *that* ten seconds after seeing her for the first time in two years?

She looked incredible, of course. Her minimalist wardrobe—a taupe-colored skirt and chestnut brown boots with a white button down today—always let the woman shine and not the clothes. Her one sexy accessory was her long, dark hair woven into a thick braid.

"Did I say something wrong?" he asked, pinning his eyes to the road and keeping them there. He headed west, ready to put distance between them and the media hounds sniffing out a story about his retirement.

In his peripheral vision, he could see Lark leaning into the leather seat, hear her heavy plait falling from her shoulder to rest beside her with a soft *thunk*. He had fond memories of the silky mane rarely seen loose. He'd found it sexy as hell to be the man who saw her undone at the end of a day.

"Just surprised you'd be glad to see me after the way we parted." Her voice always had a note of authority in it, like she'd never second-guessed herself in her life. He'd always assumed that it must be reassuring for her patients, who had to trust in her judgment. "You told me it would be best not to contact each other anymore."

Ah, damn. Just hearing his emotional words flung at him dragged him to the past and that painful day when she'd ended their marriage. His fingers flexed against the steering wheel as he turned onto the road that would lead to Catamount.

"I didn't mean we shouldn't ever speak again," he clarified, checking his rearview mirror to make sure they weren't followed. "At the time, I'd hoped taking a breather from one another would make it easier for us both to move on."

In the silence that followed, he mentally laid odds on her response. Something sharp without being downright cutting. He could envision her perfectly, recalling the way she preferred the thoughtful consideration of her words over blurting out anything to fill a conversational void. His gaze might be on the county route winding alongside the Yampa River, but his mind's eye saw only Lark, her lips pursed in thought.

Which led him to think about her mouth and how she never wore lip color. He'd loved that about her, the way she never hid behind makeup, never felt the need to camouflage herself. With Lark, you got exactly what you saw, and when it came to her lush mouth, that was an excellent thing. Her lips required no help to be seductive.

And the lack of cosmetics made it simpler to taste *her*.

"Did it?" she asked softly, her thoughtful tone surprising him as much as the question itself. "Did the absence of contact make moving on easier for you?"

The confidential note in her voice catapulted him back to late night pillow talk. Long distance calls from the road when he'd been in some nameless hotel with the team, and she would pick up the phone even if she were half-asleep to ask him about his day. Why hadn't he asked about hers more often? Why hadn't he thought to put her first in his life?

"Tough to say since it was still…difficult," he admitted, downshifting as he slowed for a stop sign. "But I thought maintaining a friendship would only make it harder to get over you."

He'd been vocal about wanting to stay together. To work through her problems with his career. But there had been more to it than that, and he'd never been able to pin down what had been the final straw for her. She'd always kept some part of herself tightly closed. She'd given him her body, but he'd never been sure what was going on in her mind. One day, he'd returned to their Los Angeles home from an eleven-day road trip through Canada and she'd had her bags packed.

That had been the second worst day of his life, topped only by the last time they'd been in a courtroom together to dissolve their brief marriage. He couldn't bear a repeat of that pain, her rejection rattling him to the core.

He hated failing at anything. From when he was young and his father abandoned the family, his job was to fix things for the people he cared about. His family and teammates. But Lark didn't need any fixing. And it had left him unsettled—not always in a good way.

"Right." She bit out the word, a chill creeping into her voice as she shifted in her seat. "You didn't want us to be friends. So why bother offering me a ride when the wolves are at our heels, all thanks to your decision to retire in Catamount? It wasn't difficult enough when we both lived in LA? Now we need to be neighbors here?"

Gibson ground his teeth together as he accelerated.

"I like Catamount. And just because I couldn't handle a friendship two years ago doesn't mean I would allow those reporters to hassle you. I know how much you value your privacy." All of which was true.

Yet, as he glanced her way again, his gaze snagged on the vee of her blouse and the shadowed patch of skin that hinted at her cleavage without being revealing. And he acknowledged that part of the reason he'd offered her a ride today was because he'd been floored to see her again.

He'd been in the Routt County Courthouse to establish conservatorship of his mother, who suffered from dementia. And he'd recognized Lark immediately, even from twenty-five yards behind her. Her all-business walk. Her feminine shape that her conservative outfits could never fully hide. And that perfectly straight hair, plaited with precision and clamped with a soft scrap of white cotton instead of a hair tie.

He'd tied those thin strips of cloth himself many times in the past, and he happened to know that it protected her from tresses from split ends. Watching the braid sway ever so slightly while she walked had been his downfall today, distracting him from the sports media who'd been lying in wait for him. How the hell had they learned he'd be in court today? He needed to keep out of the news cycle, damn it.

"In that case, thank you for the lift." She reached for the air vent and tilted it to blow higher on her face. "I want no part of the spotlight."

He didn't blame her. The media hadn't been kind to her. In an effort to shift the conversation away from unhappy memories, he asked, "Should I take you to Crooked Elm? Or do you need to return to the courthouse later? If we wait half an hour, the press will clear out."

"My car is back there, but I'd rather not chance returning for it." Folding her arms, she crossed her legs at the same time, her body language broadcasting how much she'd rather be almost anywhere besides in this car with him. "If you don't mind dropping me off at Crooked Elm, I'll ride in with my sisters tomorrow."

"Not a problem. I'm headed home anyway." The ranch he'd bought for his retirement from hockey shared a property line with the Barclay land, in fact, so taking her home couldn't be easier. He remembered from their talks before they split that she wasn't happy he'd decided to keep the home they'd once planned to live in together.

When she spoke again, her words were clipped, cool. "I appreciate it, Gibson. But this should be the last we see of each other while I'm in town. As you pointed out two years ago, there's no need to maintain a friendship."

Way to draw the battle lines, Lark.

He shouldn't be surprised, and yet the pinch of disappointment caught him off guard. He *had* moved on since their divorce, hadn't he? He'd dated, but nothing serious, and no one around here.

"If that's your preference, I'll certainly honor it," he

said carefully, driving around a tractor with tires that spilled over into the opposite lane. "But let me know if you need any help managing the media."

She pivoted in her seat, her arms wrapping tighter around her midsection. "What do you mean?"

"You heard them back there. They recognized you. I'm sure someone snapped a photo of us together before you got into the car." He wasn't sure why she'd looked at the reporters when he'd offered her the ride, but then, her life hadn't involved ducking the media for the past two years so maybe she'd forgotten the drill.

Head bent. Avoid. Avoid. Avoid.

Her small moan of dismay was so unlike the self-possessed woman he recalled from their marriage, that he did a double take. Had that sound emanated from Lark Barclay?

And how wrong was it for him to feel a sharp bolt of need to inspire that sound again—for purely carnal reasons?

"I forgot about that," she admitted, seeming to recover herself. Or at least, she shifted to look out the window again, away from him. "But I'm sure I'll be fine."

With an effort, he swallowed the urge to pull the car over and face her head-on. He wanted to look into those forest-green eyes. Try to read what was going on in her thoughts. Or maybe finally understand what had happened to send her running from their marriage.

"I heard about your father contesting your grandmother's will." He'd liked Antonia Barclay tremendously. She was strong, feisty and endlessly competent, managing a large property on her own long after her family had left the area. During the occasional visits he made to Catamount to set up his home here, she had encouraged him to try his hand at ranching even after things went to hell between him and Lark. "I assume you'll be at the court-house again soon. And there's a good chance the sports media will figure that out too, so they could be waiting to ambush you next time. If there's anything I can do—"

"Definitely not." She reached into the small brown bag she carried at her hip and withdrew her cellphone, an obvious social cue that she was done with the conversation. "Whatever happens, I'll handle it. Alone."

Same as ever.

Gibson increased his speed and refocused on the road, determined to end Lark's ordeal of having to sit beside him as soon as possible. He'd known she'd been hurt when things ended between them, but he'd always assumed she'd be happier without him. That she would move on faster since she was the one who'd decided to call it quits in the first place.

Now? He wondered if she'd recovered from their split any more than he had. He could have sworn he'd seen a hint of the old spark in her gaze when she'd first locked eyes with him today.

He'd felt the answering heat.

Fought the desire to act on it. For now, at least.

But his fierce competitive streak had helped drive him to the top of his career. And right now, that same hungry instinct hounded him to rekindle an old flame.

Two

The morning after her encounter with Gibson, Lark moved through the brightly tiled kitchen that had once belonged to her grandmother, flipping on the coffee-maker as she glanced outside the open window above the apron sink. The scent of late summer wildflowers filtered in on the warm breeze.

Dragging in deep breaths of fresh air, Lark told herself to enjoy the time here in her grandmother's house. This was real life, not whatever was happening online in the sports media world where she'd been photographed with Gibson the day before. Picking out the scents and sights of wild bergamot, fireweed, blanket flowers and columbine, Lark used the grounding technique she often taught in counseling sessions to calm her morning's anxieties about being back in the media spotlight, if only for the day. She'd also downloaded an app on her phone to try to minimize her exposure to social media, a trick she'd learned while still married to Gibson. She wouldn't get caught up in the old spirals of negative thinking that had always resulted from being married to an elite athlete.

She'd never thought for a moment that Gibson cheated on her, physically or romantically, but his energy had so often been focused on everyone around him, she felt overlooked at times.

Opening her eyes, Lark noticed out the window that Fleur's car was gone, which meant her chef sister was still at the Cowboy Kitchen, a local diner where she delivered fresh baked goods each morning. It was a way to earn money to finance Fleur's dream of opening a tapas place, and the Catamount community—small though it might be—had embraced Fleur's culinary skills. Now Fleur was doing local catering gigs too, preparing their Catalan grandmother's recipes and offering unique menus at weddings, birthday parties and other events.

When the coffee machine started to burble in earnest, Lark tugged open the old-fashioned refrigerator that contained bottle after bottle of goat's milk thanks to the three dairy goats Fleur kept. Bypassing these in favor of some soy milk she'd picked up at the store, Lark shut the fridge and poured herself a cup of coffee, the vibrant tiles echoing hollowly under her dishes.

The kitchen wasn't the same without Antonia Barclay. Back when Lark had been married to Gibson, and she'd helped him choose the house next door to this one for their off-season residence until he retired, she'd been so excited to spend more time in Catamount. She'd imagined shared summer afternoons with her grandmother at the very table where Lark carried her mug now to sit alone.

Then came the divorce, and she'd told herself she'd

find another time to spend with Gran. And then, last spring, time ran out. Her chest ached at the knowledge that she wouldn't have another chance to visit with her warm, wise grandmother, the wave of sudden grief stronger than she would have expected after all these months…

The slam of a car door outside yanked her from the painful memories.

Voices followed. Happy laughter punctuating words she couldn't hear through the open window. Fleur had returned home with Jessamyn. For a moment, Lark wished she could join their easy conversation. She'd missed so much time with her sisters after their parents' bitter divorce had torn the family apart, requiring everyone to choose sides, a decision no child should have to make. It had been a no-brainer for Lark to choose their mother, Jennifer, since she'd done no wrong. Their father had been the one who'd cheated. But Jessamyn, for reasons known only to her, had always sided with their dad. Fleur, who on the surface had the most mild-mannered personality of the three of them, had been the only one to steadfastly refuse to choose, working double-time to maintain lines of communication with all, even when their father cut off financial assistance the moment she turned eighteen.

Lark had admired Fleur's stance, even though she'd never been tempted to mirror it. Their father was a self-absorbed asshat. End of story. Now that he was attempting to steal their inheritance from Antonia—the beautiful house and lands of Crooked Elm Ranch in Catamount—Jessamyn had left his company and Fleur had stopped trying to keep the peace.

The door burst open as Jessamyn strode inside, Fleur on her heels. They were both dressed in tennis shoes and denim cutoffs, a far cry from Jessamyn's usual clothes. As a New York City resident with a high-profile real estate job, Jessamyn normally wore designer everything. But maybe, now that she was transplanting herself to Catamount to make a life with Ryder, that would change. Funny how something simple like a change in clothes could make Lark see her sister differently, but it did. Maybe because the luxury wardrobe items had always reminded Lark that Jess had put her bank account over family.

"Big news!" Fleur squealed as she settled her burden of empty baking containers onto the counter near the sink. Fleur's copper-colored hair was tied in a ponytail, a pink scarf keeping the strands from her face. "You'll never guess what happened to Jessamyn."

Lark shifted her gaze to her other sister, walking into the house more slowly, her hands shoved in the back pockets of her shorts. Yet her face glowed with happiness even though she tried to suppress a smile.

"More big news?" Lark shook her head while she mused aloud, grateful to think about her sisters' lives rather than her own. At least Fleur and Jessamyn weren't talking about Gibson, or the damnable photos of Lark with her ex that were surely circulating online. "Let me think. Jessamyn's already knocked up. I don't think she'll top that for big news—" She stopped herself as a very real possibility came to mind. "Oh wow. Are you having twins?"

Fleur's laughter tripped through the kitchen. Jessamyn removed her left hand from her pocket and extended it for Lark to see.

Diamonds caught the morning sunlight, refracting tiny rainbows everywhere. A chevron shaped band pointed toward Jessamyn's fingertip, a cluster of diamonds surrounding the pear cut stone in the center.

Lark's focus went from the engagement ring to her sibling's face. The joy she saw there outshone any jewel. In that moment, Lark forgot all about their old enmity. She wanted to share her sibling's happiness. She even opened her mouth to congratulate Jess.

"I'm so happy for you—" she began, but her voice cracked with emotion that she had to clear her throat to hide. Memories of another ring lambasted her, along with all the hopeful optimism she'd felt when she'd said yes to Gibson. Would her regret over their lost bond ever stop hurting? Cursing herself—and her ex—she tried again. "For both of you."

The kitchen remained quiet for a moment, and as Jessamyn's smile dimmed a few shades, Lark sensed she hadn't been as effusive as the occasion called for. She sort of hoped her sisters would write it off to her strained relationship with Jessamyn before they guessed the truth—that the failure of her own union still weighed heavily even after two years.

Forcing her lips into a smile, she poured soy milk into her coffee and made another effort. "So when's the date?"

"That's the other huge news," Fleur answered, drawing close to Jessamyn's side and sliding an arm around her shoulders in a squeeze.

A show of solidarity. Fleur was good like that.

"We're getting married in three weeks," Jessamyn announced, the brightness returning to her face, the happiness irrepressible.

And yeah, Lark remembered that feeling, too. Luckily, the time frame for a wedding was so ludicrous, it

gave her something else to think about besides the endless optimism of new love.

"Three *weeks*?" Shaking her head, she stirred in the
milk with her spoon while Fleur moved to the pantry
and withdrew a dome-covered plate containing pastries
visible through the clear glass. "Is it even possible to pull
together a reception that quickly?"

Shrugging, Jessamyn reached into a cabinet to retrieve a bottle of prenatal vitamins and shook one into
her hand. "We didn't want to wait with a baby on the
way."

Fleur set the glass dish on the table and removed the
dome with a flourish while Jessamyn brought over three
plates. Lark eyed the almond croissants and slices of tra-
ditional Spanish sponge cake called *piononos*, but she
already knew she'd choose the spiral pastry called *ensaimada de Mallorca*, one of her favorites their grandmother used to make.

Fleur had inherited the baking gene.

"I told her we'd help," Fleur added as she took a stra-
tegic seat between her siblings. She gave Lark a mean-
ingful look. "They're going to have the reception here."

"At Crooked Elm?" Lark blinked in surprise, her hand
pausing midway to the pastry she'd been reaching for.
"Or do you mean here, as in Catamount?"

Jessamyn swiped the *ensaimada* Lark had been eyeing, spilling confectioners' sugar as she transferred it to
her plate. "At Crooked Elm," she replied firmly. "Ryder
offered to have it at Wakefield Ranch, but I've felt a
strong pull to this place since I've been here. Besides, I
think Gran would have loved a wedding here."

Loss echoed through her as Lark took a caramel and
pecan *pionono*, memories of Gran vivid in her mind.
Their grandmother was a practical woman, as down-to-

earth as they came. She milked her own goats and grew her own vegetables, carving out a simple life here from the work of her own two hands. But she'd had a romantic side, especially where her granddaughters were concerned. They'd all seen photos of Antonia's backyard wedding where she'd taken her vows under an awning of honeysuckle. An errant pain stabbed at the thought of a future Lark would never have now that she'd ended her own marriage.

She blamed being back in Catamount for dredging up that hurt.

"That she would have," Lark admitted, recognizing she'd have to find a way to come to terms with her own negative feelings toward marriage so as not to mar her sister's day.

She'd promised Fleur she'd try, after all.

"Right?" Fleur chimed in cheerily. "Gran would have been all over this. So I think it will be a fun sister-bonding thing for the three of us to work on wedding planning a little each day, especially since we'll have some time now that the probate hearing is delayed."

Fun?

Lark suppressed a groan by gulping her coffee. She needed to figure out a way to get a handle on her feelings ASAP if she wanted to survive a day—no, *weeks*—of wedding planning. Potential excuses circled through her mind. A patient emergency in LA? Or she got called for jury duty? Contracted a contagious disease?

"It shouldn't be that big of an undertaking." Jessamyn licked sugar off her thumb between bites of pastry. "I mean, we can only do so much in three weeks anyway. I don't want the emphasis to be on a fancy gown or pricey party. What's important is sealing the deal with the man I love in front of our friends and family."

Lark's chest ached at the sentiment. A brief moment of superstition making her wonder if things hadn't worked out for her and Gibson because they'd done a courthouse wedding, circumventing the need to contend with complicated Barclay family politics. But of course, that wasn't the reason her marriage had crashed and burned. Gibson's travel and lack of commitment to a home life were to blame.

And, partly, Lark's inability to bridge the growing emotional gap his absences had created. The more charming he tried to be in those final months, the less she felt like he knew her at all. She'd craved reality, not the side he showed to the press.

"Aww," Fleur sighed happily at Jessamyn's words while Lark stuffed the final bite of pastry in her mouth in an effort to end this visit. "That's a beautiful idea, Jess, but we're going to do everything we can to make the day memorable, too. Aren't we, Lark?"

Fleur turned pleading gray eyes her way.

Mouth full, Lark nodded. Stretched her facial muscles into another semismile.

But this visit to Catamount now multiplied in difficulty by about one hundred. She'd thought it had been complicated by Gibson's presence in town. But now she had to contend with her ex next door all the while planning a wedding.

Salt? Meet wound.

Lifting aside the heavy plastic sheeting on the work site, Gibson toured the new addition on his house, taking note of the progress the builder had made over the past few days. The scent of freshly cut wood permeated the air as he stepped around a pile of white twelve-inch tiles delivered that morning.

The brick annex to the main structure of his home would be all on one floor, an addition that would make it easier for Gibson's mother to get around. Not that she was old. Stephanie Vaughn's physical body remained strong. Vigorous. It was cruel that early onset dementia was slowly stealing her mental health.

Gibson wandered into the bathroom, where the first walls to go up were the ones that would be tiled for a walk-in shower. There would be no step up, and no threshold, necessitating a large space to keep water off the rest of the floor. He wanted to make life as easy as possible for his mom, and for his mother's full-time caregiver. Yet he couldn't move either one of them to the house until the annex was complete. He lifted his phone to text his builder again and ask when he'd be onsite today.

It was a far better use of his time than scrolling through the photos of Lark and him that had started appearing online the day before, even though he couldn't help but see the picture again since he'd left a browser window open on the device.

Damn, but she still took his breath away.

The warmth of the day already filtered through the half-finished space, but he could hardly blame that for the rush of heat through his veins as his gaze swept over Lark's image, from her high cheekbones and forest-green eyes to the conservative clothes that never fully camouflaged the pinup-worthy body beneath.

Her shoulders were tense, her spine straight. Because of him? Or because of the media chasing them? He regretted bringing stress back into her life.

Gibson didn't know how much time elapsed while he stared at the photo, telling himself there was still a spark evident between them. But the next thing he knew, the device vibrated in his hand, a banner appearing across the photo with his agent's name for an incoming call.

Again.

Stifling an oath, he jabbed the button to connect them since he couldn't duck the guy forever. Better to get this conversation over with.

"Hey, Dex. What's up?" Gibson asked casually, moving out of the half-built annex and into the sunlight.

"Just wanted to let you know your stock is going up, my friend. The longer you stay silent on the rumors about your return to the ice, the more teams are wanting you. I had a third general manager call me this morning after your mug was all over the place online this morning."

"I'm retired. Remember?" It had been tough enough reaching the decision without the added pressure of his agent trying to keep him in the game. "I've remained silent on the subject because I've already made a public announcement about my retirement."

Dealing with his mother's illness had forced him to take a long look at his priorities. And he'd realized that he hadn't been paying enough attention to the people who were most important to him.

"Just until we get the right price for your comeback though," Dexter responded smoothly, ever-confident in his ability to negotiate terms. "I don't think you're going to find much to fill your days in that no-man's-land of a town you're living in after the excitement of professional hockey."

Gibson couldn't deny that he would miss playing. The ice had always been the one place in his life where he excelled—the one arena where he'd found success.

Unlike the failures of his personal life. The stress of his decision—knowing he'd have to fight hard every day to resist the temptation to return to his sport—combined with the worry over his mom's health and knowing that he'd upset Lark all over again, was a two-ton weight on his chest. He entered the garage from a side door to edge past his sports car and climb into his pickup truck.

He needed a break from the building site his home had become. A break from the media and the pressure of getting back in the game. He hit the button to open the garage door and started the truck's engine.

"I'm looking forward to some downtime," he reminded Dex, for what seemed like the tenth time, as he swapped the phone to Bluetooth through the vehicle's speakers.

He hadn't said much to his agent about the situation with his mom since, at the end of the day, they weren't really friends. Gibson respected Dex's business savvy, but he wasn't all that certain the guy had a life outside of sports.

Dexter spoke over the background noise of city streets, traffic and whistles, horns and air brakes. "You thought that once before though, remember?"

Of course he did. He'd been ready to retire to save his marriage. After a tough road trip through Canada, he'd told his agent he needed to retire, that the time had come to make his marriage a priority. But by the end of that playing season, Lark had already moved out of the home they shared. She'd packed up while he was on the road, not even bothering to inform him they were through until he found the last of her boxes in the foyer of their Los Angeles home.

He'd made the decision to retire a little too late, apparently. So he'd called Dex and told him not to schedule the retirement announcement. He'd played two more seasons until his mother's health worsened to the point where he couldn't ignore the decline.

"I remember all too well. But this time is different."
Now his mom needed him.

Hell, Gibson had to prove to *himself* that he could
be the son she needed. He'd messed up too many other
things in his life to get this wrong.

Gibson backed out of the driveway just as his general contractor arrived for another's day work on the
house addition. Gibson gave the guy a wave as they
passed, then he stepped on the gas to head toward one
of his favorite Catamount retreats, an old stone bridge
that had fallen into disrepair along a backroad not far
from his place.

Lark had taken him there once and they'd dangled
their feet into the creek. He visited it often whenever he
was in town now, always in hope of the peace they'd experienced there—together—that first time. Somehow,
the spot was never quite the same without her, but that
didn't stop him from returning there anyway.

"But the offers are only going to be available for so
long, Gibson. You know that as well as I do." Dexter's
warning felt more than a little ominous. "The clock is
ticking."

Nothing like piling on the pressure.

Gibson nodded absently, even though his agent
couldn't see him, as he drove along the feeder creek for
the White River. The road had shade trees on either side,
cooling the interior of his truck as they blocked the sun.

"I realize that, and I appreciate you looking out for
me. But I don't see myself changing my mind about this."
No matter how tough it would be to ignore all the texts
from his teammates urging him to return for one more
season, a year when a playoff run was finally a real possibility. Tough enough to ignore the social media stories
from fellow players touting their off-season workouts.

Normally by this time of year, Gibson would be deep into endurance training to prepare for the fall, traditionally his favorite time of year.

Disconnecting the call on his dash, he planned to leave his phone in the truck cab once he reached the bridge. That way, he wouldn't be tempted to scroll.

And he wouldn't be distracted by any more photos of Lark.

Even though he was *sure* he'd seen signs of a spark between them in that picture that had run of them together. He was grateful when the bridge came into view up ahead since he needed some peace.

Except he wouldn't be finding it anytime too soon because he could see the tall, sexy figure of his ex-wife already there.

Three

Fingernails digging into the soft bark of a birch tree, Lark heard an approaching vehicle. Her breath hitched even before she turned to see her ex-husband's dust-covered blue pickup trundling along the bumpy road.

Had she come here—to a favorite spot of hers that she'd once shared with him—purposely hoping she might run into Gibson?

Of course not, she thought to herself as she turned back to the view of the shallow creek water rushing just below her feet. She was simply too stubborn to relinquish a spot she loved to him. She'd refused to take much from their marriage when they had ended things, recognizing that she'd brought little enough into the union with her very average salary and minimal belongings. But this? This quiet retreat place near the old bridge had been *hers* first.

Her spine stiffened at the sound of his truck door

slamming. The crunch of his boots across dried leaves and pine needles on the forest floor.

Belly tightening as he approached, she forced out a long breath to calm the swell of emotion.

"I know I can't keep you from living in Catamount," she reminded him, lifting a stick from the ground to swipe through the surface of the creek. "But I don't think it's too much to ask if I want to claim this spot as my own."

Even her own ears could discern that she sounded more like a wounded child than a grown-ass woman. Why was it that this man could bring out the worst in her?

His step paused. Birds chirped and fluttered through tree branches overhead as Gibson went silent, giving her a moment to rethink her approach. A moment to regret. But before she could recant the inhospitable words, he spoke.

"You're right. It's not too much to ask." The timbre of his voice shot through her, the vibration of it familiar. Entwined with happy memories, not just sad ones. "Would you like me to go?"

Risking a glance at him, even knowing how appealing she always found him, Lark lifted her gaze from the creek bed.

Gibson stood some fifteen feet from her, dressed in jeans and a black T-shirt that outlined delineated muscles. His dark hair was still damp from a morning shower and combed away from his face.

"No. Forget I said that." She shook her head, remembering she was a licensed therapist and a professional woman, not an embittered former spouse. She could share the woods with this man for a few minutes, if only to show herself that she had moved on from Gibson Vaughn. "It's just been one of those weeks."

He nodded then continued toward her, his thighs flexing as he walked, straining the denim of his jeans as he moved. She'd forgotten that about him, how his body was more than just a thing of male beauty. It was a scrupulously maintained machine, a tool of his sport and one of the keys to being an elite athlete.

Her throat dried up as he reached her.

"Sit with me?" he asked, nodding toward the flat rock where they'd settled beside one another long ago.

She supposed it made sense to move past this enmity with him if they were going to see one another around town in the future. Besides, she didn't like what it said about her feelings that her back went up every time he was near. From a counseling perspective, she recognized the signs of unresolved issues.

"For a few minutes," she agreed, carefully setting a mental boundary for herself by referencing the time limit. Giving herself an out if she needed one.

Then, stepping out onto the ledge of a rock that had probably once served as a foundation for the long collapsed wooden bridge that had spanned the creek at one time, Lark lowered herself to the cool stone. She wished she'd worn one of her long skirts today instead of the cotton shorts and tee she'd thrown on for a run earlier. From experience, she knew the more clothes between them the better if she wanted to hide her body's reaction to him.

Sometimes just the sound of his voice could give her goosebumps. His effect on her had always been so strong and at the same time, wildly unfair.

A point driven home as his knee brushed hers when he took the spot beside her. She tried not to skitter from him, but the effect of that touch, however innocuous, was potent.

But if Gibson noticed her struggle, he didn't remark on it. Instead, he leaned back on his hands and tipped his head to peer up at the canopy of trees overhead. A soft breeze fluttered the leaves in a continuous rustle, the scent of silty soil and dead leaves mingling with the pervasive smell of the pines.

"You once told me I should come out here when I needed space to breathe and think," he mused aloud. "I guess it's been one of those weeks for me, too."

Caught off guard that he recalled advice she'd given him—let alone that he still implemented it—Lark looked at him again. Really looked. Beyond the well-publicized physique and handsome face. There were shadows beneath his eyes, hints of sleepless nights and worries.

"Second-guessing retirement?" The old resentments crept in while a belted kingfisher sounded its rattling call.

While she waited for his answer, Lark glanced up at the bird, its blue head and white neck feathers easily distinguished amid the green leaves of the birch. She hadn't meant to pick a fight with Gibson but damn it, his job had been impossible to live with. Or was it just his *commitment* to the job? His endless quest for excellence had consumed his time and energies, leaving him little leftover to share with her.

"Not second-guessing so much as wondering who to be now that I'm no longer a hockey player," he answered, not rising to the bait of an old argument. A self-deprecating smile lifted one side of his mouth before he finished drily, "An end-of-career identity crisis, I guess."

Was he truly concerned about that? It was a rare glimpse behind the composed, confident mask he usually showed to the world. But then, they'd met through her practice, before she'd switched her professional focus from sports psychology to counseling kids.

Gibson Vaughn had walked into her office one day for an initial consultation, but there'd been a spark between them immediately. She'd ignored it, of course, because she was a professional and that was a sacred line to her. But he'd refused to schedule a session with her, insisting he wanted a date instead.

She'd never been more grateful for a canceled appointment in her life.

After a few weeks of getting to know one another through texts and phone calls, she'd agreed to come to an afternoon game and dinner with him afterward. He wasn't merely charming and attractive; he'd been persistent. Focused on her completely. And he hadn't given up once he'd made up his mind. What woman could resist that brand of wooing? She'd been swept off her feet.

And she was not a woman to get carried away by romance. Until Gibson, she hadn't even believed it existed. The memories of her broken family had made her distrustful of relationships. She'd had to become so independent that she had trouble being vulnerable to anyone. Gibson had broken through the first layers, but they hadn't had enough time together to work through all her issues.

"So you're going to turn your property into a working ranch?" She watched the kingfisher leave its branch to dive headfirst into the creek, coming up a moment later with a pale colored fish in its long beak. "My grandmother mentioned that's what you were planning the last time I spoke to her."

When he didn't respond right away, Lark pulled off her shoes to dip a toe in the water while she turned to observe him. He had straightened in his seat to pick a blade of grass from a crack in the rock.

"Antonia told me I had all the makings of a good rancher."

The warmth in his voice reminded Lark how much Gibson had enjoyed her grandmother. He'd said his family had never been close, but it was a subject he never lingered on. She'd gotten the impression his dad had been the stern, withholding sort before he'd left the family when Gibson was eight or nine.

After that, his mother had worked two jobs to support herself and her son, making interactions between them infrequent. Lark had liked Stephanie Vaughn a great deal and sensed she wanted to be closer with her son, but Gibson seemed to keep her at a distance.

Now, Lark's defenses crumbled at his regard for her loved one. She was grateful for the creek water flowing around her feet, the cool chill keeping a check on her emotions.

"If Gran said it, then it must be true." She watched as he wound the grass blade around one long finger, his hands crisscrossed with old scars. "But you'd be good at a lot of things. What's more important is to find something you'll enjoy."

He gave a mirthless laugh, the grass falling forgotten through his fingers. "I enjoy things that I'm good at."

The idea scratched at an old memory she couldn't quite call to the surface, the notion bothering her. She dug her toes into the silty earth beneath the water.

"Gibson, you're at a fortunate place in life financially that some people never achieve. You could follow any dream you're passionate about—"

"Not true," he corrected her, shifting to face her. Behind him, the eroded bridge pilings made a moss-covered backdrop. "I was passionate about you once, Lark. That's a dream I'll never have back."

Her thoughts evaporated like mist, the draw of this man compelling even after all the heartache he'd caused her. But she knew better than to act on it now, no matter how much he affected her. He hadn't fought for her, she reminded herself. Not even a little bit.

She wouldn't have ever asked him to retire, but she felt sure he could have found ways to be home more between road trips. Other players did. And he could have found ways to help ease her sense of loneliness and disconnect when they were apart.

"Giving up on that dream was a choice we both made." Shaking her head, she flicked her toes along the surface of the creek, sending a spray onto a nearby log. "Now, what happened with us is sort of like this…" She kicked up another small spray, startling a bullfrog on the shore. "Water under a fallen down, forgotten bridge."

Which reminded her that they really weren't going to resolve any of the old issues between them today, no matter how much she wished that seeing him didn't affect her. So, getting to her feet, she slid on her shoes again and told herself this was a good time to walk away.

Gibson let her words rattle around his head for a moment as Lark strode away from him. Retreating. He wanted to call to her, but he also recognized the need for caution in his response.

He disagreed with her. Strongly.

But he knew better than to cross swords with his clever ex-wife unless he was truly ready to dig in and stand by what he said. Her experience as a counselor made it easy for her to see through bullshit and ego. She had a way of carving right to the deeper point of an argument, even before he realized what they were arguing about.

So he weighed and considered. Chewed on the idea of their old dreams being forgotten. Water under the proverbial bridge.

And still couldn't let her indictment of their past slide. He couldn't let her pretend their time together was all bad, that it meant nothing. Shooting to his feet, he jogged a few steps along the creek toward the path that led to Crooked Elm, catching up to her quickly.

"You have to know that's not true, Lark."

"Which part?" She swung around to face him, green eyes brighter than usual, the color of spring moss. "Us both giving up on the dream? Or that our past is over and forgotten?"

Inside, his brain insisted that he hadn't been the one to give up on the dreams they shared, even though he'd moved on since then, damn it. But his sixth sense told him that was dangerous terrain for an argument. Instead, he stuck with the safer view.

They stood close now. Nearer to one another than they'd been on the rock ledge. He caught a hint of her fragrance—the lavender soap she preferred and some kind of minty shampoo she used. Nostalgia slammed him, almost as strong as the jolt of desire that was automatic whenever she was near him.

"Our past may be over, but clearly neither of us have forgotten it. Otherwise, seeing each other wouldn't be so—" His gaze dipped from her eyes to…lower. All without his permission. He forced his attention back up where it belonged even as his fingers flexed with the urge to touch her. "—*charged*."

Her lashes flicked briefly. Hardly a flutter. But definitely a sign that she'd needed a moment to collect herself.

"That has more to do with wounded pride than anything else." She tilted her chin at him, a silent dare to contradict her. "I don't think either of us enjoy failing at something we set out to accomplish."

"Is that what you think our marriage was? A failure?" And damn, but she knew how to push his buttons.

"It ended in a courthouse with you going one way and me going another." Her eyes flashed, breath quickening. "What else can we possibly label it?"

Two great years where he got to call her his wife. Then she'd walked away from him when he needed her most. But he'd be damned if he'd revisit that hurt now.

"Call it what you like. You can't deny the pull between us even now. You can file all the dissolution of marriage papers you want, but you can't dissolve attraction with a court order."

She opened her mouth, presumably to argue with him, then snapped it shut again. Clamped her teeth in her lower lip for good measure.

He felt the light scrape of those straight white teeth in his mind's eye, a phantom, teasing brush of them along his shoulder. His abs. And lower.

Yeah, the attraction hadn't gone anywhere.

His thoughts must have shown in his eyes because a slight shiver went through her, so subtle he would have missed it if he'd blinked. They stood together, breathing in the same air as the space between them seemed to shrink. His hands lifted, very ready to touch her.

Until a bird streaked past them, plunging into the creek with a splash.

Lark startled away from him, seeming to recover herself as she resurrected some space between them. Disappointment swelled even as he knew he should be grateful for the interruption. He didn't have a plan where Lark was concerned, and his record with her had proven that wasn't wise.

But it didn't make him want her any less.

"Just because an attraction exists doesn't mean we have to act on it." She tugged at the shirt cuffs on her long-sleeved tee, as if covering up as much skin as possible would somehow mitigate the chemistry. "We're adults. And obviously, we know better now."

Above the trees, the sun must have dipped behind some clouds, casting them in sudden shadow.

"You keep telling yourself that." He took a step back, dragging in a calming breath. "In the meantime, I wanted to see if there's anything I can do to help with your case against your father."

His swift change of subject was purposeful. He needed a distraction if he wanted to stop thinking about touching Lark.

And he'd been incensed on her behalf when he'd heard her dad was contesting Antonia's will. News traveled fast in a small town like Catamount. His other neighbors had been quick to fill him in on the local drama.

"I appreciate that." She regarded him with new interest. Curiosity. "But I'm not sure there's anything you can do unless Antonia articulated her plans for Crooked Elm with you."

An errant birch leaf floated down to rest on Lark's shoulder briefly before she shrugged it away, her focus staying firmly on him.

"She absolutely did. She told me more than once that she was planning to leave the house and lands to you and your sisters." He'd spent quite a few happy hours with the older woman, helping her with the goats or dropping off grocery items after a run to the store.

At first, he'd done those things to be neighborly, but in a short space of time he found himself over at Crooked Elm just for the enjoyment of talking to the wise and witty older lady. She had an opinion about everything and wasn't afraid to share it, but she also wasn't the kind of person who tried to convert him to her way of thinking. She embraced the "live and let live" school of thought, content to let those around her walk their own path. It made her easy to talk to.

"Really?" Lark clamped a hand around his wrist, her fingers cool against his bare skin. "Gran said that to you? In those words?"

Gibson's heart thudded harder in reply to the touch. Responding to her nearness.

"She said as much in many different ways. Before you and I divorced, your grandmother frequently alluded to the time when you could join your portion of her lands with mine. It made her happy to envision you here in Catamount full-time." As he shared the memory, he noticed Lark's face clouded. "But even afterward, when you and I split, she still talked about how you'd come home one day, even if it was just to sell your share of Crooked Elm."

He hadn't liked thinking about that. About Lark walking away from a place she'd loved visiting as a kid. She'd adored it when they were married, sharing her pleasure in the place with him so that he'd been eager to buy a home for them here.

Now, she released his wrist abruptly as if she'd just recalled they were touching. Her tongue darted around the rim of her lips before speaking. "That would be really valuable testimony if you were willing to share an official statement with the court."

His gaze remained fixed on her mouth, his thoughts wildly inappropriate. He nodded at first, his throat too dry to speak. Then, forcing the words, he managed, "Of course I will."

"Great. Thank you." She danced back a step, making him wonder if the pull between them was as electric for her as it felt for him. "Fleur and Jessamyn will be thrilled to hear it, too."

Her feet continued to shuffle away, shifting the pine needles and leaves as she moved. And seeing her careful avoidance made him realize all at once that he needed the leverage this good turn could earn him.

"Wait." He hated to be that guy who traded on doing the right thing. But damn it, Lark wasn't going to give him the time of day if he didn't use this as a way to see her again. "Can I ask a favor in return?"

She arched an eyebrow. "If the gratitude of my family isn't rewarding enough for you, I guess you may."

For a moment, he was tempted to ask for something selfish. A kiss. A date. A chance to see that gorgeous hair of hers falling down around her naked shoulders one more time. Any of those things would be easier to request than what he really had in mind.

"I hoped you might stop by to see my mother the next time she's at the house, Lark. Not for long. Just for a quick hello." He saw the surprise in her eyes. Sympathy, even. So she did remember his mom's diagnosis. But he couldn't think about that—about his ex-wife doing anything for them out of sympathy—or he'd lose his nerve to ask for this boon. "She speaks of you often."

He didn't mention that his mother inquired every single time she saw him. Multiple times, thanks to the early onset dementia. He'd given up trying to remind her what had happened between him and Lark. It was too tough to recount that painful time in his life over and over again.

"Oh. How kind of her." Lark nodded quickly, agreeing. "I'll definitely do that. Just let me know next time she's around."

"Will do." Bargain struck, Gibson backed up a step, hoping it hadn't been a mistake to ask. "And if you put me in touch with your attorney, I'll work on that statement for you."

"I'll text you the contact information." She seemed flustered, which was unusual for Lark. "Thanks again for offering to help with the case."

At his nod, she pivoted fast, making tracks along the path that would follow the creek to the Crooked Elm Ranch. Gibson watched her go, eyes following her every step, wondering if it would ever get easier to see this woman walk away from him.

Four

"Lark, you're just in time!" Fleur waved from the backyard.

Two days had passed since Jessamyn's engagement announcement, and the house was routinely in an uproar with wedding plans. Lark had tried to be a good sport about it even though she and Jessamyn hadn't spoken much in years. But morning, noon and night there had been talk of dresses, possible attendants, a registry, food for the reception and a million and one other details.

Until she'd been ready to pull her hair out by the roots.

Instead, Lark had locked herself in the dining room at Crooked Elm for a few hours of telehealth visits with her patients back in Los Angeles, but she'd only stepped out of the house for a breath of fresh air and already her sisters were flagging her down. Fleur stood by the picnic table with the future bride and groom. A Bluetooth speaker sat on one bench, playing a classical piece of music.

Her wedding radar clicked into high alert.

"I'm only out here for a few minutes though." Lark hesitated as she stepped off the back porch onto the grass. The sun was low on the horizon, casting a mellow pink and orange glow over the surrounding fields. "I still need to finish up some paperwork before I can call it a day."

The bane of her existence as a counselor: the reports she needed to file seemed endless sometimes.

"This will only take a second," Fleur promised, gesturing to the engaged couple beside her who were staring deeply into one another's eyes, all smiles. "Jessamyn wanted me to show her and Ryder how to waltz, and it will be easier if I have a partner."

Lark's gaze stuck on Jessamyn. Dressed in a denim miniskirt and black T-shirt with the name of a local rodeo, her sister looked like she been born and raised on a ranch, right down to the dusty turquoise cowboy boots she wore. Jess had one hand on Ryder's shoulder, the other curved around his palm, while the local search and rescue hero stared into her eyes as if she were the only woman in the world. And maybe she was, for him.

The obvious love made Lark think of her own wedding. Gibson had stared at her once just that way, and she remembered exactly how it had made her feel inside. As if she was the luckiest woman on earth. As if their love were so deep and true it would pull them through any hardship life had to offer.

Until it hadn't.

Her throat burned so badly that she needed to swallow before she answered. "I don't know how either," she began, not wanting any part of dancing lessons.

"I'll teach you, too," Fleur insisted, lacing her fingers together to pantomime begging. "Please? I need a warm body to be my partner."

Seeing no way to refuse gracefully, Lark joined them. Fleur had wanted this time together in Catamount to repair their sister bond, but she hadn't said anything about subjecting Lark to daily doses of wedding mania. From the dinnertime discussions about writing your own vows to the breakfast chats about honeymoon clothes, being in the house with her sisters this week had rubbed her emotions raw. But she didn't want them looking too deeply into her aversion to all things matrimonial.

"Okay. What do I do?" Edgy and uncomfortable, Lark forced her attention to stay fixed on Fleur while she cued up a new song on her phone.

A familiar country ballad began, the romantic lyrics scraping over Lark's skin like sandpaper while Fleur moved toward her.

"It's simple really. We'll do a country waltz since you'll have The Haymakers playing at the reception." Fleur grinned at this, still thrilled that she'd booked the popular Western band last minute because they'd had a cancellation in their schedule. "This song is on their suggested playlist for ranch weddings."

"I love this one." Jessamyn practically swooned into Ryder as she said it.

Not that Lark was watching them. Gritting her teeth, she willed Fleur to get on with the lesson so she could stop thinking about how it felt to be wildly, hopelessly in love. Lark had already given Gibson way too much space in her head today, his image filling her phone screen as she scrolled through social media. It didn't matter that she'd blocked the sports news outlets. All her local friends and nearby small businesses seemed to be buzz-

ing about the question of Gibson Vaughn's retirement.
Everyone had an opinion about whether or not he would
settle in Catamount to start ranching this time, or if he'd
return to another hockey team before the season began.

There'd even been a few old photos of the two of them
together, images that had made her shut down her phone
for the day. Who knew she'd bounce from reminders of
her failed marriage to dancing lessons beside the world's
happiest couple?

"So what next?" she prompted Fleur, while the Nu-
bian goats that had belonged to their grandmother made
a ruckus in their pen nearby.

The goats were adorable with their long ears and play-
ful ways, but they were definitely vocal, bleating to one
another and to the backyard dancers.

Fleur removed the flour-dusted apron she'd been
wearing around a pair of yellow overalls, then tossed it
on the picnic table before she answered.

"Well, the country waltz is in three-quarter time, the
same as the American waltz. Just listen for it." Fleur
hummed along with the tune for a few moments, exag-
gerating the "One, two, three" count so the rest of them
could hear it.

Lark focused on the rhythm, telling herself the sooner
she conquered the steps, the faster she could be released
from the day's romance session.

"Now, let's get into our dance positions." Fleur flipped
her copper-colored ponytail behind her and moved closer
to Lark, laying a hand on her waist. "Ryder and I will
lead, Jess and Lark, you'll follow so your first step is
backward on the count of one."

She demonstrated the basic steps and Lark mirrored
her, an unexpected memory drifting up from her childhood. She'd danced like this once. Not at her own wed-

ding of course, since she and Gibson had opted for fast and private over a public declaration of their vows.

There'd been a time…before her parents' bitter split. Before all the family fractures that had followed. Beneath all those rifts, there'd been happy times. Her singing along with the radio in the kitchen of her girlhood home. It had been a warm summer morning, and her father swooped her into his arms, standing her on his feet to dance her across the tile floor.

He'd still been her hero then. Back when she'd believed he'd been a good person.

She missed a step, stumbling on Fleur's toes.

"I'm sorry." Righting herself, Lark let go of her sister. "I probably shouldn't do this while I'm distracted by—" she cleared her throat as she produced an excuse "—my work."

What did she even do with a memory like that? She'd spent too long resenting her father—for good reason—to dwell on any redeeming qualities he might have once had. He'd turned his back on his family, not her.

"Is anything wrong?" Fleur asked, her gray eyes keen as she studied her.

At the same time, Jessamyn whirled past them in Ryder's arms, still dipping and stepping to a one-two-three count. "It's all good! I think we've got it down well enough to survive our couples dance."

This time, Lark was grateful for her sibling's starry-eyed romance since it distracted Fleur from inquiring more about what troubled her.

"I really should return to work." Lark edged away another step, seeing her chance to escape.

Between the constant reminders of her ex-husband next door, the pheromone-filled atmosphere at Crooked Elm with both her sisters in love and the pending court case with her father, she felt pushed to her personal breaking point this week.

"If you really have to," Fleur said reluctantly, moving toward the animal enclosure to scratch a friendly black-and-white goat named Guinevere. "But can you check in with Mom sometime tonight to ask for her flight details? I know she's booked her trip here for the wedding, and it would be great if you could pick her up at the airport."

"Really?" she blurted before realizing how rude she sounded. She moved closer to Fleur to scratch one of the other goats—was the brown and white one Morgan Le Fay?—who headbutted her in the hip. "I mean, of course I'll find out when she's flying and I can take care of the airport run. I'm just surprised she agreed to come to Cat-amount…" Lark's gaze found Jessamyn where she still twirled and laughed with Ryder as they worked on their waltz moves. "Er—while the court case is in progress."

She was actually sort of surprised Mom had signed on for the wedding in the first place given the way Jes-samyn had taken their dad's side in the split. While Mom had never held that against Jess, Lark knew their rela-tionship had been strained. Diplomatic avoidance had been their usual MO.

Fleur glanced toward the dancing couple too, follow-ing Lark's attention.

"Well for starters, Jessamyn reached out to Mom after she got engaged and it sounds like they had a good talk." Fleur straightened the blue collar around Guinevere's neck with a silver name tag in the shape of a crown—a recent gift from Drake. "And once they started discuss-ing the will contest case, it turns out Mom had a lot of ideas for potential witnesses who heard Gran talk about leaving Crooked Elm to us. Including Mom."

Lark's hand stilled on Morgan le Fay's neck. "You

don't think Mom wants to get involved in the case? I mean, I'm all for winning this thing, but do any of us really want to see Mom and He-Who-Shall-Not-Be-Named facing off in another courtroom battle?"

Their family had barely survived the first one.

She'd begun her college studies in psychology at first, not because she'd had her heart set on being a therapist, but in order to have a reasoned, rational approach to analyzing what had gone wrong in her family. It had been her way of coping with a hurt that was, in essence, an abandonment. One day, she'd known two loving parents. Then her mother caught her father cheating and Lark found her own home a war zone with both the adults too consumed with their anger to remember things like after-school pickups, sports practices, or to even buy groceries. One of their money arguments turned into a contest to see who could go the longest without being the one to make a supermarket run.

At sixteen years old, Lark became the one to bum rides from friends who could drive in order to obtain food for the week with her babysitting money. Later in life, she'd learned about her mom's depression and had been able to forgive her for those dark months that had turned into two torturous years. But understanding those times hadn't made them easier to survive while she'd been going through them.

Fleur shrugged, her attention shifting to a stretch of backroad leading to Crooked Elm that was visible from this corner of the yard, where a dust cloud stirred in the dry air. "Mom is in a good, healthy place now. I think it should be her call. Besides, the attorney is accepting written statements, not just in-person testimonies."

Lark didn't share her easy acceptance of the idea. In fact, her stomach tightened into a knot. "Written statements that could easily lead to in-person testimony if the judge wants more information, or if Dad's attorney wants to question any of them."

This week was tough enough with Gibson in town and facing her manipulative, self-centered father. She wasn't ready to relive the toxic family dynamics, too.

"It will be fine." Fleur's tone was placating at best as she still stared out toward the road. Distracted. "I don't recognize that vehicle coming toward us. Do you?"

Sighing at the way Fleur wasn't taking her concern seriously, Lark took a sidestep to see around a low hanging branch of a cottonwood tree.

Could it be Gibson? Her heart did a funny quickening that she firmly ignored. But the SUV moving through the dust cloud sure wasn't Gibson's truck or his sports car, both of which Fleur probably would recognize since he'd started spending more time at his house just a stone's throw from Crooked Elm.

Although he would use that road to approach the house. There weren't many places to access the quiet country lane, and Gibson's home—the one they were supposed to have shared—was one of them.

"I'm not sure." Lark took a few more steps toward the tree line that hid some of the thoroughfare, squinting to see through the dirt kicked up by the vehicle.

"I think there's a logo on the side—" Fleur began at the same exact moment Lark recognized it.

"It's the pain-in-my-ass sports media," she muttered, the knot in her stomach tightening as she headed for the back door. "And there's no way I'm letting them take pictures so they can use me for their stupid clickbait headlines."

She could already see it: "Where Are They Now? Former Hockey Wives We Loved to Hate."

At least they hadn't filmed her country waltzing in

the yard with the goats as a backdrop. They'd try to fabricate a story about how lonely she was without Gibson in her life that she needed to dance alone. That's all her family needed was an excuse to probe.

Angry at the whole pseudo-industry that was loosely labeled sports entertainment "media" and didn't have a damned thing to do with news or even *sports*, Lark slowed her step.

Why should she have to hide herself away just because she resented them so much? Did it really matter what they had to say anymore now that her marriage was already over?

She'd come to Catamount to put the past behind her, after all. To bury the hatchet with her sisters. To secure Crooked Elm from her father's greedy clutches. And, most recently, to heal her guilt about her part in a failed marriage.

Maybe it was high time she gave the proverbial middle finger to her old enemy, the sports media, too. How long was she going to allow them to write her script for her, while she ducked and hid and hoped they wouldn't notice her? How had she let herself become that woman?

She had things to say for herself, damn it. Why not use the platform rather than run from it, at least this one time?

"You can go inside," Fleur urged her as they heard the SUV tires on the gravel driveway in front of the house. "We'll make sure they know they have to stay off the property."

Shaking her head, Lark rolled up her sleeves, preparing for a showdown.

"There's no need. They want a story? It's long past time I gave them a good one."

Gibson was in the middle of a teleconference meeting with his newly hired ranch manager when his phone vibrated for the third time in a row. And even though he hadn't begun true ranch operations yet, the meeting was important if he ever wanted to get his new business off the ground.

He'd carefully researched the market for a bison ranch and found a good opportunity for profit. Plus, he admired the majestic beasts and looked forward to working with them.

"Will you excuse me for a minute?" he asked the new hire as he leaned back from the workspace he'd set up at the dining room table.

With so much of the house under construction to be comfortable for his mother's arrival, Gibson hadn't bothered to furnish much of the upstairs, preferring to wait until the dust settled on the renovations.

"Sure thing," Jackson Daly tipped the brim of his Stetson at him on the other end of the video call. "Though I've got enough to keep me busy until next week's meeting."

"Sounds good to me." Gibson had requested revenue projections for the business plan he was putting together for a few friends who had expressed interest in investing. "Thanks, Jackson."

After closing out of the app on his laptop screen, Gibson pressed the connect button on the call from—surprise, surprise—his agent.

Again.

"Dex, I'm still committed to starting the ranch." He told himself as much every day, even though the project had a huge chance of flopping.

If he ever wanted to conquer the fear of failure—of losing—he couldn't spend his whole life only taking on things that he was good at.

"Are you watching the news?" Dex blurted, his voice

sounding tenser than normal. Gibson could hear a phone ringing along with what sounded like multiple news feeds running in the background.

A sea of talking heads.

"Of course not. I'm working, and even if I weren't…" Gibson leaned far back in the ergonomic desk chair he'd bought for his long frame, tilting the neck rest so he stared up at the sleek chrome light fixture hanging over the blond wood table. "You know I didn't check out the sports headlines even when I was playing—"

"Not the sports news. Turn on your local network affiliate. They've been promoting the hell out of a story with a clip of your ex-wife. It'll be on as soon as they return from commercial."

Gibson tipped forward so quickly he nearly fell out of the chair. "They're back to chasing Lark around town?"

Pounding one fist on the table, he used his other to reach for the television remote that controlled a big screen across the great room above the fireplace. He cursed the media hounds the whole time for interfering in his personal life again, after he'd made some progress with Lark.

"From the sound bite they keep showing, it sure didn't look like she was trying to avoid them this time." Dex's words sounded muffled, as if he were covering the phone or maybe sandwiching it between his chin and shoulder. The guy juggled too much, but for once, Gibson appreciated the heads-up considering he was to blame for bringing the spotlight with him to Catamount.

Jabbing a few buttons to find the right channel, Gibson blasted the volume on the remote in time to see Lark's pretty face fill the television screen. Her sexy dark braid lay coiled on one shoulder bared by a white tank dress as she stood in front of the Crooked Elm

Ranch house. Her expression was serious as she looked directly into the camera.

"…because since when does reporting on the activities of elite athletes' wives, girlfriends and exes constitute sports news?" Lark had taken the microphone out of the hand of whoever had been trying to interview her. She moved backward now as someone reached into the frame to try to retrieve it. Lark's forest-green eyes flashed with a fire Gibson remembered well from their arguments. And from other times…

She continued now, "If you're going to cover women, why not give camera time to actual women athletes who are overlooked by the media and paid far less than their male counterparts?"

The camera work turned awkward then, the lens bouncing as whoever carried the video recorder moved to forcibly take the mic out of Lark's hands. But not before Lark could be heard saying, "Do you know how many professional women's teams there are in Los Angeles where I live? And do you know how many more times I made your stupid news feed over talented, trained women who deserve—"

The video and audio ended abruptly, the local anchor appearing on the screen with a still image from the clip behind one shoulder labeled "Gibson Vaughn's Ex Speaks Out."

Indignation on her behalf fired through him. They couldn't even give her the credit of her own name under her photo? But the local anchor moved quickly to another story, leaving Gibson to wonder when—and how—they'd obtained a clip that clearly hadn't been shot by their own team.

More than that, his thoughts were at Crooked Elm with Lark. Was she upset about the encounter? Pleased?

She'd definitely taken the offensive this time, and he couldn't be prouder of her about that. He remembered too well how frustrated the media had made her when they'd been married.

"Good for her," Gibson mused aloud, almost forgetting he had Dex on the phone in the onslaught of thoughts about Lark. She'd looked sexy as hell in that clip. "Thanks for the heads-up about this."

"I didn't call just to give you a heads-up." Again, a phone rang in the background of wherever Dex was sitting, a racket all around the guy. "I'm getting bombarded with opportunities for you. Teams that think you must be considering a comeback if Lark is putting herself in the spotlight."

Shoulders slumping, Gibson didn't know what to say to that other than that tired old refrain. "Not going to happen."

He would have pounded home the point except a notification from the security guard at his front gate chimed on his phone. Pulling it from his ear, he read the message.

Lark is out front. Should I let her through?

Surprise made him hesitate for only an instant. Then he tapped an auto-response command in the affirmative. Damn right he wanted to see her, even if he couldn't imagine what she was doing here.

Returning his phone to his ear as he rose to his feet, he strode to the door while Dex continued speaking without pause. "And there are two new teams interested in you because of this new attention. A lot of hockey clubs are trying to be supportive of women's teams and this really resonates—"

Clearly he hadn't missed much of the conversation. His agent was giving the same old spiel while headlights arced across Gibson's windows. Anticipation thrummed through him.

Gibson pulled open the front door as Lark herself stepped from a gray sedan, her long legs encased in fitted black boots. She still wore the same white tank dress she'd had on in the television clip.

And she was here. At his house.

Making him want her simply by being.

His throat was dry when he spoke again. "Dex, I have to go now. I'll call later. Bye."

Shutting the phone off and tossing it on the couch and well out of reach, Gibson held the door open wide for his too-gorgeous ex-wife who'd just set him on fire with her take-no-prisoners approach with the media.

Whatever she wanted, he was more than happy to provide.

Five

Lark's thoughts scrambled at the sight of her ex-husband on his front doorstep. The overhead porch light cast his chiseled features in shadow, his broad shoulders and strong chest stretching the fabric of a blue dress shirt with the sleeves rolled up and the top buttons unfastened. Dark gray trousers hugged his thighs, while his sock-clad feet padded onto the painted black floor of the deep porch.

Seeing him there, looking tousled after a workday, reminded her of other homecomings when they'd lived together. On his rare days off when he'd cooked for her, he would greet her this way, the scents of a simple roasted chicken or grilled steaks drifting out the door while he wrapped her in those massive arms. Just thinking about it made her gaze return to them now, the musculature so well-defined he could have been an anatomy diagram. A very hot diagram.

"This is a welcome surprise." His voice jarred her from thoughts she had no business thinking. "Will you come in?"

Shaking off the hunger that seemed to grow every time she saw him, Lark flipped her braid behind her shoulder and took a step forward. She'd driven over here, after all. She couldn't pretend it had been an accident.

She'd expected to see the media camped outside his gates, but there'd been no one there except the security guard. Perhaps the local cops flushed out unwanted visitors now and then. Whatever the reason, she needed a safe haven from reporters.

Yet setting foot inside Gibson's house with him looking at her the way he was right now would only lead to her making questionable decisions.

"That's not necessary but thank you." She folded her arms across her chest, gathering her defenses against all six feet four inches of male charisma staring back at her.

He lifted one dark eyebrow in question. "It may not be necessary, but I think we'd be more comfortable if we took a seat while you tell me what brought you over here."

Glancing around the front yard of the home they'd chosen together, Lark tried to find a good reason to remain out of doors.

"It's such a nice night though," she hedged, her heart thumping too hard, too fast. "Maybe we could sit on the porch swing? That is, if you still have it hanging up on the back side of the house?"

Already she felt foolish for driving here, of all places, when she'd been agitated from the media interview and her emotions were already scraped raw from romantic dances in her backyard. But she hadn't been able to think of anywhere else to take shelter until she was certain the reporters were gone.

"Sure thing." Nodding, Gibson waved her around to the rear of the place, leading her along the polished floor planks. "It's a good spot for watching sunsets, just like we guessed it would be."

They'd been excited to purchase the property. So hopeful that it would help heal the growing rift between them created by his long absences. But there'd been one delay after another with the sale, and in the end, they hadn't been able to hang on long enough to see if the house could be a magic elixir to fix their broken relationship.

Frustration over all that they'd lost—so much more than Gibson knew—put the starch in her spine that she needed for this visit.

"I'm glad you're enjoying this part of the estate at least." She followed him around the house to the veranda in back where a low half-moon illuminated the cedar swing painted gray. "I noticed you're renovating most of the rest of it."

Taking a seat on the far end of the swing, she regretted commenting on the home as soon as the words were out of her mouth. It didn't matter what changes he made to his house. The property was no concern of hers anymore.

Even if a tiny, ugly part of her brain wondered if there was a girlfriend behind the redesign of a perfectly good residence.

"I'm adding a suite for Mom," he told her simply, tossing aside a plump ivory-colored throw pillow before he lowered himself into the swing. "So I've been grateful for a few places to retreat from the dust of remodeling."

Surprised at the big undertaking for the mother he didn't see often, Lark regretted her snarky thoughts. The starch in her spine wilted again as she watched Gibson stretch his long legs, one knee splayed so it rested inches from her own.

"That's good of you." Tugging another throw pillow out from behind her back, she hugged it in front of her instead. If she kept her hands gripping the cushion, she couldn't possibly reach out to touch him. "And sorry to show up here unannounced. I had a run in with the media—"

"I saw you go on the offensive." A wide grin stole over his features, white teeth glinting in the moonlight. "That was so freaking perfect."

"That clip is already online?" She knew video snippets like that circulated fast, but that had to set a new record. "I only lost the last of the reporters half an hour ago. I was afraid they would be waiting for me at Crooked Elm and I didn't know where else to go."

And how messed up was it that the first place she thought of to duck the press was with Gibson? He'd been the one to bring them back to her doorstep to begin with.

"Wait. Someone was following you? Not the asshat who interviewed you in the first place." His brow furrowed as he shifted to face her, his voice indignant. "The guy stole your mic just when you got going—"

Confused, she shook her head. "No. He retreated to his van after that. But there was a young woman filming from an unmarked car that pulled into Crooked Elm after the first guy. I have no idea who she worked for or how she knew to show up just then."

The members of entertainment media were like bees that way. One member of the hive could spot something juicy and minutes later, a swarm amassed.

"Probably a freelancer hoping for a toe in at one of the big media outlets." Gibson shook his head, his dark hair brushing his shoulders as he splayed his arms wide in a helpless gesture. "Although how anyone rationalizes stalking people for a living is sickening. Are you okay?"

His warm hand landed on her bare shoulder. A gesture of concern. Comfort, even.

Yet given how long it had been since they'd touched, the physical contact overrode her senses and short-circuited her brain. She couldn't think. Couldn't recall what he'd just said.

There was simply his hand. Touching her.

Lark's heartbeat redoubled. Squeezing the pillow tighter, she willed herself to speak.

"This was a mistake." Bolting upright from the seat, she took two long strides away from him, the swing's chains jangling softly in her wake. "I should go home now."

"Lark?" Soft concern laced Gibson's voice as he rose to follow her. "What's wrong? Did something happen with the press that we should report? Because if they crossed a line—"

He left the sentence half-finished as his gaze roved over her, as if checking to be sure she was still in one piece.

Old angers simmered anew, a welcome outlet for the fire still heating her blood from just a single touch of this man's hand.

"Where exactly is the line these days anyway, Gibson? I'm not sure I'd have any idea what violates my privacy when you assured me that having cameras camped out around my garage every time you were in the headlines was normal." Her fingers gripped the swing cushion so tight her fingernail popped off some of the beading near a tassel.

She slapped the silk-covered pillow onto a nearby

table, frustrated at herself for letting her emotions get the best of her. For permitting the smallest caress to overwhelm her.

"They're not allowed to touch you. They're not allowed to block your way," he repeated the guidelines she remembered well, his tone betraying his own agitation. "You know that."

"Whereas speculating on our love life, asking me loaded questions to imply you were unfaithful to me every time you were on the road, and goading me to speak until they had a juicy sound bite, that's all just fine." Lark knew she needed to rein it in.

Her words were far too revealing. Not just to him, but even to herself. Hadn't she put this behind her?

Hadn't her confrontation with the reporter tonight proven she'd stopped hiding from them? That had been growth, damn it. So why was she reverting to a tired argument now?

Gibson's hand on her.

"They're gone now," he reminded her, tipping one shoulder against a porch post so that moonlight outlined him. "You did a stellar job turning the tables on that jerk tonight. But I wish you'd tell me if they hassled you because we should report it."

She wished he would argue with her. Debate the past. Remind her why they split in the first place. Any of it would be so much easier to bear than his concern. He wanted to take care of her, but she had to stand on her own. Because that was how she'd be again. Alone.

Added to the intimacy of the setting, alone in this house she'd once dreamed would be hers, and the way her skin still prickled where his fingers had sketched along her shoulder, Lark feared she couldn't combat the impulse to throw herself into his arms.

"I'm fine." She pressed her fingers to the center of her forehead, searching for the calm focus and grounded perspective that her patients always commented on in reviews of her practice.

Ms. Barclay has a way of slicing past the emotional noise of a problem to logically reason through the heart of it, read one of her personal favorites.

If only she had an inkling how to do that in her own life.

"Would you like to stay here tonight?"

Gibson's voice sliced past a whole wealth of her own emotional noise, stirring up all her fears for her self-preservation.

Her fingers slid away from her forehead as she met his dark gaze. Her pulse thrummed hard through her temples. Pounding. "Of course not. How can you ask me that?"

She leaned closer in spite of herself, perhaps with the need to press him for an answer.

"Because you're upset. Because there's a spare bedroom away from the media and away from the pressure of being around your family. Reporters know better than to drive onto my property. I've made that clear, and since the incident at the courthouse, I added extra security for the next few weeks until interest in my career fades." He shrugged one big shoulder. "I know being in Catamount has to come with a lot of stresses, especially now that Jessamyn and Ryder Wakefield are getting married here."

Blinking from the accuracy of every last one of his observations, Lark realized she was in way over her head tonight. From the moment she'd pulled into Gibson's driveway, she'd been giving up control of the situation. By now, her ex-husband was unraveling her every last protective layer with all the insider knowledge that a former spouse possessed.

"Now who's the therapist here?" she teased lightly, her hands finding the tie around the end of her braid and retying the fabric. Anything to keep her fingers busy.

Away from him.

"Just calling it like I see it, since you never seem to extend the same grace to yourself that you'd give to anyone else in your life. It's okay to say enough is enough with your father. And your sister, too."

The locked box where she normally kept her emotions opened wider, the overflow too messy to stuff inside.

"Thank you," she managed finally, seeing no way to maintain an argument with him when he insisted on being kind. Letting go of the hair tie, she straightened to her full height. "It has been a rough week, but I'm committed to healing my relationship with Jessamyn. I'm even helping plan the wedding."

She caught herself before she rolled her eyes. Gibson knew how much she'd regretted losing Jessamyn to their father's side for so many years.

"Is that right?" Mischief skipped through his tone as he reached toward her forgotten braid.

Mesmerized by the careful movements of his fingers, she watched as he straightened the lopsided bow she'd left in the scrap of cotton fabric used to secure the tail.

Technically, he wasn't touching her body anywhere. Weren't the cells that made up hair supposed to be dead? Yet his efforts shifted the silky rope in a way that made her whole scalp tingle with awareness.

"Jessamyn and Ryder are in a hurry to make things official since she's pregnant," Lark rambled, needing to fill the air between them with words before the tension became too thick. Plus, the mention of any pregnancy still felt loaded for her after the way she hadn't been able to tell him about that one time when the stick had shown two distinct pink lines. Dragging in a breath, she continued, "And she's having the ceremony at Crooked Elm, so Fleur thought if we all helped, it would speed things along and give us a way to spend time together."

It really had been a sweet gesture on Fleur's part, now that she thought about it.

"I'm glad you're trying to work things out with Jess." Gibson had finished with the hair tie, but he hadn't let go of her braid. He smoothed his thumb and forefinger over the links, his gaze tracking the progress.

Sensual memories bombarded her. She had never understood his fascination with her hair, but she recalled vividly how many times he'd done this very same thing as a prelude to kissing her. Undressing her. Coiling the length of the braid around a wrist. His or hers...

Her breathing grew shallow. Her body heating with want.

When he tipped her face up to his with his free hand, she wouldn't have been surprised if he'd lowered his mouth to hers.

Instead, his voice was pure gravel when he spoke.

"Let me be your date for the wedding."

Gibson didn't know where the suggestion had originated.

He only knew that there was unfinished business between them, and he had to find a way to see it through—had to find a way to see *her* again so they could explore it together.

Because fighting off the urge to wrap her in his arms and kiss her until they were both breathless was taking every ounce of his strength. But he knew if he gave into that hunger too soon, he could stoke the fiery resentment that lurked inside his ex-wife.

Well, sure, he could distract her with the chemistry that sizzled into a full-blown blaze when their lips touched. Yet sooner or later, she would remind him of all the reasons they didn't work. Reasons that didn't even apply anymore now that he was retiring.

Not that she believed him. And it shouldn't matter so much to him when she'd walked away at the lowest point of his career, when he'd needed her most. But the effect she had on him had never made sense.

He only knew that if he wanted a chance to be with her again, to explore the chemistry that had them both sizzling right now, he needed to bide his time. Not push for too much, too fast.

"You want to be my *date*?" Lark's eyes were wide. Her fast breaths worked the top of her fitted tank dress in a way that made his hands ache to mold to her curves.

Instead, he kept his left around her braid and his right cradling her cheek. Her skin was even softer than he remembered.

"Damned right, I do." He also wanted her to spend the night under his roof so he could make sure that she was safe, that no reporters hassled her, that her complicated family dynamics didn't steal focus from the important work she did in counseling troubled kids.

He hadn't realized until he saw her again on the courthouse steps how deeply the urge to protect her and pleasure her were both still ingrained in him. He regretted not putting her first when they were married. His mistakes were clear to him now, but how could he ever make Lark see that? He'd hurt her enough already, and he refused to do that again. Yet he needed to free himself of that hold she had on him.

Too bad the only way he could envision it happening was if he had the chance to be with her again. To indulge the chemistry until it flared out. To excise the attraction along with the hurt so they could both move on.

"That makes no sense." Her jaw tensed in his palm as she gritted her teeth.

He knew big league goalies who weren't as tough as this woman, let alone as stubborn.

"We have things to work out between us, Lark. You know it as well as I do." He skimmed lower on her braid, using the tasseled end to stroke up her bare arm like a paint brush. "Why not use your time here to end things between us the right way?"

"By dating? By attending a wedding?" She gave a half-hearted shrug of her shoulders, but he hoped she was also feeling twitchy because of his nearness.

Even in the moonlight, he could see the gooseflesh raised on her arm.

"By spending time together. We shut down everything so fast we never had a chance for closure. To say goodbye to the good times we had instead of just the bad." He heard her swift intake of breath and stepped closer, needing to press any advantage before she shut him down.

"We might end up tearing open old wounds instead. From a counseling perspective, I don't think there's any value to revisiting a broken relationship that way."

"Then it's a good thing you're not my counselor, isn't it?" He could feel her response to his words in the rapid tattoo of pulse at her neck.

Still he waited. In life and in hockey, timing was everything.

Her gaze narrowed. "If I agree to a date, will you kiss me already?"

His heart slugged harder. Blood surged south.

"If you say yes," he teased a touch along her plump lower lip, "I'll kiss you until you ask me to stop."

Her tongue darted out to dampen the seam of her mouth. He couldn't wait to taste her.

"In that case, you can come with me to Jessamyn's wedding." She gave a small nod, sealing the deal. "You can be my date one more time."

Victory bells rang in his head, the triumph sweeter than any game seven overtime win.

"You made me a very happy man tonight." He still wrestled with the urge to run his hands all over her, but at least he had the green light for taking that sweet, sweet mouth of hers.

He closed the last of the distance between them, her curves brushing against him.

"So start making me a very happy woman." Her clear-eyed challenge was meant to provoke him to haste. Maybe to goad him into taking her hard and fast against the side of the house.

She had to know how much he wanted that.

But he wouldn't mess up this chance with her by rushing or taking more than what they'd agreed on.

"Soon enough, I promise." Slowly, he wound the end of her braid around his hand until he tugged her head back. Her lips parted as her chin tilted up.

Damn, but she was a vision with the moonlight turning her skin to cream and her lips still glistening from where she'd wet them. He pressed his thumb into the soft fullness of her lower lip, pulling it down. A fire roared inside him.

But he didn't kiss her there yet.

He brushed his lips along her ear instead. Whispering, "First, you need to let me taste you the way we're both dying for."

Six

Breathless, needy and quivering like a virgin bride after two years of abstinence, Lark couldn't wait another second.

Gliding her hands up Gibson's strong chest to hook her fingers over his shoulders, she tugged him closer so their bodies fit together. Her sigh of pleasure sounded in stereo since Gibson echoed it, his grip on her tightening as they stood alone on the shadowed porch.

Yes. Please.

She could feel exactly how much he wanted her, his body hot and hard against hers. Emboldened, she arched on her toes until their lips brushed.

Desire streaked through her like wildfire, burning away everything but the need for more. This man had always had her number when it came to pleasure, and that hadn't changed just because she'd quit using his last name. He loosened his hold on her hair, using both hands to skate down her body, thumbs barely skimming the sides of her breasts, so that she shivered into him, her nipples tightening into hard points.

By the time he cupped her hips it took all her willpower not to rock and wriggle against him, to create the friction she desperately needed. The ache between her thighs was sharp. Intense. Made all the more so by the knowledge of how easily he could satisfy the hunger.

But she couldn't let this encounter get any more out of control, could she? Instead, she pressed her thighs together in an effort to ease the throbbing. She concentrated on the way his tongue stroked along hers. Just the right amount of pressure. The perfect amount of patience. He knew her body so well, and had always taken a pride in being able to give her orgasm after orgasm. What woman walks away from that kind of sensual attention?

Already, his slow, thorough kisses were turning her inside out. His fingers had rucked up the hem of her tank dress just enough to allow his touches to trail over the tops of her bare thighs. Her feminine muscles clenched tighter, her body speeding toward the finish she needed even though they were just kissing.

Couldn't happen.

Or, rather, *shouldn't* happen. Because the logistics were all in place for her to go there. One brush of his fingers between her legs and she'd be flying apart…

"Wait." Breaking the kiss, she tried to catch her breath while Gibson studied her through half-lidded eyes.

He'd complied with her request for space instantly, a mark of gentlemanly restraint she should admire. And she did, of course. But she wouldn't have minded if he'd looked half as breathless and starved for her as she felt for him.

Gibson had always been that way though—relentlessly controlled. A lifetime of being a hockey star—from the time he was a preteen until this moment—had schooled him to be the spokesperson for every team he'd ever been on. His charm, his media savvy, his consummate composure didn't break for anyone.

A welcomed reality check.

"What made you change your mind?" he asked, releasing his hold on the hem of her dress.

Letting go of her.

The summer evening felt cooler all of the sudden. The soft chirp of crickets and katydids filled the air. Farther away, a bobcat screeched its distinctive call.

"I haven't changed my mind. I'm still going to honor the date." She didn't hate the idea really. Gibson's long absences had hurt her, but their marriage was over so she had no expectations where he was concerned.

His charm and composure might be welcome at a family wedding where she would inevitably feel out of her element. Gibson would smooth her way through the day, talking to people and keeping the focus off of her.

"That's not what I meant. You changed your mind about the kiss." He regarded her closely, like she was a puzzle to solve.

His dark eyes saw too much.

Especially when she'd let her guard down. Her whole body felt raw from that kiss. From the orgasm that she hadn't allowed to happen. Her pulse remained thready. Erratic.

"We kissed," she reminded him, backing away a step to insert some space between them. She really needed to retreat before she thought too much about how good they could make each other feel. "It was…" not nearly enough "…nice. Like always."

"Nice?" He bristled. Predictably.

Was she *trying* to goad him into a do-over? A way-ward shiver tickled over her skin at the thought.

"Okay, better than nice. Obviously." She hugged her arms around herself, missing his hands on her.

Satisfaction gleamed in his eyes. "Then why stop something we were both enjoying so much?"

His voice stroked over her as surely as any touch. How could mere words set her on fire so easily?

Retreat!

"Because unfortunately, sometimes the things we like aren't good for us." She knew that from personal experience.

With him.

His head tipped to one side for a moment. Then he nodded, the speculative look fading from his expression. "Because you had a rough day with the press and your family, I'm going to accept that as an answer tonight."

"Magnanimous of you." Despite the sarcasm in her tone, she appreciated him letting her off the hook. Her defenses were in tatters and in need of serious reinforcement. Backing up another step, she bumped into the porch swing and set it rocking before she stilled the chains with one hand. "Thank you."

Gibson followed her, his moon shadow falling over her as she headed around the side porch to the front of the house.

"Just keep in mind that next time I'm going to remind you in detail how good kissing can be for both of us." He said it as confidently as if he were on camera in the locker room, trotting out an opinion on an upcoming game.

We're just going to play with the puck more and remember how effective it is to stay in our zone.

Lark shoved away the imagined sound bite in her

head, telling herself she needed more sleep and less kissing to clear her mind of this man.

She arched an eyebrow. "Who says there will be a next time?"

His smile unfurled the deep dimple in one cheek that had cinched his spot on the "Men of Hockey" calendar for the last decade. "I'm already looking forward to it."

Returning to Catamount from an all-day tour of a bison ranch over the Wyoming border, Gibson slowed his truck as he neared the local diner close to supper time. Thunder rumbled in time with his stomach since he hadn't eaten all day.

He was hungry, yes. But he could have waited to grab a bite until he returned home.

The bigger draw was the place's connection to the Barclay sisters now that owner Drake Alexander had offered for his chef fiancée, Fleur, to take over operations. She hadn't done so, preferring to open a restaurant of her own down the road, or so he'd heard from the extremely forthcoming rumor mill that was the Cowboy Kitchen dining room. Still, Fleur provided baked goods daily for the operation, and Gibson had noted that one or both of her sisters frequently stopped by to give her a hand in the mornings.

Flipping on his directional as storm clouds gathered, Gibson suspected his chances were slim he could catch a glimpse of Lark now, an hour before closing time. That didn't stop him from hoping. She'd been quiet for the last few days, ever since she'd stopped by his house and flipped his world upside down with that kiss. He'd been thinking of her nonstop in the meantime and hoping she wouldn't change her mind about their date.

He hadn't intended to push her about a follow-up kiss,

all but guaranteeing there would be a second. But at the time, with the memory of her body pressed tight to his, her hands stroking over him like she craved more, taking things further between them felt inevitable. Imminent.

A date with destiny.

Her silence had him second-guessing, however, and he didn't like that one bit.

His tires crunched over a pothole in the parking lot situated near the building that housed the restaurant along with a post office and hardware store, the latter a two-for-one shop. The place was as close as Catamount got to a shopping plaza, the sum total of downtown business fronts in a rural community.

Yet the parking area was more than half-full. Diner business had been booming since Fleur had taken the food offerings up a notch.

Gibson steered the truck into a space at the far end of a row and switched off the headlights while another bout of thunder rolled ominously, the sky growing dark even though the sun wouldn't set for over two hours. He saw no sign of Lark's rental car or the silver compact that belonged to Fleur, but he recognized Drake's Super Duty pickup near the entrance. Did that still leave a small chance Lark could be inside with her sister?

Trying to ignore the surge of hope as he stepped from his vehicle and settled his hat on his head, Gibson heard the bell chime over the diner entrance followed by a male voice.

"...as soon as the case is closed. You know I'm good for it." Something about the speaker's tone—the bluff confidence of someone who thought highly of himself—made Gibson glance up sharply.

He recalled that voice.

Worse? He recognized the speaker—an overdressed

out-of-towner from his too-slick suit to custom cowboy boots that had never spent a moment off of pavement. A careful comb-over and the flash of gold jewelry marked the guy as Lark's estranged father, Mateo Barclay.

Grinding teeth at the sight of the man who'd cut Lark out of his life long ago, Gibson stalled his step, still unseen near a stake body truck from a local farm. He couldn't have said what made him hesitate, perhaps an unwillingness to acknowledge the guy actively trying to steal away his daughters' inheritance.

"I'll make sure you are since your case goes nowhere without me." The man who'd exited Cowboy Kitchen with Mateo was a weathered looking rancher in worn coveralls and boots. He dropped a battered Stetson onto his gray hair. "See you in court."

A streak of lightning flashed in the sky while the two men seemed to size one another up on the step outside the diner. Gibson remembered the second guy was Antonia Barclay's tenant, Josiah Cranston. Gibson had heard from Drake that the Barclay sisters tried to evict him from the old Crooked Elm foreman's quarters, but with the estate tied up in probate, the eviction hadn't been enforceable and the guy had refused to leave.

What did Lark's slimeball father want with the disgruntled Crooked Elm tenant? Could it be as shady as it sounded?

Gibson's feet were already moving toward the entrance while the men shook hands and Cranston lumbered toward a truck towing an empty horse trailer.

"Barclay, hold on." Gibson hailed Lark's father before the snake slid away.

The man paused in the act of smoothing his pinstriped tie over a slight paunch, his comb-over lifting off his head in a sudden gust of wind.

"If it isn't my former son-in-law." An oily smile spread over his face as Lark's father walked toward him, one hand extended.

Grateful there were no reporters around to witness the encounter, Gibson disregarded the offered hand. Too bad he couldn't ignore the indignation—no, the anger— he felt on Lark's behalf.

"Paying off your witnesses already? Your case hadn't even started yet." Tension strung his shoulders tight as he stared the other man down.

Not missing a beat, Mateo shoved his hand in the pocket of his blue jacket and jingled his keys.

"I'm sure you're not referring to my business dealings with my mother's tenant," he said easily, rocking on his heels and toes. "Our association goes way back."

"I think your daughters' attorney will be interested to hear about the shared business interests." For a moment, Gibson wondered how any parent could so actively work against the kids they raised.

But then, his own father had no use for him, preferring to belittle and berate his sports endeavors, until Gibson reached the highest professional level of hockey. And while Gibson had thought he'd outgrown the need to please his absentee father, hadn't his lifelong commitment to his sport and his team been a leftover attempt to fulfill his dad's wishes? He regretted every time he'd put his team before his wife.

So yeah, he understood that it was all too common for people to use their offspring to work through their own baggage.

"Not being a man of business yourself, you might be surprised at all the ways I try to give back to the community where I was raised." Mateo gave a fake, too-jovial wave to an older couple exiting the diner as a few fat raindrops of a summer storm began to fall.

Could the guy really get away with bribing witnesses to give testimony in the court case? Maybe it would have been helpful if there had been a few reporters following Gibson around today after all. It would have been nice to have someone else's word about the shady conversation he'd overheard. Or better yet, to have to it on film.

"Generous to a fault," Gibson muttered, backing up a step since his appetite had fled.

"How about I buy you dinner and we can discuss how I can help you, too?" Mateo jerked his head toward the Cowboy Kitchen behind him. "I hear you have plans for ranching the property near Crooked Elm. I'd be glad to invest, especially since you must have known my mother intended Crooked Elm for me."

Another lightning bolt scissored across the sky as the rain accelerated. The shower pattered onto the brim of his Stetson and the tops of his shoulders while Mateo Barclay's hair molded to his head.

"You're asking me to lie under oath for the sake of a payday?" Gibson couldn't believe his ears. The unmitigated gall of the guy. "I think my finances can do without the bribe."

A steely gleam lit Barclay's avaricious gaze as he jingled his car keys faster. "You're out of hockey now, son. It's not going to be easy maintaining the lifestyle of a sports star now that you're…not."

Gibson's fists tightened at his side. Not that he was tempted to deck the guy. He'd taken cross-checks to the kidneys from vicious blueliners and skated away without saying a thing. But if he could be this insulting to someone who'd once been married into his family, how must he have treated Lark? That ticked him off a whole lot.

Unwilling to waste words on someone like Mateo, Gibson pivoted on his heel and walked to his truck, the rain drops steaming off him as he fumed quietly. Lark had never confided many particulars about her family dynamics. She wasn't one to dwell on unhappy parts of her past. Gibson had known that her father was a liar and a cheat, and that he'd shamelessly hidden financial assets to make sure his wife and daughters didn't receive their fair share of spousal and child support. He'd played the daughters against one another, showing a different side to Jessamyn than he had to Lark and Fleur, capitalizing on a rift between Jessamyn and their mother. But hearing those spare details didn't compare with experiencing the manipulation for himself. Sliding into the driver's seat of his pickup, Gibson tossed his hat in the back and fired up the engine.

He couldn't wait another day to see Lark. Not when he needed to share the news about Cranston's testimony with her and her sisters.

Pulling out onto the county route that would take him to Crooked Elm, Gibson was still pissed off. Yet he couldn't deny that just the thought of seeing his ex-wife again, of watching her green eyes darken when he stood a little too close or hearing her fast gulp of breath when he found any reason to touch her, lifted his spirits.

He'd thought about her often, even dreamed of contacting her after his retirement, but his focus had turned to caring for his mother. And he'd come to realize that with all his doing for others, he hadn't taken the time to figure out what he really wanted.

Letting the possibilities play out in his mind, Gibson

pressed the accelerator harder, more than ready to close the distance between them.

Rain battered the windows of the ranch house at Crooked Elm while Lark finished a telehealth visit with one of her older teen patients, Misty. The autistic high school sophomore had been seeing Lark for over a year, and her life seemed on track after her parents' divorce to the point that Lark had told the girl's mother they could end their sessions. But Misty herself had lobbied to extend the visits, and between that display of faith in Lark as a counselor, and the lower pressure conversations now that Misty had worked through her most difficult challenges, Lark really enjoyed the talks.

In fact, she'd purposely scheduled Misty's session for the end of the day in the hope of shoring up her personal defenses before the inevitable wedding planning.

Even now, Lark could hear her sisters charging up the staircase, laughing and juggling packages from a shopping outing to Denver. Plastic bags crinkled as they tumbled through the open door to Lark's bedroom, half falling over from the burden of dress bags, accessory boxes and paper sacks bearing designer labels.

"You won't believe all the good stuff we found," Fleur announced, dropping her armful of purchases onto the bed where an old-fashioned chenille spread and handmade quilt that dated from Lark's childhood still covered the full-size bed. "Rehearsal dress, honeymoon outfit—"

"All vintage," Jessamyn interrupted, dropping to sit on the cedar hope chest at the foot of the bed. "The store was stuffed with treasures."

Lark took in the sight of her siblings, damp from the rain but overflowing with good humor, and wondered how she could resist the lure of being part of her own family again. She'd once thought that her anger at Jessamyn's defection would last forever, but if she were counseling herself about a grievance as old as theirs, she would have to say that holding a grudge was only hurting herself.

"Very cool. Am I getting a fashion show?" She sat in the bedroom's window seat, folding her legs beneath her, content to watch them and maybe even a little grateful they'd pulled her into the fun. She'd excused herself from the outing in her ongoing attempts to avoid too much romance.

The evening planning hours with her sisters reached her personal threshold of love and marriage talk. Especially now that she'd foolishly agreed to a date with Gibson. She couldn't allow herself to get soft with her boundaries around him.

"Actually, no," Jessamyn replied, a sly look stealing over her face as she glanced at Fleur and then to Lark. "We were hoping you'd put on the fashion show for us."

"What do you mean?" Trepidation tickled her spine faster than the rain tapping the windowpane at her back.

Standing, Fleur bustled over to one of the bags while Jessamyn moved closer to Lark, finally sitting beside her on the cushioned bench of the window seat.

"I know you aren't crazy about all the wedding stuff," Jessamyn began, her dark curls growing slightly frizzy from the rain. "And that you aren't even necessarily crazy about me."

Jessamyn's eyes, the same green as her own, darted around a little. Was she nervous?

Lark couldn't remember the last time she'd witnessed Jessamyn unsure of herself. Yes, she'd seen her cry her eyes out before she'd gotten engaged to Ryder, when they'd briefly broken up. But this was different.

"I like you fine," Lark retorted, unwilling to break the accord they'd been working on for the past week in their grandmother's house. "We're working on this sibling thing, remember?"

She even slid an arm across her sister's shoulders, remembering Jessamyn was pregnant and that carrying babies surely required extra emotional reserves. The pang in her chest reminded her that she'd been pregnant once too, however briefly.

The miscarriage she'd never told Gibson about. Lark swallowed the hurt she'd thought she'd put behind her, needing to focus on this moment with her family.

"I hope so." Jessamyn blinked fast. "I know we don't have it all worked out yet, but I do appreciate you trying. And I want you to be a bigger part of my life. You know that, right?"

While she spoke, Fleur carried over a dress bag, holding it up in front of them with the black plastic protective cover still in place.

Lark glanced between the two of them before answering Jessamyn. "Um, yes?"

"I do." Jessamyn rose to her feet and dragged the dress bag up to reveal a striking navy blue gown—silk satin with a plunging neckline, skinny straps and clean lines. "That's why I hope you'll be my co–maid of honor with Fleur."

Gaze shooting from the dress to the bride, Lark tried to follow her sister's words. "You're asking me to be an attendant?"

"Yes. Just you and Fleur. I can't choose one sister to stand up there with me when I need both of you in my life."

Surprised and yes, touched, Lark met the eyes so like her own as she stood.

"I'll be there." Wrapping Jessamyn in a quick, hard hug, she realized her voice wasn't quite steady. "You didn't even need to bribe me with the dress."

Fleur squealed, joining them by tipping her head onto Lark's shoulder while wrapping one arm around Jessamyn. She was careful not to crush the gown she held. "But the dress helped, don't deny it."

Grateful for laughter after the unexpected swell of emotion, Lark stepped away from them. Outside the rain-spattered window, a swirl of headlights flashed in the driveway below. She seized on the sight as a way to reclaim a little space.

"Looks like one of your suitors is here." Nodding toward the diffused beams of light showing through the pane, Lark lifted the hanger from Fleur's hand. "While you figure out which Romeo is calling, I'll try on this gorgeous piece to see how it fits."

Fleur and Jessamyn agreed quickly enough to the plan, disappearing out of her room to greet whoever had come calling. And despite the warmth in her heart from the moment of healing her siblings had just given her, Lark couldn't deny a small twist of yearning for the happiness of their new relationships.

Voices sounded downstairs in the kitchen as she peeled off her shirt and bra to shimmy into the low-backed gown. Ignoring the thrum of a male voice too deep to distinguish through her open door, Lark told herself that tiny bit of envy was a symptom of the wedding planning. She'd hit her personal quota of romance for the day, thank you very much.

Lark had her jeans off, her hair down and the dress in place by the time Fleur's voice called up the stairs.

"Gibson is here to see you, Lark. I'm sending him up, okay?"

No!

Unfortunately, she thought the word instead of shouting it. So a moment later, she had no one to blame but herself when she stood facing her sexy-as-sin ex with nothing but a whisper of silk to shield a body suddenly very, very aware of him.

Seven

Gibson knew he had a perfectly good reason to be here, visiting the Barclay house this evening.

But for a minute, hovering at the threshold of Lark's bedroom door in the Crooked Elm main house, he couldn't recall what it might be for the life of him. Not when Lark stood in the middle of the room looking like his every fantasy brought to life. Backlit by two small sconces that bracketed an old-fashioned window seat, the woman he'd once vowed to love forever wore a navy-colored silk dress. The thin gown skimmed her curves, outlining her body in a way he hadn't been privileged to see for over two long years. Thin spaghetti straps left her shoulders exposed while the neckline dipped deeper than anything she normally wore.

Best of all? Her dark hair was loose, the way she only wore it in the evenings after her workday was done.

Glossy strands framed her shoulders like a cape, catching the light as she moved to cross her arms over her chest.

A too-late effort to hide the telltale peaks of her nipples that he hadn't been able to enjoy for nearly long enough.

"I wasn't expecting you." Her voice scratched along a dry note.

"It was my turn for a surprise visit," he returned absently, using all of his willpower to draw his gaze up from her body to look her in the eye.

Then, her green gaze only took his breath away more.

"In that case, congratulations." She turned away from him to drag a small lap blanket off the window seat bench. "You've caught me completely unaware."

Her words floated around his head without penetrating his brain since the back of the gown was even more jaw-dropping than the front. The navy silk dipped so low that he could see the two dimples bracketing the base of her spine, just above the sweet curve of the world's most bite-able ass.

He swept a hand over his mouth and held it there for a second to silence the hungry sounds he made in his mind.

When she turned around to face him again she was draped in the plush white lap blanket, the corners held in one fist clutched just below her breasts. When she lifted one raven's wing dark eyebrow, an impatient expression on her face, he realized he'd better start talking fast or she'd shove him right back out the front door.

"Actually, I'm here because I ran into your father at the Cowboy Kitchen." Recalling the unhappy reason he'd driven to Crooked Elm in the first place, indignation returned. "I overheard him talking to Josiah Cranston in a way that suggested your dad would be paying Cranston off in exchange for his testimony in the case."

"Right in the middle of the diner? Where anyone in town could hear?" Her brows knitted as she seemed to weigh the news. Then she waved him into the room with a quick gesture of her hand. "Come sit. Tell me everything."

Lark dropped onto the edge of the mattress as he entered, the blue silk gown pooling around her legs as she crossed them. Even as he debated the wisdom of sitting beside her—on a bed, of all places—Gibson lowered himself to a spot near her.

"I heard them outside the restaurant, but they must have started the conversation indoors." He realized now that it had been a mistaken to drive away before going inside himself. "I was so ticked off after talking to Mateo that I didn't—"

"You spoke to him, too?" Her gaze held his, questioning.

Quickly, he recapped what happened, including her father's offer to buy his testimony and Gibson's failure to enter the Cowboy Kitchen afterward to see who might have overheard something valuable. "It never occurred to me at the time," he explained, feeling like he'd let her and her sisters down by not thinking that through. "But maybe if I made note of the patrons inside the eatery, your attorney could have found someone else who heard your dad bribing Cranston."

Lark was already shaking her head, one long lock of hair falling in front of her shoulder. "I doubt it. My father is an expert in knowing how much he can get away with. If he was that obvious about suggesting he could bribe you, he must not be worried about blowback from potential testimony that he's unethical."

Gibson eyed the fallen lock of her hair, imagining the texture against his skin while the room seemed to shrink around them. The scent of her lavender soap teased his nose along with her mint shampoo while he remembered what it had been like to kiss her on his veranda just two days ago.

He wanted more than a taste, needed more than that. But he wouldn't rush the chance to have her in his bed and risk having her bolt. If he wanted any hope of letting this chemistry work its course, he needed to let Lark set the pace.

"He should be," he forced himself to say, dragging his gaze away from Lark to glance around the room and looking at anything that wasn't her enticing figure beside him. Unfortunately, the first thing his attention fixed on was a pile of her discarded clothes in the corner.

Crumpled jeans. Black blazer. A barely-there ivory-colored bra in a model he knew so well he could unfasten it in less than a blink. The temptation of being alone in a bedroom with her weighed heavy on him, infusing his every thought.

"I'll tell my sisters and let them decide if it's worth sharing with the attorney." Her tone was careful. Circumspect.

It was so startlingly unlike her when it came to discussions of her dad that Gibson found his gaze swiveling to her again.

"Don't you want to go after him? After the way he cut you and Fleur off from all financial support—"

"I wouldn't take his money under any circumstances," she retorted, her shoulders straightening to cover any hint of vulnerability he knew still lurked inside. "Although I definitely hate what he did to Fleur, and I resent him for hurting my mother, I'm not interested in retribution for my own sake. I won't lose any more personal happiness because of some childhood hurt."

Admiration for her pulled a smile from his lips, even as his protective instincts surged. He'd do everything in his power to ensure her father didn't succeed in his quest to steal Crooked Elm from his daughters.

He also had the power of a media following. And if he could leverage that to help Lark, he intended to use it.

"That's impressive considering—well, considering what I know of the guy," he said finally, guessing she wouldn't approve of his tactics if he told her about his plans. "Good for you, Lark."

"It didn't happen overnight, believe me." Her gaze slid over to his as an answering smile curved her lush mouth. "Therapists know the best therapists."

All at once, the lightness faded from the moment for him as he recalled asking Lark to see a marriage counselor with him before she left for good. She'd only shaken her head and kept walking away.

Perhaps he should have welcomed the reminder of why they weren't right together for anything more than the chemistry. But the memory still nicked an old wound. And it underscored all the reasons he needed to find closure.

"Then I'll leave it up to you." He rose to his feet, doing his best to keep his eyes off the discarded pile of her clothes.

There was no point in thinking about what his ex-wife wasn't wearing under that blanket.

"Thank you for coming over." She stood with him, the movement stirring the scent of her hair again. "I appreciate you letting me know what Dad did."

"Of course." Nodding, he bit back the urge to ask her how she was holding up in the new spurt of media interest in her since that small video clip of her lobbying for more coverage of female athletes went viral. He'd tested his ability to resist touching her enough for one day. "I guess I'll see you in court then?"

"I'll be there. So will my mother, actually. She flies in tomorrow and will stay with us until Jessamyn's wedding."

He'd always liked Jennifer Barclay, but then, Lark's feisty spirit was a lot like her mother's.

"I'll look forward to saying hello," he told her honestly.

At the same time, Lark said, "I haven't forgotten about my promise to visit your mom. You'll let me know when it's a good time?"

Thinking about how often his mother asked about his "wife," Gibson knew that couldn't be soon enough. Still, he was glad Lark didn't seem to mind.

"My contractor assured me the annex on the house will be finished by the end of the week." He'd already called the moving company to bring their things permanently. "With any luck, maybe when the trial wraps up, my mom will be around."

He moved toward the door, knowing he should cross the threshold. Drive home before he looked into Lark's forest-green eyes for too long.

"Sounds good." She walked a step behind him and when he stopped to take his leave, she bumped into him lightly.

Just a brush of the blanket where it wrapped around her elbow, but the touch still jolted him.

Her gaze darkened a fraction as she looked up at him. His heart thudded harder.

Restraint, he counseled himself.

Still, he couldn't halt the final words she deserved to

hear before he took his leave. "For what it's worth, that dress looks incredible on you."

She gasped softly, then glanced down at herself, parting the blanket slightly as if to recall what she'd been wearing. The renewed glimpse of her in the midnight-colored silk had him swallowing his tongue.

"Thank you. It was an unexpected gift from Jessamyn." Her fingers smoothed along one skinny strap at her shoulder. "She picked it out for me today and then asked if I would be a co–maid of honor with Fleur."

Recalling her fractured relationship with Jessamyn, he couldn't help but wonder how that went.

"She couldn't have chosen anything more perfectly suited to you," he observed, even as his hands ached to feel the fabric and Lark's warm body beneath it.

"I'm not so sure. I've never worn anything this revealing in my whole life." Wrapping her arms around herself again, she gave a small shrug.

"There are no ruffles, frills or lace. It's not a flashy color and it's perfectly tailored for you. I'd say she put a lot of thought into finding something exactly right."

"Maybe so," she acknowledged, her attention dropping from his eyes to…his mouth.

She was killing him.

One hundred percent.

And he didn't stand a chance of leaving just yet.

"Are you going to do it then? Be one of her maids of honor?" he pressed, his whole body heating.

Wanting.

Downstairs, he could hear her sisters working in the kitchen, talking and laughing. Outside, the rain still pattered lightly on the windowpane. But right here, at the threshold of Lark's bedroom, there was only the slow burn of longing.

"Yes. I'll be there for her." She dragged her focus up to his eyes. "It's a new era of sisterhood for the Barclays."

He released a long breath, trying his best to ignore the pent-up hunger. He had to walk away now before he took the kiss that she was thinking about every bit as much as him.

"Good for you." With a nod of approval, he backed up a step, inserting more space between them. "And me, too."

"For you? How do you figure?" She scrunched her nose as she stared at him, her long hair a dark ripple in the shadowed hallway as she followed him toward the stair landing.

He gripped the banister, forced himself to keep moving.

"Not only will I get to see you in that dress again, but you'll be wearing it for our date." His pulse jackhammered at the vision that created in his mind. "At a *wedding*. Where I can ask you to dance as an excuse to have my hands all over you."

He didn't know how he'd wait to touch her until then. But at the soft, quickly stifled gasp that Lark made at his words, at least he knew he wasn't the only one who'd be fantasizing about seeing each other again.

"Lark, look this way!" the voice of a reporter outside Routt County Courthouse called to her as she strode toward the municipal building on the first day of the court challenge.

A small throng of camera operators hovered behind a few on-the-spot media members. Lark kept her feet moving, remembering Gibson's advice. Reporters couldn't hassle her or impede her. She didn't have to talk to them. She had the control—not them.

Still, she felt glad to be entering the court with her sisters. Jessamyn and Fleur were two steps behind her. Her mother had wanted to attend the session, but a long day of travel had left Jennifer Barclay under the weather. Privately, Lark worried the stress of facing their father in a courtroom again had taken a toll of its own on their mom. They'd left her to rest in a spare room at Crooked Elm.

"Lark, are you hoping Gibson returns to Los Angeles this coming season?" A petite woman asked, taking two steps to Lark's long stride in order to keep pace with her on the left side. The awkward gait made the woman's microphone bob up and down around Lark's chin. "Is it true he's testifying here today to support you?"

On her right, a man's voice added to the noise. "Lark, have you spoken to any of the female athletes who've come out in strong support of your campaign to re-center media attention on women?"

Is that what she'd been doing? Campaigning?

It took all her effort not to snipe back that her campaign must not have been very successful since journalists like him still followed around the former wife of a major athlete rather than an *actual* athlete. But today wasn't about her battle with the superficial entertainment media types. Since her rant on camera, she'd been disciplined about blocking as many news sources as possible that might speculate on her relationship with Gibson in hurtful ways.

Eyes forward. No comment.

While a part of her regretted not figuring that out in time to help her marriage, another part of her knew that Gibson's extended absences were more to blame than the media. The press interference just added fuel to the fire. And how was it she ended up thinking about Gibson so often lately? She still couldn't believe they'd parted ways two nights ago without touching. She'd been on edge ever since.

Beside her, Fleur's voice pulled her from her musing at the same time as the distinctive rumble of a helicopter's rotor sounded overhead. "You okay?"

The aircraft must be flying close by, the sound growing louder still.

"Perfect," she lied, needing it to be true. "Ready to show the court what a liar our father is and secure Gran's legacy."

They were halfway up the stairs into the building when raised voices from the parking area made Lark turn to see what was happening.

At first, she couldn't quite make sense of it.

The reporters—mostly a ragtag collection of freelancers trying to invent a story to sell, although there'd been one local network affiliate—were swarming in the opposite direction of the courthouse. They moved as one toward the grassy space behind the court while the *whap-whap-whap* of the helicopter blades increased in volume.

A shadow fell over the open green area, and Lark realized that the aircraft she'd been hearing was descending onto the lawn across the street.

It didn't look like a rescue vehicle. The gray bird touching down was unmarked. Yet why would the press think it was a big deal?

"Do you think it's Dad trying to make a showy entrance?" Fleur asked, shading her eyes as they all watched.

"Dad hates helicopters," Jessamyn murmured, craning her neck to see around a few other pedestrians who'd been on their way into the courthouse building. "I could never get him to take one in or out of Manhattan even though it's often the fastest way."

Then, the door opened and a tall man with unmistakably broad shoulders stepped from the craft.

Three-time league scoring champion Gibson Vaughn had arrived.

"What would he pull a stunt like that for?" Lark asked herself as much as her sisters. Surprised she still had air in her lungs to talk after his drool-worthy entrance.

She understood that Gibson had always been good with the media. He was often the face of the league, sought out for his opinions on big-picture issues that affected all of hockey. He'd always been able to steer negative press away from his teammates, shouldering blame for hard losses himself where he could as a long-time captain.

But for a man who was supposedly retiring, he sure was working the media now.

"You seriously don't know?" Jessamyn asked her, spinning around to pin Lark with narrowed eyes. "Lark, he's been on a quest all week to make sure the media knows he supports your efforts to draw more attention to women's sports."

Frowning, Lark wondered why he hadn't mentioned it to her when she'd seen him at Crooked Elm two nights ago. Did he have an ulterior motive? Even as the thought formed, she felt guilty for doubting him.

"But here? Today?" She failed to see the connection between that thirty-second sound bite of her on camera with the court case today. "Why stir the press to a frenzy at the trial when we need his testimony?"

Fleur looped an arm through hers as they all watched Gibson work the crowd like a celebrity at a premiere. He walked at a normal pace, nodding and acknowledging the sidling members of the media as he moved toward the courthouse.

"Gibson has also been vocal about supporting your efforts to retain your claim to Crooked Elm," Fleur explained, withdrawing her phone and scrolling to a social media post with an image of Gibson engaged in one of his rare on-ice fights. Beneath it, the tagline read, "Hockey hero praises ex's fight for family land." Fleur flipped past it to the hundreds of comments following the post. "If you ask me, I think it's really nice he's spoken out publicly in favor of Gran's will."

Lark hadn't known any of this. But of course, she'd been so proud of herself for blocking mentions of herself and Gibson wherever possible.

"Do you think that helps our cause?" She glanced between her sisters while Gibson drew within fifty yards of them, bringing the buzzing media circle with him. The sound of excited voices and shouted questions came with him, the volume increasing each moment.

"Absolutely," Jessamyn answered definitively, her ring-bearing hand straying to her still flat belly. "Rallying public favor makes our fight sympathetic. It sure can't hurt."

And somehow, seeing Jessamyn's fingers brush lovingly over the place where her future child rested chased every other thought from Lark's mind save one—her own baby that might have been.

She'd thought of the miscarriage all the more since returning to Catamount and seeing Gibson so often. Yet it was a hurt she couldn't have weighing on her heart through the probate trial.

"We'd better get inside ahead of the crowd," she urged her sisters. Keeping Fleur's arm looped through hers, she used it to tug Fleur toward the main doors with her. "Gibson might enjoy the media, but no matter how hard I try to flip the script, I'd still rather avoid them."

The last thing Lark wanted was more attention from the press, especially now that she knew how expertly Gibson had wound them up regarding this case. Because all it took was one reporter asking the right questions about her past—about the time of her split from Gibson—to uncover the secret she could never bear to share.

Eight

Settling into the witness stand in the Routt County Courthouse almost six hours later, Gibson's gaze went automatically to Lark seated between her sisters.

She wore a gray shirtdress cinched at the waist with a narrow belt, the knee-length hem and conservative cut of the outfit a far cry from the siren's gown she'd worn the last time they'd met. Her hair was in its signature braid, her green gaze darting around the courtroom so that she looked anywhere but at him.

Because she was frustrated with the proceedings in the first day of the hearing? Or because she was unhappy with him for leveraging his media influence to garner public support for her and her sisters?

"State your full name for the record, please," a court official intoned while a stenographer typed away silently nearby.

Gibson had already given a deposition prior to the

hearing, but today was an opportunity for the attorneys to question one another's witnesses and for the judge to ask questions about the information submitted. After sitting through hours of garbage testimony like Josiah Cranston's insistence that Lark, Fleur and Jessamyn exerted "undue influence" over Antonia Barclay in the last year of her life, Gibson was eager to set the record straight for the court.

"Gibson Vaughn," he replied into his microphone, mentally recalling the advice from Lark's lawyer to be succinct and clear in his remarks.

And he would be. He planned to nail his part of this hearing so Lark would have the portion of her grandmother's estate that was rightfully hers. He knew how much the land meant to her. He'd bought his ranch next door to Crooked Elm just to be sure they could both enjoy all the things she loved about the remote region.

Even though they weren't together anymore, he still wanted her to have what made her happy.

So after a brief swearing in and a recap of his deposition by Lark's attorney, Gibson was made available for questions from Mateo Barclay's attorney, who was allowed to remain seated at his own table. The process seemed less formal than trials dramatized for the screen, with much of the day given to dry exchanges of information for the record.

Now, the plaintiff's counsel, a tall, heavyset man with jutting brows and a weathered face leaned closer to his own microphone to speak.

"Mr. Vaughn, your statement to this court about Antonia Barclay's personal confidences suggests you had a close relationship with the decedent in the final year of her life, but isn't it true you were divorced from her granddaughter at that time?"

Lark's eyes lifted to meet his.

And just like that, despite all the worry that he'd upset her today by stirring up the media, Gibson felt a bond with her that no divorce paper would ever erase. He could practically see her thoughts in her eyes—her silent caution to tread carefully. He hoped she could read him the same way, because he was mentally telling her he had no intention of letting her down.

"Yes, but Antonia remained my neighbor and friend."

The attorney raised one protruding brow. "Even though your divorce from her granddaughter was acrimonious?"

Heat crept up at the insinuation. His hands clenched beneath the wooden stand as he spoke evenly, "My divorce was the worst loss of my life, and I can assure you I did everything in my power to ease any pain that I may have caused my ex-wife."

Lark's right eye twitched. It was the smallest hint of a reaction, but Gibson read that one, too. Despite her disappointment in him for the failed marriage, she still cared enough to be touched by his words.

Somehow that made anything else he faced today easy.

"The photos of you with another woman online preceding your split say otherwise," the attorney continued, approaching the bench to flash a series of papers in front of Gibson before laying them in front of the presiding judge. "As does the receipt from the moving company that loaded your then-wife's things into a truck the same weekend."

Gibson knew enough to school his features into a semblance of composure. He'd been doing as much his whole life in front of cameras, so he could perform the trick now even when the desire to lash out at the guy was

strong. His divorce hadn't been about the stupid photos—taken at a charity event with a drunken attendee
who'd asked for a picture with him and turned it into an
opportunity to plaster herself to him. Still, he understood
how the timing had looked suspect.

That charity event had prevented him from taking
calls from Lark when she'd been upset about something
different—something that happened hours before the
drunk photos. It had been one of many times he hadn't
been there for her, and he'd come to regret that bitterly.
He'd been so focused on trying to lift that struggling
team of young guys who'd all looked to him to turn
their season around, he'd hurt the person who had mat-
tered most.

At the time, he'd only been upset that she couldn't
understand how much they needed him.

Fortunately, Lark's attorney objected to the other lawyer's remarks for all the obvious reasons, while the judge
urged the man to ask a relevant question if he had one.

"Very well." Mateo Barclay's legal counsel continued,
returning his attention to Gibson. "Mr. Vaughn, is it true
you're planning to win back your ex-wife?"

Schooled though he might be in maintaining his composure in front of a crowd, the question still rattled him
while the attorney for the Barclay sisters objected to the
personal question. They'd worked out a few scenarios in
case the lawyer asked about the future grazing or sale
rights, but hadn't expected it to get so personal.

While lawyers and judge sorted out whether to allow
it or not, all Gibson could think about was the direct
query.

Memories of kissing Lark on his porch fired through
him. Of the way she'd promised to visit his ailing mom.

The way she'd looked at him when he'd stood at the threshold of her bedroom, her eyes full of heat.

Was he trying to win her back?

A moment later, with the objection overruled, Mateo Barclay's lawyer circled closer to the witness stand. The older man tapped a knuckle on the wooden rail separating them as he zeroed in on Gibson.

"Mr. Vaughn, is it your intention to resume a relationship with Lark Barclay?"

Gibson knew where the question would lead. Him wanting Lark back in his life would give the impression that his testimony was self-serving because if they ever married again, Lark's portion of the Crooked Elm property could potentially belong to him as well.

His gaze flipped to Lark's, her green eyes shooting him a warning. But since he was under oath, he had no choice but to answer with a truth he'd just come to acknowledge himself.

"Only a fool wouldn't want her back," he said into the microphone, watching every nuance of Lark's expression while her full lips tightened into a frown. "And I assure you, I'm no fool."

After the bombshell of Gibson's surprise revelation, Lark sat through the remainder of the day's hearing in a sort of fog. Dimly, she'd been aware of the aftermath in the courtroom. Her father's counsel had tried to make it sound like Gibson was a washed-up hockey player who needed his ex-wife's inheritance to make his new bison ranch venture a success now that his sports career had ended. All of Gibson's helpful testimony about Antonia assuring him she wanted Crooked Elm to go to her granddaughters certainly came into question.

Of course her father's legal team would try to undermine him, and Gibson had played right into their hands.

Since when did he want her back? The idea tied her emotions in knots. Because surely he wouldn't have lied under oath. More importantly, what did his words mean?

"Lark?" On her left, Fleur nudged her with an elbow. "Did you hear what I said?"

Dragging her thoughts from the drama of Gibson's declaration and the probate hearing, she refocused on her sister. At the same time, she realized the judge had exited the courtroom, signaling the end of the day's session. Her father was giving his lawyer a hearty slap on the shoulder while Jessamyn and Ryder were listening intently to their attorney. The few other attendees were standing to leave.

Gibson, however, still sat in the place he'd taken after he'd been excused from the stand. At the far end of her row, he scrolled through his phone.

"I'm sorry. I must have zoned out for a moment." Lark reached for her cross-body bag that had slid to one side of her on the seat, preparing to leave the courtroom. "What did you say?"

"I said you should have an exit strategy for leaving the building. When I turned my phone on, I got a million notifications about Gibson's support for us today." Fleur waggled her device for emphasis, the photo on her screen showing a split-frame image of Lark and Gibson with a dividing line between them. Words had been printed over the image reading, "Her Ex to the Rescue?"

"I'm guessing the number of interested bystanders and media hounds has tripled by now," Fleur continued. "But they're not all here for Gibson. There are memes all over the place from when you confronted the media about the lack of coverage for female athletes. That story has taken on a whole life of its own."

Tension coiled in her belly at the thought. She didn't want to be a spokesperson for a cause that wasn't really hers to champion. She'd just been sounding off. And as for Gibson's sudden declaration about their relationship, how much interest would that draw? She might have gotten a little better with handling the media, but she didn't look forward to a slew of uncomfortable questions when she walked through the band of assorted media types.

Unlike Gibson, Lark didn't have the knack for schooling her features into a neutral expression when someone asked her something upsetting. It was one thing to control her visible response to distressing news in the course of her patient appointments. It was entirely different to remain poised when someone came at her personally. Shooting to her feet, she wished she could sprint from here to Fleur's vehicle without looking back.

"Lark?" The deep rumble of Gibson's voice sounded behind her.

Sensation raced up her arms and down her spine, a strong physical reaction to his nearness that she did not want to feel. Especially when at any moment the press could be racing up to snap a photo which might capture her feelings for the world to see.

Spinning around to face him, she whispered furiously, "Haven't you done enough to upend this hearing already?"

"You're right." He laid a hand on her shoulder, a gesture meant to comfort perhaps, but it only stoked the sensations zinging through her already. "And I'm sorry if my testimony proves to be a roadblock for you."

On the other side of her, Fleur whispered in her ear that she'd be by the door if Lark needed her.

Great. There went her support system.

Her heart pounded in her chest, her emotions knotted more than ever as she faced Gibson. She didn't want this kindness from him. Didn't know what to do with it when he'd publicly admitted he still had feelings for her. Why hadn't he tried to show her that when they were married and she'd needed him desperately?

Agitated, she couldn't help but flinging back, "It's not just the testimony though, is it? What about the media interest you've purposely stirred so that no one can escape the building without being bombarded by microphones, cameras and questions?"

She looped the strap of her bag over her head, adjusting the zippered pouch to lay flat on her hip, her movements abrupt with her shaken nerves.

Gibson's hand remained on her shoulder, his broad fingers rubbing lightly as he leaned closer to speak quietly in her ear. "I know how much you hate that kind of thing. That's why I've asked one of the bailiffs about taking us out the back exit so we can reach the helicopter quickly."

She stilled. For a moment, with the cedar and sandalwood scent of his aftershave so close to her nose and the warmth of his fingers playing along her spine, she could almost pretend they were still together. There'd been a time when she would have trusted him to be by her side through anything. To be her partner.

Maybe old habits died hard because in spite of everything that had happened between them, her instincts still leaned into that feeling.

"I don't need a ride in your helicopter," she retorted, trying to preserve a measure of distance between them. A small part of her defenses against this man's appeal. "But I would be grateful if you can show me another exit that would get me closer to Fleur's car without tripping over twenty reporters."

He hesitated, his dark eyes searching hers for a moment before his chin dipped in acknowledgment of her request.

"All right, but I hope you'll reconsider sticking with me once you see the kind of crowd that's out there." His hand slid down her back to settle at the base of her spine. He guided her toward the rear of the courtroom. "At least text your sisters to let them know we're together."

Lark wanted to argue that she wouldn't be riding home with him, and yet one look out the front windows of the courthouse to the throng of people gathered around the main entrance made her rethink that stance. Two guards had been posted by the doors to the building, a security measure that hadn't been necessary when she'd arrived that morning.

Now, with the press of dark shapes all around the oversized doors and the hum of excited voices through the glass, Lark understood how much interest in Gibson's personal life had grown exponentially in the last few days.

Stomach sinking, she withdrew her phone to text Fleur and Jessamyn. It wasn't fair to them to drag them through the media spotlight if she could avoid it by leaving with Gibson.

"Are you ready?" Gibson prompted as she sent the group message. "We need to follow Officer Kincaid."

"As ready as I'll ever be." After sliding her cell into her bag, Lark greeted the young court official dressed in a blue uniform. The man spoke into a walkie as he led them to a side staircase, taking them in the opposite direction of the way Lark had entered the building that morning.

When they reached an unmarked steel door at the base of the stairwell, Officer Kincaid spoke some kind of alert into his walkie again, then clipped the two-way onto his belt.

"Officer Bracey says your driver is waiting, Mr. Vaughn," the young man assured them, something about his straight bearing and at-ease stance suggesting a military past. "If you need to use the entrance tomorrow, just let us know in the morning and I'll meet you here."

"Thanks a lot." Gibson placed one hand on the door to push it open, keeping the other around her waist. "I'll make sure to bring a signed jersey for your nephew tomorrow. I appreciate this."

The younger man's military reserve disappeared as he grinned. "Spencer will be over the moon."

A moment later, Gibson's hold on her tightened as he ushered her from the building into the waiting black Range Rover with heavily tinted windows. Lark was too distracted by the pinpricks of awareness all through her body at Gibson's palm fastened around her hip to notice who drove the vehicle on the other side of a shaded privacy panel.

Why was his touch affecting her this way today of all days when he may have very well cost her family their case?

"Can't we just let the driver take us home?" she asked as she scooted, breathless, into the far side of the vehicle.

Away from the temptation Gibson's touch presented.

As the SUV lurched forward in the direction of the grassy expanse where the helicopter sat, Lark tried to get her bearings. A police car with its lights on sat in the middle of the court parking lot now, as if to control the extra crowd drawn by the hearing and the celebrity taking part in it.

Besides the media, there were fans from Gibson's former team there, obvious by the number of hockey jerseys and signs bearing messages to him.

"Through that crowd?" He pointed toward the mayhem now visible around one end of the building. He leaned partially over her so he could peer out the tinted window on her side of the vehicle. "I don't think that would be fair to ask of the car service since that sort of driving goes above and beyond a routine fare."

Not to mention, having to stop and inch their way through crowds of pedestrians would slow their escape and give the media hounds more time to take photos and shout questions through the windows.

Clearly, Gibson's exit strategy had been better thought out than hers. She just resented that they had to use it in the first place. Swallowing her pride, she took shallow breaths so as not to inhale more of his distinctive scent. Having his arm braced on the window near her, his chest leaning close to hers, made her twitchy inside.

Restless. Hungry.

Was it true that he wanted to win her back? Lark shut down the question as soon as it floated to the top of her thoughts.

"If the offer is still open, I'll accept the ride home," she said instead, keeping her gaze on the gray metal aircraft whose rotors were already in motion.

"Good. It'll be safer for everyone this way. Your sisters, too." Leaning into the seat beside her, he withdrew his cell phone and thumbed a text. "I'm letting the pilot know she can take off as soon as we're on board."

A moment later, the SUV pulled to a stop near the helicopter that sat on private property behind the courthouse. She guessed it hadn't been difficult for Gibson to obtain permission to land there from the owner. Just like with Officer Kincaid, a signed jersey went a long way in getting the hockey star whatever he wanted in life.

Right now, it was tough to be upset about that because she wanted no part of facing the sports media after the eventful first day of the probate hearing. After texting her sisters once more, she took a deep breath as Gibson opened the passenger side rear door for them to exit.

"Thank you for arranging this, Gibson." The last part of the sentence was shouted, the noise of the helicopter blades drowning out all other sounds.

Taking his hand, Lark stepped from the vehicle. He didn't let go as he led her a few steps to a set of flip-down stairs leading into the chopper.

"It's my fault that all the media are on site," he returned, his own voice only slightly raised to be heard over the racket from the engine. "So it's only fair that I find a way to get us out of here."

Lark stepped into the aircraft and dropped into a sideways-facing seat while Gibson raised the stairs and pulled the door shut behind them, turning the lock mechanism for safety.

Immediately, the aircraft ascended. Gibson rocked on his heels for a moment but righted himself easily before lowering into the spot beside her. He passed her a headset and microphone before strapping one into place on his own head.

Lark fumbled with the mechanism, but a moment later, she could hear Gibson's voice through it. "Testing. Testing."

She gave him a thumb-up while he buckled his seat belt and then double-checked that hers was locked.

The small gesture of simple caring reminded her of all the ways he'd confused and stirred her emotions today. Swallowing past the lump in her throat, she spoke into her microphone as she watched the shapes on the ground move as one big shadow toward the spot where their helicopter had been.

"I can hear you," she said over a dry throat. "And I'm very ready to go home."

Gibson was quiet for so long that she wondered if he'd heard her. But then, swinging her attention back to him, she saw he watched her intently, his brow furrowed.

"What's wrong?" she asked, grateful that they were in the air and not on the ground near all those questioning eyes.

"I'm not sure going home is the best idea, Lark. The media will be waiting at the edge of the property. Particularly if they see you're there."

Spirits sinking fast, she clenched her hands into fists.

"Of course they will be," she muttered, wondering how she'd get through this week until the hearing ended. "I should warn my mother—"

Taking her phone from her bag again, Gibson stopped her with one hand covering hers.

"In a minute." A lopsided, apologetic smile lifted his lips. "Before you do that, I want you to think about how returning to Crooked Elm will only bring all of that crowd from the courthouse to your doorstep."

Anger and dismay warred in her gut. "So what do you suggest I do, Gibson? I don't have that many options."

The roar of the engine and the rotor were dulled through the headset so that Lark could hear her own breathing. Her pulse pounding in her ears with the stress of the day.

"Come with me to a private retreat in the mountains."

His voice was a silky rasp in her ear, the words enticing her when they shouldn't. "We can escape all the media."

The knots in her stomach suddenly didn't feel like the result of her too-emotional day. Right now, the tension there turned sensual.

She guessed that her eyes reflected those feelings too, because Gibson's dark gaze went molten as he looked at her.

"I don't know," she half whispered the words, more unsure of what tomorrow would bring than she was about what she *wanted*.

Desire for this man still ran through her veins like he had space reserved in every blood cell.

"Just for one night, until we can make arrangements for security," he urged, his broad palm sliding over to land on her knee. His thumb grazing her thigh.

Call her weak. Call her susceptible to the Gibson Vaughn charm. But she didn't have a prayer of saying no after the day she'd had.

Licking her lips, she struggled to form words over her dry throat. At the prospect of being with him, her body tingled from head to toe, every inch of her aware of him. She knew this wasn't just about a place to lay her head for the night.

This was about *them*.

Alone. Together.

"I'll go with you," she agreed, deciding that taking pleasure for herself wasn't an act of weakness after all. She wanted him, and she owned her feelings. There was a kind of strength in that. "As long as you understand this really is just for one night."

The gleam in her ex-husband's eyes should have warned her that his notorious competitive streak had been stirred by the challenge.

But far from sending her running, the knowledge that he would do everything in his power to make tonight amazing for her only made her look out the helicopter window and wonder how fast they could land.

Nine

She'd said yes.

Gibson couldn't quite believe his luck. Even though he'd screwed up in the courtroom by drawing extra media attention to Lark's case, then added to the trouble by admitting he wanted her back, she had still agreed to spend the night with him at his retreat in the mountains.

His gaze swept over the gray shirtdress that covered her incredible curves, her shape only hinted at by the slim belt that tucked in at her waist. The silken rope of her braid had come to rest between her breasts at some point during the flight, making him fantasize about unbuttoning her dress beneath it while leaving her hair right where it lay. He would use the velvety ends of her tresses to paint lightly along her skin until she arched closer to him for more contact…

And damn, but the helicopter ride couldn't possibly pass quickly enough.

Finally, twenty minutes later, the chopper descended at a location just outside the Flat Tops Wilderness area. The pilot touched down in a clearing ringed by tall aspens, less than twenty yards from a two-story rustic log cabin.

"This is your place?" Lark asked through the headset, pointing to the structure with wide porches on the rear of both levels. Her dark brown braid shifted forward as she leaned toward the window.

With an effort, he pulled his gaze from her to glance out at the property that he hadn't visited in months. In a nearby detached garage, a truck awaited them along with a snow machine and a dirt bike, but none of that was visible from their seats in the helicopter as the rotor slowed.

Nodding, he unbuckled his seatbelt and tugged off the headset while she did the same. "It is. I bought the cabin last year, thinking I might need a place to retreat. My mother's medical team mentioned that it's important for caregivers to schedule time to unwind, and it got me thinking I might appreciate having another property nearby. I purchased the cabin in the name of a limited liability company as well so the media can't track me here."

She hesitated before answering, her expression pensive.

"You've put a lot of thought into transitioning your mom into your house." Lark rose to her feet while he pushed open the aircraft door.

There were no houses around for miles, the view of the Flat Tops Wilderness a breathtaking sweep in front of them. And even though it was a warm day, the weather was cooler at the higher altitude.

"Maybe now you'll believe I really am retiring from hockey," he commented drily, holding out a hand to help her down.

The scent of pine rose to meet him as he stepped to the ground, the clean mountain air a welcome respite after the claustrophobic atmosphere of a small-town courtroom.

"I do. And now that I know you're committed to retiring, it helps me understand what a big change this is for you." Her hand in his felt so natural. So right.

But he let go, mindful of letting her set the pace tonight. As much as he wanted to take her inside and make her remember how good they could be together, he needed to feed her. Give her time to unwind from the hellish day she'd had in court.

"From team captain to rookie owner of a bison ranch? You'd be right about that." He signaled to the pilot once they cleared the rotors and the helicopter took off again, sending branches and saplings nearby into a frenzy of movement until it was well above the tree line. Then, not wanting to discuss the drastic U-turn his life was taking now that he'd walked away from the one thing he'd always been good at, he redirected the conversation. "Are you ready for dinner? I had a catering service deliver some options for meals tonight."

Beside him, she tensed as they walked onto the gravel driveway in front of the cabin. "Was my visit a foregone conclusion?"

How could she think that? He had championship trophies in his den that he hadn't worked half as hard to win as this time away with Lark.

"Absolutely not. I ordered the food since I planned to spend the night here either way. The construction is almost finished on the annex to the ranch house, but it's still disorganized. I've got a cleaning crew coming in later in the week to make things habitable again." Waving her ahead of him onto the wide front porch, Gibson studied her face in the early evening sunlight, hoping to gauge her reaction to the cabin. "What do you think of it?"

He stepped past her to open the security panel so he could tap in the entry code.

"It reminds me of that chalet we stayed in when we went to Vail." A sexy smile curved her lips as she ran one hand over the rough-cut log porch rail and slanted him a sideways look. "Remember?"

The shared memory lit a fire inside him again despite his efforts to be a considerate host. "Hell yes, I remember. We never did get around to skiing."

In fact, thinking about that time now—and the possibility that she might want a repeat of that incredible weekend—made him forget the security code to the cabin. His finger hovered uselessly over the panel, his attention drawn to Lark as she moved closer to where he stood.

Green eyes fixed on him like a woman who knew what she wanted.

"Lark." He'd need her help if he was going to resist her for even five more minutes. Every inch closer she came, the thinner his restraint stretched. "I'm trying my damnedest to be a gentleman—"

"Please stop," she ordered, laying her palm on his chest, right over the place where his heart pounded a demand only she could meet. She tilted her chin up to meet his eyes while she walked her fingers lower. "I'm not here for the gentleman tonight. After the day that I've had, I want the best player in the game who smokes through every defense to get to the goal."

Heat streaked through him so fast it left scorch marks. Possessiveness surged along with fiery need.

Wrapping his arms around her, he pressed her against him. Lifted her so her feet dangled off the ground.

At the feel of full body contact—even through the layers of their clothes—his breathing accelerated. He dipped his head to her neck to taste her there, the skin bared thanks to her braid.

"You taste so good," he said against her skin, his fingers flexing to cup her ass, molding her to him. "I need you so much."

Her fingers speared into his hair. Stroking. Petting. Driving him out of his head.

"I need you, too." She arched her back in a way that tilted her breasts up, demanding his attention. "What's the code so we can get in?"

She stretched a hand toward the security screen by the door while he debated the fastest way to bare her breasts.

"Our wedding anniversary," he informed her, the answer blared into his brain now, as if all his system functions operated at her command. "Eight digits."

"You're not supposed to use dates people can guess," she chided even as she punched in the numbers.

After a series of beeps, the code cleared and the door unlocked. He never lifted his head from where he kissed his way down Lark's neck, however, he just heard the electronic cue in the back of his consciousness.

"I'll change it tomorrow," he promised, the scent of her lavender soap stronger as he nudged open the neckline of her dress to kiss the soft swell above her bra cup. "Right now, I have a goal."

Shivers raced over her.

Lark had deliberately put herself at this man's mercy and the result was every bit as tantalizing as she knew it would be. Gibson Vaughn unleashed was a power to behold. Stark male strength and raw masculine appeal made him a formidable bed partner.

Tomorrow she would contend with the complications of this night. For now, she needed one more time in his arms, one more chance to experience the way he could make her forget everything but pleasure. No one else had ever possessed that power for her, and she feared no one else ever could again.

So by the time he shoved his way inside the cabin and locked the door behind them, she was almost dizzy with lust while he strode through the foyer with her in his arms. The erection swelling against her was impossible to ignore, the heat and length of him branding into her belly. And of course, his mouth did wicked things to her breast, his tongue flicking beneath the satin of her bra cup to tease close to her nipple.

"Gibson," she panted his name as she shifted against him, needing more. Wanting everything. "Just to be clear, your goal is to be inside me, I hope?"

He lifted his head to meet her gaze, his pupils dilated so that the brown ring around them was barely visible. Around them, she grew vaguely aware of the high ceilings and open floor plan where weathered woods in gray and sandy tones dominated the space. A lamp glowed on the big plank mantel of a floor-to-ceiling stone fireplace, the golden glow the only illumination save the pink shades of sunlight from the waning day slanting through big windows.

"You thought wrong." Setting her on her feet again, he shifted his attention to the gaping neckline of her dress where he'd been kissing her moments before. Hooking a finger into the placket, he began unfastening the buttons, his work-roughened knuckle grazing first one breast and then the other. "My first goal is bringing you pleasure."

Her knees buckled as she questioned the ability of her legs to support her through whatever he had in mind.

"That *would* bring me pleasure," she argued weakly, her words breathy and ineffectual since she swayed on her feet at his touch. Her fingers scrabbled against the expensive cotton of his dress shirt, his jacket from court long ago discarded.

Beneath her palms, she could feel the muscles of his arms working as he continued to slip her buttons free. Her nipples tightened unbearably against the satin of her bra.

He shook his head, his expression resolute. "It's been too long since I've touched you. Being inside you again is going to rip away my control, and I can't allow that until after you reach your peak at least once."

A hungry, helpless sound rose from her throat. How was it he could turn her into this needy creature at just a touch? His cedar and sandalwood scent intensified as his skin warmed. Or maybe it was the pine of the cabin walls that teased her nose with every breath.

"I want that, too," she admitted, her own fingers clumsier than his as she unfastened his belt, the smooth leather slipping in her grip. "But maybe hurry? Because I want you to feel good, too."

His eyes were molten as they fixed on hers. "I already feel better than I have for over two years."

While she tried to absorb that, Gibson walked her backward through the great room, steering her to a far corner of the cabin. Her feet stalled a little when her boots shuffled from smooth plank flooring to a throw rug, and he plucked her off her feet again, carrying her the rest of the way to a first-level bedroom suite.

More muted colors surrounded them, whitewashed grays, tans and cream. The room contained little beyond a bed and a fireplace that was bracketed by French doors on either side. He strode with purpose to the bed but didn't lay her on it. Instead, he set her on her feet and peeled off the dress he'd already unfastened, leaving her in her boots and underthings.

Another lover might have fixated on her erogenous zones, but Gibson's attention to detail had continually surprised her when they first started dating. He could spend an hour washing her hair, for example. Or endless minutes unbraiding it.

And she happened to know he liked her legs in boots. That may have been why she'd chosen today's calf-hugging pair that came over the knee. She wasn't vain about her limited looks. But a woman would have to be supremely well-adjusted to not care how she appeared around an ex.

"Were these for me?" he asked now, dropping to one knee in front of her and wrapping one strong hand around the back of her thigh so he could steady her while he unzipped the boot.

Slowly.

Oh so slowly, he lowered that zipper.

Midway down, he paused the action to stroke a finger into the skin he'd bared, from midcalf to just above her knee.

She tried to press her thighs together against the throb of need between her legs, but she only succeeded in balancing her hands on his shoulders to keep herself upright.

"Maybe. Yes." Her fingers flexed against the heavy muscles of his arms, wanting all his warmth and strength on top of her, pressing her into the bed. "Please, Gibson."

For an extended moment, she became hyperaware of his knuckle skimming up and down, up and down just inside her knee while he seemed to consider the request. But just when she thought she couldn't bear the wait another second, he shucked off one boot and made quick work of the other, tossing them aside.

In another moment, he was on his feet, tugging off his half-undone shirt and stepping out of his pants. When he wore only a pair of black cotton boxer briefs that outlined his erection, he pivoted her around so she faced the gray linen-draped bed, her back to his front.

Breathless, she leaned into him, savoring the heat of his chest. The hard ridge of his desire trapped against her ass cheek. His arms wrapped around her, one securing her just beneath her breasts, the other sliding along her belly and into her underwear.

"Do you remember my goal?" His voice had deepened. The sound vibrated against her back, tripped over her skin.

"I—I remember it." Her words stuttered as she shivered from the sensation. He stroked through her wetness, sure fingers giving her precisely what she needed, where she needed it. Not just the lush caresses that made her body weep with pleasure, but him surrounding her with his strength. His scent. His warmth.

The familiarity of it, of all the things she'd once thought she'd have forever, made a shadow dart through the pleasure for a moment. But she forced it aside, focusing instead on the circling, insistent fingers that demanded she give him everything.

"I want to feel you come." He spelled out the goal in no uncertain terms as he spoke into her ear, the words warm and damp against her skin while her body flushed with heat. "Can you let yourself go for me?"

Her head tipped against his shoulder. She couldn't

have answered him if she'd wanted to since the coiling
tightness inside made her breath catch. Hold.

Suspended in one perfect moment, she opened her
mouth on a soundless cry before sensation slammed
through her. Pleasure unspooled in one heady spasm
after another, her whole body in the grip of the fiercest
climax she could ever remember feeling.

Moments later, sagging with relief from it, she wanted
to tell him how incredible he'd made her feel, but the
throb of his body against hers reminded her that he
hadn't shared in the pleasure yet.

Something she intended to correct immediately.

"It's your turn now." Spinning to face him, she
gripped her braid in one hand and slid her fingers down
the length of it until she reached the tie at the end.

His dark eyes latched onto the calculated move.

"Making you feel good is my turn," he told her, stub-
bornly never acknowledging the heavy weight in his
boxers. "You came so fast the first time, you must need
another orgasm."

With each plait that she sifted free, his muscles tensed
and twitched, making her feel empowered. Attractive in
her own way, no matter what the world saw when they
looked at her.

"I need you," she reminded him, determined to
break past that competitive pride to the man beneath.
Had it been a mistake to invoke the hockey hero in the
first place? She'd only done it to convince him that she
wanted fire and passion, not caution and restraint. "Inside. Me."

When she reached the end of the woven pieces and
shook out the strands, Gibson's rough growl was music
to her ears. The sound hummed through her while he
unhooked her bra with one hand and shoved down her

panties with the other. A moment later, he tipped her back onto the mattress, the nubbly texture of the linen spread the only fabric against her skin now.

Gibson tucked a thumb in the band of his boxers and dragged them down. Off.

She stretched toward him to pull him to her when he turned away. Confused, she followed his movements as he reached into the bedside table and withdrew a new box of condoms.

Surprise shook her. She'd forgotten about protection completely. Because of course, when they'd been married...

Emotion blindsided her.

The memories of her secret—the one time she'd been pregnant and hadn't been able to tell him before she'd lost it again—swelled in her chest. Crowding everything out. Threatening to spoil this night. This coupling that he deserved after she'd thrown all her seductive powers at the chance to savor pleasure.

Thankfully, it took him an extra moment to rip away the shrink-wrap on the unopened box, and another moment to unfold a sleeve of packets and tear one open to roll the protection into place.

Lark used that time to breathe deeply. Pull herself together. Recall the generous way he'd given to her just now.

She wouldn't allow her mistakes to steal anything else from him. Or from her either.

When his big body met hers on the bed, pressing her into the mattress with the fraction of his weight he gave to her, Lark gave herself up to sensation again. She'd enticed this incredible man, this world-renowned athlete with a body that was a finely tuned machine, into her bed.

And she would do anything in her power to make him feel amazing.

"Now, where were we?" His hips wedged between her thighs, the heat of his erection rubbing against her folds.

A whimper stole from her throat.

"You were going to make this a night neither of us would ever forget." Reaching between them, she stroked him from base to shaft, remembering how he liked to be touched. "And I was going to help."

His eyes rolled back for a moment, his nostrils flaring.

"Promise me one thing," he breathed the words on a slow exhale, moving his hips in a way that rubbed their bodies together again.

"Mmm?" She arched beneath him, ready for him.

"Remind me to feed you tonight," he told her as he entered her in one long, incredible stroke. "Because if you don't, I might forget to let you out of this bed."

A sensual thrill raced over her skin as he filled her, the possibilities of being with him this way all night enough to make her forget everything else.

"I promise." Hooking her ankles around his back, she anchored herself to him.

His pectoral muscles flexed as he kept most of his weight off her, his chest grazing hers as he set a rhythm to please them both. It felt so good. He knew her so well, understood all her cues, fed her every need.

She'd known she missed this, but that still didn't seem to account for how desperately hungry she was for his touch. His kiss.

Their eyes met again, and she wondered if this was overwhelming him, too.

Because there was no denying that what they were sharing right now felt better than ever.

"I'm going to need you more than once." He said the

words with a gravity that reminded her he might consider that a personal failing.

He'd always enjoyed being able to hold back so that she could reach peak after peak.

Why hadn't she ever considered that there might be a darker side to that need? That maybe Gibson found it a challenge to be anything less than perfect?

Tightening her thighs against his hips, she cupped his handsome face in her hands.

"I'm going to need you twice as often," she vowed, only too glad to indulge them both this way. "So I hope those meals you've got in the kitchen have enough protein to fuel hourly sex."

He fell on her then, his lips tasting her deeply, tongue exploring her all over again. Then when her tongue followed his, he thrust his hips harder. Faster.

Her breath sped up as she held tight to him. Let his body carry hers over the edge with him.

This time, with him buried inside her, the sensations were different. Stronger. Better.

Plus she got to see him enjoy the finish, his gorgeous male physique shuddering with the power of his release.

Pleasure flooded through her. His and hers. Not just from what they'd shared, but from the thought of the hours they still had ahead of them to feel this way again and again. If she was only going to have Gibson back in her life for one night, she would make every second of it count.

She just hoped she could maintain her focus on the physical—the intimacy that rocked her to the core— rather than all the unresolved feelings between them. The tenderness that she felt for this man, the realization that maybe he'd found it tough to be there for her every day because he only wanted to give people his absolute best, were feelings that didn't have any place in her life anymore.

They weren't together. His decisions and problems were his own.

Yet as Gibson stroked her hair in the bedroom that had grown cool and dark now that the sun had set, Lark worried she didn't have nearly enough emotional self-discipline to keep her heart out of this night.

Ten

Balancing drinks and two warmed meals on a bamboo serving tray, Gibson padded barefoot from the kitchen into the living area of the cabin. Lark sat on a carpet in front of the fireplace, her back against the low leather sofa.

The blaze in the hearth picked out a few burnished highlights in her dark hair where it spilled over her shoulders, still damp from a shared shower. She'd wrapped herself in a gray cashmere throw blanket while he prepared their food, but he remembered only too well what she wore beneath it. Clothes from his dresser—a black pair of cotton running shorts and one of his white silk undershirts.

Nothing else.

His grip tightened on the tray at the thought, which was amazing considering the release he'd found just half an hour earlier in the shower. And before that, in his bed.

Yet already, he couldn't wait to finish their meal so he could hear her sweet cries of completion all over again.

"Here you go." He joined her on the floor, settling the tray between them. "Are you sure you're comfortable enough?"

She tucked her knees under her as she reached for one of the cut-crystal glasses of water. "Never better," she quipped, winking as she brought the drink to her lips. "I have enough feel-good endorphins floating through me right now to make me serene and relaxed most anywhere."

"Then dig in," he urged her, grateful for the way she could put him at ease even though the aftermath of this night had the potential to be awkward tomorrow. "I hope you like it."

"Are you kidding?" She lifted the lid from her stoneware plate to reveal the almond chicken and brown rice meal she'd chosen from the options of catered meals he'd given her. "I haven't been able to spoil myself like this since we…" Hesitating, her gaze slid to his. "Since we were together."

The ease he'd been feeling evaporated. He'd tried his best to provide for her when they'd split, but she'd refused every effort, insisting she wanted nothing from him.

It had hurt knowing she rejected everything he had to offer, right down to his money.

"I don't like to think about you economizing—"

"It's not a financial issue. I didn't mean that," she hurried to explain, laying a hand on his wrist, stroking softly. "It's just that I don't make time for food planning anymore, let alone order things ahead of time. And it's not as much fun cooking for one."

At his nod, she forked up a bite of her food while he tried the whitefish in lemon sauce he'd heated for himself.

"That's fair," he acknowledged, even though the lingering reminder of rejection still made it tougher to settle into the moment again. "But I've been with the same meal service for over a year, and by now they know all my favorites. I don't have to cook or plan anymore."

He was about to launch into a pitch for her to share the service with him, but before he could, Lark spoke again.

"So tell me about this bison ranch you mentioned before." She tucked into her meal again, looking at him expectantly.

The fire crackled while he thought about his answer, a spark shooting from the logs to glow briefly on the dark brick hearth before fading.

"I have a ranch manager and a business model already in place. I won't purchase livestock until next spring so I can have all the necessary facilities built." As he warmed to the subject, he explained about the animals' ranging habits, their preference to remain out of doors.

He appreciated that she was interested. Her eyes didn't glaze over the way other people's tended to when he spoke about his plans. His agent had about a ten second attention span for bison.

"You don't bring them into a barn?" she asked, brow furrowed in thought.

He'd forgotten what a good listener she was, how she engaged with him in a way that seemed effortless. No doubt, that was part of what made her successful as a counselor. In fact, long ago when she'd still been a practicing sports psychologist, Gibson had stepped into her office the first time because of a recommendation from a teammate.

But as soon they'd exchanged hellos, he knew that

having her as a counselor wouldn't be enough. He hadn't continued his search for professional help, throwing himself into wooing Lark instead. But the past year he'd visited a therapist for a couple of sessions and realized some things about himself. His need for perfection in his sport. His relentless commitment to a team. Both qualities tied to his relationship with his father. The insights had helped him confirm his retirement was the right choice at this time.

Forcing his thoughts back to her question, he explained, "No barns for bison. They are tolerant of all kinds of weather conditions and get agitated if they're in an enclosed space." He told her about his trip to the Wyoming operation and his visit with the owner.

Which reminded him that she came from a long line of ranchers herself, her father notwithstanding. That made Lark's input all the more valuable since she knew a lot about the life, having spent plenty of summers at Crooked Elm.

He didn't tell her about her father's jab about Gibson's business future.

It's not going to be easy maintaining the lifestyle of a sports star now that you're...not.

The insult shouldn't have gotten under his skin to the degree it had, but the affront had lodged in his brain. He had lucrative endorsement deals that would pay out for another decade. He'd invested a big chunk of his earnings yearly. No matter what Mateo Barclay said, Gibson knew he could afford to retire and live well for the rest of his days. Yet as a real estate developer, Lark's father possessed a level of wealth well beyond Gibson's portfolio.

"Can I ask what made you choose this direction? I mean, it sounds great. I'm just surprised. When we first talked about buying property here, I thought you were more interested in a recreational ranch." She readjusted the blanket around her shoulders, the movement stirring the scent of his soap on her skin.

Stirring him.

And he welcomed the distraction from thoughts about her dad's insults.

"Well, I mentioned that your grandmother encouraged me," he reminded her, making sure Antonia received the credit for all the time she'd spent talking to him in those lonely weeks after Lark had left him. "She told me about her grandfather's horse ranch in Vallromanes, Spain, near Barcelona."

Lark's fork stilled midway to her mouth. "She did? I'm not sure I remember much about her family."

"She was trying to show me how I could build the ranching operation while I let the bison mature by exploring agritourism." He'd been intrigued by her ideas, doing online research of his own between their conversations so he could get her opinions on things as he expanded his plans. "Her granddad supported his ranch with horseback riding tours and a small bed-and-breakfast, and she thought I could grow interest in my bison if I had guided bus tours or four-wheeler expeditions. Maybe add a seasonal farmers market and pumpkin patch to draw business and build awareness of what I'm trying to build here."

When he realized how much he'd been speaking about himself, he took another bite of his dinner, not wanting to dominate the conversation. He didn't run that risk with many people, but with Lark he had to remember to turn discussions back on her sometimes.

"Wow. Now I'm not only impressed with you, I'm also super proud to hear how much Gran helped." She set aside her empty plate, covering the dish with the lid again and returning it to the bamboo tray on the floor between them. Then, smoothing her hands over the gray cashmere that covered her knees, she said carefully, "So obviously you're committed to staying in Catamount long term."

Something about the way she said it made him wary. He took a sip of his water before answering.

"Will that be a problem for you, having me next door to Crooked Elm? I hadn't counted on keeping the land at first since it was supposed to have been ours." Actually, thinking about that now still hurt, so he shoved aside memories of what might have been between them. "But I've grown to feel more at home here than anywhere else I've ever lived."

For a moment, he allowed himself to imagine what it could be like for them living next door to one another. They could see each other this way again and again. Indulge the connection he'd never experienced with anyone else.

"Of course it's fine," she rushed to say, her fingers moving brusquely over the blanket to brush aside invisible crumbs. "I won't be in Catamount much longer anyhow, even if we win the court case. After Jessamyn's wedding, I'll fly home to LA, so it's not like we'd be seeing each other here anyway."

There was so much upsetting in those few sentences that he didn't know where to begin addressing the problems. She had to win the case, for one thing. He wasn't going to allow Mateo Barclay to bribe his way into controlling the legacy Antonia had left to her granddaughters.

For another? He wasn't ready for her to leave Colorado. Especially not after he'd finally admitted to himself—and a Routt County courtroom—that he wanted

Lark back. But what bugged him most of all was the way she seemed to whisk away any feelings she had about him living next door to her as easily as she swiped at those nonexistent crumbs.

She'd strolled out of his life once before and she seemed destined to do it once again.

Setting aside his plate, he slid the tray out of the way and took her restless hands in his, needing to reroute her thoughts. Fast.

"Just remember who you're bringing to that wedding." Threading his fingers through hers, he watched her eyelashes flutter with his touch.

Her breathing quickened.

"How could I forget I promised you a date?" She shrugged a shoulder in a way that sent the blanket sliding down her arm, revealing more of her body in his T-shirt.

Her braless body.

And his T-shirt didn't hide the tight points of her breasts pressing against the white silk fabric.

The vision proved too tempting to resist. He fell on her, his tongue swirling around the dark outline of her nipple through the material. Her back arched as she gasped, giving him more access. He sucked the peak into his mouth, greedy for the texture of her skin on his tongue.

They shifted and moved together, finding more space on the carpet so they had room to lay. Her on her back. Him levered up on one elbow to admire every inch of her in the glow of the firelight.

"I can't get enough of you." He hadn't meant to say it aloud, but the thought reverberated through him with every rapid beat of his heart.

He'd scarcely dated since their divorce, failing to find enough interest to invest in more than a night out here and there. Yet with Lark, he was all in. Aching for contact.

Needing more time.

She cupped her fingers around his neck, twining them through his hair and drawing him near as she whispered, "Try anyway."

Be careful what you wish for.

Or, maybe when it came to sensual wishes with the sexiest man imaginable, it was just as well for Lark to aim high. Because, oh my, did he deliver.

He raked off the T-shirt she wore, baring her breasts to firelight and his avid gaze. He stared for so long she knew he was strategizing a game plan for her, and she rolled her hips to urge him on. Then, his lips returned to her nipples, suckling lightly before edging back to blow a cool stream of air over one and then other. He nipped at the undersides.

All the while she worked to undress him. Finally, she peeled away the blue tee he wore from an old hockey team, revealing the compelling strength and size of his shirtless form.

"Gibson." Breathless as she said his name, the word came out in too many syllables. She wriggled her lower body closer to his and stroked the heavy ridge outlined by the sweats he'd pulled on after their shower earlier. "I need you."

He throbbed against her hand, but his concentration never broke from the attention he gave her breasts. He did move his hand over her bare belly though, his knuckles rasping over her tender skin in a way that gave her shivers. Her thighs fell open in invitation, and he cradled her core in his palm, easing the ache there with skillful fingers.

Or was he adding to the ache?

Both things seemed to happen at once, one pleasure driving the hunger for another.

How would she ever walk away from this—from him—in the morning?

Refusing to think about it, Lark reached into his sweatpants, ignoring the drawstring to find what she wanted. He'd gone commando, so there was nothing in her way as she stroked the velvet-over-steel feel of him.

"Did you bring condoms out here?" she asked, thinking the bedroom seemed a million miles away when she wanted him now.

Her heart rate galloped. She felt quivery everywhere at once.

"Left pocket," he informed her as he plunged two fingers inside her.

Making her cry out with pleasure.

Her hands forgot what they were doing as he crooked his fingers forward, finding the spot only he knew how to find deep inside her. He'd been the one to introduce her to the exquisite sensations there in the first place, and she'd never bothered seeking it out on her own. For her, solo play had always been quick and efficient. Not the hours-long extravaganza that this man could make of intimacy.

But now, it felt like a million years since she'd come this way, the pressure and tension building fast.

"Hold on to me," he entreated, one strong thigh sliding over hers to keep her still.

Wrapping her arms around him, she steadied herself, meeting his dark gaze in the firelight. Intense. Sexy.

"I'll take care of you next," she promised, wondering how he could stay so focused when she was spinning out of control already.

She bit her lip, not sure if she wanted to ward off the finish or let it roll over her.

"I know you will. But first, you're going to let me take you where you need to go." There was something about the way he said it. His absolute assurance that he knew what she craved.

Because the words sent her over the edge, her feminine muscles contracting hard and fast around his fingers where he touched her. Her whole body shuddered with it, hips lifting off the floor, spine arching.

And through it all, he worked every sweet sensation free, leaving her thoroughly pleasured and more than a little dazed. It took her long moments to come down, but when she did, she returned trembling fingers to the drawstring of his sweats, tugging it loose so she could slide off his pants.

Fishing in the left pocket, she found the foil packet and rolled it into place.

"Your turn," she reminded him, pushing him over.

He went without argument. If anything, his brown eyes flared with fresh flames as he watched her straddle him.

"I dream about this moment," he admitted, his voice rough with desire.

Or at least, she told herself it had to be desire and not emotion. Her chest throbbed an answer anyhow. Possibly because she'd dreamed about this, too.

Her throat was too dry to speak.

Instead, she gripped the length of his shaft and guided him home. His moan mingled with hers as she remained there, fully seated so she could feel him deep inside her. Then, lifting up on her knees, she stroked him up and down. Up and down.

Remembering the slow build he liked.

Remembering everything.

The rhythms that had belonged solely to them. There was nothing boring about sex that was fine tuned for maximum pleasure. Sex that fulfilled one another's every hidden need. They'd sought out all the erogenous zones. Knew how to drive each other to the precipice over and over again.

"Go as slow as you want, gorgeous," he drawled from beneath her, his eyes still fixed on her with that intense heat. "I could watch you this way forever."

He slid a hand up her hip and into the curve of her waist, his gaze tracking the movement as if she was the most fascinating woman he'd ever laid eyes on.

"Then you'd better not say things like that, or I'll get too excited." She thrust her hips twice to demonstrate.

His eyes narrowed. "You wicked, sexy girl."

But as fun as it might be to tease him, she owed him exactly what he wanted after all the ways he'd already brought her to release. Besides, she needed to make the night last as much as he did.

More.

Because while Gibson might deceive himself that they still belonged together—that he could win her back and there would be more nights like this—Lark knew better.

He'd never want her back if he knew her secret. That she'd been selfish about something she had no right to keep from him.

So she took her time giving him everything he could want from her. Every slow slide of her flesh over his. Every kiss. Every graze of her breasts over his chest.

She rolled her hips. Rocked them. Rode him.

And when her legs could take no more, she let him roll her to her back and take everything else. When he came at last, his hand buried in her hair and his other arm wrapped around her, Lark wanted to weep with the perfection of it.

Or, maybe, she needed to weep from everything they'd both lost. Everything they were losing all over again. Because as the world seemed to contract to just the hammering of their hearts against one another, one thing had become abundantly clear during the course of this night with her ex-husband.

She still loved Gibson Vaughn. And that was still a very, very bad idea.

Eleven

A phone ringing woke Gibson in the morning.

Disoriented at the full sunlight streaming through his bedroom windows onto the king-size bed, he blinked a few times to remember why he was still sleeping at this hour. Almost nine, according to a sleek black clock on one wall. But then, with the scent of Lark in the sheets wrapped around him, memories of their time together returned.

Where was she now?

R-r-r-ing!

His cellphone hadn't stopped, prompting him to retrieve it from the bedside table even as he rose to find Lark. Would she be in the shower? The need to see her, to touch her and assure himself that last night hadn't been a dream became his primary goal. His feet headed toward the en suite bath while he connected the call from—surprise, surprise—his agent.

"Dex, I'm not fielding any offers except for endorsement deals," he said preemptively as he passed through the walk-in closet to enter the bathroom. "What have you got for me?"

"Gibson, you're going to love this," his longtime professional representative began. "A contract's already drawn up and everything, with the best money we've seen to date. Plus, it's from a team guaranteed to make the playoffs this season."

The bathroom remained dark, and there were no signs that Lark had been here at all. Gibson's stomach clenched as he pivoted fast. Maybe she was in the kitchen?

"There's no such thing as a guaranteed spot in the playoffs," he said wearily, recognizing Dex's call as yet another attempt to woo him back into the game. "And it doesn't matter anyway because I'm not playing anymore."

He paused in the bedroom to throw on his T-shirt and sweats from the night before, noting that Lark's clothes were gone. Which only meant she'd already dressed for the day, right? Glancing out the bedroom window at the Flat Tops Wilderness all around the cabin, he reminded himself she couldn't have gone far. They'd taken a helicopter in, for crying out loud. It wasn't like she could walk to Crooked Elm from here.

Why hadn't she curled up next to him and awakened him with a kiss, the way she had when they'd been married?

"Gibson, you're the biggest story in sports media this week. I couldn't have scripted a better way for you to command a new contract—"

"And that's part of the problem," he shot back, unable to scavenge even an ounce of the composure he'd been famous for on camera throughout his career. Had his agent's machinations behind the scenes helped ratchet up interest in Gibson's career transition? Was Dex planting seeds around the media to drive coverage of an angle that wasn't ever going to happen? "My life is more than a sound bite, and I'm not a clickbait story anymore."

Striding into the kitchen with fast, angry steps, he knew at a glance Lark wasn't there. A piece of paper lay on the butcher-block countertop that hadn't been there the night before.

A note?

Knowing it wouldn't contain anything good, he approached it slowly, still hoping she'd walk through his front door. Say she'd been out for a morning walk and couldn't wait to shower together.

"But, Gibson, as your agent it's my job to share all offers with you—"

"Not anymore it isn't." Gaze fixed on the torn scrap of notebook paper held in place by a black pepper grinder, he wouldn't let himself look at it until he'd dealt with the call. "If you want to keep repping me for the occasional speaking appearance or ad deal that may come through in the future, you're going to have to spread the word with the media that I'm out of hockey for good. Do we understand one another?"

He regretted not taking a more aggressive stand on the issue earlier in the summer when it might have kept Lark from being hassled. But he was done being the face of any franchise. Done being the last guy to leave the locker room so the media had all the quotes they needed to file their stories. Done sacrificing everything—including his personal life—for the sake of the game.

"Loud and clear," Dexter said finally, his tone thoughtful. "I'll share your intentions on my end. But keep in mind it hasn't been me working the media all week to garner public support for your ex-wife's court case."

The comment found its mark.

"True enough. That's on me." He'd used the media when he thought it might help Lark, but now that he knew how vehemently she opposed those tactics, he wouldn't be tempted to leverage that tool again. "I've got to go now, Dex. I'm expecting a visit from you next spring when I've got my bison on the property. We'll catch up."

He tried to end on a positive note, not wanting to burn bridges to make his point. Losing Lark once had made him realize he needed to work harder to be a better man.

"For you, I might take a whole day off," his agent mused before they disconnected.

Gibson might have felt relieved to have gotten his message across since it meant he'd at last made peace with retiring. He had a new career to look forward to, and whether it was a financial success straight out of the gate didn't matter. Or rather, he couldn't allow it to matter. He needed a path in life that wasn't predicated on society's metrics for success.

He intended to find something that would bring him some happiness and a sense of purpose so he could re-wire all the negative habits of his brain to associate success with the stat sheets. From now on, he wasn't going to be tracking goals and assists or number of all-star appearances.

Too bad he'd learned how to do those things just in time for Lark to leave him nothing but a note on his kitchen counter.

Sliding the paper out from under the pepper grinder, he unfolded it and read,

I asked Fleur and Drake to pick me up on the way to court this morning. I'm behind on my share of maid of honor duties, so I'll be busy this week, but I won't forget our date.

No mention of their night together. No hearts or smiles to indicate any warmth of feeling for what they'd shared. And yes, call him ten kinds of sucker for caring that she hadn't drawn any damn smiles in the margins.

He cursed softly, swiping a hand over his unshaven jaw. The kitchen felt too big and impersonal with only him standing in it, like all the warmth of the day had faded when Lark walked out of his house.

Again.

She wanted space from him, obviously. He'd given it to her the first time she'd run off when they'd been married, and he'd regretted it. Now? He wasn't sure he could let her go again.

Gritting his teeth, he stalked toward the bathroom to shower. He had a court trial to attend.

From her seat between her sisters in the second row of the Routt County courtroom, Lark had a clear view of Jessamyn's fiancé, Ryder Wakefield, as he shared his testimony for the record.

She discreetly checked her smart watch for messages while Ryder related some background on himself. Still no word from Gibson. Not that she expected any given the cowardly way she'd left his cabin early that morning. By dawn, with her body thoroughly sated, her heart tender and hopeful, she'd known she didn't have the emotional reserves to paste on an "everything's fine" morning-after smile. So she'd called Fleur and crossed her fingers Drake would know the location of Gibson's cabin to retrieve her.

And while Lark had been relieved to slip out unheard, she still felt like a first-class heel for not being able to face Gibson after all they'd shared. Even now her body ached pleasantly from his attentions. Too bad the twinges in her chest were far from pleasant.

Straining to ignore the feelings, Lark looked to Ryder on the stand. His story was compelling, even as it revealed the very worst of her father's character. She'd heard secondhand about Ryder's presence in a search and rescue mission on a mountain peak after Mateo Barclay's then-girlfriend had been critically injured. But the tale was even more upsetting to hear from Ryder's point of view now.

Mateo had been frustrated with the girlfriend who couldn't hold her own on skis and had explained to Ryder that he "preferred strong women who could keep up." That alone made Lark feel ill—not only because that was the mindset of the man who'd raised her, but also because of all she'd learned as a counselor about the way a parent's biased gender views could undermine a child's sense of self. Yet, Ryder wasn't done.

While the Barclay sisters held their collective breath for the rest of the testimony, Jessamyn reached to hold Lark's hand. Surprised, she glanced to her left to see a tear slide down her sibling's cheek, a reminder that Jessamyn had striven to be the "strong woman" in their father's eyes for nearly a decade after Fleur and Lark had quit trying to please him. For the first time, she saw Jessamyn's journey through a therapist's eyes instead of a sister's. Lark knew all too well the way an adult child could continue seeking approval without being aware of how damaging it could be when that approval would never be given. She guessed that same sort of need for approval had driven Gibson for most of his career too, not that he'd ever said as much.

As for Jessamyn, had the pricey education and career opportunities she had received ever made up for the love she hadn't gotten?

Squeezing Jessamyn's hands in hers, Lark reached to take Fleur's palm in her other. Braced together, they listened as Ryder continued.

On the stand, Ryder cleared his throat, his eyes seeking his fiancée's before he went on. "Mateo said that's why he left his wife when Jennifer Barclay began to struggle with depression. He viewed that as weak."

Lark felt a fierce stab of relief that her mother hadn't attended the trial, even as Mateo's lawyer interrupted Ryder to remind the court that his client had likely been suffering from shock that day. The attorney had already tried twice to have the statement suppressed on the grounds that Ryder had been serving in an EMS capacity that day, and that Mateo's remarks were subject to doctor-patient confidentiality. The judge, thankfully, had not agreed.

While the legal representatives argued, Lark heard a murmur in the back of the courtroom. Turning, she caught sight of Gibson slipping into a seat at the rear of the room.

"Gibson's here," Fleur observed quietly in her ear.

As if Lark didn't have every sense attuned to the man at all times.

He'd come to the trial even though he hadn't been scheduled to testify today? Her heart fluttered at the proof of his caring. The support warmed her in spite of the swirl of tangled emotions at the sight of him—guilt for leaving, hunger for his touch, regret that she might never feel his kiss again.

He wore a gray suit today, his white dress shirt unbuttoned at the throat while he made himself comfortable at the end of a bench. A moment later, his dark gaze met hers, as if he'd felt her watching him.

What did he discover written in her face, she wondered? She didn't know how she felt about seeing him, so she couldn't imagine he could glean any more understanding about her feelings than she had herself. Her belly tensed with nerves.

As the lawyers finished their debate, Lark returned her focus to Ryder on the stand. After prompting from the judge, Ryder continued to speak.

"Mateo Barclay went on to tell me that his mother had disinherited him because of how he'd treated his ex-wife," Ryder explained, giving what Lark considered to be the most important piece of evidence in the defense.

Because Ryder's testimony proved that Mateo knew nine years ago that he wasn't receiving an inheritance from his mother.

More questions followed from Mateo's lawyer, but Lark didn't pay much heed to the back and forth. The key statements had been made for their case, so now they needed to trust the process. That the court would find Gran's will valid and Crooked Elm would rightfully belong to Lark, Jessamyn and Fleur.

If the judge decided in their favor, they'd be able to kick Josiah Cranston off the land for good, and they could send their father packing.

And whether or not the judge decided in their favor, Lark had done all she could here.

Once the decision was in she'd be free to leave Catamount—and Gibson—right after Jessamyn's wedding. Lark would be able to say she'd made progress toward healing her relationships with her sisters, and she'd done what her grandmother would have wanted by spending time here with them for the summer.

There was nothing left to keep her here. Right?

Surely, that knowledge should bolster her as she started the next chapter of her life alone in Los Angeles once again. Or maybe it would if she could look herself in the mirror and feel like she'd been honest with Gibson, too.

She really did owe him the truth she hadn't been able to share during their marriage. He would be angry. Rightfully so. But that didn't excuse her from something she should have confided to him long ago. Maybe then, she'd be able to leave town with a clear conscience.

Too bad she'd also be leaving with a heart more tattered than ever. Without thinking, she squeezed Jessamyn's hand again. Taking comfort for herself when she should have been giving it.

"How are you doing?" Lark whispered to her to cover the action.

At the same moment, the judge announced a short recess for lunch, then rose to leave. The participants in the case began conversations of their own, gathering bags and keys in preparation for the break.

Jessamyn nodded quickly, sliding her hand free from Lark's. "I'm okay, thanks. I just hope Ryder's testimony is enough to prove that Dad knew Gran's wishes long ago."

"Me, too." Standing, Lark's gaze went to where Gibson had been sitting, but there was no sign of him now. "But we've worked hard to find as many people as possible who knew what Gran wanted. Now we need to let the legal process play out."

Even as they moved toward the exit, Lark's eyes

scanned the room for Gibson. She should be relieved, perhaps, since she'd been the one to flee his house the morning after their amazing night together, telling him she'd see him on their date for Jessamyn's wedding. Implying, of course, that she wouldn't be seeing him before then.

Yet she couldn't deny the twinge of disappointment at his absence.

He'd come to support her family, perhaps. But now she realized it hadn't been to see her.

Cursing herself for being sad about getting exactly what she'd told him she wanted, Lark stuffed down the pain her chest and told herself to get over it.

Especially as Fleur and Drake paired up in the corridor outside the courtroom. And then Ryder and Jessamyn did the same.

Leaving Lark very much alone.

Gibson stared at the desk calendar in his home office, mentally checking off how many days he'd managed to stay away from Lark since she'd vanished from his cabin.

Five.

Five endless days of scarcely seeing her face except for their brief acknowledgments of one another at the courthouse, surrounded by other people. He'd continued to attend the sessions in case he was needed to clarify a point of his testimony and also to show public support for the Barclay sisters. At least the media interest had died down after Dex had issued a statement to the press that Gibson was committed to retiring, but a few stubborn freelancers still stuck around Catamount, hoping for a story.

The coverage of the estate case had slowed down too, and that was just as well since Lark hadn't been pleased at Gibson's efforts to involve the media. Yet another way she hadn't wanted what he'd had to offer. Still, he could see her point since the intrusiveness of the cameras and questions bothered him more than it used to. He understood why it had upset her so much during their marriage.

He just hoped the judge in their case reached a decision soon. And he hoped like hell Lark and her sisters would receive the lands Antonia had intended for them.

"Gibson, are you in here?" His mother's voice called to him from the annex on the far side of his kitchen.

She and her caregiver had moved in with him the day before since the renovations on the house were complete. The transition had seemed to go well enough, even though his mom had told him several times that she really needed to get home soon.

"I'm on my way, Mom." Dropping his pen onto his desk, Gibson strode out of the office and into the kitchen where his mother stood at the door, peering out through a side light. Her blond hair was pinned back from her face, her frosted pink lipstick the same shade he remembered from childhood. She didn't even look her age, let alone old enough to be suffering from dementia. He swallowed a swell of emotion before he asked, "Is everything okay?"

"Someone's in the driveway, Joe. Come see." His mother called him by his father's name, a slip she'd never made before.

Was she getting worse? What other signs might he have missed?

"It's Gibson," he reminded her gently, draping an arm over her shoulders to hug her to his side before he glanced out the leaded glass windowpane. Outside, the tall, familiar figure of his ex-wife made her way up the walk, her dark braid bouncing with her step.

Lark was here.

The emotions that knowledge stirred were too dense and multilayered to name. But first and foremost, he was grateful as hell that she was going to be able to visit with his mom before the illness stole even more of her.

"Who is it?" his mother asked, peering up at him with confusion in her eyes.

A pang filled his chest. He hated the unfairness of this disease with every fiber of his being.

"That's Lark, Mom," he explained, rubbing an encouraging hand on her shoulder. "You've been wanting to see her."

Recognition flooded her expression along with genuine joy.

"Lark's here." His mother smiled, every trace of confusion fading as she swatted his chest good-naturedly. "Of course I want to see her, you silly man. Open the door!"

Before Lark could lift her hand to knock, Gibson did as his mother asked, swinging the door wide, bracing himself for the impact of her presence.

He only had a moment to make eye contact with her before her gaze darted to his mother at his side. And then Stephanie Vaughn stepped forward to fold Lark in her arms.

"Hello, my favorite daughter-in-law." His mother squeezed her tight while, over her shoulder, Lark shot him a questioning glance. "It's so good to see you."

It was too late for Gibson to give Lark any warning or explain how much his mom's condition had progressed, but Lark was a mental health professional.

She would surely assess the situation quickly enough for herself.

Even though it might be awkward.

Really awkward, actually, considering his mom thought they were still married.

Twelve

Lark's reasons for coming to see Gibson all moved to the back burner when she stepped into her former mother-in-law's warm embrace.

She'd come to tell him the judge had ruled in their favor. To announce that their father's claim had been denied. And to celebrate that Crooked Elm and all of Antonia Barclay's estate would be legally distributed between Jessamyn, Fleur and Lark. Their father had already left town, swearing never to return. She'd wanted to thank Gibson for his testimony and support, but her joy in a victory over her father had been overshadowed by her need to tell Gibson about the secret she'd been carrying. The one she feared would sever their connection for good.

Now? With Stephanie Vaughn looping her arm through Lark's and leading her into the new addition

Gibson had built for her, how could she do anything but settle in for a visit?

"This is really beautiful," Lark remarked sincerely, glancing around at the wide windows overlooking the pool house and backyard, the separate entrance from the driveway in front, and the two first-floor bedrooms to accommodate Gibson's mother plus the caregiver that he'd mentioned.

The small kitchen had a Scandinavian appeal with its clean, modern lines and spare, blue and white touches, the open floor plan connecting the living area with dark blue couches and lots of greenery.

"Thanks to you and Gibson," Stephanie told her, waving Lark toward one of the couches. "Let's sit."

Confused, Lark lowered herself onto the seat she'd indicated. "Oh, but it's Gibson who—"

"Lark, can I get you anything to drink?" Gibson interrupted her, something she'd never known him to do.

But then, his whole manner seemed anxious. He hovered close to them, staring hard at her. Meaningfully. Like he wanted to communicate with his eyes.

She had no idea what he was trying to tell her though.

"No, thank you. I'm fine." Scooting deeper into the corner of the sofa, she glanced toward his mother, thinking she looked the picture of good health. Not that her appearance necessarily meant she was thriving. Lark understood better than most how mental health challenges could hide behind deceptive facades. "Are you all settled into the house now, Stephanie?"

Tall and lean, Gibson's mother tucked her ankles to one side as she leaned forward to visit, her spine arrow straight. She'd always had that noble bearing about her, making Lark want to improve her own posture. Yet there was nothing else remotely intimidating about her. She was warm and chatty, the kind of person content to carry on a one-sided conversation if her companion felt quiet, and that worked for Lark just fine.

Given how her job necessitated drawing people out conversationally, it had often felt like a relief with her former mother-in-law to just listen. And it had been ages since they'd spent time together. Gibson had been away so much during the last six months of their marriage that Lark had few opportunities to see his mom.

"I am all situated, thank you." Stephanie smoothed a manicured hand over a blue throw pillow. "Gibson moved my furniture so I'd feel at home," she mused as she stroked the soft pile of the fabric. Then, she lifted her gaze to look at Lark. "But it won't really feel like home until we all sit down for a meal together."

Surprised at the invitation, Lark hesitated. Things were uncomfortable enough for her since she needed to speak to Gibson privately and tell him about the secret she'd kept from him. But to suspend that task in order to sit through a tense meal with him?

Before she could answer, Stephanie hastened to add, "But it's your house, dear. I don't mean to invite myself over before you're ready. I just think it will be nice for us all to catch up as a family." Reaching across the couch cushion to Lark's side of the sofa, she squeezed her hand. "Gibson, you should bring your wife that water after all. She looks a little pale."

Realization swept over her. Hard.

Stephanie thought they were still married.

Lark's gaze shot to Gibson's face. She read the apology in his eyes this time. His helplessness in the face of his mother's merciless illness.

When had Stephanie gotten so much worse? She was only in her early sixties.

"I will get her some, Mom," Gibson assured her, coming to Lark's rescue. "Why don't you show her where we set up the doll collection?"

Stephanie's blue eyes brightened as she nodded. "Of course." Rising from the couch, she gestured for Lark to follow her toward the bedroom. "I'm preserving the dolls for my granddaughter one day. I hope it won't be much longer, you two!"

Lark's step faltered, the lighthearted remark smacking her like a two-by-four to her midsection. Her hand went to her mouth to stifle a gasp.

How much crueler could this day get?

Pretending she was married for the sake of Gibson's mom. Smiling through prompts to make a baby with the man she'd once loved and now loved all over again without him knowing. All while carrying this awful secret that weighed on her like lead shoes.

It hurt that Gibson hadn't bothered to tell her about his mom's deterioration when he'd invited Lark to visit. He must have known even then how tough it would be for Lark to smile through the pretense that they were still a couple.

Or what if she'd unwittingly revealed the divorce to Stephanie?

Still, she had zero right to be indignant about his secrets considering her own, but that didn't stop her from feeling frustrated. Hurt. And battling the urge to flee.

"You okay?" Gibson's voice sounded low beside her as he caught up to her in the corridor. He passed her a glass of water, his fingers brushing hers while his mother led them into one of the bedrooms.

"Not even close," Lark fired at him, edgy and overwhelmed. "We need to talk."

"And we will. She tires more quickly these days, and

her caregiver will return in an hour." The sadness in his voice at the mention of his mom's health reminded her how much he'd been dealing with on his own. "We'll speak then."

Heart softening, she nodded. "Fair enough."

Until then, she would visit with her former mother-in-law and look at the dolls for the baby Lark wasn't meant to have.

He should have warned her about his mom.

Gibson had recognized it the second Lark's panicked eyes had sought his when his mother referred to her as his wife. He'd had years to watch the slide of his mom's mental health, but the last time Lark had seen her, she'd been merely forgetful.

Not overtly confused and disoriented.

Now, as his mother's caregiver ushered him and Lark from the annex he'd built for them, Gibson prepared himself for whatever Lark wanted to discuss with him. Sure, he recognized that she was probably frustrated that he hadn't prepared her for this visit. But she'd made the trip to his place even before she knew his mom would be there, so clearly there was more on Lark's mind than just what had happened today.

He knew better than to hope that she wanted a repeat of their night together. Her silence for days on end had assured him she viewed that as a one-time event. And yes, that still stung.

"Do you have any tea?" Lark asked him now as they moved into his kitchen.

Her voice sounded weary. And of course, tea was her comfort drink, so he knew she felt stressed.

"Chamomile or orange spice?" he flipped the switch

on the countertop kettle before pulling two mugs from an overhead cabinet.

"Chamomile. Although I'm not sure there are enough calming vibes in those tea leaves to soothe the frustration I'm feeling that you didn't tell me your mother thinks we're *still married*." She dropped into one of the seats at the kitchen island, her head slumping forward to rest in her hands.

Regret pinched. He cleared his throat to explain, but her head popped up, her eyes blazing.

"Gibson, how could you not mention her condition to me? When I asked her caregiver how long she'd been with your mother, she said over two years. Which means you hired her while were still together." Her volume rose at the same time the kettle beeped for the water. "Regardless of what happened between us, I care about your mom."

Grateful for the extra moment to formulate a reply, he took his time pouring two cups of tea.

"I hired her during a stressful time for us. The media coverage had really intensified for you and we were dealing with our own problems. I didn't want to add to that." Lifting the mugs, he pivoted to the island, sliding one in front of Lark and keeping the other one for himself.

"But she's family. At the time, she was my family, too."

He rubbed his nape. "I know that, Lark, but I worried you might feel an undue burden to help because you're a mental health professional, and that wouldn't be fair to you." He slid into the seat next to her at the island.

"I would have wanted to help, but you robbed me of the chance." She pushed aside the cup he'd poured and swiveled on her barstool to face him fully. "You carried everything in your world on your shoulders, never sharing with me. So is it any wonder I felt like I had to do the same?"

"You felt like you had to shoulder your burdens on your own," he repeated, recognizing that she was upset and not quite following why she was *this* upset. He'd been trying to protect her, damn it. Why was that so wrong?

Sure, he understood that she had wanted to be a bigger part of his life and he'd denied her that by trying to manage his problems alone. In retrospect, that hadn't been fair to either of them.

But he felt like he was missing something more.

"That's right," she snapped, sliding off the stool to pace the length of the kitchen, agitated energy fairly vibrating off of her as she moved. "In case you missed it, I pride myself on being independent, too. That's why I never asked to travel with you, because I knew you liked the time on the road to bond with your teammates."

Surely he hadn't heard her correctly.

"Wait. You would have come on the road with me?" He wanted to slow down and talk about that, because he would have appreciated her steadying presence in that last crap year when he'd been with the LA team and the media had lambasted his team and him at every turn.

"So no matter how hard it was to stay at home and live like a single woman while my husband kept an existence separate from me, I did it because I knew what I had to deal with was nothing compared to the pressure the team and the media put on you." She reached the window and swung around to pace the length of the room again, her arms crossed tight around her body. "And you, Mr. Calm and Composed, Face of the Franchise, never complained that you had too much on your plate."

Gibson was out of his depth. But then, he'd never seen

Lark this upset. Except, of course, for the night she'd walked out on him.

Rising to his feet, he moved closer to her without interrupting her path. He wished he had the right to wrap his arms around her and slow her down. To hold her tight and tell her everything would be all right. "Lark, please. What's going on here? Is this all about me downplaying Mom's problems? Because I know I should have told you—"

"No. It's not about that." Stopping her restless prowling, she pinched the bridge of her nose. "Although I'm hurt about that, I didn't come here to argue with you about what happened in the past."

Her tone shifted. Growing cooler. Calmer. And yet, the change made him wary. She stared at him with steady green eyes, as if steeling herself.

"Okay." He reached for her, wanting to take her hand in his, but she sidestepped him to move back to the counter stool. "What did you want to talk about then?"

He rested his elbows on the gray-and-white quartz but remained standing. His eyes followed Lark's movements as she sipped her steaming tea. The scent of chamomile filled the air.

She continued, "We had a chance to chat after the judge gave his decision. Jessamyn and Fleur plan to stay in Catamount. Fleur can go ahead with her ideas for a restaurant on the land. And we'll give Josiah Cranston thirty days to vacate the premises."

He'd be glad to see the last of the ranch's shady tenant who'd been willing to lie under oath for a payday.

Gibson reached across her for his own mug of tea, wishing they could return to the night they'd spent at the cabin. When every conversation hadn't been fraught with land mines, and they'd been deliriously happy just to touch each other. Take care of each other.

"There will be a celebration at the Cowboy Kitchen for sure," he mused as he took a sip of the drink. "Fleur is the most talented chef this sleepy town has ever seen."

For an instant, he thought he spied an answering light in Lark's eyes. But it faded again, and she drew a long breath.

"I also came by to let you know that I'm leaving right after Jessamyn's wedding this weekend." When he made to interrupt, she held up a finger to indicate she needed another moment. "And it only seemed fair that I let you back out of our date ahead of time. I think you'll want to when you hear something that I should have shared with you a long time ago."

Warning prickled the skin at the back of his neck. Wariness tightened his muscles. The feeling was reminiscent of the foreboding he'd had the day he'd pulled up to their house, only to discover she was leaving. But this couldn't be the same because they weren't together now.

"We agreed to attend the wedding together. I'm looking forward to it." He knew there was nothing she could tell him that would change his mind about wanting to work things out between them.

But had he urged things forward too fast with his public declaration under oath? Was this her way of pushing back?

"Please listen, Gibson. This isn't easy for me." Her gaze fell on the double-sized refrigerator. The open shelving near the sink. Shifted down to her tea mug. Anywhere but on him. "I never told you why I was so upset that night of the charity event when you were on the road and couldn't take my calls."

He mentally rewound to the time she referenced. The

evening of the photos of him with an intoxicated patron of the event, photos that showed the woman stuck to him like a second skin and him wearing an awkward smile since he hadn't known how to peel her off.

Had that played a larger role in their split than he'd realized? Lark had never seemed ruffled by incidents like that before.

"Those pictures were misleading, like I explained in court." He'd always tried to make himself accessible to fans when he'd been playing, knowing they made his lifestyle possible. For the most part, he didn't regret it since the vast majority of fans were incredibly supportive.

But he fiercely regretted that evening when a woman had taken advantage of their proximity.

"I know that." She met his eyes finally, her expression sincere. Compassionate. "I've seen with my own eyes how some fans cross boundaries." A sad smile lifted one corner of her lips. "As a woman, I understand a thing or two about being the object of inappropriate touching, believe me."

A surge of protectiveness roared to life inside him, and he was seized with the need to right the whole world for her. But he knew better than to trail down a tangential path when she wanted to share something important with him.

"Then what about that night?" he asked gently, hating that he hadn't tried harder to find out before now. But he'd been so caught up in his own problems with his mother and his team, compounded by the pain of Lark leaving him, that he hadn't had the emotional wherewithal to seek out the "whys." Or at least, not as tenaciously as he could have. "What happened?"

"I miscarried."

The two words rattled through him on a discordant note, making no sense.

"You…" He struggled to remember that night. The long weeks apart that had preceded it when he'd been on a road trip, exacerbated by a home stand with one charity event after another as part of the team's PR during a year of poor performance in the rink. He and Lark had hardly seen each other. But still, she hadn't said anything to him about… "You were pregnant?"

He didn't even dare think about what that meant. Had she been happy about it? Unhappy, given how disconnected they'd grown in those last few months together? The idea that his child might have been unwelcome news was a sucker punch he would have never predicted. Still, he tried not to let his thoughts run away with him until she finished explaining.

She swallowed hard, her eyes downcast. Slowly, she nodded.

"Yes. I was only ten weeks along, but—"

"Ten weeks?" He did a double take, brain casting back even further in the past to remember the circumstances in their lives during that time. "How long did you know about it?"

She exhaled a long breath, as if trying to calm herself. He needed some serious calming too because the news was pummeling him.

"About three weeks. It took me a while to realize I was late, and even then I thought it was just stress because of everything we were dealing with. The increased media scrutiny, the insinuations about our marriage, your travel schedule—" She stopped herself. Shook her head. Arms wrapped around her stomach. "Anyway, by the time I took a pregnancy test and saw a doctor, I was already over six weeks. And I knew the exact window of conception since you weren't home very often."

Regrets about that and so much more carved a hole in his chest.

"I knew we'd grown apart, but for you to not even tell me you were pregnant..." He let the words trail as he traced the rim of his mug with his thumb, the scent of chamomile not nearly enough to soothe the raw parts inside him.

"I tried at first. I swear I did." She laid a hand on his knee, her touch urgent. Squeezing. "I made a dinner for us, with a cake that had the pink lines on it, just like the pregnancy test."

He was afraid to ask where he'd been for that dinner that hadn't happened. "I know I wasn't around much—"

"You decided to do a training camp for kids with your friend in Nova Scotia that weekend instead of coming home. Which was fine, but I really wanted to tell you in person." Her words came faster now, her fingers still clutching the denim of his jeans above his knee. "After that, I figured I'd settle for any night when we were together. Except the next time you were due for a home game, your goalie was getting traded and you went on the road to talk the new guy into signing with your team. Remember?"

He recalled. Hurt for her and what she'd gone through alone wound with the hurt he felt now. Yes, he'd been trying to arrange help for his ailing mom at the same time, but he hadn't shared that with her either. Could he blame her for shouldering the pregnancy news alone?

"I wish you'd called me. I know telling me over the phone wouldn't have been ideal, but at least I would have known." His throat burned with what might have been, even if only for a short while. He could have known about his child, had the opportunity to place his hand on Lark's stomach. Over their baby. "I could have alerted the team that I needed to be there for you. They would have made sure your call got through that night of the charity event if I'd told them you were newly pregnant."

"I know," she said softly, her hand sliding off his knee. She swiveled away from him on the counter stool and took a sip of the tea he'd made her. "One of my many regrets the night I miscarried was that I didn't let you know about the baby. Afterward, it seemed cruel to tell you when we couldn't change the outcome."

"So you packed up and left." He'd never forget the cold, echoing foyer of the home they'd shared with her boxes stacked and waiting for the moving truck.

But he'd allowed the hurt he'd felt to prevent him from going after her. From demanding answers about why she was leaving. He'd assumed it was because he hadn't been home enough.

After a childhood with a father who'd never found anything redeeming in him, Gibson had grown the thick skin that had allowed him to thrive in his sport. But it had prevented him from forming deep attachments. Something he'd sought professionally counseling for, once upon a time. Except that when he'd walked into the therapist's office, he'd seen Lark and wanted to date her more than he wanted counseling.

No doubt he'd been just as glad to set aside the idea of therapy in favor of romance with the sexiest woman he'd ever seen. But he'd done them both a disservice that day.

"I'm sorry I didn't tell you before," Lark said finally, slipping off the stool to loop the strap of her cross-body bag over one shoulder. "I should have explained myself to you long before now. Being in Catamount again, and seeing my sisters grow to be stronger people capable of loving relationships, has made me want to be a better person, too."

He recognized the blame wasn't all hers. But did it matter now when they'd already tried and failed to be together? What if love wasn't enough?

The last thing he wanted was to hurt her again.

For that matter, he wasn't sure he could survive losing her a second time when their divorce had been so painful.

"I'm glad you told me now so we can both have closure." He would be thinking about what might have been for a long time.

He didn't ask her again about attending Jessamyn's wedding together. Part of him wondered if she'd told him about the pregnancy now in order to push him away because she was afraid of getting too close to him again.

For all he knew, maybe that was for the best. Hadn't he promised himself he wouldn't hurt her again?

So when Lark pivoted on her heel and quietly let herself out of his back door, he didn't follow her.

Thirteen

Lark had to dig deep into her emotional resources to fulfill her co–maid of honor role with the grace it deserved. Dressed in the stunning navy blue gown that, until today, only Gibson had seen her wearing, she rushed up the stairs at Crooked Elm with a glass of water and some crackers for the pregnant bride who was getting dressed for the big day.

"Here you go, Jess." She called out to her sister as she entered the largest bedroom in the house that now legally belonged to them. Before today, none of the Barclay sisters had used this particular space since it had been inhabited by their grandmother. Instead, Fleur, Lark and Jessamyn had gravitated to the smaller rooms they'd occupied as children when they'd visited the Colorado ranch. But in their planning sessions for the wedding, Fleur had declared their grandmother's former chamber as the best place for a bridal suite. Jessamyn and

Lark had agreed it would be a wonderful way to make new memories in the space, and to feel like Gran was with them.

"I've got your morning sickness cure."

She crossed the dark plank floor, the grapefruit-colored walls providing a vibrant backdrop for the bride dressed in her ivory chiffon, off-the-shoulder gown.

Fleur scurried around the hem of the dress, fluffing the fabric so that Lark had intermittent peeks at Jessamyn's hand-stitched ivory lace shoes where she stood in front of the antique cheval mirror. Fleur had draped the mirror with one of Gran's white lace mantillas so that Jessamyn's reflection was surrounded by the fabric.

Seeing her framed that way made a lump form in Lark's throat. She told herself to focus on her sisters and the beauty of the moment, not the memories of her own love story gone so far awry. But how could she not remember her own wedding today?

These weeks in Catamount with Gibson had made her remember all the ways they'd been good together. He'd supported her through the trial. Applauded her courage in standing up to the media. Given her a safe haven from them when she'd wanted a retreat.

And then, there'd been the hours in his bed when everything else had fallen away and their love—because yes, that's still what she'd shared with him—had been the only thing in the world.

"I'm feeling better now that I started to move around again," Jessamyn declared, waving away the cracker offering, her French manicure showing off her engagement ring on her right hand, where it would remain until Ryder slid the wedding band on her left. Then, she would transfer the pear-shaped diamond to her left finger as well, fitting the V-shaped platinum pieces together. "The scent of the hair spray just made me a little woozy."

"I'm glad your stomach settled," Lark said briskly, setting the silver tray on the bedside table near a framed photo of the Barclay sisters when they were girls. "Because it's almost time to head downstairs."

Her gaze lingered on the old picture of herself at thirteen, standing next to one of the four-rail fences to support six-year-old Fleur as she leaned to stroke the nose of a buckskin-colored mustang. Jessamyn would have been nine at the time, and she had one foot on the fence to stroke the horse's neck on the other side of the animal. All three of them looked thoroughly happy, cheeks pink from the summer sun and fresh air, hair in careless ponytails and feet in matching turquoise-colored cowboy boots, a gift from Gran that year. She'd loved those boots.

She made a mental note to buy new pairs for herself and her sisters, too. She might not be staying in Catamount, but she could take that happy memory home with her, along with the knowledge that her sisters would enjoy them. Her visit to Colorado had returned her to her family, and that was a very good thing, no matter how much she hurt today for the love that had slipped away from her.

Again.

"It's that time already?" Fleur stood, her face flushed from all the gown straightening. Her navy blue dress was styled differently than Lark's, the strapless sweetheart neckline and slight flare to her skirt giving her dress a more overtly feminine appeal that suited the former rodeo queen. She peered out the window overlooking the yard where wedding guests had been arriving for the last twenty minutes. "Oh be still, my heart. The men are a sight to behold."

Lark's heart smarted at the thought of the man who was missing from the small ceremony. The ex-husband who hadn't wanted his date with her after learning how she'd robbed him of those weeks where he could have—albeit briefly—celebrated the news of being a father.

She hadn't told her sisters about the split with Gibson since she'd never mentioned that sparks had been flying between them throughout her stay in Catamount. It was easier that way.

Although, even as she thought it, she wondered if she was once again robbing herself of the chance to share her hurts and maybe find better healing. She'd done the same thing with Gibson. But she was saved from having to overthink that realization when a new voice spoke from the threshold of the bedroom.

"Is there room for one more in here?"

Jennifer Barclay stepped tentatively inside, wearing an elegantly draped blue mother-of-the-bride dress, the silk hand-painted with swirls of cream and tan. Far from matronly, the dress skimmed her curves to show off an enviable form. Her dark hair was in a sleek twist, while pearl and gold earrings winked in the sunlight as she gazed at Jessamyn.

The daughter she'd only just begun to reconnect with after the family rift.

"Of course there's room," Jessamyn replied as she waved her inside. "Mom, you look beautiful."

"No, honey. You're the one who is absolutely radiant." Striding deeper into the bridal suite, their mother stopped in front of the bride to admire the ivory chiffon wedding gown. "I can't tell you how happy I am to be a part of your day."

Lark knew the two of them had made steps toward healing their relationship, and she hoped today would cement the progress since Jessamyn had asked her mother to walk her down the aisle. Their father had opted not to attend the wedding even though Jessamyn hadn't revoked his invitation.

Mateo Barclay hadn't spoken to them since he'd left town after losing the ranch.

Now, Jessamyn stepped forward to take her mom's hands in hers. "I'm really happy, too. Especially now that I'm going to be a mother." She gave a self-deprecating smile. "I'll have a new take on the mother-daughter relationship now."

Mom squeezed her hands before spinning to face all three of them. "You'll be a wonderful mother. Better than I've been."

All three of them opened their mouths to argue, but their mom shook her head, cutting them off. "No, listen to me. I had a duty to my family, and I failed you all when my life went off the rails once your father left us."

Lark refused to be silent. "Mom, you were ill. No one can fault you for depression. We had a duty to you, too."

She'd tried to be there for her mother. But Jennifer Barclay's road to wellness had been a long one, worsened by setbacks with her personal life. Lark realized now it might have helped her mother more if she'd reached out to Jessamyn herself, to be a good older sister and substitute maternal figure through Jennifer's illness. Instead, Lark had been too wrapped up in anger with her sibling.

"I know that, sweetheart. I've accepted that I couldn't change my illness. But it doesn't take away the fact that I checked out of my job as a mother during those years." As she spoke, a warm breeze stirred the curtains behind her, even lifting the lace mantilla to flutter softly.

All their eyes went to the movement.

Lark wasn't the superstitious sort, but even she saw it as a sign. Gran was there. Approving of the moment. Being a part of this day.

Fleur cleared her throat, her gray gaze bright with emotion. "I think Gran is saying that it's okay. We forgive each other, and we all want to do better. To *be* better for one another."

And they were, Lark knew. She'd tried harder this week, reserving judgment, not assuming a negative motive on anyone else's part, and it had paid off. She was in this wedding, a part of Jessamyn's life once more.

What if she'd tried that hard in other areas of her life? Like with Gibson?

Her mother stepped forward, reaching a hand out to Fleur and Jessamyn, who in turn both reached out to Lark. So they stood in an unbroken circle of four. From the backyard, strains of country love songs drifted through the window from a guitar and fiddle player who'd been hired for the day.

It was almost time for the vows.

Drawing a deep breath, her mom spoke softly. "Each of you has filled me with pride in your own way. You might seem different from one another on the surface, but in your hearts, you're all strong, independent women, brave enough to live the lives you imagined for yourselves. That takes courage."

Lark felt a twinge at the words that were meant as a compliment but felt hollow for her personally. She could see how her sisters had done that. Fleur had taken a chance by coming to Catamount with nothing but her dreams of owning a restaurant, determined to sell the property for a profit so she had the resources to start her business. But she'd adapted her dream to encompass the town and the man she'd grown to love.

Jessamyn, too, had followed her heart to Catamount, and now she was planning to use her real estate development skills to initiate agritourism in the area, finding ways to showcase Ryder's off-grid living initiatives in ways that would inspire others. She had plans for self-sustaining yurts in a range of wilderness locations so tourists could experience the beauty of the region as well as a commitment to the land.

All while preparing to have a baby.

But what had Lark done besides show up for the wedding and make nice with her siblings? She was planning to catch a flight in the morning to return to Los Angeles. Was that really living the life of her dreams? Or had she been playing it safe with Gibson, pushing him away before he could hurt her?

Yes, her parents' disastrous marriage had made her gun-shy. But she'd told herself she'd grown beyond that when she took a chance on romance and married Gibson. When the going got hard, however, had she fought for her dreams? Or their shared dreams?

Not by a long shot. She'd cut and run, scared he wouldn't be there to support her when she needed him. Afraid to give him a second chance after he hadn't rushed to her side on that night she'd needed him.

But she wasn't the same woman that she used to be. Two years apart had only reinforced that Gibson was the only one for her. And she'd had time to appreciate the way her sisters has fostered the love in their lives, even when there were obstacles.

She needed more courage. Before today, she hadn't known where to find it. Yet right now, feeling the love of her family around her in a way she hadn't experienced in over a decade, Lark felt a welling up of new fortitude.

And yes, love.

She had more to give, and she wasn't going to leave Catamount without trying harder to live her dreams with Gibson at her side.

After the circle of four disbanded, Lark, her mom and sisters picked up their bouquets and descended the stairs.

Lark was the last one to step outside into the sunshine while the guitarist picked out the strains of a wedding march. Ahead of her, forty white folding chairs adorned with tulle and flowers sat in rows facing an arbor with four rough log posts where an officiant waited to perform the ceremony. The posts were draped in pink roses, white hydrangeas and grape hyacinths, the stems wrapped in clouds of white tulle. More white tulle fluttered around the top of the posts to provide a thin canopy from the sun.

The effect was country elegance, a perfect blend of Jessamyn's refined preferences and her love of Western life. Ryder waited for her under the canopy in a dark gray suit, an ivory rose boutonniere complementing the bride.

With every fiber of her being, she wished that Gibson was in the crowd waiting for her. Looking toward her with even a fraction of the feeling that she could see in the groom's eyes as he awaited his bride.

Then, as Lark blinked into the brightness of the day, her eyes adjusting to the noontime sun, she spotted a tall, broad-shouldered figure sliding into one of the white folding chairs.

A heart-achingly familiar figure.

Was it just a wishful imagining of a heart tied in knots by the romance of the day?

Hurrying to stand beside Fleur for their procession up

the white carpet to the arbor, Lark couldn't take her eyes off those shoulders. An athlete's unmistakable, well-muscled form. Just like in the courtroom day after day, he'd shown up today when she'd needed him.

Was he quietly making up for the way he hadn't always been around while they were married? For weeks, he'd been showing her a different side of himself and she'd been too caught up in her own fears to recognize that he'd changed. She'd accused him of always putting his team first, but for the last year—even when he'd still been on the active roster for his club—hadn't he been overseeing his mother's transition to living with him? She'd seen firsthand how much thought he put into making a comfortable home for her, providing her with both love and security. Even providing himself with an outlet in the mountain retreat for days when caregiving grew more difficult.

Not to mention, all his plans for a future outside of hockey with a bison ranch. His future wouldn't be tied to a sport, and that had to be a tough transition for him.

He was changing. But had she changed enough to make a relationship between them really work?

When Gibson rose to his feet to watch the procession, she was staring at him when their eyes locked.

Held.

And she hoped some of the day's wedding magic would rub off on her so that, after the ceremony, she could find the words to convince him to give their love one more chance.

She still took his breath away.

Gibson watched the subtle sway of Lark's hips as she made her way up the aisle, her navy blue silk dress molding to her curves whenever the breeze blew. He wouldn't approach her today since she'd made it clear that he wasn't her date. But Drake had invited him, and he wouldn't ignore the duty to a friend, so he sat in the back. Alone.

His eyes returning to Lark again and again. She'd worn her dark hair half-up and half-down, forget-me-nots woven through a braid coiled at the back of her head while the rest of the tresses fell over her shoulders, hiding the mostly backless dress.

He'd always liked that about her. The subtlety of her beauty that was never showy, as if she reserved it for those who took the time to pay attention.

And man, did he ever pay attention to this woman as she settled into her place beside her sister for the ceremony. Even as the officiant spoke, Gibson kept his focus on Lark. He'd shortchanged her during their marriage, taking her strength and independence for granted. But just because she could deal with whatever life threw at her didn't mean she should have to. She'd deserved a partner who put her first.

Something he would do now that he'd learned to draw his own boundaries. To step away from the old pattern of being the best, being the guy his team could count on. The people he loved were important than the game.

His mom.

And yes, Lark.

His thoughts were interrupted by the sound of Ryder's voice as he faced his bride.

"I give this ring as a sign of my love." The words rang out over the yard, the guy's eyes fixed, unwavering, on Jessamyn Barclay as he lowered the band into place on her left finger.

While he spoke his vows, Gibson's gaze sought Lark's. Was she remembering their wedding day, too?

He thought of the vows he'd spoken four years ago, and how deeply he'd meant them. Yet he hadn't delivered on them when push came to shove. He hadn't been there for Lark when she'd needed him. Hadn't let himself need her either, always so damned confident he could take care of his own problems thanks to his father's earliest admonitions that a hockey player needed to be invincible.

Which of course, he wasn't.

When it was the bride's turn to speak, Lark's green eyes shifted from his to land on her sibling.

"…to have and to hold, from this day forward, for better or for worse…" Jessamyn's voice was steady as she spoke the words that would unite them as a couple in front of their friends and family.

He hadn't done that with Lark, opting instead for a courthouse ceremony. They'd been deliriously happy at the time, but how could they have known what life would have in store for them? How could they have guessed how much they would need the support of a network like this one—people who'd born witness to the vows?

With the ache in his chest deepening with every word spoken, Gibson couldn't wait for the end of the ceremony. His time he had to win back the woman he loved was running out, with her flight leaving in the morning.

So as soon as the officiant announced the couple as husband and wife, and the musical duo began a triumphant wedding recessional song, Gibson calculated the fastest way to win an audience with Lark.

There was no receiving line with such a small wedding. The reception would begin soon, with an informal meal under a nearby canopy. But for now, the wedding guests simply congregated around the newlyweds, offering congratulations and teasing marital advice. With Fleur as Lark's co-maid of honor, those duties would be covered for a few minutes if he could sneak a little time to speak to Lark privately.

Except, in the shifting crowd around the bride and groom, he'd somehow lost sight of her.

"Looking for someone?" a woman's voice asked to his left.

Glancing down, he saw Jennifer Barclay, Lark's mother.

"So good to see you, er, Mrs. Barclay." He'd briefly called this woman "Mom" when he and Lark had been married. While Lark had been comfortable calling his mother by her first name, Gibson had opted to move right to the more familial name for her mother. "And yes, I was looking for Lark."

"I had the feeling you were." She beamed, her expression happy and her cheeks glowing. No doubt she was pleased to have mended the rift with Jessamyn. "She asked me to let you know that she's waiting for you by the creek. She seemed to think you'd know where she meant."

Lark had asked to see him?

"I do." He told himself it might not mean anything. Maybe she only wished to say goodbye privately. But he couldn't help hoping that this could be a sign she wanted something more. "Before I talk to her though, do you have any advice for winning her back? That is, if I promise to be a much better partner for her in the future?"

He had no way of knowing what her mother thought of him and the role he'd played in their breakup. But he wasn't going to shy away anymore from asking for help when he needed it. And there was nothing more important to him now than telling Lark how much he wanted to try again.

Nearby, a server recruited from the Cowboy Kitchen

strolled past with a wooden tray of champagne glasses. Lark's mom took one, but Gibson wasn't ready to celebrate yet.

"Gibson, I always thought you were a good balance for Lark." She lay a hand on his arm as if she could impress her thoughts on him. "Before she met you, she worked nonstop, as if she needed permission to have fun. But when you were together, I saw her take time away for vacations with you and for road trips to your games."

He'd forgotten about that. Once he'd moved to the Los Angeles team and taken on its problems as his own, his marriage had suffered.

"I appreciate you saying that." His gaze lifted toward the path to the feeder creek for the White River, where Lark waited for him even now. "I hope I can convince her to give me another chance."

"I won't claim to be an expert on love, but I do know my daughter." Mrs. Barclay smiled, her face shifting in a way that made the resemblance to her oldest daughter clear. "And I can't help but think you should speak from the heart when you talk to her. Lark has enough practicality in her life. She deserves to be wooed with romance and flowers. A man who sees past her tough exterior to the sweet and vulnerable woman beneath."

It was sound advice, and it settled around him with a new rightness. He'd gotten to know Lark better this week too, and he'd been reminded of her deeply tender side. She'd talked to his mom for almost an hour about her doll collection, patiently listening to the stories from Stephanie Vaughn's childhood to learn how she'd acquired each one. And she'd done it while she'd had every right to be angry with him, right after she'd learned that he hadn't confided in her about the severity of his mom's disease progression.

"You're right." Leaning down, he kissed his former mother-in-law on the cheek—hopefully soon to be his current and forever mother-in-law. "I'm going to do just that."

Spinning away, he started toward the tree line to find Lark.

Trailing a long blade of feathery reed grass across the surface of the creek, Lark had started to get nervous Gibson wasn't coming when she finally heard the sound of pine needles crunching underfoot.

Branches slapping against a body moving through them.

She tensed, equal parts hope and anxiety twisting her insides. Turning, she spotted Gibson in his dark suit and white shirt just a few yards from her. Through the trees behind him, she could still see the wedding party on the lawn. The white canopy set up for the meal with a few picnic tables on loan. The huge floral arbor where Jessamyn had said her vows.

The music carried easily, upbeat country tunes but no vocals. Later, her sister and Ryder would test their country waltzing skills, but for now, the guests milled around with cocktails and passed hors d'oeuvres.

"You're going to ruin your shoes," Gibson warned her, his dark gaze going to her feet where she stood in the tall grass.

"Nope." Lifting the hem of her dress, she showed him a pair of her old cowboy boots. "I grabbed a pair of these from the porch before I walked here."

"Very practical," he admitted, his attention shifting to her hand where she still held the long reed grass. "But you're still going to get your gown wet if you're not careful."

Releasing the slender reed, she wiped her hands together and shrugged. "Maybe. But at least I got through the ceremony looking like I belonged in this dress. I don't think Jessamyn will be surprised if I return with a few wrinkles."

"You can take the girl out of the country, but you can't take the country out of the girl?"

She smiled. "Something like that." Her smile faded again as she realized… "Although technically, I'm supposed to leave this part of the country tomorrow."

"I want to speak to you about that." He took a step closer to her, his big body parting the reed grasses until he stood toe-to-toe with her.

Her breath caught at his nearness, the cedar and sandalwood scent of his aftershave teasing her nostrils. Her heartbeat jumped erratically.

"Actually, it was me who wanted to talk to you regarding that. My mother must have told you?" Nervous, she brushed one palm along the top of the fluffy reed grass, the tiny filaments tickling her skin.

He frowned. "She told me where to find you but didn't say what you wanted."

Hadn't she told her mother that she hoped to have another chance with Gibson? But then, Jennifer Barclay had displayed a huge amount of confidence in Lark and her sisters this weekend. It had been nice when Mom talked about being proud of them, touching a part of her soul she hadn't realized had been hungry to hear words like that.

Perhaps her mother had been sure Lark could handle the situation on her own.

And live the life she'd imagined for herself.

"For starters, I wanted to say that I've learned a lot about myself this month. About where I went wrong in our marriage." She hesitated a moment, still uneasy about sharing the full extent of her insights. But was that being brave? Living courageously?

"Lark, I made the mistakes," he said somberly. "Far more than you ever—"

"Please, let me just say this." If she wanted a better relationship, she needed to take bigger risks. She could even picture herself telling her patients as much. Why hadn't she taken the advice seriously for herself? "After telling you about the miscarriage, I wondered if part of the reason I'd kept it to myself for so long was just another way to keep you at arm's length. To not risk being…" She had to pause to clear her throat, and when she spoke, the words were raspy. "Vulnerable with you again."

Gibson's warm palms moved to her shoulders bared by the thin spaghetti straps of her gown. His fingers flexed into her skin, and she had to close her eyes against how good it felt to have him touch her.

"And that's understandable. I wish I had been a better man for you while we were married, but I wasn't present enough for us to build the kind of relationship I think we both wanted." His thumbs sketched small circles on her arms where he touched her, soothing and inciting at the same time.

"It's not understandable, Gibson. It was wrong of me." She'd been so upset with herself—and him, too—that she hadn't been able to face the mistake. Not then, and not for a long time afterward.

It had been easier to run than to face all the frustrations she'd suppressed in her marriage. To articulate her hurt and work toward solutions. She'd told herself she'd handled the breakup well—better than her parents had survived the dissolution of their relationship. But she'd only been holding it together on the surface. Deep inside, she'd fallen apart, too.

In spite of all her precautions not to let love wreck her.

"You're too hard on yourself." He pulled her into his arms now, surrounding her with his strength and warmth. His scent.

She breathed him in, grateful for the chance to be close. Grateful that he'd listened to her and didn't hate her for keeping the news of his child from him.

After a long moment, she realized he was stroking her hair over the middle of her back, his cheek pressed to her temple. And nothing in her life had ever felt as right as being in his arms.

Angling back from him, she laid her palms on his chest, feeling the expensive silk of his suit. The warm heart beating beneath. Taking a slow breath, she reminded herself that she was here to take risks. To live the life of her dreams.

"I don't want to leave Catamount."

Her words were met with silence as he stared at her. His eyebrows lifting. Jaw working slowly as if he was warming up to speak.

Her stomach twisted. Her chest ached where she craved this man's love.

At last, he lifted a hand to her face and tilted it upward another degree.

"I don't want you to leave Catamount either. Not tomorrow. Not ever. Unless you take me with you wherever you go." His thumb grazed her cheekbone, rubbing lightly.

Her pulse leapt. And she suspected her eyebrows were the ones arching high now. Because she had not expected this for even one second.

"What?" She shook her head to clear her ears, her

heart hammering too loudly for her to hear him over the whoosh of it echoing in her head. "What are you saying?"

She tried to listen hard. In her degree program, she'd learned about generous listening, where you opened your mind to people without anticipating what they would say or how you would respond. It was a tool she used often in her practice, and she leaned into it now to hear what Gibson was saying, because it was wildly different from how she'd expected this conversation to go.

"I love you, Lark. I don't think I ever stopped loving you." He spoke with a gravity she'd never heard from him before, a sincerity that matched up with the dark intensity of his eyes.

Hope sparked brighter. Still, she had to be sure. "But when I left your house the other night, I thought—"

"I didn't handle the news well, but mostly because I was so disappointed with myself for not being the man you needed me to be while we were married. That you couldn't even have me in the same room as you to share your pregnancy news—news that would have been so welcomed—it hit home what a rotten husband I'd been."

On the lawn behind the trees, a roar of laughter went up over the romantic melody of the guitar and fiddle. A champagne cork popped, and then another and another.

"That's not true." She'd been frustrated with his travel and with the media, but despite their problems, she'd never stopped loving him. "When we were together, I was happy. And I thought I was being a good wife not to complain about the long separations, but I know now we owed it to ourselves to find solutions instead of just wading through those hard times."

"I owed you far better than I gave you," he said resolutely. "But you're not the only one who has learned things this month. I know I can do better now."

Excitement tickled along her nerve endings as it occurred to her this was really happening. Gibson Vaughn loved her. He wanted to be with her again.

She couldn't suppress a smile. It bloomed over her face like the new happiness filling her insides.

"I never stopped loving you either. And I already know that you've changed. I saw you in court for me every day even when I pushed you away. And you came to the wedding today when I desperately wanted to see you." She looped her arms around his neck, pressing herself even closer to him.

"You did?" He stroked his fingers through her hair.

A dislodged forget me not drifted to her bare shoulder, and all she could think about was getting through the reception to be alone with him later.

"I did. At first I thought I wished you into being there, but it was really you, turned out in your custom suit, looking all kinds of edible."

His eyes darkened and he bent to brush a kiss over her lips.

"You're the edible one," he breathed the words over her damp mouth. "And I'll prove it to you later."

Desire pooled in her belly even though it was the wrong time for that. They had so much to navigate if they were going to be in one another's lives again, but first they needed to celebrate her sister's big day.

Still, all of that would be a joy because on the other side of it would be Gibson. Not just for a night or a week.

Forever.

A yellow leaf drifted down from a nearby tree, an early sign of fall that came to rest on Gibson's shoulder before she brushed it away.

Summer was ending, and a new chapter of her life would begin. Here in Catamount. In a house next door to both of her sisters. She could work remotely for a while. Start a new practice here.

Become the wife of a bison rancher, which made her smile again.

But all of that would wait until tomorrow.

"We should rejoin the party," she murmured. "Everyone will wonder what happened to us."

"I bet they could guess," he argued, smoothing his hands down to her waist. Over her hips. Lower. "And I don't think anyone will worry."

Her smile returned. She couldn't seem to keep it off her face, not that she wanted to try.

"We're really doing this? Getting back together?" She ran a hand along his freshly shaven jaw. Her heart full.

"If you mean are we really going to be together forever the way we once promised each other we would be?" He lifted her higher against him, so they were eye to eye. "The answer is yes."

"Thank goodness." She tipped her forehead to his, breathing in the man and the moment. "And to be perfectly clear, this time I'm never letting go."

It was his turn to smile as he turned toward the tree line so they could return to the wedding party.

"That's what I was hoping you'd say. Now, it's the perfect day to drink a toast to the happy couple and celebrate happy-ever-afters." Gibson lifted their joined hands to his lips so he could lay a very deliberate kiss on the ring finger of her left hand.

Where a ring used to be.

She knew him so well. She felt the promise in that kiss. Knew that a ring would rest there again one day.

For now, she simply planned to celebrate this love they shared, the love they couldn't walk away from.

Every. Single. Day.

* * * * *

CROSSING TWO LITTLE LINES

JOSS WOOD

One

"Can you *please* stop breaking into my apartment?"

Jamie Bacall-Metcalfe shook her head at her brother, who was sitting at the small table in her kitchen, eyes on the screen of *her* tablet and drinking *her* coffee. Greg, just eleven months older than her, was dressed in shorts, sneakers and a less-than-fresh T-shirt, his dark hair wet with perspiration.

"I gave you a key for emergencies, not so you can use my place as a rest stop during your run," Jamie reminded him, keeping her tone mild. They both knew she was chastising him because she thought she should, not because she wanted him to stop dropping by. She adored her brother. He and his husband, Chas, were her best friends.

She nodded at his grungy T-shirt. "Can't you go home and shower and then break in?" Jamie asked, reaching for a coffee cup.

Greg patted the table, looking for his own coffee cup, his eyes still on the tablet. "Chas likes me nice and fresh. He's weird that way."

"So do I, actually," Jamie told him, walking over to peer over his shoulder. "What's caught your attention?"

Greg held up one finger, asking her to wait. Jamie sipped her coffee and allowed her eyes the supreme pleasure of looking at a headshot on the screen of a guy in his midthirties. Square jaw, straight nose, sexy mouth, brown hair with natural, streaky blond highlights. The right amount of stubble. But it was his eyes that caught and held her attention. They were an intense blue, the color of the wings on a blue morpho butterfly. Like the insect, all that intense blue was contained in a black ring. If he had a body to match the face, she could cast him in advertisements. Who was he, and how could she track him down? Sexy, masculine, handsome men who could look both sophisticated and sporty weren't easy to find.

Greg lowered the tablet to the table and leaned back in his chair, pushing his hand through the same dark brown hair they shared. Jamie took the seat next to him and nodded at the now-black screen. "So what's the news?"

And who was that guy? Jamie felt a frisson of attraction skitter up her spine, and it took her a few seconds to recognize it for what it was. Wow. So she wasn't a dried-up husk of a woman after all. Good to know.

"I was reading an article about Rowan Cowper."

Greg spoke as though she should know who Rowan Cowper was. She shrugged. "Who?"

Greg rolled his eyes. "Cowper Construction? He built the new hospital?"

"You are an architect and know builders, Gregory. I own an advertising agency, remember? I wouldn't mind putting Cowper in some of my ads, by the way."

"I wouldn't mind him putting his shoes under my bed," Greg commented.

"Your husband might object," Jamie said wryly.

"Chas is such a killjoy," Greg grumbled, and Jamie rolled her eyes. Her brother, being one of the most loyal men she knew, was all talk and no action.

"So why is he on the front page?" Jamie asked.

Greg rose and refilled his coffee mug. "Ah...he was working late at one of his building sites and was heading back to his car when he came across a group of thugs mugging a college kid. It was three to one, and the kid was on the sidewalk, curled up, and they were kicking the crap out of him. Cowper arrived and proceeded to take down all three muggers solo... And the kid who was attacked is the governor's son. Cowper is being lauded as a hero."

Ah, now the picture was clear. Governor Carsten was a personal friend of her parents, who owned the very paper featuring Cowper. He had two children, the younger of whom had recently made a splash on social media when they came out as bisexual and nonbinary.

"Hate crime?" Jamie asked, feeling a little sick. Sometimes people sucked.

"The police aren't saying, but we know how often it happens. His father is the governor, the family is high profile, so it's not a stretch to believe he might've been targeted because of his family rather than his gender identity," Greg replied, wrapping his hands around his mug. "What isn't up for debate is that Cowper saved his life. The muggers had knives and were planning on using them."

Thank goodness he was there, Jamie thought.

Greg leaned back against the counter and looked

at her, his expressive eyes narrowing. "Changing subjects—how are you doing, James Jessamy?"

Jamie scowled at him using her full name. What had her parents been thinking when they named her? Thank God they'd settled on calling her Jamie. "I'm fine, Gregory Michael Henry."

She knew what he was really asking. He had that worried-about-you look on his face. The fifth anniversary of her husband's death was coming up in a month, and it was her family's cue to check up on her more than usual.

She often wanted to tell them that the anniversary of Kaden's death wasn't particularly horrible. She thought about Kaden and relived the accident *every* day and felt as guilty now as she did five years ago. The guilt didn't come in waves; it was a constant presence. It was her fault the car had rolled, her fault he'd died.

"I'm fine, brother," she lied.

"No, you're not."

No, she wasn't. But she could pretend to be.

Rowan Cowper drained the whiskey in his glass and rolled his shoulders, wishing he could remove his tuxedo jacket and yank off his black tie. As his companion droned on, Rowan pulled back the sleeve of his jacket and took a discreet peek at his Patek Philippe Aquanaut, his most recent indulgence, and swallowed a sigh of relief. It was close to eleven, and soon he could leave this boring black-tie charity dinner that had been organized by the governor's wife.

He'd contributed a significant amount of cash but couldn't remember the cause. Children's cancer? The homeless? He should start paying attention or, better yet, stop coming to these stultifying events.

Option number two, please.

Rowan dropped out of the conversation and moved from the bar to the exit, making his excuses as people tried to talk to him. Not that long ago, he had been just another construction-company owner. Rich, sure, but not part of the highest echelons of Maryland society. Stopping a fight had resulted in an invitation to dinner at the governor's mansion and a sudden slew of invitations to the best society events in the state.

Not bad for a boy originally from West Garfield Park, Chicago, one of Illinois's most dangerous areas.

He wasn't a fool. He knew how the game was played. Connections to the people who influenced decisions were a smart business move and would make his life easier.

A *lot* easier.

Rowan exited the ballroom, resisting the urge to pull down his tie, and headed for the bank of elevators on the far side of the entrance hall. His time hadn't been wasted. He'd heard about land about to be rezoned for commercial development on the outskirts of the city and that a plastics plant was building a new premises. He was interested in both the land and the factory and had the names of people to call.

Not a bad night's work. The downside, of course, was having to duck the offers of dinner, drinks, a night in bed. He'd refused them all.

Standing by the bank of elevators, he jabbed the button with his finger and rubbed the back of his neck, sighing when he heard a feminine voice calling his name.

Shona…something. They'd had a few dates, but when she'd hinted he should meet her family, he'd backed off. Way, way off.

He wasn't a meeting-the-family type of guy. The only

commitment he was capable of was to Cowper Construction. It was his only love.

"Shona." Rowan winced when she rose up on her toes to kiss one cheek, then the other.

Dropping her heels, she play-swatted his chest. "I'm so glad I ran into you! I haven't seen you for ages… Did you change your number? I've left you so many messages."

He was trying to think of a way to extricate himself without hurting her feelings when he felt an unfamiliar hand on his back. He whirled around and looked into the sparkling sherry-colored eyes of a brunette dressed in a slinky beaded silver dress. Her perfume, light and sexy, drifted up to his nose as she slipped her much smaller hand into his and leaned her temple against his shoulder.

His heart triple-thumped in his chest. Weird. It had never done that before.

"There you are! Sorry, I got caught up talking to Terry. He sends his best," she said, tipping her face up to look at him, smiling. It took him a couple of beats to remember that Terry was the governor.

God, with her flawless skin, big eyes and curvy body, she was heart-stoppingly beautiful.

She lifted one eyebrow in a challenge and turned her attention back to Shona, who now looked both bemused and belligerent. "Shona, are you well? How are your parents?"

Shona opened her mouth to speak, but Gorgeous Girl got there first. "Please send them my best wishes, but we must fly." She turned, slapped her hand on one of the closing doors to the elevator and tugged on Rowan's hand. "Babe, I've got a bottle of Moët on ice and whipped cream and strawberries in the fridge."

Strawberries and cream? Champagne? Yeah, he could

easily imagine painting her skin with cream and licking it off. Dipping strawberries into champagne and sliding the plump fruit between those sexy lips?

Yes, please.

Rowan allowed her to pull him into the elevator. He looked back to see Shona standing there staring at them, her bottom lip wobbling. He was known for being a hard-ass, but he was still a sucker for a kick-me-when-I'm-down expression. He was about to speak when he felt Gorgeous Girl's grip on his hand tighten.

"Don't you dare. She's playing you," she muttered.

Right. Okay, then.

The elevator doors slid closed, and he pushed his free hand through his hair, feeling like he'd stepped through a portal into a strange new world.

Lovely, but weird.

What was she thinking, trying to rescue the very tall, very hot Rowan Cowper?

Did he even need rescuing? Maybe he wanted to take Shona back to his place and she'd just derailed his plans. Jamie shuffled from foot to foot, her hand still swallowed by his—so warm.

She looked up into those deep, intense eyes and bit the inside of her cheek. His face held no expression. She couldn't begin to imagine what was going on in his head, but she thought she caught the corners of his lips edging up, the start of a smile.

Well, at least he wasn't pissed.

She looked down at his hand holding hers. "You can let me go now."

He followed her gaze and immediately released her. "Sorry."

Her hand wanted to be back in his; it felt good there.

"No need to apologize, I was the one who dragged you in here," Jamie replied. She pulled a face. "Did I read that situation wrong? Did you not need rescuing?"

Finally, that stern mouth morphed into a smile. "I've never needed rescuing, but thank you for trying."

She tipped her head to the side, hearing the truth in his words. He looked strong, powerful and incredibly capable. His eyes radiated a quiet intelligence that suggested there was no situation he couldn't get himself out of.

To be honest, now she felt foolish. She'd rushed in, thinking she was helping him but maybe she'd messed up. "Sorry if I spoiled your plans for this evening."

"You didn't. I was just heading home," he replied.

Right. That didn't tell her anything. What was it about this man that made her feel jittery? She met good-looking men all the time—both at work and at these social events she occasionally attended—but none of them made her feel warm in places that hadn't felt heat in a long while.

She recognized him earlier, immediately remembering him from the article Greg pointed out six weeks ago. He was even better looking in real life, and because she hadn't been able to keep her eyes from straying in his direction she'd noticed the slight shifts in his demeanor, from attentive to resigned to bored. And that was why she'd noticed he looked uncomfortable talking to Shona.

He made her think too much, see too much, feel too much. Suddenly, Jamie wanted to step out of the elevator, desperate to put some distance between her and the inscrutable Rowan Cowper. She was comfortable in her numb cocoon woven by guilt and grief. After what happened with Kaden, it was safer for her to stay distant, to not engage.

And yet she met Rowan's eyes instead.

Zzzztzzzt...zap.

She'd heard of sparks flying, but this was the first time it had happened to her. There was a force within her, urging her to wind her arms around his strong, tanned neck and taste his mouth. She couldn't go one more second without knowing whether he tasted as dark and dangerous as she suspected...

His eyes dropped to her mouth. She felt—rather than heard—his sigh, saw his eyes deepen to an inky blue and held her breath as he leaned down to...touch the console behind her.

"I presume you are heading for the lobby?" Rowan asked politely.

Well, damn. She'd been imagining a hot kiss and he couldn't wait to get away from her.

Way to go, Jamie. Your imagination is on fire tonight.

"Basement garage, actually," she replied, cursing the heat in her cheeks. Rowan stared at the console, his brows pulling down into a frown. "That's weird."

"What?"

"We're going up, not down. And the numbers are jumping out of order." The car dropped a floor, then shuddered, stopped and started heading up again. Rowan punched the button for an upcoming floor. "We need to get this thing to stop and catch another elevator."

"Okay," Jamie agreed.

The elevator started heading down again.

"Eight, seven, six, five..." Jamie counted down the floors and waited for the elevator to stop and let them out. It shuddered again, sighed and then stopped.

"Shit," Rowan muttered. "That's not good."

He turned to look at her and shrugged. "We might be here for a while. If ours is stuck, then they may all have problems. It might take them a while to get to us."

Fabulous.

Two

Rowan finished his call, looked down at his smartphone and grimaced. His eyes connected with Gorgeous Girl's as he pushed his phone into his pants pocket. "It's as I thought—all the elevators are malfunctioning. They are going to get the older people and kids out first, so we'll be the last to be rescued, I'm afraid."

To his surprise, she just shrugged before bending and lifting her right foot. "If I'm going to be stuck here for a while, then these instruments of torture are coming off."

He didn't blame her. Rowan shrugged out of his jacket, pulled down his tie and released the top button of his shirt. Feeling like he could breathe, he turned his jacket inside out and placed it on the floor. "I don't think it's a good idea to get that dress dirty. It looks like hell to wash, so sit on my jacket."

She sent him a grateful look, her hand skimming over her beaded bodice. "Thank you. And, yes, it is a pain to wash, but it's worth it. I shouldn't be wearing it, but every couple of years I pull it out, fall in love again and can't resist slipping it on," she told him as she sat down, her back against the wall of the elevator and her legs stretched out. She had a tiny bumblebee tattoo on the inside of her ankle, and her toenails were painted shell pink.

Rowan dropped down to sit next to her, keeping a decent nonthreatening distance between them.

He looked into those fabulous eyes and realized that he couldn't call her Gorgeous Girl for the rest of the evening. "I didn't catch your name."

"I'm Jamie Bacall-Metcalfe."

Jamie...it suited her. He looked down at her dress, puzzled. "Sorry, I'm trying—and failing—to work out why you shouldn't wear the dress. Did you steal it? Borrow it without asking?"

He was surprised at the words flowing from his mouth; he rarely spoke so much, and never to a stranger. Then again, most people were strangers.

Her laugh was surprisingly deep and very sexy. "No, I didn't steal or borrow it," she replied, smoothing the fabric over her slim thighs. "It's a rare dress from the twenties, so it's over a hundred years old."

He turned his head to stare at her. The dress looked like it had been made yesterday. "Really?"

She nodded, then sighed. "I'm a sucker for old clothes, vintage jewelry, the twenties and thirties. I knocked over a glass of red wine, and I narrowly missed having it land on me. So I thought it was time to leave."

He saw something flicker in her eyes, and he knew she spoke the truth—just not the whole truth. "What else happened tonight?"

Those amazing eyes widened, then narrowed. "How on earth do you know something happened?"

He could tell her that six years spent in some rough foster homes had made him a master of reading body language. His ability to see the smallest change in someone's eyes, shoulders or lift of the lips had saved his skin on more than a few occasions. But he didn't explain. Nobody knew of his past and never would.

He watched her turn a solid gold band around and around the ring finger of her right hand. Her left hand—thank God—was bare. He didn't want her to have a husband, fiancé or significant other waiting for her at home.

Why? God only knew.

"What else happened tonight?" he repeated his earlier question.

She dropped her hands into her lap and rested the back of her head against the wall. She turned to look at him and grimaced. "I was with my parents and grandmother, and a guy sitting at our table invited me to have dinner with him. I tried to get out of it gracefully, but my family was pushing me to accept. So I knocked over a glass of red wine so I could leave."

She sighed. "I keep telling my family that I'm fine on my own, but they believe I need to get back on the horse."

She'd lost him. What horse? "Sorry?"

She looked down at her hands. "I haven't dated for a long time, and they want me to." She released an annoyed sigh. "And that's only partly true. They want me to date, then marry, then produce a child, because I'm the only hope for carrying on the family line."

He winced. He'd never experienced family pressure, but it didn't sound like fun. "Is passing on the family genes so important? Do you have a rare genetic advantage the world needs?"

She laughed at his teasing, and he felt his throat tighten, his stomach warm. When was the last time he had made a woman laugh? Years ago? Never?

"None of the above, sadly. Have you heard of the Bacalls?"

Of course. Everyone who lived in Annapolis knew of the family. The Bacalls owned a media empire and had interests in tech. Old money, they were the bluest of Maryland blue bloods.

"Sure, I've heard of the family—but when you say 'Bacall,' my mind immediately goes to Greg Bacall. He's an incredible architect who specializes in designing green buildings."

Pleasure lit up her eyes. "Greg is my brother. I'll admit he is brilliant, but he's also a pain in my ass."

He heard the affection in her voice and felt a little envious. He would've loved a brother or sister. More than that, he would've loved a parent who cared about him enough to keep him around. But he was over wishing for a family, for things that wouldn't come true.

People had a habit of leaving him. He was destined to live his life solo. That was a truth he'd accepted a long time ago.

"Can't your brother help out with the continuation of the family line?" he asked, fascinated by her family dynamics.

"Greg is gay, and while he and Chas could have kids—surrogacy, adoption, whatever—they don't want any. So I'm my mother's and grandmother's last hope. They are both obsessed with the idea of a baby to coo over," she said.

He couldn't help the next question. His curiosity was burning a hole in his head. "Two questions… Why isn't there a Mr. Jamie at home? And do you want kids?"

He caught a distraught flicker in her eyes, saw her jaw tense. "It's a long story and, no, I don't want kids either."

Oh, now that was a lie. He cocked his head to the side. "Really?"

She nodded. "Oh, yeah. Not interested." But when she refused to meet his eyes and glanced at the elevator door instead, as if looking for an out, his suspicion that she was fudging the truth was confirmed.

But because he hated people digging into his own psyche, he decided not to pursue the topic. Her body, her life. Her mother's and grandmother's disappointment.

"God, I'm hungry," Jamie said after a long sigh. As if to emphasize, her stomach rumbled.

Rowan grinned when she blushed.

Jamie bent her legs and rested her forearms on her knees. "Distract me, Cowper."

Her eyes connected with his, and he felt the pull, saw the hot flare of desire in her eyes, the way her breath caught and her shoulders tensed. He couldn't ignore the flush on her cheeks and the throbbing pulse point in her neck. And another good clue—underneath those tiny beads on the bodice of her dress, her nipples were tight and erect. She was as attracted to him as he was her.

He could dip his head, hold her face, kiss her sense-less. And, God, he wanted to. He was very sure she wouldn't object. If they reacted to each other the way he thought they might—with bone-melting intensity—they'd probably take this too far.

And that wasn't wise. Not in an elevator…

So he hunted around for a neutral topic. "How do you know me?" The answer came to him before she could answer. "That damn newspaper article," he muttered.

"Yep." Jamie nodded. "I've been coming to these cial events since I was a teenager, and I've ne you around before. I take it your newfound popularity is due to the governor's gratitude?"

Bluntly put but true. "Accurate."

"And you're here because making friends with the power brokers might help your business."

A frown pulled her dark eyebrows together as she glanced at his watch. He knew she was curious as to how much help he needed if he could afford one of the most expensive watches in the world.

He wondered if she'd understand that it wasn't a matter of money. Having grown up in this world, would she understand that being invited to these events was the equivalent of being asked to join an exclusive club? To someone like him, someone who hadn't been born with a silver spoon in his mouth, these types of invitations had been nonexistent before his chance encounter with the governor's son.

Bigger and better construction deals, the ones with prestige, had also been out of his reach.

"Sometimes it's not *what* you know but *who* you know," he told her. "I work hard and I work smart, but sometimes that's not enough." He wouldn't say more. He'd run his mouth too much already.

"I get that. My dad gets so frustrated with the great and the good of Annapolis. He says the snobs cut off their noses to spite their faces, because they deal with the same incompetent, inefficient, lazy people just because they went to boarding school or played polo together."

"I think I'd like your dad."

"You probably would," Jamie admitted. "Despite being the fifth generation to run Bacall Media, he's the most chill, low-key, unsnobby guy you'll ever meet. My mother is equally down-to-earth but my grandmother…" Jamie threw up her hands in despair. "Well, to put it mildly, she thinks she's Annapolis's answer to the Dowager Countess Crawley."

"Who?"

"You haven't watched *Downton Abbey*," she accused him.

He had the urge to apologize. "I don't watch TV."

"Never?"

"I catch a game now and then. The news."

"How do you relax, wind down?" she demanded.

He didn't. "I exercise, sometimes read." Though he couldn't remember the last book he'd read for fun. Or when. "I mostly work."

Her expression suggested that work made Rowan a very dull boy. She wasn't wrong. Needing to change the subject again, he asked, "Do you enjoy these types of events?"

She wrinkled her nose. "Not really. I'm expected to show my face. Not to be boastful, but my family is influential, and I am what they call 'a catch.' Powerful family, lots of money, reasonably good-looking."

If *reasonably good-looking* was a euphemism for *freaking gorgeous*, then okay.

"But I'm not naive, and I know most of the men who ask me out are more interested in the family fortune and connections than they are in me."

He thought she was underestimating her appeal but he knew where she was coming from. He never knew whether he was being hit on because he was wealthy and fresh on the market or because his face had been plastered across the front page.

Nobody really knew him. Mostly because he never let himself be known. He kept people at a distance and, if pushed, he'd admit to being emotionally stunted. Could he be blamed for being that way? Throughout his life, every time he made a personal connection—whether it was with a social worker, a teacher, a friend or a foster parent—that person had been ripped from him in one way or another.

He protected his emotional core and never indulged in personal conversations…until now. With Jamie.

But only because they were stuck in an elevator, and not talking would be weird. He was reticent and uncommunicative but not weird. He hoped.

"I wish I could hang up an 'I'm off the market' sign. I just want to be alone. I'm not interested in dating or a relationship or being one-half of a couple."

Wow. That was quite a statement. And since every word she'd uttered was coated with sincerity, he believed her. This wasn't a woman playing hard to get. This was a woman who wanted her freedom and her solitude.

Jamie nudged his side with her elbow. "I bet you get hit on all the time too. Here? Tonight?"

He wasn't the type to boast, so he just shrugged.

Jamie grinned and nudged him again. "You so did!"

He didn't kiss and tell.

After a surprisingly comfortable silence, Jamie spoke again, her tone wry. "Here we are, sitting in an elevator after spending far too much money on a ticket to a charity fundraiser. We've drunk expensive booze, eaten expensive food—"

"Not a lot of it," Rowan corrected.

She nodded. "Not a lot of food but expensive, nonetheless. And now we're complaining about the fact that people want to date us. I think we are whining, because those are such first-world, one-percent, rich-people problems."

Yeah, they were. But he'd come from poverty, knew what it was like to have nothing, to not eat for a day or two, to struggle to make a rent payment. "I hear you, but being rich doesn't insulate you from loneliness, from problems, from feelings and, in your case, from interfering relatives."

Their eyes connected, and Rowan watched as hers darkened with desire. His heart sped up when her mouth curved into a small genuine smile. "That's pretty deep, Cowper."

"I'm a pretty deep guy."

"Are you?" she whispered, her eyes moving from his mouth to his eyes and back again.

"Yeah. I'm also a guy who wants to kiss you."

Jamie half turned to face him and hooked her arm around his neck, pulling him closer. "Kiss away."

Rowan didn't hesitate. He covered her mouth with his, learning its shape, testing the softness. He placed his hand on the side of her face, tipping her head to the angle he preferred as he nibbled her full bottom lip and stroked his thumb over her high cheekbone. Needing to taste her, he probed the seam of her mouth with his tongue, and she opened, allowing him to slide inside. She tasted of wine and wonder.

They spent a few minutes exchanging long, lazy kisses, her fingers in his hair, his one hand on her back. But further exploration was hampered by their position. He needed her breasts pushing into his chest, his cock against her stomach. Without thinking, he wrapped his arm around her waist and hauled her onto his lap so that she sat sideways across his thighs. A loud rip of fabric made them jerk back to stare at each other.

"Shit! Was that your dress?" Rowan demanded, his heart sinking.

Jamie looked down and gasped when she saw a six-inch gap revealing the curve of her breast. "Oh, dear."

Oh, dear? He'd damaged her hundred-year-old dress and that was her reaction? "God, I'm so sorry."

She shrugged, seemingly unconcerned. "It tore at the seam. I'm sure it can be repaired." She placed her hand on his cheek, her thumb swiping over his bottom lip. "Now, where were we? Here, I think," Jamie said, lowering her mouth to his.

His head spinning, he leaned into her to take everything she was offering. He fell into her scent, her taste, reveling in the feel of her slim body in his arms, her hip pushing into his cock. Delicate, sexy, feminine as hell. His hand curled around her breast, and he sighed when she arched her back to push into his palm.

Yeah, she wanted him. The thought made his head spin.

Rowan brushed his thumb across her nipple, lost in the moment, in her mouth.

"Folks, we have a team on their way to you, and they'll be pulling you out soon. Thank you for your patience."

Rowan stiffened at the sound of the strange voice floating through the elevator's speakers and winced when he remembered that most elevators these days had cameras that livestreamed video into a manned security room. They'd given someone quite a show.

Rowan banged his head against the back wall and muttered a hopefully indistinguishable curse. He patted Jamie's hip and gently lifted her off him before bounding to his feet. Holding out his hand, he took hers and pulled her to her feet. Standing, he saw the rip in her dress was worse than he'd thought. She was about to give their rescuers a very nice view of her right breast.

He winced. "God, I'm so sorry about your dress. That's far worse than red wine."

She looked down and grimaced. "Good thing I know a really good tailor."

"I'll pay to have it fixed," Rowan offered, bending down to pick up his jacket. Digging inside the pockets, he removed his slim wallet containing his credit cards and his car fob. Jamming both into his pants pocket, he flung his jacket around Jamie's shoulders.

"Put this on."

Jamie pushed her arms into the sleeves, and his jacket covered her to midthigh. She flapped her arms, and the ends of his jacket jumped up and down. He rolled up the fabric of one arm until her wrist was exposed. Then he started on the other arm. When he was done, he buttoned the jacket lapels together.

Jamie looked up at him, amused. "You're very good at taking charge and getting things done."

He supposed he was. *When there is nobody to look after you, you get on and look after yourself. And then you look after the people younger and smaller than you.* It was what he knew, how he lived his life.

"Folks, we're coming in," a voice said from outside the elevator doors.

Rowan picked up Jamie's shoes and bag before pulling her away from the door. He bent his head to speak in her ear. "This is the most fun I've had in an elevator—ever."

Jamie flashed him a brilliant smile. "Me too." She placed her hand on his arm and squeezed. "Thanks for not making this weird by asking me out on a date or asking if you can see me again."

He'd been about to do exactly that… *Shit.* "We did kiss," he pointed out. "And it's obvious there's chemistry."

She shrugged. "Yeah, there is and the kiss was fantastic but…"

His heart dropped to his toes. "Not interested?"

She shook her head. "Interested? Sure. Ready? No."

He heard the sadness in her voice and wondered what put the devastation in her eyes. "Will you ever be ready?" he asked. Though why he was asking, he had no clue. It wasn't like he wanted a relationship—with her or anyone.

"Probably not," Jamie replied. She squeezed his arm again and reached up to kiss the corner of his mouth. She'd no sooner dropped back down to her toes than the elevator doors opened, and Rowan saw the smiling faces of their rescuers. Their elevator car was at least two feet down from the hallway passage.

The younger of the two responders grinned at Jamie and held out his hands. "If you give me your hands, I can pull you up."

"I've got her," Rowan brusquely told him. Standing behind Jamie, he gripped her hips and easily lifted her so that her feet rested on the ledge. A small push on her butt and she was in the hallway. He handed up her bag and shoes and hoisted himself up onto the ledge.

"Thanks, guys," she told the responders.

Rowan held her elbow as she put her shoes back on, then escorted her to the door leading to the stairs, where a line of people stood, slowly edging their way through.

"Hey, my folks must've gotten stuck in another elevator," Jamie exclaimed, gesturing to a tall, distinguished man and his pretty wife, who looked a lot like Jamie. "I'll walk down with them."

Their time together was over. Rowan briefly clasped

her hand. "If I ever get stuck in an elevator again, I hope it's with you."

She flashed him another blinding smile and nodded. "It was nice being stuck with you, Cowper."

Then she, and his jacket, walked out of his life.

Three

Two weeks later, Jamie walked into the reception area of Cowper Construction—pretty, swish offices in a multistory high-rise in downtown Annapolis—and looked around at the sleek couches and bold art on the walls. A buff guy stood behind a granite counter, a headset over his shaved head. He held up his finger, asking her to wait. Jamie nodded and walked over to the wide window looking down at the busy city street below.

She draped Rowan's jacket, recently laundered, over the closest chair and looked at her watch. It was ten before six, and she knew she shouldn't be here. She had a pile of work sitting on her desk, and her parents expected her for dinner tonight.

Her family seemed to need to constantly take her emotional temperature. Was she lonely? Was she coping?

She was a widow, someone who'd loved her husband, despite their issues. Yes, she still felt guilty; she always would. But she wasn't miserable. Unfortunately, it seemed her mom and grandmother would only accept that she was fine—whatever that meant—when she was in another relationship.

Not going to happen.

They would be thrilled to know she'd kissed Rowan—such a weak description!—and part of her was tempted to tell them. But a bigger part of her wanted to keep their kiss to herself. It was amazing and precious and unexpected and...

Well, lovely.

Everything about being in his arms had been sensational, from the heat rolling off him to the heady combination of his cologne and masculine scent; from the hardness of his thighs to his spice-and-sex mouth. She could've kissed him for millennia, lost in a world created just for the two of them. One filled with bright colors, intense sensations...heat.

The loud jangle of the receptionist's phone pulled Jamie back to the present, and she shook her head. What had she been about to do? Oh, right. She was going to text her mom.

Won't make it tonight. Sorry. Xxx

Her return message landed ten seconds later.

I expect you here by eight. Not one minute later. Love you!

Blergh. Her mother was persistent.

Jamie scrolled through her messages and saw a couple of invitations to upcoming events. She sighed. Her folks would be disappointed if she didn't attend the Gordons' private beach picnic—a catered affair for a hundred people—and the Jacksons' thirtieth wedding-anniversary party. The Bacalls, Gordons and Jacksons had a friendship that went back generations. She'd attended the same schools as their kids.

Her presence would be expected, and if she went to either function solo, as she usually did, there would be the same old clucking behind her back: "Poor Jamie. She still hasn't recovered, you know. She hasn't had a relationship since Kaden died…"

And she doubted she ever would.

Jamie placed her hand on the window, easily conjuring up Kaden's face, his green eyes, the red-gold stubble on his cheeks and chin. His mouth had been quick to smile, and she'd hoped their kids would inherit his dark red hair.

Their kids… The kids they'd never have.

Their inability to conceive had been the subject of the argument they'd had as they'd made their way to what was supposed to have been a sexy weekend away. Jamie couldn't remember how the fight started, but she did remember shouting at him to stop harping on the subject. He'd yelled back and taken his eyes off the road for too long. He'd missed the corner, skidding on the icy road.

She very much remembered hearing the car ripping apart, the screech of metal, the smell of blood, looking at Kaden's face when the world stopped spinning. For as long as she lived, the labored sound of his breathing would haunt her nightmares. Then the light in his eyes dimmed and he slipped away…

"Jamie?"

She whipped around, hand on her heart, to see Rowan standing a few feet from her, looking puzzled. Guilt, sorrow and sadness faded as she took in his big body, his quizzical expression. How was it that he could pull her into the present, grounding her in the here and now?

"Hi." The small word was all she could manage.

"Hi," he replied, frowning. "I called your name, but you were zoned out."

Jamie worried her bottom lip between her teeth. Whenever she went down that wormhole of memories, she zoned out, sliding into the memories of those horrible hours on that lonely road—praying, crying, screaming for help, begging for forgiveness.

"Sorry," Jamie said, pulling up a smile. She looked around, saw that the reception area was now empty and that the lights had been dimmed. "Wow, this place clears out fast."

"You've been standing for a while, ten minutes or so," Rowan told her.

That long? Dammit. She'd lost time before but never for so long and not in someone else's space. "I'm so sorry. It's busy at work, and I have a lot on my mind."

He raised his eyebrows, his expression telling her that he didn't believe her off-the-cuff explanation. Rowan was dressed in chino pants and a navy button-down shirt, his sleeves rolled up. His brown leather belt matched his shoes, and he looked as good as he did in a tuxedo. Frankly, Cowper could wear a brown paper bag and still look hot. If she ever got to see him naked, she might spontaneously combust.

"It's nice to see you, but why are you here?"

Jamie quickly gathered her thoughts. There was a reason she was here, right? What was it? Her eyes fell on the packet containing his dry-cleaning, and she gestured toward it. "I brought your jacket back. I had it dry-cleaned."

"Thank you," Rowan replied. "I appreciate that. Oh,

did you manage to get your dress fixed? I said I'd pay for the repairs."

She winced and shook her head. "I didn't, unfortunately. My tailor said the fabric ripped in a bad place and can't be repaired."

"I am so sorry. I know how much you love that dress."

She shrugged. "It was my fault for wearing it." Jamie placed her hands behind her back, her palms resting on the glass behind her. She looked around. "I like your offices. Very smart."

"What were you expecting?" Rowan asked, smiling. "A double-wide with battered desks on a construction site?"

Well, sort of. Okay, yes—not that she'd admit that to him. She nodded toward a corner office with glass walls. "Is that yours?"

"Mmm-hmm. Since you're here, would you like a drink?" Rowan asked.

She very much would. She should be sensible, hand his jacket over and leave. But she didn't want to. She wanted to have that drink, look at him some more and, yes, kiss him again. Maybe even do more than that. She knew she was playing with fire, but she'd step back before she got burned.

Her heart was encased in steel and ice. It was impenetrable. She could handle a mild flirtation, maybe even a one-night stand, with the very sexy Rowan Cowper. She'd walked through hell. A few flames didn't scare her.

Jamie picked up his dry-cleaning with one hand and hoisted her bag up onto her shoulder with the other.

"Sure."

Jamie followed Rowan across the reception area to his glass-walled office.

He hadn't been in his office earlier, or she would've

noticed him sitting behind his wide, messy desk, the incredible view of downtown Annapolis to his right. At the open door, Rowan stepped back and gestured her inside his sanctum. There was a low couch situated against the wall and a small boardroom table tucked into another corner. But his view of the city dominated the space, and Jamie headed over to the L-shaped bank of floor-to-ceiling windows, enchanted. Dusk was falling and the city was starting to light up. What a magical time of day.

"Your view is amazing, Rowan," she said, her voice husky.

"My view *is* pretty spectacular."

Something in his voice made her turn, and she immediately noticed he wasn't looking at the buildings or the harbor but at her. Their eyes connected. He smiled and moved his gaze across her face, taking in her hair pulled into a high ponytail, the bold necklace she wore around her neck. He skimmed over her white silk top tucked into no-nonsense wide-legged black pants. His lips kicked up at the corners when he caught sight of her red-painted toes. He spent a moment looking at them, and she felt a low throb deep in her womb.

Feeling jittery from his intense look, she yanked her eyes off him and looked around his office. The glass walls had turned dark, and she could no longer see into the reception area.

"Is there a reason you've switched the walls from clear to opaque?" Jamie asked him, her heart rate climbing fast. She wasn't scared to be alone with him—not in the least. If anything, she was scared he *wouldn't* kiss her or touch her.

And maybe that was why she was here.

She wanted to be in his arms, to feel her mouth under his, to lightly rake her nails across the skin of his back,

his butt. He was the first person in five years to make
her feel alive, like a woman who had wants and needs.

"There are still people working late, and I thought we
needed some privacy."

"For what?" she asked.

He quickly crossed the space between them, standing so close she felt the heat radiating off him, inhaled
his cologne, brushed her shirt against his. He bent his
head, his mouth a whisper from hers. "This. Let me kiss
you again, Jamie."

Of course she would; wasn't that why she was here?
To experience the magic of being in his arms again?

"I thought you'd never ask," Jamie whispered, moving her body closer to his.

She caught his smile before his mouth covered hers
with devastating accuracy. He didn't hesitate, and his
confidence was sexy as hell. Jamie grabbed his shirt and
twisted it around her fist, using her grip to keep herself
steady as he decimated her self-control.

She wanted this man—more than she'd ever wanted
anyone, ever. She wanted him naked, on the couch or the
floor or the desk, while the lights of Annapolis bathed
their bodies.

This was unexpected and scary. What was it about
this man, this stranger, that made her act so out of character? She didn't do one-night stands, never had. When
she chose a lover, she did so with deliberation and after
some time second-guessing herself.

And those choices had only happened in the years before she'd met and married Kaden, when she was young
and far more impetuous than she was now.

But she couldn't walk away from Rowan. Not until
she knew what it felt like to make love to him.

Even if it was in his office on a Tuesday evening in July.

Rowan wrapped her hair around his fist, gently pulling her head back to look up at his face. "I want to see you naked."

He was so very honest, so damn forthright. She liked that about him; she knew where she stood. She loosened her grip on his shirt and ran her hand over his rib cage, down his hip. "I've been imagining you naked too."

His eyebrows raised. "You've been thinking of me?"

Yes, far too much. "Only in an X-rated nighttime-fantasy type of way," she clarified.

He kissed her nose, then the corner of her mouth. "Good to know. I've been thinking of you too. In a double-X all-day-fantasy type of way."

Her inner romantic sighed, but her pragmatic side immediately reminded her that this was about sex, nothing more. She touched his cheek with the tips of her fingers, loving the feel of his stubble.

"Want to go somewhere?" she asked.

"If we do, will I get to see you naked?"

She thought about hedging, playing it coy, and brushed off the urge to play games. He was a blunt guy; she could be blunt too. "There's a damn good chance."

Rowan flashed that rare pirate grin that made her skin goose bump with pleasure. "Excellent," he said, grabbing her bag with one hand and her hand with the other. Tugging her to the corner of his office, he opened a floor-to-ceiling door concealing an elevator. Rowan pushed her inside, stepped into the small space after her and hit the only button on the panel. They immediately started flying up.

Twenty seconds later the elevator door opened, and Rowan walked backward, pulling her into his spacious penthouse apartment. She looked around, her jaw dropping at the double-volume bank of windows that offered even more sweeping views of the city's skyline and the harbor. Her quick visual sweep of the apartment told her it was dotted with the occasional piece of high-end Italian furniture, that she was standing on hardwood floors and that his kitchen was small but state-of-the-art.

Rowan clutched her hand and pulled her down a hallway, passing one bedroom, then two more, before pulling her inside a corner room dominated by a massive bed. Doors led onto his private patio and what looked to be a hot tub.

She could just imagine sitting there on a warm summer evening—or in the snow—kicking back and taking in the view.

Rowan gently gripped her jaw and forced her to look at him. "You with me?"

Was she? Did she want this?

Yes. Yes, she did.

She didn't *want* to want it, which was a totally different thing. Over the years, Greg and Chas had urged her to get her head, and body, back in the game. They'd told her, repeatedly, that she was too young to hide away, to sacrifice herself on the altar of regret and grief. Up until that Saturday night, she hadn't had the energy or the interest, but Rowan stirred her comatose libido to life. Now, it was demanding she engage.

And that was why she'd made the trek across town to his offices, why she'd used the return of his jacket as an excuse to see him. Because he made her feel alive, more *Jamie*, than she'd felt for years and years. With him, her guilt was sidelined, subdued.

He didn't expect anything more from her than this moment, wasn't asking for anything but for her to share her body with him. There was such freedom in living in the moment and not worrying about tomorrow, or next week, or next year.

"Your apartment is huge."

"I'll give you the tour later," he promised. "Right now, I want to explore you."

His words should've sounded cheesy, like a smoothly delivered line, but she saw the sincerity and admiration in his gaze and slowly nodded. She closed her eyes, hauled in a deep breath and felt his hands drop away.

When Jamie looked at him again, she saw that he'd put a healthy amount of distance between them, and his small action reassured her. If he could pick up on her nonverbal cues, then she knew he would stop if she needed him to.

"If this isn't something you want, we can walk back into the lounge, have a drink—or we can go back down to my office. No questions asked."

He was a good guy, no doubt about it. Jamie shook her head, stepped toward him and placed her hand on his chest, above his heart. "This isn't something I've done for a long, long time but..."

"But?"

"I want to, okay? I'm just not sure how to tell you."

His mouth quirked up at the corners. "You just did."

His smile took her breath away, and when he placed his mouth on hers, his lips were still curved. Then he put just enough distance between their lips for him to speak. "I want you so much, Jamie."

She curled her hand around his neck and stepped closer, pushing herself against him, enjoying the way his hard body complemented hers. Opening her mouth, she fell into his kiss, shocked by the hunger in his eyes. For her.

"You're so much more than what I dreamed," Rowan muttered, clasping the side of her face and tipping her head up. His eyes—the color of a midnight sea—flared with passion. "Can I undress you, take you to bed?"

Knowing what she wanted—him—she didn't hesitate. "Yes. Please."

Jamie heard Rowan's sigh of relief, and she released one of her own when his hands gripped her hips close to his, allowing her to feel the hard length of his erection pushing into her stomach. He lifted his hand, covered her breast and his thumb found her nipple, brushing over it with perfect pressure. He hadn't done much beyond kissing her and her panties were damp.

But if he didn't kiss her again soon, she would die from frustration. Jamie stood on her tiptoes and slammed her lips onto his, her tongue tracing the seam of his mouth, demanding he open up.

She didn't push like this, Jamie thought from a place far away. Before Kaden, even *with* him, she waited for men to make the first move—to kiss her, to lead. She followed.

But not today.

Rowan made her feel reckless, confident. Powerful.

Rowan held her tightly and let her kiss him. When he didn't open his mouth or kiss her back, Jamie started to pull away.

Rowan growled a harsh "no" and moved his hand from her breast to the back of her head to keep her in place. "I was loving that," he told her. "Your mouth is… heaven."

Then Rowan started kissing her—hot, drugging kisses—and she was lost.

This was why she was here—to experience this. To share this with Rowan. He was a stranger, but she knew him, and he knew her. He knew how to touch her, kiss her, build her up, pull her back. To make her yearn. And burn.

Jamie pulled his shirt from the back of his pants and put her hands on his hot masculine skin. Rowan groaned his approval, and as her palms drifted over his gorgeous ass, she became annoyed at the barrier of clothes between her fingers and his flesh.

Rowan kissed the corner of her mouth, trailed his lips over her jaw, nipped her neck as he slowly stripped her of her clothes. Standing in her bra and panties, she realized it had been a long time since a man had made her feel like she was something infinitely marvelous and ravishing.

And, God, she'd missed this. Missed being in a man's arms. The heat and the strength, the yin and the yang. Needing to touch him, to know every part of him, she stroked his hard shaft with the pad of her finger, from base to tip, and was rewarded by the sound of a low curse.

Needing more, Jamie opened the snap on his pants, pulled down his zipper and released his straining erection from his underwear. Using both hands to hold him, she arched as Rowan nipped and sucked on the tender skin where her neck and shoulder met.

He walked her backward and gently turned her around and asked her to put her hands on the wall. She gasped when his mouth touched every bump on her spine, barely noticing her bra falling to the floor. Stepping close to her, both his hands covered her breasts, his fingers teasing her nipples into hard points.

"I want you," he muttered.

Rowan pulled her panties down; but before she could feel embarrassed about being naked while he was still dressed, his fingers slid in between her legs, finding her bundle of nerves with ruthless efficiency. Jamie was close—she wouldn't be able to hold on—and she started to moan.

He pushed a finger into her, then another, and she climbed…reaching, teetering, desperate.

Rowan pulled his hand away and turned her around to face him. His eyes, rich with desire, held hers as he stripped, and as soon as he was naked—his gorgeous body more muscled than she'd expected—he gripped the back of her thigh and lifted her leg to rest over his hip. She groaned when his erection brushed her sweet spot.

Pulling her backward, Rowan moved toward his enormous bed, pulling her down so her legs fell on either side of his thighs, as close as they could be without him slipping inside.

He rested his forehead against hers. "As wonderful as this feels, we need a condom."

Jamie dragged her core up his erection and smiled when Rowan groaned. "Just give me a minute more."

"I don't have that much patience."

But Rowan gripped her hips and lifted her, the muscles in his stomach and arms contracting. *Whoa. So hot.* He slid inside her, still unsheathed. He rocked and she closed her eyes, swept away by the feeling of perfection.

Rowan cursed then and pulled out. He gently placed her on the bed and rooted around in the drawer of the bedside table before pulling out a strip of condoms and abruptly ripping one off. He removed the latex without dropping his eyes from hers.

There was something sexy about a guy who engaged in so much eye contact.

He stared down at her, pinning her with all that deep blue. Without asking, Jamie lay back on the cool cotton of his duvet, and her legs fell open. She watched, fascinated, as Rowan rolled on the condom and then lowered his body to cover hers, his erection nudging her opening.

"I can't wait to be inside you."

Jamie touched his jaw with her fingers. "Nobody is asking you to wait," she told him.

He used his hand to test whether she was ready, to tease her a little more, and then he slid inside her, hot and big and wonderful.

And she stepped oh-so-willingly into a giant sparkler, the heat igniting a series of fireworks under her skin. Rowan placed his hand under her butt and yanked her up at the same time he plunged inside, and those individual fireworks amalgamated to create a firestorm, the explosion ripping her apart from the inside out.

It was the best, brightest, most intense orgasm she'd ever experienced, and no sooner had it died down than she wanted another.

And then another.

Sex with Rowan, she decided as she watched the kaleidoscope of colors dance behind her eyes, was immediately addictive.

That might be a problem.

She'd forgotten how good sex could be.

Jamie lay facedown on Rowan's big bed, one arm dangling off the side, her fingertips resting on the cool hardwood floor. She couldn't move, couldn't think... In fact, she was doing well just to pull air into her lungs.

She was wiped.

And it was all Rowan's fault. He'd flipped her inside out and turned her upside down, and she'd loved every second of it. Every kiss, every slide of his hand, every way he made her body and soul sing. She wouldn't be averse to round three—or four—as soon as she recovered, rehydrated and refueled.

Jamie yawned and her eyelids dropped closed. She gathered one of Rowan's pillows, wrapped her arms around it and hiked up her knee. She'd take a nap. Just a small one…

A gentle hand tapping her sheet-covered butt made her groan. "Go 'way."

Rowan's deep laugh washed over her, and he bent and laid a kiss on the side of her neck. "I see you like to sleep," he teased, his voice in her ear.

She couldn't tell him that she never slept through the night without a sleeping pill and, because she hated taking drugs, she only averaged around three hours of rest a night. The ghosts of her past, specifically Kaden's, visited her between midnight and four and demanded she replay the events of that life-changing road trip.

Sometimes she did, sometimes she didn't—choosing to read, work or watch a movie instead. But either way, sleep was in short supply.

She rolled and was caged by Rowan's hands on either side of her shoulders. She noticed he'd pulled on a pair of sweatpants and a T-shirt, the hem of his sleeves tight around his biceps. Biceps she'd licked and kissed, amazed at their definition and size. There was no doubt about it: Rowan Cowper was ripped.

Big shoulders and arms; washboard stomach; truly excellent bum; and long, athletic legs. *Yum*…

"If you keep looking at me with those come-to-bed eyes, I'm going to…" He narrowed his eyes as his words trailed away.

"You're going to do what?" Jamie asked, her voice sounding sexier than she'd ever heard it.

"Climb back into bed with you," he reluctantly admitted, his expression rueful.

She was about to ask whether that would be such a bad thing, to tease him a little, but she caught the hint of wariness in his eyes. She didn't blame him for feeling that way. Their connection had been intense, a roller coaster of sensation, and they needed to put some physical and emotional distance between them.

Theirs was only a physical connection, a couple of hours of fun, nothing serious. Jamie sat up and pulled the sheet under her arms. "We made love twice, but it's been a while for me so..."

He nodded, stroked her sheet-covered thigh before standing up. "Absolutely."

Okay, then. Right. She dropped her head, a little embarrassed, thrown off her stride by his quick understanding.

Rowan handed her a T-shirt. "I've opened a bottle of wine. Do you want a glass?"

She looked at him, tipping her head to the side.

Was he just being polite? Should she accept? What if she did and he didn't want her to stay? What were the protocols here? Why wasn't there a standard policy for these types of situations?

"It's a glass of wine, Jamie, not an invitation to move in," Rowan stated wryly.

She shrugged and felt her face heat. "I don't know how to act. I feel like I should go."

"Why?"

"I'm not sure if you want me to stay or whether you're being polite," Jamie admitted.

"I'm never polite. Ask anyone. And I asked you to stay because I'd like you to share a glass of wine with me. And if we can still stand each other after an hour,

I'll ask you to share a pizza with me. And if we are still enjoying each other's company after that, I'm going to ask you to come back to bed with me. And then I'll make you scream. Again."

"I did not scream," Jamie said. Kaden had always said she was incredibly silent during sex. "I'm not a screamer, moaner or whimperer."

"Trust me, you did all three," Rowan assured her as he stood up and walked out of the room.

Jamie flopped back on the pillow and covered her eyes with her forearm. She'd had a one-night stand, and she'd liked it. She'd been uninhibited enough to let go, to verbalize her pleasure. She'd felt comfortable enough to explore Rowan's gorgeous body with her teeth and her tongue, had allowed him access to her body after a couple of brief conversations. Somehow she'd temporarily left her guilt and grief at Rowan's bedroom door. She didn't recognize herself…and neither would anyone else.

Maybe, just this once, that was a good thing.

Four

Hearing her footsteps on his living room floor, Rowan poured some red wine into his glass and placed the bottle back on the coffee table. He sat on one of the lounge chairs next to his plunge pool, his legs stretched out, feeling lazy and, for once, stress free.

Early-evening sex was the bomb.

He watched out of the corner of his eye as Jamie stepped onto his private balcony and heard her gusty sigh. He knew why: his view of downtown Annapolis and Spa Creek from his apartment was kick-ass. He loved his three-bedroom apartment and sometimes couldn't believe that he—the kid from the worst suburb in Chicago, the kid who ran wild, boosted cars, shuffled from foster home to foster home—now owned various buildings on the East Coast, including this one.

Rowan watched as Jamie walked over to the infinity railing and rested her arms on the top, the fabric of his shirt riding up as she bent forward, showing him a glimpse of her panties. Of course she'd put on panties; he couldn't quite imagine her walking around commando, especially outside.

Jamie acted sophisticated, but he suspected that underneath the glossy hair and expertly made-up face was a woman with unexplored depths. She wasn't fragile or brittle, but he sensed she had demons nipping at her heels.

Don't they all?

"Your place is fantastic," Jamie told him, turning to face him.

"Thanks. I like it," Rowan replied, standing up. He picked up her glass of wine and walked it over to her. He gestured to the plunge pool. "Feel free to jump in. The water's warm."

"Naked?" Jamie asked, a hint of shock in her eyes.

Rowan tapped his bare foot against the transparent panels. "Clear looking out, opaque looking in. Nobody could see you from down below, and no one can look at you from up above." He looked up and squinted. "Maybe helicopters, birds and satellites."

"Funny," Jamie replied after sipping her wine. "Thanks, but I'll pass."

Rowan sat down again on the two-seater lounge chair and patted the space next to him. After a moment of internal debate, she sat down next to him, rearranged his shirt so she kept her decency and leaned back with a contented sigh, her small shoulder resting against his. "This is nice."

"It is."

A few minutes passed, and Rowan turned his head to see if she'd fallen asleep again. He smiled when he saw that her head was back and she was staring at the few stars in the now-black sky. She looked relaxed and content, and he was happy to see her that way. "Why did you come over tonight? I never expected to see you again."

She rolled her head to look at him. "I came to drop off your tuxedo jacket. I had it dry-cleaned."

"Very thoughtful of you, but we both know you could've had it delivered."

He half smiled at her busted look. Jamie sipped from her wineglass, her fall of hair blocking his expression from her view. "Why, Jamie? And is Jamie your full name or a nickname, by the way?"

"James Jessamy is my full name, but Greg shortened it to Jamie."

"Not JJ?" Rowan asked and grinned when annoyance jumped into her eyes.

"Not if you want to keep living."

He grinned once more before returning to the subject at hand. "So, your impromptu visit?"

"You're like a dog with a bone," Jamie muttered.

"It's been said," Rowan replied, not offended. Determination had gotten him his first job and kept him going when he lost money on his first solo building gig. It had helped him grow his business despite numerous cash flow crises, bad faith suppliers, and con men wannabe investors.

Jamie placed her wineglass on the side table next to her and clasped her linked hands between her thighs. "I'll admit, the tux jacket was just an excuse to see you. I'm not sure why, because I promise I'm not looking for a relationship."

She'd said that before, in the elevator. Then, like now, his curiosity was piqued. He knew why he wasn't interested in anything long-term—to him, love meant being let down, being abandoned, and he vowed he'd never be disappointed like that again. But something about Jamie made him think she should be married and have kids, and that she belonged in a permanent relationship.

He'd known many women in his life, knew how to read them. He could tell who was greedy, who was clingy, who needed constant love and assurance. He sensed that Jamie functioned best when she was one-half of a whole.

Her brow was furrowed, and Rowan knew she either didn't want to answer him or couldn't, so he asked another question. "Earlier, downstairs, you were zoned out. What were you thinking about?"

"Ah, um… I have a client who keeps asking me out. He's being unusually persistent."

Mmm-hmm. He didn't believe her. She'd looked too sad and too lost to have been thinking about some dude she didn't want to date.

"I was also thinking about my mom and her campaign to find me a man—oh, shit!"

Her eyes widened and she grabbed his right wrist, turning it so that she could see his watch. Then she swore again. "Oh, I'm in such big trouble."

"What's the problem?" Rowan asked.

"I missed dinner at my parents' house!" Jamie muttered, leaping to her feet. "Where's my bag? I need my phone. In another half hour, they are going to start calling hospitals and morgues."

Right, that seemed like an overreaction. She was around thirty, give or take—a grown woman. "Your phone is downstairs, in my office."

She swore again and rocked from foot to foot. "Can I run down to get it?"

"You could, but if you know your folks' home number, you can just use my phone." He picked up his phone from the side table and handed it over.

Jamie sent him a thankful glance. "Thank you. And, yes, I do know the number." She punched in the digits, and he heard the call ring through.

A squawking voice came from the other end of the line. "Are you okay? Are you hurt? You're ninety minutes late!"

Jamie gripped the bridge of her nose with her thumb and index finger. "Sorry, Mom, I was... I am... My phone died."

God, she was a terrible liar. "And I got held up at work," she added.

Squawk, squawk.

He listened to her end of the conversation. "I'm sorry I worried you, Mom... No, I'm not coming over... It's been a long day... I'll talk to you soon..." Her mom wasn't ready to let her end the conversation. "Dinner? Maybe next week... Got to go, Mom... No, I didn't watch *The Bachelor*... Mom, I've *got* to go. Love you."

When she was done, Jamie smacked his phone on her forehead a couple of times before handing it back to him. "Thanks. My mom worries if she doesn't know where I am."

"I gathered," Rowan stated. Leaning across, he picked up her wineglass and pushed it into her hand. "Drink."

Jamie took a few sips and eventually sat down on the edge of the lounge chair, draping one long leg over the other.

"Why the panic?" Rowan asked after she'd taken a few more sips. "You're an adult and fully capable of looking after yourself."

"I am and I do, but there's a reason, a good one, why

they worry." She shook her head. "And, no, we're not getting into that tonight."

He saw the stubborn look in her eye, the way her chin lifted, and realized that there would be no budging her on that topic now. He'd retreat and circle back if she gave him the opportunity. "Tell me about your client, the one who keeps asking you on a date."

"His name is Drake, and he's pretty persistent."

Rowan tasted something sour at the back of his throat. The thought of her dating someone else, sleeping with someone else, made his skull shrink, his skin tighten. He wasn't the jealous type, so he couldn't understand what it was about this woman that threw him off his stride. Not only did he feel jealous but he also wanted to know more, to dig and delve into her life and explore her fascinating personality.

He didn't recognize himself.

Jamie didn't offer any further explanations and her reticence was strangely, and ironically, frustrating. Maybe if he opened up, just a little, she would too. Yeah, he was definitely becoming a stranger to himself.

"I know how that feels… My ex-fiancée keeps asking me for another chance."

Her amazing eyes connected with his. "And you don't want to give her one?"

"I'd rather shove my head into a vat of concrete," he replied. "She left me because I wasn't taking her to fancy parties and because we didn't live in a mansion on the water. She wanted unlimited access to my cash and walked out on me when I wouldn't give it to her."

Jamie winced.

"I didn't have unlimited cash back then. I was mortgaged to the hilt, trying to get a project done on time and facing late-delivery penalties. I was barely keeping my head above water." This was information he'd never shared with anyone, but he couldn't keep the words behind his teeth.

Jamie rested her wineglass on her knee. "Let me guess—you did deliver on time, and had she held on for a couple of months, she would've been living on easy street."

He smiled at her accurate summation of the situation. Not about living on easy street, but he had made a helluva killing on that deal. From then on, the cash and projects had started flowing in.

"She's seen pictures of me, in the papers and online, attending these A-list events, and she's angling to reconnect, to get in on that action."

"Have you told her that the food portions are terrible and the company can be a bit handsy?" Jamie asked, amusement in her eyes.

"I don't talk to her at all, but the texts and emails keep rolling in."

Jamie wrinkled her nose. "And I suppose you can't change your email address or phone number because they are linked to your business?"

He nodded.

"It's difficult when the lines between business and personal become blurred."

Difficult and annoying. And time-consuming. He routinely worked sixteen-hour days and had enough to deal with without weeding out unwelcome emails and deleting text messages. Besides, *over* meant *over*. When and how would she get the message?

"You have a clingy ex, and I have a persistent admirer…"

Rowan sent Jamie a sharp glance, wondering where she was going with that statement.

"And…?" he asked her, sounding wary.

She sent him a quick look, obviously picking up on his chary tone, and he wondered what was coming next. What he didn't expect was her laughter, or how the joyful sound danced on the summer air and made his head spin. Women didn't normally make him feel off-center, but she did. She also made his hands itch to touch her, his mouth needed to be on hers and, yeah, he needed to slide inside her…

She felt like home.

An asinine thought because a woman couldn't be home. No person could.

"Relax. Despite you rocking my world, I'm not about to make any demands on you. I'm not interested in a relationship."

He'd rocked her world? He knew she'd had fun—he made sure his partners enjoyed sex as much as he did—but "rocking someone's world" was a helluva compliment. So, yeah, he'd take it.

To mask his confusing reaction of disappointment and relief—relief he understood, but he had no idea why he was feeling disappointed—he slapped a hand on his chest. "I'm wounded."

"No, you're not. You don't want a relationship either."

Jamie leaned back and looked up at the sky. His heart kicked up as he took in the pretty picture she made—dressed in only his T-shirt, bare legs, incredible eyes and messy hair, smelling all feminine and wonderful. The woman short-circuited his brain.

"Do you want to see me again?" Jamie asked, placing her hand on his leg and squeezing. "We can keep it light, on the surface, enjoy each other in bed. And out."

She sounded like she was ordering coffee, giving directions to a cab driver, speaking to a stranger—calm, cool and under control—and it pissed him off. Dear God, his emotions—usually buried deep—were wreaking havoc on his heart. He had to get himself under control.

Rowan ran his hand over his jaw, his eyes on the hand she had on his thigh. A couple of inches higher and it would be on his package, and his brain would completely shut down. No one had ever made him lose his shit like this.

Needing to put some distance between them, Rowan stood up and walked over and gripped the railing. He stretched out his arms, looking through the glass panels at the busy street below. The car lights made pretty red, yellow and white streaks as they moved through the city.

He pulled in a few deep breaths and considered Jamie's question. Of course he wanted to see her again, but he didn't know if he should. She had the ability to slide under his skin, make him feel things he shouldn't, mess with his self-control.

He rarely dated, and he never continued seeing anyone, even when there was an intense attraction, whether that attraction was sexual or emotional. His dates, if you could call them that, were always with women he could easily walk away from. He didn't like, or trust, excess of emotion. He didn't want to find himself liking a woman too much, being in the position of craving her company, missing her when she wasn't around. It was human nature to seek companionship—he knew that—but he couldn't allow himself to get used to having someone in his life.

Because people always, always left. And it hurt like hell when they did.

He'd taken one chance in his life, and that was with his ex-girlfriend, Marisa. He hadn't fallen in love with her, but she'd been nice, interesting, bright. She'd told him she wasn't interested in the long term, that she just wanted a fling, but somehow that morphed into her becoming his girlfriend, spending most nights at his place, carving out a place in his life for herself. And he'd thought he could deal. Being one-half of a couple wasn't so bad. In fact, it had been nice to come home to someone after a long day.

He'd been surprised at how much it hurt when he discovered she was cheating on him, how empty his life felt when she left. Not because he missed her, particularly, but he missed not feeling alone. But she—like his mother, like the various foster parents he'd encountered—had made promises that never materialized. Everyone he forged an emotional connection with left.

He was mentally, sexually *and* emotionally attracted to Jamie.

It was a wild chemical reaction, a hunger he'd never experienced before. He had an undistilled physical craving to make her his—lust in its purest form.

But he was old enough to understand that when the chemistry between two people was that powerful, a sexual relationship could morph into something more. And that was why he could only allow himself one night with her. He couldn't risk anything developing between them. It had happened before with Marisa, and she couldn't hold a candle to Jamie.

He did not doubt that loving and losing Jamie would emotionally sideswipe him.

And really, he'd had enough of those types of losses in his life, thanks very much. He had no choice but to protect himself.

"I'm sorry but…no."

He'd said no? What the hell?

Jamie looked at his broad back, took a moment to

admire his truly excellent butt and then yanked her thoughts back. No? *Really?* What the hell was wrong with the man?

Jamie stood up and walked over to him so she could see his face. "Are you kidding me?"

His hard expression said he obviously wasn't. Jamie tapped her foot in irritation. She didn't see a problem with them meeting up again. He didn't want a relationship and neither did she. They could keep sleeping together until they tired of each other or one of them wanted to move on.

It was a clever unemotional arrangement that would benefit them both. She couldn't see a downside.

Rowan's expression was implacable. "Sorry," he said, shrugging.

Jamie ignored the knife in her chest that was tearing a hole through her heart. "I thought you enjoyed yourself with me," she stated, proud of her calm voice.

"You know I did."

His cold tone didn't reassure her, and she was immediately assaulted by a wave of doubt. Had she done something wrong? Did he not want a repeat? Was she so out of practice? There was no way she'd let him know she was having doubts about her performance. Of course she was; she hadn't had sex in five years... More, because she and Kaden hadn't been active in the bedroom in the last few months before he died. They'd argued about their fertility issues, and those fights had cast a pall over their sex life.

"I think sleeping together again would make things complicated," Rowan said eventually, and it was obvious he was choosing his words carefully.

Complicated? How? She wasn't asking for more than a few hours in bed. But Jamie was damned if she would continue this conversation. She would not beg. She had more pride than that. But, man, it hurt knowing that she wanted him far more than he wanted her.

It had been stupid to suggest an affair anyway. What had she been thinking? Right…she hadn't been. She'd just been confused by hormones and outstanding orgasms. She liked who she was when she was with Rowan, felt connected to the old Jamie—the person she'd been before life slapped her around.

She held up her hands, forced herself to smile and gestured in the direction of his bedroom. "I'm just going to get changed, and I'll get out of your hair. Thanks for the…"

She stopped, not sure how to continue. *Thanks for my multiple O's? For making me feel like a woman again? For doing that thing with your tongue?*

"Thanks for the wine," she said, turning away.

Rowan gripped the hem of her T-shirt, stopping her from stomping inside. She whirled around, scowling at him. "What?"

"I really did have a good time, Jamie."

She nodded and faked a smile. "Me too."

She turned to go back into the bedroom to get dressed. Pulling on her clothes, she blinked away her tears, wondering if she'd ever meet another man who could make her feel the way he did, make her feel safe and excited, tempted and turned on.

She was probably just the newest entry on his list of one-night stands, but he was the man who'd made her feel alive and attractive, feminine and free, for the first time in years.

Whenever she was with him, she forgot about her grief and guilt and felt like the best version of herself.

Maybe that was why she wanted to see him again: with him, she could step out of the past and into the present.

Whatever the reason, it didn't matter, she thought, tucking her shirt into her pants and slipping on her shoes. He didn't want a repeat, and that was his prerogative.

Unfortunately, his rejection hurt far more than it should. And that was stupid because he was little more than a stranger.

A stranger she seemed to know all too well.

Five

Come for a family and friends barbecue this Saturday and stay for an outdoor movie. We'll have some time during the socializing to talk business. Bring a date.

Rowan reread the text message that had just landed on his phone from one of Maryland's most successful real estate developers, a man he'd been trying to meet with for months now. They'd shaken hands at social events and exchanged small talk, but every time Rowan had asked for a meeting, he was blown off, with Matt finding one excuse or another.

So a personal invitation to visit Matt's on-the-water property was unexpected and very welcome indeed. Rowan just needed a half hour to pitch his vision of developing the land he owned north of the city into an eco-friendly residential, business and shopping park.

Piquing Matt's interest would lead to a formal meeting and, hopefully, a partnership.

Rowan could do the project on his own, and would if he had to, but having someone like Matt—and his marketing machine—on board would boost interest and lead to quicker up-front sales. He didn't *need* Matt, but his involvement would be helpful.

But to pitch his idea, Rowan had to attend the function at Matt's mansion in Whitehall Beach. And he needed to bring a date. Rowan did a mental run-through of the women he could ask, finding fault with each one as he went along. *Too clingy, too political, her laugh sounded like nails on a chalkboard...*

Shit. He wanted Jamie and no one else. And that was just one of the reasons why he was standing in the reception area of her advertising agency without an appointment. But it was the end of the day and, hopefully, she was done. Hey, it had worked for her when she unexpectedly dropped in on him; he was hoping to have the same luck.

He wasn't a guy who blew hot and cold, who played with women, but from the moment she'd walked out of his apartment weeks ago, he'd deeply regretted saying no to her "let's do this again" offer. He had to be the only guy in history to turn down mind-blowing, uncomplicated sex.

Over the time away from her, he'd convinced himself that he could sleep with her and not allow his emotions to get involved. When a person was aware of the pitfalls, he or she could dodge them. If he kept clear parameters in place—no intense conversations and no sleepovers—he wouldn't make the same mistake he'd made with Marisa, and there would be no chance of him ending up feeling dinged and dented.

As lovely as Jamie was, he wouldn't let himself feel more for her than he should. He refused to watch another person he cared for walk away. Sleeping with her could oh-so-easily lead to authentic dating, and that had to be avoided at all costs.

Unfortunately, he couldn't stop remembering how incredible they were together, and he wanted her back in his bed.

Or in *her* bed, on the floor, up against a wall...

Rowan gave himself a mental slap and told himself *again* that this would only be a fling. He wouldn't cross any lines or allow any lines to be crossed.

All presuming, of course, that she gave him a second chance at saying yes.

He wanted to see her again, wanted her naked under him, but it felt crass to walk into her office and just ask. Luckily, he had an icebreaker—a damn good reason for getting in touch with her once more.

The morning after setting his bed on fire, he'd remembered that Jamie's vintage dress couldn't be repaired, and he felt compelled to spend hours online trying to track down another. But since he knew less than nothing about vintage clothing, he'd gone down various rabbit holes online before admitting defeat. After returning to his senses, he commissioned a vintage-clothing collector to track down a suitable replacement for Jamie's ruined dress.

Thanks to finding a picture online of Jamie wearing the dress at another society event, the collector had a frame of reference. Earlier this week, he heard that she'd tracked down another dress—a little older, a slightly different style, gold instead of silver—and the garment had arrived today. He'd forked out an obscene amount of money for it, and he hoped it fit. And that Jamie liked it.

But, because he didn't want her staff to wonder, and then gossip about why he was giving her a dress, he'd left the garment in his car. He'd hand it over when he could get her alone.

The receptionist cleared her throat to attract his attention. "Ms. Bacall-Metcalfe is currently with someone, Mr. Cowper. And then she needs to leave because she has a dinner engagement across town."

Dinner engagement? The thought of Jamie going out with someone else left a bad taste in his mouth. Jealousy, it turned out, tasted revolting.

The receptionist turned away to answer a call, and he tuned back into her conversation when she mentioned the name Drake. "Despite the many conversations we've had, Mr. Cummings, I really can't call you Drake. And I'm sorry, but Ms. Bacall-Metcalfe is in a meeting. She asked that you direct any queries to our creative director."

So the persistent Drake hadn't given up. Rowan jammed his hands into his pants pockets and, gritting his teeth, stared past the receptionist's head to an oversize black-and-white photograph of downtown Annapolis.

He had to get himself under control! He had a plan, and he needed to stick to it. He'd give Jamie the dress, ask her to accompany him to Matt's barbecue; and if she said yes—which wasn't guaranteed—he'd then see whether there was any chance of revisiting her offer.

One step at a time…

"Rowan Cowper?"

Rowan turned and saw a masculine version of Jamie walking down the hallway toward him, his hand outstretched. "Hey, I'm Greg Bacall."

Rowan shook his hand, pleased. Greg was the architect he wanted to design his green residential park but hadn't approached yet because he'd hoped to get Matt on board first.

"Are you looking for an ad campaign?" Greg asked.

Ad campaign? "No, actually, I was hoping for a word with Jamie."

Greg's eyebrows rose in surprise. "She's in her office, getting ready to leave. We're going to dinner at my parents' house, and she's dawdling."

Greg jerked his head in a "follow me" gesture, and Rowan fell into step beside him. A minute later Greg knocked on the office door at the end of the hallway and opened it. "You have a visitor."

Jamie, who was zipping up her laptop case, looked up in surprise. "Rowan? What are you doing here?"

"Hi there," Rowan said, stepping into her office. He gave her a quick once-over, and his breath caught in his throat. She wore a short, body-skimming white dress that ended midthigh, and his gaze was immediately drawn to the gold zipper running from her throat to her cleavage.

Sexy. And damn tempting.

Their eyes clashed, held. Within hers, he saw bemusement, embarrassment and, thank God, a healthy dose of desire. At least he wasn't alone in this madness.

She dragged her eyes off his to look past him. "I thought you had gone, Greg."

Rowan turned and caught the smirk on Greg's face. "I was on my way. Then I saw Rowan and decided to come back."

Jamie narrowed her eyes. "You need to fetch Chas, and I'll see you at dinner."

"Dinner *with the parents*," Greg said, emphasizing the words.

Jamie spread out her hands, silently asking him for an explanation.

"Where they'll be discussing, ad nauseam, their thirty-fifth wedding-anniversary party next weekend and demanding to know who you're bringing as your date. So here's a suggestion…ask Rowan to be your date," Greg added.

Jamie released a low growl. "Go away, Gregory."

Greg winced. "Going." He held out his hand to Rowan. "Hope to see you again. We must talk buildings some time."

"I'd like that," Rowan replied, nodding.

"Maybe at the party next weekend," Greg said, winking at Jamie.

A pen flew past Rowan's nose toward the door, but Jamie missed Greg's head by a foot or two. She shook her head and sat down on the edge of her desk. "Sorry about that, Greg has all the subtlety of a sledgehammer." She gripped the edge of her desk and tipped her head to the side. "Why are you here, Rowan?"

"I need a date for a barbecue this Saturday. Would you come with me?" he asked, biting the bullet.

"I thought you didn't want to see me again," Jamie stated.

He ignored her flat tone and kept going. "So I was thinking—"

"Did you hurt yourself?" Jamie asked, her voice sweet but her eyes cool. Her words hardly had time to settle before she waved her hands in the air. "That's not fair, sorry." She pulled her bottom lip between her teeth. "You had every right to turn down my clumsy offer. Sorry, it's been a while, and I'm out of practice."

"It wasn't clumsy, Jamie. It was up-front and honest, and I appreciate that. Admittedly, it was unexpected."

She waved the words away and placed her hands on her hips and tipped her head to the side. "So what exactly are you asking, Rowan?"

"Will you be my date on Saturday? I'd like to spend a few hours with you... No pressure and no expectations." That sounded loose and casual, didn't it? Pity he didn't feel that way.

Strangely, whether they slept together again or not, right now a few hours of her company was enough. Right. That was a first. "Come with me, eat some great barbecue and watch an outdoor movie."

"Mmm."

Rowan caught himself rocking on his heels, the action suggesting he was anxious to hear her answer...

Curious? Sure. But anxious? Not a chance.

That was what he was telling himself, at least.

"I'll come to your barbecue thingy on Saturday if you come to my parents' anniversary party."

He felt a flash of pleasure at her response and then jerked when her words sank in. *Parents? Family? Oh, hell no!* Family functions were a nightmare. He felt his throat close. Having never had a family of his own, he didn't *do* families.

He cleared his throat, desperately looking for a decent excuse until he pushed a question past his lips. "Surely you don't want a virtual stranger at your family event?"

She raised her eyebrows. "You're looking a bit flustered, Cowper. Haven't you met a girl's parents before?"

Actually, no. Marisa had been estranged from her parents, and his previous relationships had never gotten to the meeting-the-parents stage. He'd never allowed them to.

"Won't they get the wrong idea?"

Jamie rolled her eyes. "It doesn't matter if they do,

because we both know the truth—neither of us wants a relationship! But, yes, maybe if they see that I'm dating, they might stop with the 'it's time you moved on' speeches!"

Now he was very curious. "Moved on from what?"

"So will you come?" she asked, ignoring his question.

He knew that if he said no, she would tell him she was unavailable on Saturday night. And as much as he wanted to talk to Matt, he didn't want to be the lone male surrounded by happy couples and kids.

She had him between a rock and a hard place and, judging by the amusement in her eyes, she knew it.

"I'm not the meet-the-family type," he warned her.

"Relax," Jamie told him. "You're not facing a shooting squad." She grinned. "An inquisition, maybe, but not a firing squad. Do we have a deal?"

He nodded. "We have a deal."

They were trading one date for another—a simple arrangement. So why did he feel like he was tiptoeing through a minefield?

Jamie gestured to the door. "Great. Not meaning to rush you, but I do have to leave."

If she was in a hurry, then now would be a great time to hand over the dress with minimal explanations. She could examine it later, when he wasn't around. Flora, the woman who found the dress for him, had nearly put him in a coma talking about beads and bodices, skirts and sequins, and he now knew more about vintage dresses than he wanted to.

"Sure. But can you spare five minutes? I have something for you. It's in my car."

Jamie nodded, popped her head into an office and asked someone to lock up before leading Rowan to the front door. They stepped onto the sidewalk, and he placed his hand on her back to guide her a short distance down the road to where he'd parked his new Lexus LX 570.

"Nice car," Jamie commented, not sounding overly impressed.

"I like it."

Rowan opened the back door and picked up the garment bag that lay across the back seat. After slamming the door shut, he handed the bag to Jamie, who took it, a small frown pulling her eyebrows together.

"What's this?" she asked, puzzled.

He had gotten what he wanted, so it was time to go. Besides, he knew nothing about gifts or how to hand them over, and he'd prefer not to make an ass of himself.

"I'll text you the arrangements for Saturday." He bent his head to kiss her cheek. "Bye, James."

He saw the flash of irritation in her eyes at his use of her full name and decided he didn't care. Sometimes *James* suited her better than *Jamie* did.

He turned away to open the driver's door to his car, but a feminine hand gripped the back of his shirt, keeping him in place. "Not so fast, mister."

Rowan was acting like a cat on a hot tin roof, and she wanted to know why.

She'd spent too much time thinking about him lately.

It had taken all her willpower not to rock up to his office in the hopes of repeating the fabulous hours she'd spent in his arms. One night with the blasted man wasn't enough.

Rowan shifted on his feet. He was normally so cool and contained; it was weird to see him acting angsty. "Why are you acting weird, Cowper?"

He immediately stilled, and his expression turned

inscrutable. "I'm fine." He tapped his expensive watch. "You need to get going. You don't want to be late," he told her. "Where is your car parked?"

His eyes kept darting to the garment bag as if it were radioactive. He very obviously didn't want her opening it now, so that was exactly what she intended to do. She handed him her laptop and tote bag to hold and holding the garment bag up with one hand, she slowly drew down the zipper, sending him a teasing glance. "Did you buy me a dress to replace the one we ripped?"

That dress was irreplaceable, but if she had to choose between a ripped dress and being kissed by him in a stuck elevator, she'd choose the kiss every day.

"Yeah," Rowan muttered.

Really? She hadn't expected him to remember her torn dress, never mind going to the effort of replacing it. Rowan was full of surprises. No doubt the dress would be a 1920s rip-off, but it was the thought that counted.

Jamie pulled one edge of the garment bag aside and stared at the rhinestone-covered silk, her breath leaving her body. There was no way... No damn way.

"Oh. My. God."

"I know it's not the same style or color, but the vintage clothing dealer assured me it was an adequate replacement."

Jamie's eyes flew to his face, and through her shock she noticed the flare of disappointment in his eyes, the way his mouth tightened.

"Adequate? Are you kidding me?" Jamie cried as she took the dress out of the garment bag and watched the rhinestones shimmer in the early-evening light. "God, Rowan, my dress was from an unknown designer. This is an Edward Molyneux!"

He shrugged, obviously clueless.

"He's one of the superstar designers of the twenties. He opened his couture house in 1919 in Paris and then opened several other branches in Europe, including London. He was a true artist, and his clients included aristocracy as well as stars of the stage," Jamie explained.

Rowan's eyes lightened as he started to realize he'd done well. Or his collector had. But she still couldn't accept his exceptionally generous gift. "Rowan, Molyneux's dresses can be seen in the Metropolitan Museum. This dress belongs there. I can't accept it."

But, man, she wanted to. Owning an Edward Molyneux had been on her bucket list, though she never thought she would.

She looked at the dress again, sighing at the exquisite beading and handwork. The longer strands of beads, dripping off the bottom of the skirt, gave the dress movement, and she could easily imagine a fashionable flapper doing the Charleston in a jazz club in Manhattan or Mayfair. She was instantly in love with the dress, but she absolutely couldn't keep it; so she, very reluctantly, covered it with the garment bag.

She pulled the zipper up and bit down on her bottom lip. Her rabid inner collector wanted to keep the dress, but she knew how expensive it was. Rowan's bank balance would've taken a hell of a hit. And it was at least twenty times more expensive than the dress that had ripped.

"It's a really sweet gesture, Rowan, but I can't keep it."

He stared at her, still holding the bags she'd given him when she took the dress. "Yeah, you can. Because I sure as hell do not need it."

"It's too expen—"

"Do you like it?" Rowan interrupted her.

How could he even ask her that? Hadn't she been drooling over the dress a minute before? "Of course I do. I love it!"

He shrugged. "That's settled, then." He draped her purse over her shoulder and put her laptop bag in her free hand. "You're going to be late."

"Nothing is settled!" Jamie retorted. "You need to send the dress back and get a refund."

"No can do," Rowan told her, dropping a brief kiss on her cheek. "The seller told me it's nonrefundable. Unless it doesn't fit you…"

Jamie's mouth dropped open in horror. "It's way too precious to wear!"

Rowan flashed her a small smile as he pulled open the door to his vehicle. "I'd still like to see you in it. See you on Saturday, James."

He climbed into his car and slammed the door shut. Frustrated, Jamie knocked on his window, and when it slid down, she glared at him. "Rowan, I'm not done discussing this! I don't think you understand the importance of—"

As he grinned at her, the window slid up and he started the car. He smoothly pulled onto the road and left her standing on the sidewalk, holding her bags and an exceedingly expensive and rare vintage dress.

Which she now owned.

And when Rowan's car disappeared, she did a quick but furious happy dance on the sidewalk.

Six

After parking his car, Rowan walked around the hood to open her door and held out his hand. Jamie saw the spark of appreciation in his eyes, and she, foolishly, preened a little as his gaze skimmed over her sexy, blindingly white summer dress. The bodice was lace. Spaghetti straps flowed over her shoulders and crisscrossed down her back, and when she walked, the soft cotton skirt parted to show off her legs. It was perfect for a beach barbecue, and she felt feminine and sexy.

"You look lovely," Rowan told her.

"You look pretty good yourself, Cowper." And he did. He wore a lightweight steel blue button-down shirt over tailored white shorts and expensive sneakers. A designer pair of sunglasses covered his eyes, and his hair looked more tousled than usual. Casual was a good look on him.

Everything was.

She sighed as she put her hand in his. She wanted

his approval, loved seeing the flare of attraction in his eyes, waited for that soft, quick smile. With him, she felt lovely, warm from the inside out, like a desirable woman who could take on the world.

Rowan excited her, made her think—and smile. God, he made her feel. He was smart and hot and successful, but more than that, he was a good man. Someone she could fall for, if she wasn't careful. She refused to do that. She would not risk loving and losing someone again. For a year after Kaden's death, she'd barely functioned. The next year had been a little better; she'd started taking an interest in her business again, and being at work helped keep her mind off her devastating loss. Year three had still been brutally lonely, but then guilt—kept at bay by the strength of her grief—strolled in to keep her company.

The same questions plagued her day in and day out. What if she hadn't started that argument? What if she'd agreed to try again, not given up? She'd failed him, failed *them*, and her punishment had been watching him—and the life they'd planned together—die on that lonely asphalt road.

Years four and five were much the same: she worked, she attended some social functions—normally at her mom's and gran's urging—and tried to win at life as best she could. She dated…if you could call dinner and a kiss on the cheek at her door *dating*.

Then Rowan strode into her life. A couple of hours in an elevator resulted in a comet-hot kiss. Returning his jacket had led to the raunchiest, most addictive sex of her life.

Sorry, Kaden, but… Yeah. That.

And then Rowan had bought her a Molyneux dress. Yes, it was expensive, but the dress could've been a knockoff and she still would've been impressed. He'd remembered her ripped dress, and while the rip hadn't been entirely his fault, he'd made an effort to rectify the situation. He'd gone to a lot of trouble, and she appreciated and respected that.

Underneath that gorgeous packaging was a nice guy...

Great sex or not, nice guy or not, she and Rowan weren't going anywhere. They *couldn't*. He was openly uninterested in a commitment and so was she. But because he was a good guy underneath that gruff exterior, she had to protect herself against liking him more than she should. She couldn't let that happen. *Like* could lead to *love*, and when *great sex* was part of the equation, it sped up the process.

Although she loved being with him, and she'd been the one to originally suggest they continue, she didn't think she was blasé enough for a no-strings affair. When he took her home tonight, she would be strong and tell him she couldn't see him again, that she wasn't ready to dive into an affair.

He'd understand, and if he didn't, well, he'd just have to live with it. She wasn't brave enough to love and lose someone again.

"Are you okay?" Rowan asked, his fingers lightly resting on her bare lower back as he led her up the path to the enormous lakeside mansion.

She stopped, looked up at him and shook her head. If they had this conversation now, they'd be at odds for the rest of the evening, and it would be awkward and uncomfortable. She took a breath and pulled up a smile.

"I'm fine. Let's go in and have a good time, okay?"

His eyes lightened, and his mouth lifted into that half smile, half smirk that made her tummy flutter. "Thanks for coming with me."

Jamie slid her hand into the crook of his arm and held up her floor-skimming dress as they walked up the wide steps leading to the open front door. As they stepped into the hall, a waiter holding a silver tray offered them a cocktail—a classic piña colada, judging by the color, decorated with two colorful paper umbrellas.

She took one; Rowan didn't. She raised her eyebrows at him in a silent question.

"I make it a point to stay away from fruity paint-strippers," he told her as they glanced around the overdecorated double-volume hall. Looking beyond the floating marble staircase, Jamie saw a set of wide open doors leading to an entertainment area filled with people. Her eyebrows raised again when a tanned blonde dressed in a tiny bold-pink thong bikini walked through the doors.

Right. Maybe Jamie was a little overdressed.

"So what's the plan?" she asked Rowan, who, to his credit, barely gave the busty blonde any attention.

"I've been trying to get an appointment with Matt Blunt, and he keeps blowing me off. But he told me he'd spare some time for me tonight."

She rolled through her mental database, then pulled up Matt's face and the few details she knew about him. He was a good guy but rarely did business with anyone outside of a handful of trusted associates. Rowan would need to work hard to break into Matt's inner circle.

Matt was on wife number three, a woman who was quite a lot older than him, French and shy. Matt was protective of her, a collector of vintage watches and a coach for his grandson's Little League team.

"After we circulate a little, we'll find his wife, Odile, and make nice. Trust me, he'll soon come to you."

He sent her an appraising look and nodded. "You do know your way around Annapolis's social scene."

She did. Not as well as her parents did, obviously, but well enough. And she'd learned so much from Kaden. He'd been the life and soul of every party, the guest everyone wanted to talk to, wanted to know. He'd loved this world—the buzz of socializing, the high that came from being in the know.

Frankly, she'd far prefer to be at home, drinking a glass of wine and polishing off a pizza.

She blamed her family for bullying her into going to events, but she knew that wasn't completely fair; they never hassled her when she gave them an unequivocal no. The question remained: Why did she still accept invitations to functions with people she barely knew and sometimes didn't like? Because it was something Kaden loved? Because these people were a link to the life she'd had with him? Because socializing with the A-list was what her family did?

Or maybe it was because if she attended the occasional function, she could convince herself she wasn't lonely, that she *did* have a social life. That she wasn't still grieving her husband, their marriage and the life they'd planned on having.

Was she simply conning herself?

The thing was, after having slept with Rowan, being around Rowan, she felt more alive than she had even before Kaden's death. Since meeting Rowan, she was more in tune with her surroundings; the sky was bluer; the air, softer; the fruit tasted sweeter.

And because there was always a yin to the yang, her attraction to him made her feel scared. And when she wasn't with him, her solitude—normally a protective friend—felt oppressive. Him dropping into her life made her realize how much she'd isolated herself, how lonely she was.

But he didn't want a relationship, and she was too scared to have one. So where did that leave them?

Precisely nowhere.

She'd acted impulsively when she suggested to him, weeks ago, that they have an affair. She wouldn't hold him to their agreement that he attend her parents' party with him, so this would be their first and only date.

But maybe it was time to live again, just a little. Maybe she could open herself up a bit more, and she could reach out to her old girlfriends, wonderful women she'd pushed away when Kaden died. Maybe she could join a book club, accept some of those "women in business" lunch invitations she always declined.

She'd never fall in love again, but maybe she could have friends.

Jamie sipped her drink and wrinkled her nose at the odd taste on her tongue.

"Everything okay?" Rowan asked her.

She lifted the glass to smell her drink. "It tastes and smells funny."

Rowan took the glass from her, smelled it and sipped. "Pineapple, coconut, rum." He shrugged. "It tastes as it should."

He tried to hand it back, but she shook her head. "I can't. I'm sorry. I smell it and I want to gag."

He looked around for a waiter and caught the eye of one, and within seconds, he was by their side. Rowan handed him the glass and asked Jamie what she preferred to drink. She winced. "Some cold water?"

The waiter nodded and looked at Rowan. "A light beer, thanks," Rowan said as they stepped onto the enormous entertainment deck that was heaving with people.

Jamie looked around, taking in the lavish surroundings. Three pools dotted the lush yard, one holding a ten-foot waterfall and a massive slide. Rowan gestured to the waterfall. "The pools are connected by underwater tunnels."

"Nice," Jamie replied as two young kids disappeared behind the falling water. "Especially for the kids."

Rowan looked down at her. "Fun for all ages. Did you bring your bathing suit?"

"I did not," Jamie replied as they walked down the steps to the fake beach that led into the pool. Matt stood in the center of a group of gorgeous people, all of them dressed in board shorts or bikinis. His wife, wearing a conservative cover-up, stood a little apart from them, looking uncomfortable.

Jamie's heart went out to her. She was on intimate terms with feeling alone. Ignoring the boisterous group, she went straight up to Odile and put out her hand. "We've never met, but I believe you know my mom, Haley Bacall? I'm Jamie and this is Rowan Cowper."

Rowan greeted her in what sounded like fluent French. Odile's face immediately brightened, and she machine-gunned her reply. Rowan listened intently, nodded and spoke again. As they conversed, Jamie wondered where he'd learned to speak the language.

There was so much she didn't know about him. And, she reminded herself, she never would. She pushed her surge of disappointment away, reluctantly accepting that was the way it had to be. She couldn't take another chance on another man. Her heart couldn't stand it.

A blast of cold water on her back yanked Jamie out of her reverie. She spun around to see a little boy holding a water gun. A red-haired girl raced past her and nailed the boy with a stream of water in his face.

Good job, honey. But Jamie still had a wet back, and a stream of water was heading south…

Rowan immediately whipped a towel off a nearby chair and turned her around, rubbing the water off her skin. "Are you okay?"

She smiled at his concern. "Fine. It's only water."

"I'm so sorry, Jamie. You got caught between a battle that has been raging all day," Odile told her in accented English. "Those two are my oldest grandchildren—the son of my daughter and daughter of my stepson. Mortal enemies."

"No harm done," Jamie assured her.

Odile smiled at her. "Thank you for being so understanding. If you'll excuse me?"

They nodded, greeted Matt, were introduced to his group of friends and received their drink order from the waiter they'd spoken to earlier. The conversation resumed but was frequently interrupted by the shrieks and yells of the kids in the pool and a boom box the teenagers had set up by another pool.

Within minutes, Matt suggested they move back up onto the entertainment deck so they could hear themselves think.

"That's better," Rowan said after tipping his beer bottle to his mouth. "God, kids are noisy."

"That they are," Jamie replied, raising her eyebrows when a group of preteen boys pushed three posing girls off their pool chairs. They came out of the water cursing and spluttering.

"War has been declared," Rowan said with a grin. He gestured to a pair of toddlers—both wearing inflatable armbands, their mothers close by—who were splashing around at the water's edge.

"Do you like kids? Do you want them?"

It was a question she hated. One she routinely lied about. Most of her and Kaden's friends, all of whom had babies and toddlers, had thought she and Kaden struggled with infertility, and Jamie had found their pity, and condescension, hard to swallow.

They'd never had difficulty getting pregnant. Every time they tried, she conceived right away. No, conception was easy—but *keeping* the baby was something she'd never managed to do.

For her, pregnancy was a roller coaster of hope and expectation, then grief and despair when she inevitably miscarried. After she lost baby number four, she was done. She told Kaden she couldn't put herself through that again. She'd started to tell people, in the months leading up to Kaden's death, that they'd changed their minds about having children, that they were happy to be childless.

Lying served her well back then, so she shrugged. "You asked me that before," she reminded him. "No, I'm not interested. They are not on my agenda."

She didn't ask his opinion on having children, as it wasn't a subject that would ever affect her. Needing a distraction, she saw Odile slipping into the house and remembered Rowan's excellent French.

"Where did you learn French?" she asked, changing the subject.

"Movies."

"Movies?"

"Yeah."

"I'm going to need a bit more of an explanation than that, Rowan."

He jammed his hands into the back pockets of his tailored shorts. He looked around as if checking whether or not anyone could hear their conversation. "One of my foster mothers was French Canadian and had a bunch of French movies on DVD. I watched a few and got hooked on them. From there, I rented more movies and started reading French books, and I got better. A few years ago, I went to France and realized that I picked up more than I thought. I'm not fluent but I can converse."

He certainly could. As interested as she was in his ability to speak the sexy language, she was more curious about the nugget of information he'd dropped about being a foster kid. "How long were you in the system?"

His eyes cooled and his expression tightened. "Between the ages of four and eleven, I was in and out. I became a permanent resident about six weeks after my twelfth birthday and left, as we all do, when I was eighteen."

There were a million questions she wanted answered, but his flat eyes and rigid mouth suggested she not pry further. Still, she was never any good at following suggestions. Or orders. "Why did you go into foster care? What happened?"

"That's something I don't discuss, James."

Ouch. Jamie winced. Right. His past was a subject he didn't want to discuss. Neither was hers, so fair enough.

Jamie heard Matt calling Rowan's name from the door leading into his house. Rowan lifted his hand in acknowledgment and turned back to Jamie. "Looks like I'm getting my meeting sooner than I expected. Will you excuse me for a half hour or so?"

Jamie nodded. "Sure."

Rowan looked around. "Will you be okay? I don't like leaving you on your own."

That was sweet. "Rowan, there are at least a dozen people I know. I grew up in this world, remember?"

He pushed his hand through his hair and nodded. "Okay. I'll come find you when I'm done."

She nodded and watched him walk away—so con-

fident, so masculine, so at ease in his big, surprisingly
graceful body. Jamie glanced at her bracelet watch and
grimaced. She rather resented Matt taking Rowan away,
because if she was going to end their association later
tonight, then she only had a few hours left with him.
After he dropped her off at her place, she would rel-
egate him to being a nice guy she'd once slept with,
someone who cracked open the seams of her heart and
let in a little light.

Just a little.

And that was more than she could cope with.

After he met with Matt, Rowan felt like he was dancing on air. In his direct, no-nonsense way, Matt all but
promised—subject to the numbers checking out—that
he'd invest in Rowan's project. Matt was impressed by
how far Rowan had come in such a short time. Matt said
he'd had his eye on him for ages, that it was past time he
was involved in an eco-friendly project.

They'd shaken hands and Rowan instinctively knew
an agreement had been reached as soon as their hands
connected. Oh, contracts would be drawn up and haggled
over, but the deal, sealed by that handshake, was in place.

He needed a drink, to celebrate. More than that, he
needed to share his good news with Jamie.

About to walk down the shallow steps to the grassy
area where Jamie stood with a group of young mothers,
he stopped abruptly. Did he need to tell Jamie? Why?

For the past fifteen years, he'd been celebrating his
successes solo, and he was very used to enjoying the
quick high, then tucking his pride away and getting on
with the job. Because he'd never had anyone to celebrate his successes with or to commiserate with when

he failed, he simply put his feet back on the ground or picked himself up and carried on.

Yeah, sure, it was lonely, but he was used to it.

Yet seeing her standing there, her expression full of wonder as she gently stroked the cheek of the sleeping baby she held in her arms—bullshit, she didn't want kids!—he wanted to grab a bottle of champagne, swing her up in his arms and fall into her eyes. Eyes that would be misty with excitement for him.

She was the type who would celebrate her partner's successes or support a man when things weren't going as planned. She was a woman who'd pull her weight.

God, he liked her. More than he'd liked any woman, ever. Yeah, yeah, lust was there—she was gorgeous; how could he not want her?—but *like* was so much more dangerous.

He hadn't liked many people in his life. And because he liked her too much, he should let her go.

But he wasn't going to. Not yet.

Jamie handed the baby back, said something to the moms that made them laugh and stepped away. She caught his eye and nodded to the path leading down to the beach. Rowan grabbed a bottle of champagne from an ice bucket and two flutes off the table. He exchanged pleasantries with the other guests as he walked past groups huddled around the pool. Stepping onto the beach, he admired the two long piers and the sleek boat preparing to take guests—mostly teenagers—for a ride. A teenage boy put his cap on back to front, zipped up a life jacket and jumped off the boat into the water. A wakeboard followed him, and the kid slid his feet into the footholds, expertly attaching himself to the board.

Rowan watched as the boat slowly backed away and chugged into deeper water. Another boy tossed the kid a rope; thumbs-up signs were exchanged between the two. Ten seconds later, the kid was skimming across the lake on the board, flying from one side of the boat to the other, doing trick turns and showing off.

At eighteen, Rowan had been too busy trying to survive, finish high school, feed himself, pay the rent. Did the kid have any idea how lucky he was?

"Are you going to drink that or just hold it?"

Rowan poured the champagne into the flutes, handed Jamie one and gestured to the wooden bench on a small knoll. They sat down, and Rowan placed the champagne bottle between them. "You persuaded Matt to invest," she stated, sounding completely confident.

He grinned and tapped his glass against hers. "I did."

Jamie congratulated him before tipping her head to look at him, her eyes cutting through to his soul. "You should smile like that more often. You have a hell of a smile, Cowper."

He blinked, caught off guard. He did? Well, then. "Thank you."

"I'm happy for you, Row."

Row? He'd never liked to hear his name shortened, but he didn't mind it on her lips. He was making all sorts of excuses for her, though that could be because he was happy, excited, he'd had good news. Later, he'd go back to being his cynical self.

"Now that I have Matt's buy-in, I can approach Greg and see if he wants to take my rough drawings and turn them into something workable."

Her eyebrows lifted, and pleasure curved her lips. "You want to work with Greg?"

"I'm *going* to work with Greg," Rowan corrected her. "I called him the day before yesterday and mentioned the project to him. He told me he'd come on board when

I have my investor in place. Investor in place. So, yeah, Greg will be my architect."

"Nice," Jamie said before lifting her glass to her lips and sipping. He watched her frown, lower her glass and squint at the bubbly liquid. "This doesn't taste good."

It was the second time he'd given her a drink she hated. Needing to check, Rowan took another sip and shook his head. "It's great champagne, Jamie."

She frowned and looked at her glass again. Her face turned white, and her stunning eyes looked huge in her shocked face.

"What? What is it?"

"Hand me your phone…" she demanded, her voice shaky. "Mine is in my bag on the entertainment deck."

Rowan pulled his phone from his back pocket and handed it over. Why did she need his phone? Who was she going to call?

She punched in some numbers, listened to the phone ring, and when it was answered, Jamie didn't bother with a greeting. "When was your anniversary dinner? At the end of May, right?"

Rowan heard Greg's clear yes, followed by a "Why?" before Jamie abruptly disconnected the call without further explanation. She then thrust his phone at him and told him to open up his calendar. Seeing the wild look in her eyes, he did as she asked, hoping he'd get an explanation.

Jamie poked her finger at the screen, cursing as she did so. Then she repeated the process, her curse words becoming louder.

He placed his glass next to the bottle and folded his arms. "Want to tell me what has you in such a dither?"

Jamie placed her hand on her stomach and shook her head. "Dear God, how?"

How what? What was going on?

Jamie rubbed her hands up and down her face. "I just did a couple of mental calculations, and I don't know how to tell you this but—"

He hated it when people prefaced an announcement with those words. "Just tell me, James!" he snapped, frustrated.

Jamie bent over and rested her face between her knees. She mumbled something, and Rowan demanded that she repeat herself.

Jamie turned her head to the side, her eyes wide. "I think I'm pregnant. And since you're the only person I've had sex with in a long, long time, you're the father."

Seven

Jamie kept her face buried in her knees, needing a few more minutes to stabilize her thoughts and emotions. She fought the urge to look at Rowan's screen again, to count the weeks, hoping and praying she'd made a mistake.

She hadn't. She was three weeks late, and she was never late.

Jamie did a body check, thinking back on the past couple of weeks. She'd been a little tired, but nothing serious. She'd had no morning sickness, and her breasts felt perfectly fine. But, like before, her taste and smell were affected. During her other pregnancies, she'd never been able to tolerate the taste of alcohol.

And, big clue—she was three weeks late. Three freaking weeks!

Jamie sat up slowly, her elbows on her knees and her head in her hands. Gathering all her courage, she looked at Rowan, who was staring at her like she was one of the walking dead.

"Would you like to run that by me again, please? I thought I heard you say that you are pregnant."

Jamie sat up and nodded. "Yeah, I think I am."

"'Think'?" Rowan demanded.

"Well, I can't be sure without a test but, yeah, there's a damn good chance."

Rowan released a harsh curse. "You are shitting me, right?"

She wished she was. She didn't want to have a child with a man she'd planned to never see again. A man who made her feel jittery, like she wasn't sure which way was up. "I wouldn't joke about something like that."

"But… But…we used condoms."

They had.

"Except for that one time, that first time. You slid inside me without a condom."

"I didn't come!" Rowan protested.

"You didn't need to," Jamie told him before waving his words away. In between losing babies two and three, she'd done a lot of research trying to find out why she couldn't stay pregnant. Along the way, she'd discovered other bits of baby-making knowledge, including the fact that ejaculation wasn't the only vehicle for sperm. But she didn't think Rowan would appreciate a lecture on super-super-safe sex. The deed was done…

"The *how* isn't important—"

"It's pretty important to me," Rowan replied, looking stubborn. "How do I know that you didn't sleep with someone else and now are trying to pin this pregnancy on me?"

Jesus, really? Jamie started to blast him, tasted the hot words on her tongue, but then she caught the fear in his eyes, his absolute bewilderment. She swallowed, and clenched and unclenched her hands.

"You are the only guy I've slept with since my husband died, Cowper—"

"You were married? How did I not know this?" he demanded.

"We haven't spent that much time together, Rowan. And the time that we did spend together, we didn't talk much."

"Fair point," he conceded, rubbing his jaw.

"Anyway, the last time I had sex was with my husband, and he died about five years ago. So, yes, if I am pregnant, the baby is yours."

Rowan rested his forearms on his knees and dangled his hands between his legs. He now looked as pale as she imagined she did. "I didn't even know that you were married, that you are a widow. And now you're telling me you're pregnant. I'm trying to process everything at once."

Jamie resisted the urge to put her hand on his back, to tell him that they'd get through this together, that he didn't need to overreact. Now that the shock was starting to recede, she could think. She had a little human growing inside her, the baby she'd always wanted—*craved*. Excitement bubbled and then spread its warmth through her veins as sparks danced on her skin...

She was going to be a mother...

Then reality rushed back in—cold, dark and relentless.

Jamie slumped and fell in on herself, her excitement evaporating. There was no need to get excited, no cause to overreact. She knew how this went. She'd lived it before. She'd have a couple of weeks of exhaustion, some morning sickness and then, between weeks ten and twelve, she'd start to bleed.

By week thirteen, all traces of the baby would be gone.

She'd been through this four times before—they called her condition recurrent pregnancy loss—and she had no reason to believe she'd carry this baby full-term. Nobody knew why, but it wasn't something she could do.

She started to tell Rowan, but stopped at the last minute. Maybe she should confirm she was pregnant before confessing that she was bound to lose the baby, that he shouldn't get excited.

If that was what he was…

Scared or weirded out might be more accurate.

Do the pregnancy test, see what it says and then take it from there. Horse before the cart, Jamie. Horse before the cart…

Back at her house, Rowan followed Jamie into her living room—cream walls, bold colors, interesting art—and shoved the brown paper sack into her hands. They'd stopped by the first pharmacy they'd come across, and he'd bought every type of pregnancy test they sold, much to the pharmacy assistant's bemusement. She'd tried to tell him all the tests were pretty accurate these days and that he only needed one, but he'd insisted on buying every brand they stocked. He had ten, twelve different tests in the bag, including a more expensive digital test. Apparently, that one could tell how far along Jamie was.

Jamie looked into the brown bag and raised her eyebrows. "How many did you buy?"

"Do them all," Rowan told her, feeling a little light-headed. He knew he wasn't handling this well, but how was one supposed to handle a pregnancy scare?

"I am not peeing on all these sticks," Jamie stated.

"Can you just go and do it already?" he growled, shifting from foot to foot on her carpet.

Jamie rolled her eyes. "Can I put my bag down, have a cup of tea first?"

He pulled the bag off her shoulder, tossed it onto the nearest chair and jerked his chin toward the hallway.

Jamie threw up her hands, silently admitting defeat. "Okay, I'm going."

She tipped the packet of pregnancy tests onto the coffee table, pushed them around before picking up two boxes. "I'll do two—a standard test and the more expensive one."

He wanted to argue, but saw that she held the digital test in her hand and nodded. Heart in his throat, he watched Jamie walk away, taking in her slim back and rounded hips.

One time? One time and she was pregnant? How the hell did that happen?

And how was he going to handle a child?

Rowan paced the area of her living room agitated. He was a child of the system. He'd never known his real dad, and his mother hadn't had a maternal bone in her body. She'd been constantly looking for the next party, the next man, the next high. Rowan had been, at best, an inconvenience; at worst, a pain in her ass.

When she took off shortly after his twelfth birthday, he hadn't been surprised. When they told him, he was shocked she hadn't done it sooner. But her running away was a pattern that plagued him for the rest of his life. He'd had a teacher he liked but who soon moved on. He'd had a couple who were prepared to adopt him, but they left the state. One of his oldest friends, another kid who grew up in the system with him, was killed in a gang-related shooting.

By the time Rowan had hit his teens, he was cynical. In his twenties that cynicism had hardened to flat-out mistrust. He'd had girlfriends, but no one he allowed into his inner world. Marisa had gotten closer than most, but even she didn't stick around for the long haul.

Now he made damn sure he walked away first. Because he never wanted to watch someone walk away from him again, to be hurt again.

Just like he'd planned to walk away from Jamie at some point in the future.

But now she might be pregnant.

She couldn't be. Surely it took more than a one-night stand to fall pregnant? It had to!

But if she was, how would he handle the situation? He wouldn't repeat his mother's mistake and walk away from his child. Neither could he allow Jamie to raise the baby alone. Dammit! He'd never planned on having kids and had constructed his life so that he'd never be emotionally entangled. If Jamie *was* pregnant, he'd be in a position he'd never wanted, or even imagined, he would be in!

He looked down at his shaking hands and reluctantly admitted that the only silver lining of this situation was that he was in this with Jamie, that his kid would have her as a mom. She was smart, lovely, successful, and she had her life together. If he'd had the option of choosing the mom for his child, she would have been his first and only choice.

Rowan glanced at his watch, impatience building. Wanting to know what the delay was, he walked down the hallway, opening doors. Study, guest bedroom, family bathroom.

At the end of the hallway, he nudged a half-open door with his foot and stepped into a feminine bedroom, white with touches of lavender. The bed was made, but a pile of unfolded laundry sat in the middle of it, along with an open book, facedown.

Her room smelled like she did: lovely and light, sexy and subtle, with a hint of wildness.

"Rowan? Are you in my bedroom?" she asked from her en suite bathroom.

"What's the holdup?" he demanded.

"It hasn't even been three minutes!" Jamie shouted back. "Keep your pants on, Cowper."

"Can I come in?" Rowan asked.

"No, you absolutely cannot!" Jamie yelled. Wincing, he sat on the edge of her bed. Needing to do something with his hands, he picked up a T-shirt from her pile of laundry. He efficiently folded it and made a new pile.

The toilet flushed, and he heard the water running, the splash of it against her hands. His heart rate increased, and his hands moved faster, folding a pair of jeans and matching socks. He glanced at his watch and saw that five minutes had passed... *Any minute now.*

If he didn't get an answer soon, he might just lose it. *Might?* He *would* lose it.

Jamie walked back into her bedroom, carrying the two small tests. Surely something that could change one's life should be bigger than that? Then again, little explosives could make big bombs.

He looked up at Jamie and jumped to his feet. "Well? Are you?"

She looked from him to the pile of folded laundry on her bed. "You folded most of my laundry? In two minutes?"

He shrugged, not bothering to explain that he'd been folding laundry since he was four or five. That in the system, he'd learned how to work fast and accurately so he didn't give people a reason to punish him. "I needed to do something. Are you pregnant?"

She handed him one stick. "I told you I was."

He looked down, saw the two blue lines and frowned. "Two lines means you are pregnant? Are you sure?"

Jamie sat down on her armchair in the corner of the room. "Very sure, Rowan. I've done more than a few pregnancy tests in my life."

He looked down at the test and shook his head. "I'm not sure how to react."

Jamie placed one leg over the other and tapped her elegant fingers against her thigh. "I can help you with that, Cowper, if you'd just let me explain."

An explanation would be good—excellent, in fact. He'd listen to anyone about anything in an effort for the world to right itself again. He hadn't felt this rattled since he'd first landed in the system.

He took a couple of deep breaths and finally nodded. "I'm listening."

Jamie played with her dress, folding the fabric as she gathered her thoughts. "We haven't talked much, and I seem to blurt out random facts in the heat of the moment. Like earlier, when I told you I was married."

He nodded. "And your husband died? How?"

"We were in a car wreck. But that's not what we're going to talk about, okay? I don't talk about the accident. Ever."

Rowan jerked at the fierce note in her voice. Right.

She sighed and when she spoke again, her tone softened. "I seldom talk about Kaden and our marriage, but because of *that*—" she pointed at the pregnancy test he still held in his hand "—I suppose I should. But I'd appreciate it if you keep this information between us."

Whom was he going to tell? He had acquaintances,

not friends. Besides, he knew the value of keeping his
mouth shut. Another skill he'd learned in the system.

"I'm listening. Go on."

She looked at him as if trying to decide whether to
trust him or not. He knew that nothing he could say
would sway her, so he opted to remain silent and prayed
she wouldn't clam up.

"Kaden and I were married for five years, and we
never used contraceptives. We wanted children, and I
got pregnant quite easily—that was never the problem.

"I was pregnant four times in five years, and not one
of those pregnancies managed to stick. I don't believe
this one will be any different," she stated. She came
across as calm and effortlessly realistic. But he saw the
flash of pain in her eyes before she buried it deep.

He placed his hands on the bed next to him, trying
to make sense of her statement. "You miscarried every
time?"

"Yeah. I've had what feels like a million tests, but they
still aren't sure why I can't carry a baby to term. They
call it recurrent miscarriage, or recurrent pregnancy loss,
and they don't always find a reason why it happens. It's
an uncommon condition."

He rubbed the back of his neck. "Shit."

Jamie laid a hand on his knee, her elegant fingers
warm on his bare skin. "The thing is, whether you are
mad, excited or scared, there's no point. The digital test
measures hormone levels, and that three-plus sign in-
dicates that I am more than three weeks pregnant. I got
pregnant on the night we spent together."

In Jamie's eyes, he saw the truth: she *had* conceived
on the night they'd spent together. Okay, then.

"Accepted?"

He nodded. Sighed. "Yeah."

"Let me explain how this works… Sometime in the next six to eight weeks, I'm going to miscarry. It's what I *do*. So there's no point in having any discussions about the baby, about the future, your role in it—anything. It's not going to happen."

He felt a hint of relief, but also, surprisingly, a hefty dose of sadness. "Are you sure about that?"

"Four times is a good clue, Cowper," Jamie told him, her tone even.

Fair point.

Jamie was handling this so much better than he was, and with a lot more class. He knew if he said that to her, she'd tell him she'd had a lot of practice, that she'd come to terms with the situation.

Anyone looking at her would think she was discussing the weather, but he'd caught a hint of devastation in her eyes, the flattening of her lips, the hunch of her shoulders. She wanted him to think she was resigned to the situation, but she wasn't.

She wanted kids; any fool could see that.

Four miscarriages and a dead husband. And an accident she wouldn't discuss. His heart ached for her.

"Did you love him? Were you happy together?"

Why was he asking, and why did he care? He was supposed to be putting distance between them, not asking about her history.

Jamie touched the bare skin on her ring finger. "We were—in the early days, at least." She touched her top lip with the tip of her tongue before continuing. "Later on, the miscarriages and our fertility issues made things harder."

As they would. "I'm so sorry."

She managed a tight smile. "Thanks." She bent over to remove her sandals, her hair falling so that her face was completely covered. "So, as I said, you don't need to worry about me and the pregnancy. It's not going anywhere."

"Does your family know about the miscarriages?" he asked.

Jamie pulled a face. "They know about the first one. We never told anyone about the others. I didn't want them to worry."

And she wanted to protect them. Just like he wanted to protect her. And there was no way he could walk out of this house, and out of her life, knowing she would miscarry his child sometime in the future. It didn't matter that there wasn't a thing he could do to change it—she was not going to do this alone. She wanted to, that much was obvious, but he was damned if he'd let her. He stood up and paced the area at the end of her bed, trying to think of an excuse to temporarily stay in her life.

But the truth was more powerful than any excuse he could concoct. "We're going to carry on seeing each other."

Jamie shot up, and the hand holding her sandal shook. "What? *Why?*"

He sent a pointed look at her stomach before his eyes reconnected with hers. "You're pregnant with my kid. You didn't get that way by yourself, so you're not doing this by yourself. For as long as that baby is around, I'm going to be around."

"There's nothing for you to do!" Jamie protested. "It's not like I can hand it over to you."

He shrugged and felt his stubborn rise. "I'm sticking and I'm staying. I am certainly not walking away and washing my hands of you and the baby."

"There will be no baby, I keep telling you that!" Jamie growled, irritation in her eyes.

"But there is *you*. And for the next few weeks, I'm going to stand at your side. I helped create this situation, and I'm sure as hell not leaving you to deal with it on your own!"

She placed a hand on her heart, her eyes glistening with emotion. "That's sweet, Rowan—"

Sweet? Ugh, what a word!

"—but silly. I'm going to go about my business as per usual and try to forget about it."

Try being the operative word. No doubt she'd be on tenterhooks for weeks. And, while he didn't consider himself particularly sensitive, he knew she was wishing this pregnancy would turn out differently—he'd seen that glimpse of hope in her eyes. When the miscarriage came, she'd be disappointed all over again.

"Despite your pragmatic approach to the situation, I suspect that waiting will be hell, and the days and weeks after your miscarriage won't be fun either. I don't bail when things get tough, so I'll be around to help distract you, and then I will be around after as well."

"It's not necess—"

"It is," he interrupted her. "It's *very* necessary. You didn't get pregnant on your own, James. And I do intend to distract you, as much as I can." He leaned back on his elbows and deliberately looked at her pillows before handing her a sexy smile. "I can think of one way…"

He'd meant it as a joke, but knew that if she so much as gave him a hint that she was up for sex, he'd have her clothes off in a flash.

Genuine humor lightened her eyes. "Funny, Cowper."

He shrugged. "It was worth a try." He stood up and held out his hand to pull her up. "Let's be friends, Jamie."

His hand swallowed hers, and he effortlessly pulled

her up and into his arms. Resting his chin on her hair, he held her easily, gently.

She pulled back to look at him, her nose wrinkling. "And afterward? What then? What if we draw some lines that can't be erased? What if we cross them?"

He found it interesting, and a little scary, that her thoughts echoed his. He gathered her close again. "Let's take it day by day, sweetheart." He stroked a hand down her back before patting her butt and stepping away, which was hard to do when she was soft and fragrant and made his blood boil. "We missed out on burgers and an outdoor movie."

"Do you want to go back to Matt's place?" she asked.

It was obvious that she didn't. He took her hand and led her out of the bedroom before he gave in and pulled that lovely dress off her and laid her down on the bed. "Let's make our own movie night—right here."

In her bare feet, Jamie followed him down the hall and back into her living room. She headed into the kitchen, and the sunlight streaming in from the window turned the fabric of her dress almost transparent. He could see the outline of her legs, the gap between her thighs.

Knowing she was having his baby hadn't lessened his desire for her—not in the slightest. He still wanted her with a ferocity that astounded him. Fate kept throwing them together, tossing them into its sticky web, but he wasn't trying to break those connections, fighting to get loose.

He rather liked where he was.

And that scared him shitless.

Eight

Jamie awoke on her couch, her dress twisted around her hips, her face smothered by a particularly plump cushion. She blinked a few times, yawned and looked around her dark living room.

The detritus of their pizza-and-popcorn evening had been cleared away. Jamie cocked her head, listening for sounds coming from her kitchen. Nothing. Her house was empty. She pressed a button on her smartwatch, saw that it was close to three in the morning and wondered what time Rowan had left and why she hadn't heard him go.

Neither did she remember falling asleep…

Jamie stood up and walked over to her front door to check if it was locked—it was—and looked out the narrow pane of glass to the side, frowning when she saw Rowan's fancy car still in her drive. She saw movement in the driver's seat, and then his lights came on as the sound of the car's engine broke the silence of the muggy night.

Jamie placed her hand on the door, about to open it and wave him back inside. Why? What did she want from him?

His car backed down her driveway, and she dropped her hand from the doorknob and rested her forehead on the wooden door. Three o'clock. The time of madness and magic, indulgence and idiocy.

She couldn't—wouldn't—open her door and wave him back in. She wouldn't text him to come back.

That way madness lay...

Be sensible, Jamie. Things weren't the same as they'd been yesterday. The dynamic between them had shifted. They couldn't be fancy-free, taking what they needed from each other and walking away with a smile and a wave.

She was pregnant with his baby...

A baby she would lose.

Jamie turned, placed her back against the door and slowly sank to the floor. She rested her cheek on her bent knee and forced herself to think.

They weren't lovers, and they weren't—despite Rowan's lovely suggestion—friends. Or not yet, anyway.

The thing was, friendship required trust and openness, traits neither of them possessed. He wasn't a talker. She knew very little about his past. That he'd grown up in foster care was all she'd gleaned from him. She recognized his reticence, his inability to open up, because she was the same. Her heart had spun locks and chains around itself when Kaden died, trapping all her memories. She could talk to anyone on a vast range of subjects, but sharing her innermost thoughts was utterly impossible.

How could she tell the people who loved her husband like a son, like a brother, that she and Kaden had mentioned divorce just before he died? That they'd wanted different things and could no longer find any common ground? That sometimes love wasn't enough?

Funny... The one person who would understand, or who would at least not judge her, was Rowan. Although he'd never been married, he seemed to understand people. Jamie thought he'd understand how love could become distorted, how lost a person could feel in what once had been a fairy-tale marriage.

She also suspected he'd know how it felt to live with guilt and regret.

She appreciated his offer to stand by her, respected the fact that he wasn't bailing, but a part of her wished he'd leave her to navigate the next few weeks on her own. If he did that, she could try and forget that she was pregnant—she rarely had any pregnancy symptoms except for changes in her taste and tiredness—and concentrate on her business, on living her life as normally as possible.

She didn't want to become used to having him in her life, relying on him for emotional support. She was used to living her life solo, with no emotional attachments. She liked it that way.

But Rowan was determined to see her through this, to support her and be with her—though what he could do, she had no idea. She appreciated the sentiment. She did. But, God, every time she looked at him, she'd remember that inside her was a jumble of his DNA and hers, trying to grow, trying to survive.

A baby she couldn't allow herself to want. A child she'd ultimately lose.

Jamie rested the back of her head on the door and

looked up at the dark ceiling of her hallway. Why was this happening to her? Was life punishing her?

At the beginning of her marriage, she'd been desperate for a child and had started collecting clothes and all the paraphernalia a baby required. She'd been sad when she lost her first baby, but figured number two would be healthy. After that second loss, she'd struggled to stay upbeat and tempered her excitement when she heard she was pregnant with baby number three. After *that* miscarriage, she'd told Kaden she was done, but he'd begged her to try again. She did, and the only person who'd been surprised by that loss was Kaden.

He was furious when she donated all the baby clothes and equipment, devastated when she told him that she couldn't do it again.

One argument rolled into another, which rolled into another. Misery moved into their home and lives, settled down and took root.

The headlights of a car shining through the glass side panel jerked her out of her reverie, and she climbed to her feet, feeling emotionally exhausted.

She could work fifteen-hour days for weeks on end without feeling tired, but people and the emotions they raised exhausted her.

It was so much easier being alone, keeping one's distance.

As she climbed the steps to her bedroom, she remembered making love to Rowan. While being alone was easier, it certainly wasn't as much fun.

Jamie stood on her parents' front porch, waving at the car reversing down the driveway. By her calculation, that was the last of her parents' party guests, thank God. When she arranged for Rowan to be her date, she'd expected a fun and flirty evening, a little dancing, a little necking. He was a guy she liked, someone she wanted to have an affair with. A scant week later, she was the woman who was carrying his child.

They'd crossed the line from fun and flirty to sedate and serious. *Blergh.*

Her childhood home had been full-to-bursting for most of the night, and she'd taken on the role of host so her mom could enjoy her evening as the guest of honor. As a result, Jamie had barely seen Rowan. In fact, she didn't even know whether he'd gone home or not.

She'd caught glimpses of him throughout the evening, either talking to Greg or Chas or, surprisingly, her grandmother. She remembered him bringing bottles of champagne from the kitchen and helping out behind the bar when the bartender had seemed overwhelmed. He didn't make a fuss or bring attention to himself; he was simply there, doing what was needed when it was needed.

Despite knowing only her and Greg, he didn't try and monopolize her, seeming to understand that she was busy and couldn't give him any of her attention. A few times, he did suggest she take a break; and when she didn't, he handed her a soft drink or a plate of food she could eat on the go. He'd looked after her, but so subtly she'd barely noticed him doing it.

Sneaky. And sweet.

Suddenly exhausted, Jamie sat down on the front-porch swing, kicked off her shoes and tucked her heels under her butt. She put a cushion behind her head and considered taking a ten-minute nap—just long enough to revive her so she could make the drive home.

If Rowan were still here, she'd ask him to take her.

And if he came inside with her, there was a good chance she'd jump him.

And really, who could blame her? He was hot, sexy, ripped and an incredible lover. He knew how to touch her, how to make her writhe and whimper. He seemed to instinctively know whether she needed to slow down or speed up, how to touch her, where and when to kiss her. He knew *her*...

"There you are."

Jamie turned to see him standing just outside the front door, hands in the pockets of his suit pants. He'd discarded his jacket and tie and rolled up the sleeves of his shirt, revealing his strong forearms.

"Hey. I was just thinking about you," Jamie said, patting the cushion beside her. Since she couldn't tell him about her take-me-against-a-wall fantasy, she uttered a white lie. "I didn't know if you'd left already."

"Without letting you know?" Rowan asked, sitting down next to her and resting his hand on her knee. "I thought you might need me to drive you home. You look exhausted."

Because she could, she rested her temple on Rowan's big shoulder. "Yeah, I'm pretty shattered. But I think my parents had a nice time."

"They did. Your folks told me to tell you how grateful they are for your help and that they love you. Oh, and that they were going up to bed."

"Thanks. What's Gran up to?" Jamie asked, placing her hand on top of his and linking their fingers.

"She's drinking whiskey and playing poker with Greg and Chas," Rowan told her.

Jamie released a small groan. "Gran will drink them under the table, clean out their pockets and still be awake at sunrise. They, on the other hand, will wake up with a helluva hangover."

Rowan's low laugh rumbled over her skin. "Your gran is quite a character."

"That she is," Jamie agreed. She lifted her head to look at his shadowed face. "I hope my mom didn't ask you too many questions?"

Rowan took a while to answer her. "She cornered me shortly after dinner and asked me to provide her with three character references, told me she was going to get a cop friend of hers to do a background check on me and demanded a copy of my bank statements."

Jamie stared at him. Her mother was overprotective of her—they all were—but those requests were bordering on the ridiculous. "I'm so sorry, Row. It's just that I've never brought anyone home, so she's adding three and four and getting… Oh!"

She narrowed her eyes at his smirk, and when it turned into one of his rare smiles, she punched his shoulder, an action he barely noticed. "You jerk! I thought you were being serious!"

"Who says I'm not?" Rowan asked.

"The crinkling of your eyes and the dimple in your cheek," Jamie told him, unable to hold back her own grin. "What did she really say to you?"

"She welcomed me, told me she was happy to meet me and asked me what I did, how long I've lived in the city. Normal getting-to-know-you conversation."

Jamie handed him a suspicious look. "I'm more inclined to believe your earlier nonsense than that load of hooey. What's the truth?"

His mouth twitched. "She wanted to know how long we'd been seeing each other and whether it was serious."

That sounded more like her mom. "What did you tell her?"

Rowan surprised her by turning his head and kissing her forehead. "That we're still getting to know each other and are taking things slowly."

"Good answer."

"I'm glad you approve," Rowan told her, laughter in his voice. "I liked her. Mostly because there's no doubt that she'd move heaven and earth for you. She adores you."

Jamie nodded, tears burning her eyes. "She does. I've never doubted how much I was loved." She heard her words and wished she could yank them back. She grimaced. "I'm so sorry, Row. That was inconsiderate."

"You don't need to apologize to me for having a great family, Jamie. I'm happy you do." He turned, lifted his arm and rested it on the back cushion, his fingers playing with her hair. "You look very pretty tonight. Did I tell you that?"

She knew he was trying to change the subject, and she felt a little sad that he wouldn't let her in. Then again, if he started pushing her about Kaden and the accident, would she be brave enough to open up and tell him how she blamed herself for the events of that day? How was it that this man—so emotionally detached, himself—was the one with whom she felt tempted to share her secrets?

Also, not sleeping with him, *being friends*, was killing her. She appreciated him not running from her and this pregnancy, but she'd appreciate him far more if he took her to bed. Yes, the mental and emotional connection she felt for him terrified her—she risked feeling a lot more for him than she should. But her desire for him swamped her common sense.

Maybe it was hormones, maybe he'd cast some sort of spell on her, but she needed to make love to him again. Immediately.

Rowan wrapped a strand of her hair around his finger and watched it slide off. "You have the softest hair I've ever touched." He lifted his gaze, and his eyes, deep and dark, slammed into hers. "And the most kissable mouth."

"Do I?" Jamie asked softly, feeling that warm wave of desire and need rising inside her.

"You know you do," Rowan told her, bending his head so that his lips hovered over hers. "Can I kiss you, James?"

"God, I wish you would!"

He laughed at her heartfelt response, and Jamie felt the little puffs of air on her lips. Sick of waiting, she lifted her mouth to touch his and sighed when they finally connected.

Lips locked and tongues tangled and teeth scraped, and she loved it all, every second of it. There was something magical about being kissed by a man who knew what he was doing, whose sole purpose was to give you pleasure. Jamie moaned deep in her throat, and Rowan deepened the kiss, turning it more demanding.

Minutes passed, and Jamie gave herself up to the moment, relishing being the object of Rowan's passion. When he picked her up and laid her across his lap, she leaned back against his strong arm and whimpered when his hand came up to cover her breast, his thumb gliding over her nipple. She wanted him. Here, in the dark shadows on her parents' porch while her gran and brothers played poker behind the living room window.

"Shhh," Rowan whispered. "We've got to be super-quiet or else your dad will be out here with a shotgun."

"He doesn't own a shotgun, but he does have a high-powered bow," she told him, grinning.

"Either way, I'd prefer not to be shot, by neither bullet nor arrow," Rowan said quietly, his white teeth glinting in the darkness.

As much as she wanted to make love to Rowan, they couldn't do it out here, in the open. "Take me home, Row, and let's do this properly."

"I don't know if that's a good idea," Rowan muttered. He pulled back to look at her, his brows pulling together in a small frown. "James, I'm trying to be supportive, to—"

"But you have been," she interrupted him. "Instead of ghosting me, you're here, helping as we wait for the inevitable to happen." She hesitated and then shrugged. What harm could it do? He could only say no. "I still want to have a fling with you, Rowan, and we might as well have some fun while we wait. Baby or no baby, I'm still not asking for anything more than sex."

She honestly thought he'd turn her down again and was surprised when he nodded. "Okay."

"You're agreeing?" Jamie clarified.

"I was an idiot the first time I refused and regretted it the moment you walked out my door. I've wanted you every moment since; and since I believe that you are a strong, capable woman who knows what she's doing and what she wants, I'm not going to say no again."

Yay. And thank God. "Great. So are you going to take me home now?"

Rowan's mouth kicked up into a sexy smile. "Eventually." His hand slid under her dress and stroked the length of her outer thigh. "Let's do this first." Before she could finish that thought, Rowan covered her mouth with his and slipped his hand between her thighs, stroking her with unerring accuracy.

He pulled aside her panties, and then his fingers were on her bare folds, finding her nub and stroking it delicately, building her pleasure stroke by stroke. He pulled back to look into her eyes, his expression super-serious. "You are so incredibly beautiful, Jamie."

She tried to smile, wished she could, but all her concentration was on what he was doing below, hoping he'd slide his fingers inside her. As if he'd heard her, Rowan pushed one finger into her, then another; and Jamie sighed, her head falling back, lost in the moment. His thumb swiped her clitoris, and she pushed her hips up, wanting more.

"I wish you were inside me," she told him, her whisper sounding needy. She could feel his erection, steelhard against her hip, and while his fingers were great, she wanted him to come on the ride with her.

"Later. Tonight, this is about you," Rowan told her, widening his fingers a little and tapping her inside channel. Jamie placed her fist in her mouth to keep her whimpers back and felt tears burn her eyes. She looked up into his masculine face, and her eyes clashed with his, filled with a dark blue fire.

He pushed deeper inside and rocked his hand. She felt herself peak, then fly on angel wings toward the sun. He didn't stop stroking her, wringing every drop of pleasure from her, and when she could think again, she couldn't remember ever having a rolling series of orgasms from one man's hand before.

When she was finally done, she slumped against Rowan's chest and tried to regulate her harsh breathing, feeling completely wrung out. Rowan rearranged her clothing, dropped a kiss in her hair. She should thank him, and she would—in a minute. When she remembered how to speak.

She yawned, curled up and rested her hand on his chest. She was so tired, but it would be rude to fall asleep...

Nine

"Seriously, what the hell were you thinking, tucking into Gran's homemade whiskey last night?"

Jamie scowled at Greg, then at Chas, though neither her brother nor brother-in-law noticed because they both had their heads in their hands, thoroughly hungover.

When she'd driven back to her parents' house earlier that morning, she found Greg and Chas passed out on the leather couches in the living room. She'd run up the stairs to the guest bedroom, peeked inside and found Rowan's clothes piled up on the bed and the shower running. He was alive—no thanks to her brother, brother-in-law or grandmother. Thank God, because she still had plans for him.

Jamie winced, feeling remorseful. After their conversation about sex, she'd allowed Rowan to pleasure her and then she'd passed out. She didn't believe in owing anyone anything when it came to sex, but Rowan deserved some of her undivided attention.

As soon as he came down, she'd take him home and do exactly that.

"We were feeling brave," Chas protested weakly, raising his pale green face.

Jamie rolled her eyes.

"And when did you start drinking tequila?" Jamie demanded, remembering the bottle on the coffee table and the dirty shot glasses.

Greg raised his head, squinting. "Uh, that was Gran's idea. Said she wasn't sleepy and wanted something with a kick."

Jamie covered her face with her hands. "Oh, God."

Chas frowned. "I think Rowan proposed to her at some stage. She said yes. So that's official."

Oh, dear Lord.

Jamie pushed her sunglasses up into her hair and rubbed her eyes with her thumb and index finger. While she could remember their hot and wild interaction on the porch in great detail, she didn't recall Rowan picking her up and carrying her up the stairs to the guest bedroom. When she woke, somewhere around five, her dress was lying over the back of a chair, and a light throw covered her from her chest to her toes. Her bag sat on the bedside table, next to a glass of water. She'd debated going back to sleep but decided she should find out whether Rowan was still in the house or if he'd left to go back to his place.

So she'd dressed and tiptoed down the stairs to find carnage, with Rowan curled up in a too-small chair next to her sleeping brothers. Wide awake then, she tidied up a little before deciding to head home for a shower and a change of clothes.

Because Greg had parked her in, she drove Rowan's car back to her place and returned here to find a still-quiet house. A note in the kitchen told her that her mom had gone out for an early breakfast with her friends and that her father had left for a round of golf. It was Jamie's job to revive and restore her brothers and her man.

Her *man*.

Jamie placed her linked hands on her stomach and pushed them into her sternum, trying to hold back the wave of grief that threatened to cut her legs out from under her. Kaden had been her man—the man she'd married, the one she'd adored. From the moment she'd met him, she knew he'd be the man she'd marry. He'd felt the same. Neither of them had expected the troubles that followed, and she'd never envisioned coming to a place where divorce was an option. Would she ever be able to let go of the guilt, forgive herself and move on? Would she ever be able to love Row—another man—again?

Jamie scrubbed her hands over her face, memories of Kaden bombarding her. How many times had they eaten breakfast on this deck, him kicking back in jeans and a T-shirt, sunglasses over his face? He'd played football with the Bacall men on the wide swathe of lawn that was her dad's pride and joy, practiced his putting on her dad's mini green at the end of the garden. Having a sporty father and brother, Kaden had fit right in. The men in her family played tennis and golf, went to ball games, watched games together. Losing Kaden dropped her family to their knees.

Rowan was very, very different from her red-haired, dark-eyed husband, and not just in looks. Kaden, like her, had been a child of privilege, but Rowan had a tough-ness about him. His eyes told anyone who cared to look that this man had lived a million lives, not all of them good. Kaden had held a couple of degrees, was bright as hell, and after leaving college, immediately stepped into a job at Bacall Media.

Rowan was wealthy—ridiculously so—but he was a self-made man, and he'd pulled himself up by his bootstraps. Everything he had, he'd worked for himself, and Jamie admired his guts and his perseverance. It took a special type of courage to come out on top when the odds were stacked against you.

"Gran and Rowan are engaged, by the way," Chas muttered, less green now but still pale.

Jamie smiled at him repeating himself. "Really? When did this happen?"

Chas rubbed his forehead. "I think I recall her stroking his biceps—which, I have to admit, are pretty fine—and her telling him that if you didn't want him, she'd take him. That he'd make beautiful babies."

"He told her that he'd marry her tomorrow," Greg added.

"Who's getting married?"

Three heads shot up. Upon seeing Rowan, both Chas and Greg groaned. Jamie understood why; Rowan looked as fresh as he did when he'd first arrived at the party last night. Sure, his clothes were a bit wrinkled, but he'd finger-combed his wet hair, and his eyes looked remarkably clear.

"If you're going to look all *GQ* gorgeous, then go away," Greg told him, waving a listless hand.

Rowan stopped by Jamie's chair, dropped a kiss on the top of her head and murmured, "Good morning." He pulled out a chair, sat down and reached for the jug of orange juice and a glass. He grinned at her brothers. "Feeling rough, boys?"

Greg and Chas both glared at him. "Are you human?" Greg demanded.

Rowan lifted his big shoulders. "I never suffer from hangovers. I drink, sleep for a few hours and wake up feeling normal."

"That isn't right. Or fair," Greg whined. "I feel like a couple of lumberjacks are using a chain saw to fell a sequoia in my head, and my mouth tastes like a landfill."

"Lovely," Jamie murmured.

Rowan turned to face her, remorse in his eyes. "I'm so sorry about last night."

His apology was sincere, but there was embarrassment in his eyes. He was properly ashamed, and Jamie found herself placing her hand on his bare arm and squeezing. "Relax. Gran's brand of whiskey is industrial strength, and it's felled many a man before you."

Rowan winced. "I believe you because normally I can hold my liquor and it takes a lot to make me drunk. And a lot more to make me fall asleep in a chair." He rubbed the back of his neck and looked at Jamie. "You've changed. Have you been out?"

She nodded. "I drove back to my place."

"How?" Concern flickered in his eyes. "Greg parked you in last night. Did you take his car?"

Seeing Rowan's fancy sports car in the driveway was a temptation she'd been unable to resist. "No, I borrowed yours. I didn't think you'd mind."

"You drove my Aston Martin DB11?" Rowan asked, sounding like he was choking. God, he made it sound like she'd attempted to pilot a jet fighter. It was superpowerful, sure, but still just a car.

Jamie, irritated by his lack of faith, decided to mess with him a little. "Is it supposed to make such a terrible noise when you change gears?"

She hid her smile at the three groans, and Rowan scrunched up his face, obviously in pain. "And I'm sure it won't cost much to fix the scrape on its side panel," she added, trying to look insouciant before pulling a "whoops!" expression onto her face.

Rowan gripped the arms of his chair, and Chas and Greg looked like she'd stolen their will to live. God, how stupid did they think she was? And what was it about men that made them lose their ability to think rationally when cars were mentioned?

"Chill, guys. I'm joking. The car is perfectly fine."

Three expressions lightened, and Rowan's shoulders dropped half a foot. He shook his head and laid a hand on his heart. "You took about ten years off my life. That car is my baby, and it usually spends its life in a garage."

Jamie flashed him an impertinent grin. "Next time, don't assume I can't drive a powerful car with a stick."

He winced. "My bad. I seem to be racking them up this morning." He looked around, frowning. "Speaking of, where are your parents? I should apologize."

Jamie shook her head. "Dad is golfing and Mom is out with some friends. And there's nothing to apologize for. You fell asleep. Big deal."

"But you might like to find our grandmother and start making arrangements," Greg told him, his arm casually draped around Chas's shoulders.

Rowan frowned at them. "What arrangements?"

Chas grinned. "Apparently you agreed to marry her last night."

Rowan grimaced. "Oh, Jesus. Seriously?"

"Seriously," Greg nodded. "She's enamored with your Thor-like body."

"Aren't we all," Chas said, then sighed. When Greg

growled and play-punched his shoulder, Chas laughed. "Oh, please, we've both got eyes in our heads."

To Jamie's amusement and relief, Rowan simply laughed. "Show some respect, boys. I'm going to be your grandfather-in-law."

Greg and Chas laughed, and Jamie grinned at Rowan, delighted. Delighted because he was so unfazed by her brothers, because he had a sense of humor and also because he looked so damn fine sitting next to her on her parents' deck.

Like he belonged there.

Her heart dropped to her feet, and her mood plummeted as well. He *couldn't* and he *didn't*. The only person who should be sitting there was Kaden, and he was dead. She'd watched him die, and she hadn't been able to save him. It was her fault he was gone; her fault that Rowan was sitting in his chair today, next to her, chatting with her brother and his husband as if he'd always been part of their lives.

Nobody could take Kaden's place. She wouldn't let that happen. Ever.

Jamie launched herself to her feet, pushing her chair back so hard that it scraped against the stone tiles. Her eyes fell on Rowan's surprised face. "I need to go. We should go," she muttered, cursing her burning eyes.

Rowan followed her. She couldn't look at Greg or Chas, knowing that she'd see sympathy on their faces. They might've worked out why she was so spooked.

A small frown pulled Rowan's eyebrows together. "Is something wrong?" he asked.

It was the gentleness in his voice that got to her, the tenderness in his eyes. She couldn't cope with either, just like she couldn't cope with the way she'd reacted to his touch last night, how she lost and found herself in his arms, how his deep voice caused her stomach to flip over, her heart to bounce off her rib cage.

And, intellectually, she knew it wasn't Rowan's fault that her family liked him, that they hoped she was moving on. She didn't want to move on. She liked her life the way it was: safe and stable. Since stepping into that elevator with Rowan, her life had been a roller coaster. Kisses, sex, back and forth, outside orgasms and, let's not forget, a very unwelcome pregnancy.

It was too much for her to handle.

She also couldn't bear the thought of loving and losing someone again. She couldn't bear to be happy again, feeling connected and complete, and then losing the person who made her feel that way. It hurt too damn much. She never wanted to experience that again.

Ever.

Rowan slowly nodded. "Let me see you to your car, James."

His instinctual understanding that she was suddenly in a dark place nearly dropped her to her knees.

Rowan followed Jamie home and pulled in behind her in the driveway to her vintage gray-blue house. He exited his car, and while he waited for her to do the same, he cast an eye over her property.

He'd been so freaked out the last time he was here, he hadn't taken in many details.

Or any at all.

But, having done a restoration of a similar house, he knew it was probably a three-bedroom, two-bath, with hardwood floors and a wood-burning fireplace in the living room. The house was completely fenced in, had great curb appeal and was perfectly positioned, being close to parks, shops, excellent restaurants and a train station.

He approved. Not that she wanted or needed his approval.

Rowan stared down at his shoes, remembering her sudden change of mood, the tears glittering in her copper-colored eyes. One minute, she'd been laughing and teasing him; the next, she'd looked like he'd kicked her favorite kitten. Back at her folks' house, it felt like she'd disappeared into herself, too far for him to reach her. A thought, a memory, *something* had instantaneously sucked the life and joy out of her. He wanted to know what it was. He wanted to know *her*.

God.

He rubbed a hand down his face. He was wading into quicksand and was rapidly sinking. Accompanying her to her parents' party should've been a polite in and out, no harm done. But instead of snobby rich people, he'd found a warm, loving family who teased and laughed, happy to be in each other's company. It was obvious that Jamie's parents adored her, as did her brother and his husband, but they all worried about her, judging by the concerned looks they sent her way when she wasn't looking.

And they'd been ridiculously over-the-top happy that he'd come as Jamie's partner. He'd caught that in the way her father gripped his shoulder when they shook hands, the way her mom looked at him, gratitude in her eyes.

Rowan felt like he was part of a story they'd all read and he hadn't.

He liked the Bacalls and he liked Jamie too. He loved the way she rolled her amazing eyes, the way she pursed her lips when she was trying not to laugh. He even liked the way she teased him—she'd had him going about his car!—and the fact that she wasn't scared to do so. He loved the fact that she offered her opinions easily and openly, not particularly caring whether her family agreed or not. He liked her sharp mind, lusted over her sensational body.

Adored the way she fell apart under his touch.

Yeah, he was skidding down the feel-more-than-I-should hill, and if he didn't change course, he would end up flying off a cliff.

He watched her open the door to her car, looking anywhere but at him. With her hair pulled into a high ponytail and wearing a cropped T-shirt and old jeans, she looked more like a college student than a successful business owner. She most certainly didn't look pregnant.

"How are you?" he demanded, realizing he hadn't asked after her today. He gestured to her stomach. "How are you feeling? Anything I should know about?"

She shook her head. "It's still too early. It normally happens between ten and eleven weeks."

He thought about his schedule and remembered that he was due to fly to Nashville around that time for a meeting with Matt, who'd temporarily relocated to oversee a shopping mall development. Nashville was a two-hour flight; he could be back quite quickly if Jamie needed him.

But he suspected she wouldn't. Jamie didn't want to rely on anyone, anytime. He wanted her to rely on him, though, to look to him for comfort and support. To be her primary connection. *Jesus, Cowper.* He lived his life solo. He didn't *do* connections…

What the hell? This wasn't who he was, what he wanted, how he lived his life. He didn't get this involved with anyone—ever.

Jamie gestured to her house. "I'm going in. I have chores to do, and then I'm going to take a nap."

Despite his mind and emotions being at war, Rowan didn't want to leave her. "Do you need a hand?"

Jamie's eyebrows flew up. "To do my laundry and clean my bathroom?"

He shrugged. He'd done a lot worse. "I thought you might like some company, and I don't mind pitching in."

She blew out a long stream of air and shook her head. "I'm grumpy and sad and irritable, and I think I need some time alone, Row."

Fair enough. Stepping up to her, Rowan put his hands on her hips. When she tensed, he shook his head. "Shhh. Just hang on, okay?"

He wrapped his arms around her, holding her close. Slowly, like a leaky balloon, the tautness left her body, and the hands she'd kept at her sides lifted to his waist, then inched around his back to fist in his shirt. She laid her head on his chest, and he, somehow, knew that her eyes were closed and that she was fighting the urge to cry.

He wanted to know why she felt so unhinged, what was going on behind her lovely facade. But he couldn't push—wouldn't. He respected emotional barriers and knew that it was a deeply personal and hard choice to allow anyone behind the wall. He wouldn't bulldoze his way through.

After a few minutes, he loosened his hold and kissed her temple before stepping back. "Call me if you need me. As you know, I can fold laundry."

She nodded, managing a small smile. "If your current career doesn't work out, it's something you can explore."

He touched her cheek with his knuckle. "Bye, sweetheart. Get some sleep, okay?"

Jamie walked up to her front door, and he watched until she was inside. Then he scrubbed his hands over his face.

Yep, flying off that cliff wouldn't hurt, but the landing could kill him.

Ten

I can't make dinner on Friday, sorry. Will reschedule ASAP.

Jamie reread the message from Rowan, frowned and laid her phone on her desk. Just yesterday, he'd called to confirm the invitation for them to join Greg and Chas for dinner Friday evening. He'd offered to collect her from her place at seven and drive them all to the world-famous restaurant a half hour out of town.

She'd never been to Ruby Red and had been looking forward to the gastronomic experience. It was also one of Rowan's favorite restaurants, and he'd told her he was always happy to eat there. So why had he canceled?

She didn't know him well, but she knew he wasn't one to change his mind without a good reason. And why hadn't he called her to explain instead of sending her a terse text? That wasn't like him either.

Jamie leaned back in her office chair and stared at the painting on the wall opposite her. She hadn't seen Rowan since he'd hugged her on her driveway a week ago. He'd given her space and, after a few days, called to check on her. Since then, they'd spoken a few times and texted often. He'd told her he was looking forward to seeing her Friday night and, yeah, she was longing to see him too. Preferably naked. This affair she was trying to have with him was taking a hell of a long time to manifest.

She picked up her phone and scrolled through her contacts, looking for his number. She hit the green button when she found it—and was surprised when a brisk female voice answered. "Mr. Cowper's phone. How can I help you?"

"Uh… I was looking for Rowan. Is he around? It's Jamie speaking."

"Mr. Cowper is currently unavailable. Can I take a message?"

Jamie was about to ask that he return her call when she heard the distinctive sound of a doctor being called on an intercom system.

"Would you mind telling me where, exactly, Rowan is right now?"

"At McKinley Hospital. He should be resting, but he's been glued to his phone."

Jamie's heart jumped into her throat. "He's in the hospital? What the hell for?"

"Uh… I can't tell you that. Jeez, I shouldn't have told you he is here. And now he wants his phone… Hold on."

"Cowper."

His voice sounded croaky but strong, and some of her panic receded. If he was talking and sounding tense, he wasn't at death's door. "Rowan? Why are you in the hospital? What's the matter? Are you okay?"

It was Thursday and she'd spoken to him four times this week already. Not once had he mentioned that he was going into the hospital. Or had his visit there been unexpected?

"Did you have a heart attack? An allergic reaction? What's wrong with you?" she demanded, hearing the hint of terror in her voice, tasting it on her tongue.

"A heart attack, James? No, I tripped while running and fell on my wrist, fracturing it. It needed a pin, so I had surgery."

"Oh." God, he sounded so calm. "Are you okay? Is it sore? Are you in pain?"

"They gave me something. It's in a cast. I feel a bit spacey from the anesthetic."

"They put you under?"

"Yeah, they don't like their patients wriggling while they put steel pins in their limbs," Rowan replied, and she heard the amusement in his voice.

"Can I do anything? Bring you anything?" Jamie asked, hoping he'd say yes so she'd have an excuse to fly down there to check if he was okay.

"No, I'm good…"

Rowan's voice faded out, and Jamie heard the distinct sounds of a low argument before the Irish-accented nurse spoke again.

"Mr. Cowper could do with a change of clothing and a lift home. I am not happy about him taking a taxi in his current state."

Jamie heard Rowan growl "I'm fine!" in the background.

"He vomited after surgery, and he's still a little shaky. Some people react badly to a general anesthetic, and he's one of them."

"Will you give me back my phone, Nurse?"

"Are you coming?" the nurse asked Jamie.

"I'm coming," Jamie confirmed. "I'll be there as soon as I can. Don't let him bully you."

"Ha! As if..."

Jamie asked to speak to Rowan again, and before he could argue—and she knew he would—she spoke quickly. "I'm going to your office. Tell your PA to let me up to your apartment."

"Look, it's not necessary. I'll get a taxi, make my way home."

Wow. He really didn't want her to help him. Too bad he was going to get a solid dose of exactly that. "I'll be there as soon as I can."

"Jamie, I'm good!"

"Shut up, Cowper," Jamie gently told him before disconnecting the call. Two minutes later, she was out the door.

Jamie walked into McKinley Hospital forty-five minutes later, holding a small bag containing a change of clothes for Rowan. She stepped into the elevator, thinking about Rowan and his very minimalistic apartment.

She hadn't been back to his place since the night they'd first made love. At the time, she'd had him on her mind and hadn't paid attention to his decor. Walking around on her own, she realized that his place was huge, hardly contained any furniture, and was stark and cold. With its undecorated white walls and modern furniture, it reminded her of a dormitory or institution. He had no art on display, no photographs, nothing personal. In fact, for a stupidly wealthy guy, his apartment contained little in the way of worldly possessions. There was the requisite flat-screen and a huge stereo system, but that was it.

She wondered why such a wealthy guy in his thirties

had so little, apart from his two fancy cars, in the way
of personal possessions. Why did Rowan live in a place
that reminded her of a walk-in fridge?

Jamie stepped out of the elevator and walked toward
the nurses' station. A tall nurse stood nearby, holding
a tablet. She raised her eyebrows at Jamie's approach.
The name tag fixed to her ship's-prow bosom stated her
name was Briggs.

"I'm here to see Rowan Cowper," Jamie told her,
showing her his bag.

She nodded. "Three doors down, room six."

Jamie found the door to room six, tapped on it and
poked her head inside. Rowan turned to look and gestured for her to come in.

His face held a faint greenish tinge, and his right wrist
lay on his lap, encased in a cast from the bottom of his
fingers to his elbow.

"How are you feeling? How's the—you hurt your head
as well?" she asked, seeing the trail of four stitches running across his forehead. "Holy crap, Rowan! What the
hell did you do?"

He pulled a face, looking embarrassed. "I was running and I tripped. Over what, I don't know. I landed on
my wrist and cracked my head on the side of a wooden
flower box."

She touched his shoulder, needing to connect, to reassure herself. She swallowed, blinked back her tears and
pushed away thoughts of what could've happened. She
lifted the gym bag she'd found in the cupboard of his
all-white bedroom. "I brought you a change of clothes
if you want to shower."

He grimaced. "That was the scary nurse's idea. I'd
rather sort myself out at home."

One-handed? She didn't think so. But, yes, she understood why he'd prefer to be at home. Even if his place very much resembled this hospital room. "Okay, I hear you."

"Thank God someone does," Rowan muttered.

"Having a hard time controlling the world, Cowper?"

He narrowed his eyes at her, and Jamie laughed. She picked up his bag, dumped it on the bed, opened the zipper and pulled out shorts and a linen button-down shirt. "Need some help?"

"I've got it," Rowan told her.

Jamie sat on the visitor's chair and watched him struggle to take the hospital gown off his head with one hand. She heard a couple of creative curses, and when his face drained of even more color and he bit his lip, obviously in pain, she stood up. "Ready to ask for some help yet?"

Rowan glared at her, the effect dimmed by the pain in his eyes. Ignoring his scowl, Jamie eased his hospital gown off, pulled the fabric down his arm and tossed it onto the chair. She wrinkled her nose at the blood on his chest and allowed herself the pleasure of looking at all that warm skin across his fantastically ridged stomach.

"I like it when you look at me like that," Rowan murmured. Jamie's eyes slammed into his, and she caught her breath at the passion in his gaze, the slight quirk at the corner of his mouth. "I have a raging headache and my wrist is on fire but God, I still want you more than I need to breathe. Or a pain pill."

"Then why haven't you been around?" Jamie asked.

"I thought you needed some space," he replied. "It's been hell staying away from you," he added, his tone serious.

She sent him a glance, and the serious look in his eyes had her sucking in her breath. Because she wasn't sure what to say or how to react, she opted for humor. "Exactly how hard did you hit your head, Cowper?"

"Do you always do that?"

"Do what?" she asked, nodding for him to put his good arm into the sleeve.

Rowan shoved his arm into the fabric, and Jamie pulled the shirt around his shoulders. "Make a joke when things get serious?"

She forced herself to look him in the eye. "But we aren't getting serious, Rowan. Neither of us does serious, remember?"

Looking frustrated, he pushed his hand into his hair, yelping when his fingers connected with his stitched-up cut. "Ow, shit! Dammit!"

Rowan looked down at the sleeve she was holding, and she shook her head at her stupidity. "I'm a crap nurse." She pulled his shirt off and started again, threading his cast-covered wrist through the sleeve before efficiently pulling on his shirt.

"I can do this, you know."

"Well, I'd like to get back to work before sundown," Jamie retorted.

"I didn't ask you to come down here," Rowan muttered.

True enough. Jamie cocked her head to the side as she did up his buttons. "Wow. You really are uncomfortable with someone helping you. Why is that?"

He shrugged. "It's easier. When you've never had anyone to rely on, you quickly get used to sorting yourself out."

"Nobody? Ever?"

Rowan opened his mouth to speak, snapped it closed and reached for the shorts lying next to his bag. He pulled them out of her hands. "I can manage these."

He probably could. Or, judging by the light of battle in his eyes, he would die trying. "Go for it."

He pushed back the covers of the bed, and she took a moment to admire the way his black briefs outlined his impressive package. *Not the time, Bacall!* He swung his long, muscular legs out of bed and dropped his feet to the floor. Lowering the shorts, he maneuvered one foot through the fabric, then the other, and pulled the garment up to his hips using one hand. Jamie deliberately looked at her watch, then at the ceiling, then at her watch again.

"Smart-ass," Rowan mumbled.

"Stubborn," she shot back. She placed her fists on her hips, tipping her head back to look at him. Even battered, he looked super-sexy. "How are you going to drive? Type? Work?"

"One-handed," Rowan replied.

"You can't do everything one-handed, Cowper."

"Why? Are you offering to move in?" Rowan asked, reaching inside his bag to pull out a pair of flip-flops.

She matched his challenging stare with one of her own. "I would if you needed me to."

Rowan held her eye, his turning stormy. "Just like you, I don't need anyone."

Yeah, got it. Message received. Jamie held up her hands and backed away from the bed. "I think my work here is done."

She picked her bag off the back of the visitor's chair, hoping he couldn't see how hurt she was. She got it: he was a loner, independent as hell, but she *had* left her office and her busy workday to get him clothes, to help him out. She didn't need his undying gratitude, but a thank-you would be nice. And really, she had whiplash trying to keep up with his contradictory messages. He wanted to sleep with her—*desperately*—yet he couldn't bear for her to help him?

He made her head spin—this time, not in a good way—but she wasn't going to force her help on him. The guy could take a hundred years to get things done, if he got them done at all.

His choice.

Jamie hoisted her bag up onto her shoulder, spun around and headed for the door, her back straight and her head up high. Inconsiderate jerk! She'd rushed down here to help him, as any friend would do...

Friend. She stopped abruptly. When she'd told him she was pregnant, he'd told her he wanted to see her through the next few weeks, that he wanted to be her friend. But when things went wrong for him, she couldn't be his?

There was something very wrong with this logic.

She turned around, dropped her bag onto the bed and shook her head. "Stop being a dick, Cowper. You might feel uncomfortable asking for help, taking help, but suck it up. If you can take me to dinner—a double date with my brother and his husband—or get me off on my mother's porch, be there for me as this pregnancy progresses, then you can accept my help too.

"I am going to drive you back to your morgue-like home, help you rinse the blood from your disgusting hair and help you out." She leaned down, swiped her mouth across his and saw his eyes widen in surprise. She pulled back and looked around. "Where are your clothes? The ones you came in with?"

His sigh suggested defeat, and he gestured to the bed-side cabinet. "What's wrong with my place?"

"Too sterile, too boring, too white," Jamie told him, pulling out his blood-splattered sneakers. She bundled his T-shirt and shorts and shoved them into his gym bag. She looked at Rowan, who sat on the side of his bed looking miserable and a little bemused.

Battered and bruised and hopelessly sexy.

Jamie resisted the urge to kiss him again, to wrap her arms around him and tell him she was so glad he was okay, that nothing worse had happened to him. She loathed it when people she cared about were hurt.

Hated it when they died. *Don't go there, James.*

"Can you leave? Have you been discharged?"

"James…"

Jamie sighed at the stubborn look on his face, the flash of I've-got-this in his eyes. She sat down on the bed and threaded her fingers through his. "Look, I get that you don't like help, that you are used to doing stuff on your own. I understand that our lives are upside down right now and that neither of us knows how to deal with the pregnancy, our attraction or, frankly, with each other. We seem to be dancing out of step, to a different tune. I step forward, you step back and vice versa."

He nodded, his fingers squeezing hers.

"Can we agree to be more open with each other, Rowan?" she asked. "I want to come home with you because I can't bear the thought of you struggling when I can help you." She hauled in a deep breath and forced herself to speak the hard words. "I need to help you, Rowan."

Maybe that was because she couldn't help Kaden when he'd been hurt. Maybe she just wanted this independent, lonely man to have someone to rely on. Maybe she was being too emotional, setting herself up for a fall. Or maybe this was too real. But right now, she didn't care.

She wanted and needed to be with Rowan.

She lifted her eyebrows and waited for him to speak.

"Staying away has been hell. I want to make love to you again," he stated, his expression serious. "And I want to keep making love to you until this thing between us peters out."

Because, his eyes told her, it would gradually disappear. Of course it would; both of them were scared of commitment. She didn't want to love someone again and have it blow up in her face.

She forced herself to smile. "I like the sound of that song," she told him.

He tugged her forward to kiss her, his mouth promising magic. "Me too," Rowan told her, closing his eyes. "While I'd love you to take me home and ravish me, that's not going to happen today. I just feel so…shitty. And tired."

"I can't understand why," Jamie teased him. "You only had an operation a few hours ago, and the drugs are still working their way out of your system. You're probably going to sleep for the rest of the day."

Nurse Briggs appeared in the doorway, her hands resting on the handles of a wheelchair. She looked at Jamie, her eyes bright in her lined face. "Are you getting enough rest? Taking prenatal vitamins? Folic acid?"

Jamie's eyes widened, and she laid a hand on her stomach. How the hell did she *know*?

"Uh…um…" She cleared her throat. "How do you know that I'm pregnant?"

The nurse tapped her index finger against the side of her nose. "Been around for a long, long time. Well, are you?"

Knowing that she'd get a lecture, Jamie almost lied and told her she was taking vitamins. At the last minute, she shook her head and told her she wasn't. She nearly added that there was no point, but kept those words behind her teeth.

"You should," Nurse Briggs informed her. "You also need to rest and relax."

Jamie caught Rowan's eyes and saw the sympathy within them. She jerked her shoulders up to tell him that it didn't matter, that she was used to being disappointed. But a wave of longing smacked her in the heart. She wanted a baby. Specifically, she wanted Rowan's baby. She wanted to see his eyes in another's face, kiss the same square chin and long nose.

Damn, where had that come from?

"Are you okay?" Rowan asked her, standing up. He took a couple of steps toward her and gripped her biceps, concern on his face.

Jamie pulled herself together and looked up into his still-white face. "I should be asking you that."

He cupped her cheek and sent her a soft, slow smile. "We are quite a pair. Thank you for coming, by the way. Like everything else to do with you, it was…unexpected."

Unexpected. What a perfect word!

"Okay, wrap it up. I've got work to do. Put your fine ass in this chair, Mr. Cowper, and let me parade you through the hospital."

Rowan scowled at the chair before turning to look at Nurse Briggs and handing her his most charming smile. "I'm feeling much steadier on my feet, but I just need a few minutes with Jamie. So why don't you go grab a cup of coffee and come back for me in ten?"

She stared at him, eyes narrowed and lips pursed. "You're going to leg it, aren't you?"

Rowan's wide-eyed look was more fake than the flower arrangements in the hospital lobby. He placed a hand on his chest, looking wounded. "I'm hurt by your lack of trust."

"And I'm a freakin' leprechaun," Nurse Briggs muttered. She pulled the wheelchair out of the room and shook her head. "Coffee. I need coffee."

When they could no longer hear her footsteps, Rowan and Jamie legged it, hand in hand.

Eleven

When he woke up later, Rowan felt better, less like a rehydrated corpse and more like himself. Rolling onto his back, he checked his watch, saw that it was after seven in the evening—he'd slept for the better part of the day—and switched on his bedside lamp. Sitting up, he ran his uninjured hand through his messy hair, which was clean after Jamie had helped rinse it of blood. He'd washed up as best he could before tiredness and the aftereffects of the anesthesia forced him to find his bed.

Yawning, Rowan stood up and looked around his room. He'd always thought it cool and uncluttered, but he understood why Jamie thought it was a bit morgue-like. It was unrelentingly white.

Maybe he could hire an interior decorator to bring in some color, maybe a plant or two. Right. That anesthesia must've hit him harder than he'd realized if he was thinking about redecorating just because Jamie didn't like his place.

Like everyone else, Jamie would leave his life eventually. Everyone he cared about always did. When she lost the baby, as she insisted she would, they'd move on. They'd both go back to the way they had been before—both skimming along the surface of love and life, both too damn scared to duck under the waves.

So changing anything—his apartment, his life, his attitude—was simply stupid. Nothing would come of them as a couple. Nothing could.

Unless she *didn't* miscarry his baby…

Rowan rubbed the back of his neck, realizing that he'd deliberately not thought about that possibility because she was so very convinced she couldn't carry a baby to term. But what if she did? What then? How would they move forward? What would she expect from him? What did he expect from himself?

Rowan sat down on the edge of the bed and stared at the hardwood floor. He'd be a father, a role model. How was he supposed to be either when he'd never had a dad or a role model himself?

He was cautious and cynical, deeply wary and unable to trust. How could he be expected to raise a well-balanced kid?

First things first: they needed to get past these next few weeks…

"Hey, you're awake."

He looked up to see Jamie standing in the doorway to his bedroom, still dressed in her work clothes—tailored gray pants and another of her silky T-shirts, this one a pale pink. Her makeup had worn off, and he could see freckles on her nose and the natural color of her lips. She looked messy, tired and utterly fantastic.

She stopped next to where he was sitting and looked down at his head, gently moving his hair to see his stitches. "How are you feeling?"

He inhaled her sexy scent and raised his hand to grip her hip, shuffling her so that she stood between his knees. He rested his forehead on her stomach and felt her hands stroking his shoulders, an action that was both soothing and arousing. "Thanks for staying, for looking after me. It's not something I'm used to, so if I was grumpy—" he shrugged, unable to look up at her "—sorry."

Jamie's fingers danced across the back of his neck, and he shivered. "Greg broke his arm when he was eight, and he whined like a spoiled little girl. You're behaving marginally better than him."

He abruptly lifted his head and pulled back to look at her. Had he been that bad? Jamie shook her head and smiled at him. "Relax, Cowper. I'm teasing you again. Have you never been teased before?"

He'd encountered it—of course he had—but it had always had a nasty edge, words that sliced deep. Jamie's teasing was light and sweet and held no malice. He had no way with words, but he knew he could tease in another way. He raised the hem of her shirt and placed his mouth against her warm tummy, painting her skin with soft kisses.

"What are you doing?" Jamie asked, her voice turning husky.

"Teasing you back. It's the only way I know how," he responded, surprised by his honesty. He dipped his tongue into her belly button. "How am I doing?"

"You could try a little harder," Jamie suggested, bending down to drop a kiss on his head.

Rowan felt that kiss down to his toes, warm and tender. He was used to sex, to affairs, to the tangle of limbs and chasing that orgasm high, but he'd never experienced gentle heat, tenderness and emotion when making love. He felt fear well up—fear of commitment, of being abandoned, of loving and losing another person—and pushed it away.

He wanted gentle, just once in his life. He wanted the slow and subtle and sweet.

He tipped his head back up to look into her lovely face, falling into the richness of her eyes. "Make love with me?"

"Are you…"

"I'm fine. I just…" He forced the words out. "I need you, Jamie. Be with me?"

She nodded, smiled and skimmed the back of her hand over his cheek. She stepped back and reached for the hem of her shirt, pulled it up and over her head. Her bra matched her shirt, shell pink—lacy and sexy and, God help him, low-cut. He watched, his heart in his throat, as she undid the button to her trousers, pushing the fabric down her round hips to reveal her slim, strong legs. Her high-cut panties matched her bra, the perfect foil for her olive-colored skin.

She was gorgeous, feminine and—for tonight—his.

Rowan stood and lifted his hands to cup her face, realized he could only use one hand and growled in frustration. Holding her face with that one hand, he lowered his head and covered her mouth with his, sighing as her lips softened under his. This woman, this moment… He couldn't get enough.

He deepened his kiss and ran his hand down her chest, cupped a breast and skimmed his thumb over her already-tight nipple. Doing this one-handed was a pain in the ass, but he'd manage. Curling his arm around her back, he yanked her up against him and kissed her deeper. He wanted her senseless, thinking only of him. Of how good they were together.

From a place far away, he felt Jamie open the buttons to his shirt, her hands exploring his back, his sides, burrowing under the band of his shorts to stroke his butt. Her touch electrified every inch of skin, and he fought the urge to rip off her panties and slide inside her.

He needed more than a quick bang tonight; he needed a connection. "Take off your bra, sweetheart, and get those panties off."

Jamie—panting softly, her skin flushed pink—did as he'd asked, and then she was naked in his arms. The way he liked her best.

He bent down to suck a nipple into his mouth, mentally smiling when she gasped and arched her back to increase the intensity of his kiss. He felt her hips jerk and, in response to her silent plea, he slid his hand between her legs, seeking her hot, lovely, lush places. She was wet already, and when he touched her clit, she released a soft moan.

"I love the way you touch me, Row," she told him. "You haven't done nearly enough of it."

He pulled away to clock her dazed expression, taking in her closed eyes and the soft smile on her face. For as long as he lived, he'd remember the flush on her cheeks, the way her long eyelashes lay against her skin, the curl of her mouth.

He'd wanted to wait but couldn't—not anymore. Spinning her around, he pushed her down so that she sat on the edge of her bed, leaning back on her elbows. He pushed his shorts down his hips, cursed his button-down shirt and sighed when her hand closed around his shaft.

He stood statue-still, loving the way her thumb brushed his tip, how she rolled him through her fingers.

"So strong. So masculine."

He felt strong, powerful—more of a man than he'd ever felt before. Loving this woman, being in her arms, made him feel…better than he'd ever felt before. He could stand here forever, watching her face as she touched him, wishing she'd take him in her mouth but knowing he wouldn't last ten seconds if she did.

She licked her lips and moved her head closer to him, and her tongue darted out to swirl around his head. Heaven. Hell.

He needed to be inside her. *Now.*

"Scoot up the bed," he told her, and when she did, he started to place his hands on the bed next to her and cursed out loud when he remembered his cast. *Shit!* How the hell was he going to support himself if he couldn't rest his weight on his hands? He was too heavy to put all his bulk on her.

Jamie pushed him away and quickly divested him of his shirt, releasing a low "mmm" of approval as she ran her arms over his bare chest and stomach.

"Roll on your back, Row," she told him, her bossy tone a turn-on. He was happy to oblige.

A second after his back hit the covers, she had one leg straddling his thighs, and then her core slid up and down his shaft. He barely managed to catch up when she took him in hand and slowly lowered herself onto him.

Being inside her was the best place to be. A lovely, wet, warm, safe place. But, God, they weren't using any condoms.

He stretched out his hand to pat the bedside table, looking for the handle of the drawer.

"What'cha doing, Cowper?" Jamie asked, rocking slightly and sending his blood pressure soaring.

It took some mental processing to find the word to answer her question. "Condom."

"Can't get pregnant twice," Jamie reminded him. "And I've been tested. I presume you have too?"

Caught up in the magic of being surrounded by her without a barrier, he could only think of one word: "Yeah."

"Then can we stop talking?" Jamie asked, bending down and giving him an open-mouth kiss.

"Yeah."

Rowan cupped the back of her head, pulled her down and slid his tongue into her mouth. He jerked his hips, pushing himself deeper. She whimpered and sighed and bore down on him, and he felt that familiar itching at the base of his spine—the wonderful buildup to what he was sure would be a mini cosmic bang.

Jamie sat up, her back straight, and he watched her ride him, glorious as she chased down her pleasure. Her hands came up to touch her breasts, and he found her clitoris, determined to make her fly, fast and hard.

He knew she was close—so was he—and when he felt her clench his cock, the burst of warmth and wetness against his tip, he allowed himself to let go, detonating into color and sensation.

Harder, deeper and by far the best he'd ever had.

He looked tired, Jamie decided as she slid a grilled cheese sandwich in front of him. She sat down next to him at the large white—of course—dining table on the other side of the marble island, her plate in her hand.

Then again, after a fall, an operation and fantastic

sex—twice—it was no wonder the guy looked shattered. But Rowan had stamina; she had to give him that.

She picked up her sandwich, took a bite and cursed when a blob of cheese landed on the front of Rowan's shirt. After deciding they needed sustenance, they'd opted to forage for some food. Not comfortable with walking around, or cooking, naked, she pulled on a designer T-shirt she'd found in Rowan's dresser. There was now a grease stain on its pocket.

"Sorry," she said with a grimace, dabbing it with a paper napkin.

"I can't tell you how little I care," Rowan replied. He smiled at her, and her heart rolled over. "You look good in my shirt. Not as good as you look naked, but good."

She smiled. He was a guy who wasn't comfortable with giving compliments, so hearing one fall off his lips was an amazing gift. *He's different tonight,* Jamie thought, eyeing him as he demolished his sandwich. Softer, more emotionally available.

"Why didn't you call me, or anyone else, for help today, Row?" she asked, curious.

His eyes slammed into hers before looking down at his plate. His shoulders, now covered in a sky blue T-shirt, rose and fell. "As I said, it's because I'm very used to doing everything myself. There's never been anyone to call, Jamie," Rowan added, surprising her with that very personal piece of information.

What did he mean? "Nobody? A friend? A cousin? An ex-girlfriend?"

"No, no one. I have friends. I'm not a recluse, but there's nobody I feel comfortable asking for help." He held up his hand, and she saw the defiance in his eyes. "I don't need your pity!"

"I'm just trying to understand, Row," Jamie told him,

keeping her voice steady and calm. "Most people have *someone*."

"I don't." He sighed, bundled his napkin into a ball and pushed his plate away. He rested his forearms on the table and leaned forward. "My mom took off when I was twelve, and she wasn't what I'd call responsible. She was always high, and I was in and out of foster care as a young kid. Then I went in permanently the year I turned twelve. I moved maybe eight times over the next six years."

Dear God. She'd moved once, had transferred from one school to another, and that had been hard enough. Eight times? That was inconceivable.

"Look, you don't need to be a psychologist to realize that being unsettled makes it difficult to bond with people," Rowan explained. "My mother's antics were nothing compared to how difficult it was to move."

"Were they nice places? Was that why it was difficult to leave them?" Jamie asked, trying to understand.

"No. Some of them were pretty awful," he admitted. "I mean, I wasn't beaten or abused—"

Something flashed in his eyes, and Jamie suspected that while he was speaking the truth, he might've come close to experiencing both horrors. She placed her hands on her stomach, tasting fear in the back of her throat for the child he'd been.

"Moving was difficult because I felt constantly unsettled. I could never plan. I was always worried about what came next. I'd learn the rules, figure out how to exist in a space; and then I'd be moved, and I'd have to figure a new set of rules, a new space." He picked up his glass, sipped and put it down again. "There was one family I kind of bonded with, just a little. They were awesome, and I was just starting to drop some walls. I think it was my second move, so I must've been thirteen or so. Then, out of the blue, my foster dad was transferred to another state. They couldn't take me out of state, and losing them nearly killed me. After that, I kept my distance. I still do, so that's why I find it difficult to ask for help."

Jamie nodded, understanding that on a deeper level, he was terrified of relationships, of any type, because he didn't want to be abandoned again. So it was easier not to create bonds, to pull away before anyone got hurt—especially him.

Didn't she do the same but for different reasons? She didn't allow herself to form attachments to men because she was terrified of loss. She'd lost four babies and a husband. The miscarriages were a quirk of nature, but *she* was responsible for Kaden's death.

She couldn't blame Rowan for distancing himself. She really couldn't. Why wouldn't one, as a sensible and intelligent person, try and avoid that which had scoured one before?

It just made sense, didn't it?

They were quite the pair.

Both scared, both damaged, both fighting the pull of their deep, profound attraction.

Well, she definitely was. And Jamie suspected Rowan was too.

Twelve

Another two weeks passed, and they were still sleeping together. And, yes, their friends, family and the general population of Annapolis believed they were a couple.

Neither she nor Rowan could be bothered to explain what they were or weren't. Mostly because neither of them knew. Or, at least, Jamie didn't.

After kissing Rowan's shoulder, Jamie slid out of her bed, pulled on a short robe and pattered down the hall to her kitchen. Yawning, she sleepily checked the level of the water and beans in her coffee machine and hit the button to power it up. Rowan would want coffee when he woke up, but she'd settle for tea. She and Rowan hadn't had much sleep last night—why sleep when they could make love?—and she was exhausted.

But that could also be the pregnancy hormones kicking in. She hadn't experienced any morning sickness yet, but she remembered the bone-deep tiredness she'd felt with her other pregnancies, always worse in the week before she miscarried. It would happen soon, of that she was sure.

And then either she or Rowan would start finding excuses to put some distance between them. Work would suddenly become a priority, and seeing each other every night of the week would dwindle to three times a week, then two, then nothing.

They might exchange a few text messages, a couple of emails; and in six months, a year, they'd bump into each other at a function and have an awkward conversation, exchange some strained small talk. He might be with a date; she probably wouldn't be.

It was all quite sad, really, because she and Rowan enjoyed each other, out of bed as well as in. They both loved word games, preferred books to TV, and rock to country. Their politics were mostly the same, and neither felt the need to fill extended silences with inanities. They were comfortable together, Jamie realized. Yet one look, one touch, could fire up the sizzle, and they'd start ripping off clothes.

But it would end—it would have to. Soon. Nothing lasted forever, and neither would this. Love, like, attraction—it was all as fragile as spun sugar. It shattered, dissolved, disappeared.

Jamie heard her phone chime, and she picked it up to read the text message.

So looking forward to seeing you all tomorrow afternoon. It's been too long!

She grimaced, remembering that she'd accepted the invitation to a baby shower months ago. Alice, the mother-to-be, was the wife of Kaden's brother, and a couple they'd spent a lot of time with back in the day. They'd had a huge group of friends, most of whom she'd lost touch with.

She must've been feeling sentimental when the invitation had dropped into her inbox, or nostalgic, or lonely.

"Hey."

Jamie looked up to see Rowan walking into the room, dressed in a pair of boxer shorts and a plain white T-shirt. He made a beeline for the coffee maker before stopping to plant a kiss on her temple. "You okay?" he asked after yawning. He gestured to her phone. "Bad news?"

She leaned back against the counter as he pulled two mugs out of the cupboard above the coffee maker. "Irritating news."

Rowan shoved a cup under the spout and hit the button with the side of his fist. "Why, what's up? Do you want tea?"

"Yes, please. Months ago, I agreed to go to a baby shower tomorrow afternoon. The expectant mother is Kaden's sister-in-law."

"And the problem is…?"

Where to start? She sat down at her dining table and lifted her heels onto the seat of her chair. "We have nothing in common anymore. We are nothing more than Facebook friends, and I don't know if I can spend an afternoon talking about babies."

"You have your husband in common," Rowan pointed out as he placed her cup of tea next to her elbow. "They must miss him. And you."

She shrugged. Of course they missed Kaden. She still missed him! But none of them would want her around if they knew what she'd done.

Rowan sat down opposite her, his coffee cup dwarfed by his big hand. "What happened, James?"

"What do you mean?"

Rowan's eyes didn't leave her face. "I know from experience that people talk far more about the good things in the past, and we rarely talk about the bad stuff. We never talk about the *really* bad stuff. I think I've heard you mention your husband just a handful of times since I met you."

"I don't feel comfortable talking about my dead husband to my part-time lover," Jamie retorted, feeling panicky.

"Was your marriage so awful?" Rowan persisted.

"No! I mostly had a great marriage. He was a lovely guy," she replied, feeling stung that he would think that.

"Then why don't you talk about him? If not to me, then to Greg and your family?"

Her hand tightened around her mug. "Have you been discussing me with my brother?"

"Discussing? No. But he talks and I listen." Rowan sipped, but his eyes remained laser-sharp on her face. "So why don't you talk about him, James?"

"Goddammit, Rowan, let it go!" Jamie shouted at him.

He remained calm and unfazed. "I would if I thought *you* could. Tell me what happened, Jamie. Because it's eating you up inside."

How did he know that? How was it that he knew her so well after such a short time? And why was she so tempted to tell him the truth? Because she was sick of keeping the secret to herself or was it because she trusted that Rowan, who didn't have a rosy worldview, wouldn't judge her too harshly?

The words were bubbling up, and Jamie placed her hand on her throat, to push them back down again. Once they were out, she'd have to deal with the fallout—Rowan's reaction and her emotions.

"Tell me, sweetheart."

Jamie stared at the wooden surface of the table and ran her finger up and down the handle of her cup. Could she cross this line? Maybe, but only with him.

"After years of fertility issues, losing the babies, we were struggling. Kaden wanted his own kid, his own flesh and blood. He didn't want to adopt or use a surrogate. He wanted a baby the old-fashioned way. I couldn't go through another miscarriage, and we were at an impasse. It got to a point where that was all he wanted to talk about, and whenever he raised the subject, I walked out of the room. We were so unhappy."

Rowan just watched her, his expression calm and implacable. He lifted his coffee cup in a "carry on" gesture. So she did.

"He arranged a weekend away, something to reignite the spark. He told me that we weren't going to discuss anything serious. We were just going to have fun, make love, eat, make more love. Concentrate on each other and not the problems." Jamie swallowed, her skin suddenly too small for her body. "I was ridiculously excited and so appreciative. We were going to reset our marriage. He'd made reservations at an inn, and it was snowing. Our trip started well, and I was excited. But within a half hour, he raised the subject of me trying, one more time, to get pregnant.

"I was furious and I felt like he'd ambushed me. We had a four-hour drive, and I couldn't get out of the car and leave. I told him I didn't want to talk about it, that I'd had four miscarriages and I didn't want to go through another. But he wouldn't stop talking, trying to get me to change my mind." She shrugged. "I lost it. I started screaming at him, telling him he was a selfish bastard, that he was bullying me, and to turn the car around. He started yelling back, and the next thing I remember was being stuck in a crumpled car and watching the light fade from his eyes."

"James." The word was coated with empathy, and when she raised her head to look at Rowan, his normally tough face was soft. "I'm so sorry."

"It's my fault he died. I shouldn't have lost my temper. I shouldn't have yelled or told him that I wanted a divorce. I was just so angry."

"He should've kept his word about not discussing the subject and given you the weekend he promised you," Rowan softly countered.

"And you both should've known better than to discuss such an emotional subject while driving in icy conditions," Rowan stated, his voice so calm and nonjudgmental that Jamie couldn't take offense. "You were both wrong, in different ways. As for him dying? That was an accident, James. Not your fault, not his. Just a horrible quirk of fate."

She wanted to believe him—she did. And, intellectually, she could see his reasoning. But it would take a while for her heart to catch up to her brain. If it ever did.

Jamie pulled her bottom lip between her teeth. "Maybe if I'd just agreed to try again, he'd be alive."

Rowan, surprising her, nodded. "Yeah, maybe he would be alive. But if you'd done that and lost another baby, you would've hated him and felt doubly resentful and angry. You can't play the 'what if' game, Jamie."

Couldn't she? She was rather good at it.

Rowan pushed his coffee cup away and tapped his finger on his cast. "Having had this discussion, I need to tell you how sorry I am about you being pregnant, Jamie. I could kick myself because I would never put you through pain or distress if I could help it."

Jamie placed her hand on his and squeezed. "I know that, Row. I do. Yeah, the miscarriage is going to suck, but I knew that from the moment I did that test. But we're not married, neither of us wants to be in a permanent relationship and there's no pressure on us." She made herself smile, then lie. "You're not in love with me, and I'm not in love with you."

Jamie waited for the lightning bolt to strike her, and when it didn't, she figured she had the universe's permission to carry on fudging the truth.

"We like each other, but we both know that at some point we'll drift apart, as we were always supposed to do."

God, the idea was a stake through her heart. How was she going to wake up alone instead of being curled up against his hot, muscled body? Who would she talk to about anything and nothing? How was she going to fill the empty spaces in her home and life after he left?

But she had to let him go...

He'd always been destined to leave. She might've changed her mind on taking a chance—or was considering it—but she knew he hadn't.

Rowan's expression was enigmatic, and after a couple of seconds—or maybe a hundred, who knew?—he stood up slowly and walked around to where she sat. He bent down and placed a lingering kiss on her temple, then her mouth.

"Thank you for telling me," he said, his voice a whisper against her lips. "And I am so, so sorry I put you in this position."

What position? Losing her baby?

Or breaking her heart?

Rowan stood in Jamie's shower, the bathroom door closed and locked. He rested his forearm on the tiles above his head, conscious of a deep, pervasive sadness he'd never experienced before. Up until this conversation, the subject of a miscarriage had been an intellectual exercise. It hadn't touched him emotionally. But in the last fifteen minutes, he'd connected with the idea that his kid was inside her, fighting for a place in this world. And that he, or she, probably wouldn't make it.

He knew he'd never grasp the full impact of a miscarriage. He wasn't a pregnant person, and he'd never properly get it. He'd never know the soul-deep sadness, the connection she'd had with her other babies and with the one inside her. He'd never pretend to...

But losing the baby wasn't all that was on his mind.

His guilt about impregnating Jamie was fighting a war with his realization that theirs wasn't just an I-think-you're-hot attraction anymore. Yes, he couldn't keep his hands off her. They made love often, and it was mind-blowing, but he loved their quiet moments too. Holding her as she slept was a pleasure he'd never experienced before. Hearing her laugh lifted his soul. He liked the person he was with her—calmer, less stressed, quick to laugh, strangely affectionate.

"You're not in love with me, and I'm not in love with you."

As she'd said those words, every cell in his body vibrated, yelling for him to refute her statement. The truth hit him—hard and fast—that he *was* in love with her and that she was the only person he could imagine building a life with, committing to—loving.

He loved her.

Hard to admit because he was so damn scared of losing her, but he couldn't lie to himself any longer. He'd kept coming back to her because his soul recognized hers. She was the big hole in his life he'd always had trouble filling.

He didn't want to go create a family with anyone other than Jamie. Maybe they wouldn't have kids that were genetically theirs, but he honestly didn't care if they adopted or used a surrogate. He just wanted a family with Jamie at the center of it.

But she'd made it very clear that she was better off on her own, that she neither wanted nor desired more kids or a committed relationship. He got it. She'd been married, had experienced a great loss. But he couldn't trust anyone else with his heart, his life, his kids.

It was either Jamie or no one.

And since she'd just told him she didn't love him and that she didn't want a permanent relationship, he was facing the lonely, empty life he'd thought he wanted.

Rowan rested the back of his head against the shower tiles. What should he do? How should he go forward? If he pushed her for more, told her he loved her, asked her to consider a life with him, wouldn't he be just like her ex, who'd pushed his agenda when she told him, time and again, that wasn't what she wanted?

Or should he just give her time and space, let her drive the pace of their relationship, and hope her barriers would break down and she'd let him in?

He was a guy who liked action, who worked for what he wanted, but he couldn't *make* her love him. She either did or she didn't, would or wouldn't. So, for now, he'd just stand here and curse in the shower, where no one could hear him.

They were living on eggshells, and it was making them both irritable and sensitive, Rowan thought as he walked into Jamie's kitchen early one morning. He rubbed his hand through his hair and headed to the coffee maker, intent on getting some caffeine into his system. He'd persuaded the orthopedic surgeon to remove his cast a little early, and was enjoying a wider range of movement, especially in bed.

He and Jamie might not be talking much—a wall the size of Texas had sprung up between them since she'd told him about her husband's death—but that hadn't stopped them from turning to each other in the night.

Last night had been a marathon session, and he was exhausted. A good exhausted, admittedly.

He'd toyed with the idea of yanking down that wall and telling her, openly and honestly, that no matter what happened with the baby, he wanted to stick around. That he loved her. But, judging by her remote expression, she wasn't ready to go there. He swallowed down his impatience and reminded himself that love couldn't be bulldozed through.

But Rowan also knew they couldn't keep on like this. Something had to break. And soon.

"I'll have another cup, thanks."

Rowan jumped at the deep voice and spun around. But instead of an intruder, Greg sat at Jamie's dining table, looking uncharacteristically sweaty.

Had he been running?

Rowan put his hands on his thighs and heaved in some air, trying to get his heart rate to slow. "For the love of God! What the hell?"

Greg grinned at him. "Morning. Are you always this unobservant, or did I catch you on a bad day?"

Rowan straightened and glared at him. "I wasn't expecting you at oh-dark-hundred, sitting in Jamie's kitchen."

"I am her brother," Greg mildly pointed out before

nodding to the coffee maker. "Are you going to make me one, or do I have to make my own?"

"I'm on it," Rowan grumbled, turning back to the coffee. As he completed the familiar actions, his heart rate dropped and his breathing evened out. He carried the cups over to the table and handed Greg his before taking the seat opposite him.

"Is letting yourself into her house something you regularly do, or is this a special occasion?"

"Before you arrived on the scene, I used to make it over here a couple of times a week," Greg told him. "Lately, I thought I'd give you guys some privacy."

"Nice of you," Rowan replied dryly. "And it's a good thing I don't walk around the house naked." Rowan lifted his cup to his lips, took a reviving sip and sighed. How did people start the day with tea? Or nothing? It made no damn sense.

He looked at Greg, so at home in Jamie's house. "So what's different today?"

Greg's finger traced the lip of his cup and his sherry-colored eyes, so like Jamie's, turned to chestnut brown. He frowned before asking his straight-as-an-arrow question. "What's going on with you and Jamie?"

Rowan held his cup to his lips, surprised by the question. "What do you mean?"

"You came to dinner the night before last and you were both acting...weird."

Weird? He and Jamie had laughed, joked and talked, both determined to show Greg and Chas that everything was fine. They'd acted their asses off, but it seemed neither of them would be receiving an award for their performance.

"We were acting perfectly normally," Rowan protested, mostly because he thought he should.

"While we were in the room, you two laughed and joked, but when we left, you had nothing to say to each other."

Damn. "How do you know that?"

"We spied on you," Greg retorted. "Stood at the door and peeked through, ears flapping. They say that eavesdroppers don't hear anything good about themselves, but we didn't hear anything at all. In fact, it reminds me of how Jamie and Kaden were in the months before his death." Greg nailed Rowan with a hard look. "Has she told you about Kaden?"

"Yes," Rowan replied. When Greg's eyes brightened, he shook his head. "And, no, I'm not telling you."

Greg pulled a face. "I'm presuming you won't tell me what's going on with you two either?"

"Nope."

"Is she going to get hurt?" Greg asked, and Rowan appreciated his blunt question.

Losing the baby was going to hurt like hell, but losing him? Not so much. "Yeah, probably. If it's any consolation, I will not escape unscathed either."

Greg pushed his hands into his hair and rubbed his scalp. "You two make life so damn complicated! You're crazy about her, she's crazy about you—"

He didn't need a lecture, especially at this hour of the day. "Greg, shut the hell up, okay?" Greg's head shot up, and he narrowed his eyes at Rowan. Rowan didn't give a crap. Ignoring the other man's annoyance, he leaned forward. "I need you to do me a favor—"

He didn't allow Greg the opportunity to refuse. "I'm leaving for Nashville today. I'll be there for the next few days. Matt and I are hammering out our vision for development, mostly so we can give our pain-in-the-ass architect something to work from."

"Shouldn't I be there? Wouldn't that save time?" Greg demanded.

It would, but he had other plans for Jamie's brother. Plans far more important than some architect drawings. "It would but I need you and Chas here. I need you to keep an eye on Jamie for me."

"Why?" Greg asked, instantly suspicious. "What's wrong with her?"

He couldn't explain, not without breaking Jamie's confidence. But the hell of it was, he didn't trust Jamie to let him know she was miscarrying.

Like him, she didn't like to ask for help. He suspected that when it happened, she'd go to the doctor or hospital by herself, deal with it on her own. If he couldn't be around, then he needed somebody close to her, someone he trusted, to hold her hand.

He refused for this to be just another thing she "handled."

"Look, I can't tell you, not without breaking a confidence, and I don't want to do that. I can tell you that she isn't in any danger—Jesus, will you be around or not?"

Greg stared at him, a slow smile creeping up his face and hitting his eyes. "You are so in love with her."

Yeah, yeah… So? And he was not having this conversation with Jamie's brother. He glanced at the oversize clock on Jamie's scarlet-colored kitchen wall.

"Is that the time? I need to get going." He pushed his chair back, put his hands on his hips and gave Greg a hard stare. "So will you?"

He nodded and Rowan closed his eyes, relieved.

"What is Greg going to do?" Jamie asked, walking into her kitchen with messy hair and wearing one of Rowan's T-shirts. She stopped and stared at her brother. "Hopefully he's going to stop breaking into my house."

Greg replied that he had a key, and when the siblings started to bicker, Rowan took that as his cue to leave. The sooner he got to Nashville and completed his business, the sooner he could get back home.

Because home was wherever Jamie was.

Thirteen

In Nashville, Rowan sat on the edge of his bed, looking into his phone, and Jamie sighed. He looked so incredibly good in his mint-colored collared shirt, a black-and-white geometric tie lying against his chest. She, by contrast, looked like a train wreck.

Over the past few days, she'd started to lose color in her face and felt desperately tired. She knew the time was near.

"I wish I was with you. I'm sorry this trip is taking longer than I thought. I'd fly back now, but I have meetings this morning and this afternoon," Rowan told her, looking frustrated.

Over the past few weeks, Rowan had started coming home—to her place, not his—earlier and earlier, and some afternoons he even beat her home. He'd cooked for her, ran her bubble baths, rubbed her feet and had, on more than one occasion, carried her up to bed when she fell asleep on the couch watching TV. He was taking care of her and, God, how she liked it. No—she loved it.

When he walked out of her life—because he was going to at some point down the line—how was she going to handle it?

Badly. Very badly indeed.

She'd tried so hard to put up barriers between them, to create boundaries, but Rowan, who'd never met an obstacle he couldn't overcome, just barged through them. She kept retreating, emotionally and mentally—trying to find a way to safeguard her heart, to stop herself from falling in love with him—but nothing seemed to work.

And, man, she couldn't resist his touch. One kiss, one stroke of his hand, and she was lost...

She had to call it, and soon. She was at the top of a slippery hill, hanging on to a thin tree branch, teetering, about to slide down and collide with love. If she allowed herself to let go, her world would spin out of control. And when she came to a stop at the bottom of that exhilarating ride—when he left her—she'd feel like she'd broken every part of her body.

She knew what devastation felt like, and if she couldn't stop herself from falling in love with him now, she was on track to walk through that hellscape again.

Not if she could help it.

"Why don't you take the day off, sweetheart?" Rowan asked her. Why did he have to be so sweet, so considerate? Why couldn't he just be a normal, selfish, unobservant man? How was she supposed to resist him?

"Like your business needs you, mine needs me."

"I'm just suggesting that you get some rest," Rowan replied in a far-too-reasonable tone.

"Stop fussing, Rowan!" she snapped, knowing she was being irrational. She could blame her hormones—

they were all over the place—but he was being every-thing a life partner should be: involved, engaged, kind.

It was far too real and too much.

Jamie felt her stomach cramp, and it was followed by a warm feeling between her legs. She knew that feeling. She placed the face of her phone against her forehead and wished it was all different.

Wished that this baby had stuck, that they both weren't so damn screwed up and terrified of love...

"James? What's going on?"

She lowered the phone, and her heart lurched at the panic in his eyes. If she didn't know better, she'd think that he loved her.

But she did know better.

He didn't love her. Couldn't. Never would.

"I've started to miscarry, Row. I felt... Well, I think it's starting."

"Jesus!" he shouted, leaping to his feet, panic flying across his face. "Okay, if you call an ambulance, I'll call Chas, tell him to get his ass over to your place—"

"Rowan—"

He shoved his hand into his hair. "I'll book the next flight out. I'll be there as soon as possible."

Jamie tipped her head to the side, feeling flat and dull. "Why?"

"What do you mean 'why'?" Rowan demanded.

"I've done this before, Rowan. I go to the ob-gyn, she examines me and I have a scan," Jamie explained. "I have a quick procedure and come home. There's noth-ing for you to do."

You could love me. I could love you. But neither of us is brave enough to let that happen.

"I can damn well be there for you, James!" Rowan bellowed.

Jamie briefly closed her eyes. "What's the point of you flying back here and holding my hand? It's not going to stop the miscarriage. And when it's all over, you'll fuss for a couple of days, and then, when things get back to normal, you'll look around and wonder what you are doing in my life and I'll wonder what I'm doing in yours. We'll make love, and it won't be the same as it was before. And one of us—maybe you, maybe me—will call it, and we'll go our separate ways."

Rowan scowled. "Why are we discussing our future breakup in the middle of you miscarrying?" he demanded. He released a sigh and scrubbed his face with his free hand. "But you're right. We can't carry on like this, James. We do need to talk."

Wasn't that code for "it's time to call it quits"? And, yep, it did hurt. More than she expected it to. She nodded. "We'll talk. But don't hurry back, Rowan. I've got this."

Rowan gave her a long, hard stare and shook his head before disconnecting. She didn't know if he was coming or staying in Nashville, whether to expect him or not.

Right, well… Okay, then. While she waited to find out, she had things to do. An ob-gyn to see. A broken heart to nurse.

Jamie sat in her darkened living room, her hands between her knees, staring at the black-and-white image on the coffee table in front of her, her heart thumping ten times its normal speed. Thinking she might pass out, she looked away and felt her pulse drop. Then she looked at the image again, and her heart rate accelerated once more.

At this rate, she'd need a pacemaker…

And sometime in the future…*maternity clothes*.

She was pregnant—miraculously still pregnant—and the small, grainy black-and-white printout was the proof of her new reality.

She'd seen her baby's heartbeat, watched as the doctor took measurements, listened as she'd been given an estimated due date.

She and her baby were fine. They'd made it longer than any other pregnancy, and the doctor felt that the danger had passed and that there was no reason to worry. She was going to be a mama.

At the thought, Jamie burst into tears. Again.

Greg walked into the room, holding a tea tray, followed by Chas who rushed over to her. He sat on the arm of her chair and rubbed her back. "Take a deep breath, honey," he told her, pushing tissues into her hand.

Jamie looked up at him. "You saw the heartbeat, right?"

Chas nodded as he squeezed into the space next to her. "I did. You have a happy, healthy baby, Jamie darling."

Jamie released a sigh of relief, leaned into him and closed her eyes. What a day!

After her call to Rowan, she'd dressed and brushed her teeth, then called her ob-gyn. She was told to come in immediately and that they'd decide the next steps after she'd been examined. When she got to the doctor's, she'd found Greg and Chas waiting for her, having been sent by Rowan. She tried a few excuses to get Greg and Chas to leave, but they had just stared at her, eyebrows raised and feet planted. Eventually, she just blurted out the truth. "I'm pregnant and I'm about to miscarry."

"How do you know that?" Greg had demanded.

"I've miscarried before, remember?"

Greg had closed his eyes, looking devastated. "Shit, James. You should've told us you were pregnant."

She should've told them lots of things.

After she'd been examined, her ob-gyn took her for an ultrasound. Greg and Chas followed her and the doctor into a windowless room and crowded around the tiny screen, fascinated, as the doctor made some measurements and then traced the outline of her baby. When she'd pointed to the tiny, fluttering heartbeat, they all cried.

It was now midafternoon; her brothers were still hovering, and she still had to speak to Rowan, who'd texted that he would be with her by four o'clock. She took the cup of tea Greg held out, wrinkling her nose at his serious expression.

"You are going to tell him about the baby, right?"

"Of course I am," Jamie responded. She just didn't know how to explain the 360-degree change in circumstances. She'd told Rowan, over and over again, that there wouldn't be a baby, that he wasn't going to be a father; so she had no idea how he was going to take the news.

Sure, there was a possibility that she might still miscarry—there always was in any pregnancy—but her ob-gyn had said it was very unlikely. Her baby was strong and healthy. And, weirdly, Jamie knew her child was fine. She *felt* it.

"Be honest with him, James," Greg told her.

What did that mean? Of course she'd be honest with him. But she certainly wasn't stupid enough to believe that anything would change. She wouldn't be living in a roses-and-champagne world after she told him he was going to be a father. Rowan didn't want a relationship, and he certainly didn't want a relationship and a kid.

That morning, she'd been scared of falling in love with Rowan and having him leave her, but now she had an additional reason to call their relationship quits.

Whether she loved him or not—and she probably did but couldn't make herself admit it because it was too damn painful—she didn't want him to be with her for the sake of their child. She needed him to want to be with *her*, with or without a child. But since she'd fallen for the most independent, emotionally distant man she'd ever met, that wouldn't happen.

No, it was kinder to him—and to her—to let him go. If he wanted to, he could be part of their child's life. If Rowan decided fatherhood wasn't for him, her kid would have Greg and Chas, and her dad, as great male role models.

The growly sound of an expensive engine broke their silence, and Jamie placed a hand on her stomach, panic rising. Greg and Chas rose to their feet, exchanging a long look. Greg bent down and kissed Jamie's cheek. "While part of me wants to stay, I know this is something you need to do on your own. We'll go out the back door."

Jamie heard the slam of a car door and then the faint slide of his key in the front door. The sound of his bags dropping to the wooden floor echoed through the house, and Jamie sucked in a deep breath, then another.

"James? Where are you?" Rowan called as he tossed his keys into the pottery bowl by the door.

When she whispered his name, he turned and strode into the living room, still dressed in his dark gray suit and mint-colored shirt. He looked big and powerful and lovely.

His mouth curved up, and those amazing blue eyes lightened. "There you are. Hi."

Jamie touched her top lip with her tongue before responding. "Hi."

He bent down to brush his mouth across hers, then sat on the heavy wooden box that served as her coffee table and placed his big hands on her knees. "You're looking pale. Everything okay?"

Yep, that was her opening...

"So, as you know, I saw the ob-gyn this morning because I thought I was miscarrying."

Pain flashed in his eyes. "I'm sorry I wasn't here, James. Are you okay? How are you feeling? Shouldn't you still be in the hospit—wait, did you say you *thought* you were miscarrying?"

She nodded slowly.

"So you didn't miscarry?" Rowan asked, frowning.

She shook her head.

Impatience flickered across his face, settled in his eyes. "James, stop being cryptic. What is going on?"

She stood up and looked around, wanting to delay this moment. "Do you want a drink? A beer? Whiskey?"

"I'm fine," Rowan growled.

"I think you need a whiskey," Jamie insisted. "Trust me on this."

"I *need* you to sit your ass down and tell me what's going on!"

It was easier to show than tell, so Jamie pulled the ultrasound image from underneath his powerful thigh and handed it to him. She watched as he looked at it, turned it around and looked at it again. He even checked the back before shrugging. "I know this is a picture from an ultrasound machine, but I have no idea what I am looking at," he admitted.

Right. Time for explanations. "That's my baby, Rowan. The child you made with me. That kidney-shaped blob is my thirteen-week-old baby. That's his—or her—head, the spine. I saw and heard the heartbeat."

He looked from her to the picture and back to her face,

his expression completely confused. "Are you telling me that the baby is viable?"

Jamie placed her hand on her stomach. "Not just viable—my baby is thriving."

Rowan rested the picture on his knee and pushed both his hands into his hair, staring down at it. "But you said you thought you were miscarrying."

Jamie raised her shoulders. "I had some blood, and I assumed it was just beginning. I went to the doctor immediately. I haven't had any spotting since, so she said it's nothing to worry about."

She could see his mind spinning. "Did the doctor explain why you haven't miscarried this time around like you did last time?"

"The most rational explanation is that there was a chromosomal issue between Kaden and me. She wanted to run those tests years ago, but Kaden always refused."

Rowan nodded. "Holy shit, Jamie."

Yeah, that was one way to put it.

He looked up, and the muscles around his eyes tightened, deepening the crow's-feet at the edges, and a huge smile, one she'd never seen before, transformed his face, making him look years younger. "Oh my God, we're going to have a baby!"

She wanted to roll around in his happiness, fling herself into his arms, fly away on his excitement. But she knew that when the initial shock died down and he realized the true implications of her being pregnant, he wouldn't be nearly as thrilled.

She'd just upended his calm, stable life. He'd never wanted a relationship, a commitment or kids; he was just responding to the moment. He wasn't being sensible.

She couldn't bear to taste happiness, to be filled by it and then have it ripped away.

He pulled her into his arms, whirled her around and dropped a hard kiss on her mouth. When she didn't respond, either with a kiss or to wrap her arms around his neck, he tensed and slowly lowered her to the floor. When she looked at him, his eyes radiated confusion.

"What is it? Why aren't you excited? You're having a baby!"

She touched her stomach, nodding. "I am." She sucked in a breath and lifted her shoulders to her ears. "But that doesn't necessarily mean that you are going to be a father."

His thick eyebrows pulled down. "What the hell do you mean by that?"

Jamie put some distance between them and folded her arms. "Look, I know this is a shock, but you need time to process this, to decide what you want."

Rowan pushed his jacket back to place his hands on his hips. "What the hell do you mean by *that*?" he demanded again.

"You're excited now, but in a few days, a few months, you might not be. I'm perfectly happy raising this kid myself, Rowan."

"Good God, I cannot believe I am hearing this! Why are you acting like this?"

Because she didn't want him to promise her the world and then decide he couldn't give her an inch of it. Because she'd been let down before, and she'd rather have her heart dinged now than shattered later. She raised her chin, looking defiant. "What? Are you going to offer to marry me?" she asked, her tone scathing.

"Yeah, I would marry you."

Thought so. "But only because of the baby! We agreed this wasn't a long-term thing, that it wasn't going to get serious!"

If he wouldn't go, then she would have to push him away. It was the only way to protect herself. She loved him, but she knew the consequences of love, knew how devastating it could be when it was lost forever. She'd loved Kaden, but what she had felt for him paled beside what she could feel for Rowan—if she dropped all her protective barriers.

He was everything she wanted in a man, a partner and a lover. Hardworking, smart, loving, occasionally frustrating. Sexy as hell. Her love for him was a massive wave behind a cracked seawall, desperately trying to find a path through. She had to keep it back or else it would drown her.

The anger died in Rowan's eyes, replaced by an icy intensity she'd never seen before. "Are you trying to tell me that you're not interested in making a relationship work?"

She spread her fingers apart. "I don't want us getting sucked into this false bliss and then realizing we're wrong for each other! It's better to accept that now and go back to being who we were before—two people living their lives solo."

She saw the flicker of fire in his eyes, followed by despair, and fought the urge to apologize. A little hurt now would save a lot of pain down the line. For him and for her.

He wasn't the settling-down type, she reminded herself. He'd never once suggested he wanted more. Until now. She was protecting herself. She was allowed to do that, wasn't she?

"You're dumping me?" Rowan asked in an ultra-polite voice.

Damn, when he put it like that… "I just don't want us to have unrealistic expectations of the future. You're not a settling-down type guy, and I don't want another relationship! But you're welcome to have a relationship with this baby, if you want."

"Good of you," Rowan told her, his voice scalpel-sharp. "Just to be clear—you might not want me, James, but I want that kid!"

"It's not that I—" Jamie spluttered, then pushed her palms into her eye sockets. She was overwhelmed with emotion: happiness, terror, sadness. And all she wanted, confusingly, was Rowan to take her in his arms and tell her it would be okay, that they would be okay. That they'd make it work, no matter what life flung at them.

Instead of scooping her up, Rowan sent her another icy look and walked the short distance into the hall. He picked up his keys and his overnight bag and pushed his phone into the inside pocket of his jacket. She didn't want him to go, but she was too scared to ask him to stay.

Rowan reached for the doorknob and opened her front door, turning back to look at her. "I've spent my life expecting people to disappoint me, James. But, stupidly, I never expected you to."

His words were a series of poison-tipped arrows to her heart. Jamie felt her knees buckle, and her vision began to swim. From a place far away, she saw her front door close behind him. She dropped to her knees and bent forward, hot tears dripping onto her hardwood floor.

Both Greg and Chas were sitting at her breakfast table when she came down the next morning, and the first thing she noticed was a bottle of champagne sitting in a silver ice bucket on her table. Champagne flutes, a jug of orange juice and a basket of fluffy croissants completed the early-morning picnic.

Jamie wanted to vomit, and not because she was pregnant. "You guys need to learn to phone ahead," she told them, heading for the kettle.

Chas walked over to her, pulled her in for a hug and kissed her head. "How's our favorite mama this morning?"

She had no idea how to answer that question. Luckily, Greg jumped in with a question of his own. "Where's Rowan? How did he take the news? Is he still asleep? In the shower? Is he thrilled?"

Jamie, not knowing how to answer, burst into tears. She held on to Chas's shirt and sobbed, her shoulders heaving. Chas, bless him, simply held on.

When she finally lifted her head off his chest, the champagne bottle and the glasses were gone and Greg had made her a cup of tea. She didn't want tea. She wanted Rowan.

Chas led her over to a chair, sat her down and pushed the cup toward her. "Drink. You've lost about six liters crying."

She wanted to smile at his exaggeration but couldn't. She took the paper towel Greg had thrust at her and wiped her eyes, then blew her nose. "I think Rowan and I are done."

"Why do you think that?" Chas asked gently.

"And what did you do?" Greg demanded with a deep scowl.

"Why do you automatically assume it's me?" Jamie asked him, feeling stung.

Greg snorted his disbelief. "Because that man is besotted. He would move heaven and earth for you!"

"Greg," Chas chided. He reached across the table to take Jamie's hand in his. "Why don't you tell us what happened, darling?"

Jamie, feeling utterly exhausted, closed her eyes and

swayed from side to side. She was running on fresh air and emotion, and feeling spacey. She needed sleep, but every time she closed her eyes, she saw the devastation in Rowan's eyes and knew she'd put it there. She was the last in a long line of people who'd let him down, and she hated herself for that. But she'd been scared, trying to protect herself—protect *them*—from future hurt.

"When we hooked up, we told each other that we didn't want a relationship, that we were only ever going to be a short-term fling," Jamie explained, her words coming in fits and starts. "Rowan told me he didn't want a relationship—he wasn't interested in commitment. I told him I felt the same."

"Which you probably did, at the time," Chas said, nodding.

Jamie rubbed her forehead with the tips of her fingers. "We agreed to two dates, and we both knew we were heading back to bed. But on that first date, I found out I was pregnant, and he said he'd stick around until I lost the baby, because that's what I expected to happen. I mean, why wouldn't I miscarry since I'd had so many miscarriages?"

Their spines straightened and their eyes narrowed. "What do you mean, you've had so many miscarriages?"

She had to tell them about Kaden and the argument, her lost babies, knowing that she'd done her family a disservice by not trusting them with her secret. How could she move on until the people who loved her knew the truth? In halting words and with lots of tears, she told Greg and Chas the full story of her and Kaden's struggles with having a baby and their deteriorating marriage. They listened in silence, their jaws occasionally dropping.

"We didn't know any of this, James," Greg whispered, his face pale with shock. "How could you not tell us?"

"She's told us now, babe," Chas told him, his hand squeezing his husband's knee. "She told us when she could."

Jamie sent Chas a grateful look. "Anyway, getting back to Rowan... He said that he'd made me pregnant, that he was going to be there until I lost the baby. He didn't bail."

"No, he didn't," Greg agreed.

"We got along so well, and the sex between us was so amazing! I mean—"

Greg slapped his hands over his ears and trilled, "*La-la-la!* I do not need to know about your sex life, James!"

That brought a tiny smile to Jamie's face. "Anyway, we enjoyed each other, but we knew it would end. It had to. I was prepared for that to happen."

"Then you heard that you are actually pregnant and that the baby is healthy," Greg said, his face soft. "That's a pretty damn wonderful thing, Jamie."

Jamie nodded and linked her hands across her tummy. "It really is."

"So why isn't he with you this morning?" Chas asked.

Jamie sent them an anguished look. "He was so excited, guys. Like I'd handed him the world. I'll never forget the joy on his face..."

"But?"

"But then I told him that we have nothing more than sex and a baby in common," Jamie reluctantly admitted.

"And why did you say such a stupid thing?" Greg demanded, shaking his head.

Yeah, now came the hard part—where she had to dig deep and be accountable. To face herself and her fears. "Because I was scared."

"Of what?"

"Of us being swept away by the moment, the excitement! I knew that I would still love him in six months, six years, sixty years, but I don't know if he feels the same. I lost my other babies and I lost Kaden, but I can't lose Rowan! I'll do anything I can to avoid being hurt like that again!"

"So, in your effort to protect yourself, you hurt Rowan by pushing him away." Greg sat on his haunches in front of her and looked up into her face, his eyes somber.

It was a shock to see her happy-go-lucky brother looking so very serious.

"The thing is, Jamie, you have people around you who love you—Mom, Dad, Gran, Chas and me. Rowan had *you*," Greg insisted.

"No, we weren't—"

"You can bullshit yourself that it didn't mean anything, but he came alive around you. You softened him, made him open up, allowed him the freedom to explore friendships. When we first met, he was a cold, lonely man, but that's not the man he is around you. He's affectionate, funny, caring and honorable. And he thinks the sun rises and sets with you."

She didn't want to hear his words—couldn't. "You don't understand…"

"No, *you* don't understand," Chas said. "Jamie, he loves you. Any fool can see that. Greg and I have this idea that there aren't many people he trusts, even less he's prepared to open up to, but you made him take that chance. Deep down inside, that lost and lonely man wants a partner and a family, somewhere to belong— and he found that with you."

She stared at them, wanting to bat their words away,

make them disappear. But they just hung there, refusing to budge. Truth tended to do that.

Jamie wrapped her arms around her stomach and rocked forward, then back. "Oh, God, what have I done?"

"Screwed up," Greg bluntly told her. "And you've probably broken his heart."

Her brother had never been one to pull punches, but it was a fair observation.

"James, we can't protect ourselves against love. If we do, we dilute it, make it less than. We have to embrace it and trust the idea that it's better to have loved and lost than not loved at all," Chas told her. "You don't regret loving Kaden, do you?"

"No... I...crap."

"But I've been living with soul-eating guilt for more than five years, Greg. Guilt has been my faithful friend."

I have been, it has been...

She was talking in the past tense. Her guilt had, she realized, dissipated, loosened its cold grip on her heart. And—this was harder to admit—maybe part of her pushing Rowan away was her not wanting to let go of her guilt. But she'd paid her penance and maybe it was time to set herself free.

"Rowan helped me realize that Kaden's death was an accident, that we made mistakes, but it wasn't my fault he died," she said, her voice so low it was almost as if she was talking to herself.

"Of course it wasn't!" Greg told her, protective as always.

Chas's next question was accompanied by a soft smile. "So no regrets about Kaden, then? Can you let him go?"

Jamie nodded her head. "Yes, I think I can. I regret the place we were in when he died, but no, I don't regret loving him. I still do."

"And you always will," Chas told her. "But there's a good, honorable and smoking-hot man who wants you in his life. What are you going to do about that?"

"Get him back?" Jamie asked timidly. It was easy to say, hard to do. What if he didn't want to talk to her? What if he'd written her out of his life for good?

Greg stood up, looked at Chas and smiled. "Our work here is done."

Jamie followed him to her feet. "I need to go over to his place, try and talk to him. Where are my car keys, my phone?"

She didn't see the horrified looks Greg and Chas exchanged. "No, baby girl," Chas told her, taking her shoulders and giving her a quick shake. "You need to give him some time to cool off. And you need to sleep. Then you are going to shower, brush your teeth, wash your hair. Because, right now, you look like hell."

She couldn't be that bad. When she protested, Greg walked her over to the mirror in the hallway, and Jamie gasped at her puffy raccoon eyes and blotchy, green-tinged skin. "Ugh."

Greg pulled a face. "Quite."

When Jamie started to climb up the stairs, Greg's comment to Chas drifted up to her. "Seriously, babe, babysitting the kid is going to be super-easy after looking after her. She's exhausting."

"I heard that!" Jamie shouted, not looking back.

"You were supposed to," Chas replied cheekily.

Brothers: 1, Jamie: 0.

Fourteen

In his office, Rowan heard the buzz of his phone and looked down, cursing when he saw Greg's name and number flashing on his screen. He considered dodging the call, but this was Greg's fourth attempt, and Rowan couldn't keep avoiding him forever.

The man was not only Jamie's brother but also his architect. Now he knew, firsthand, why it was never a good idea to work with family.

Rowan answered the call, put Greg on speakerphone and leaned back in his chair. He'd had a raging headache since leaving Jamie's house last night and, although he'd been popping acetaminophen like sweets, the pain hadn't shifted. A couple of times throughout the day, he wondered whether it was his heart that was hurting and not his head.

Then he dismissed that thought as overemotional garbage and went back to work. Or tried to work. So far today, he'd accomplished less than nothing.

"Row, are you there?" Greg asked.

Hearing Jamie's nickname for him from Greg felt like a stake through his heart. "You can call me Rowan or Cowper. Don't shorten my name!"

"Stop being a dick, Rowan," Greg replied, his tone mild. Rowan felt instantly chastised. And embarrassed.

"Sorry," he muttered. "I'm in a shit mood."

"That's not surprising, since my sister is being an idiot," Greg replied. "Are you okay?"

Nobody had ever, ever called him up to check on his emotional state, to ask how he was doing, and Greg's kindness made his eyes burn. *Was* he okay? No. But he would be. Maybe in ten months or in ten years. Who the hell knew?

He wanted to lie, to tell Greg that he was perfectly fine, but couldn't force his tongue to form the words. "I will be, I guess. In a hundred years or so."

"Sooner than that, I wager." Before he could ask Greg what he meant by that cryptic statement, Greg spoke again. "Congrats on the baby, by the way. You're going to be a great dad, Rowan."

"How do you know that?" Rowan asked, his voice rough with emotion. "Jesus, Greg, the way I grew up, I wouldn't know what a good dad looked like if he bit me on the ass."

He heard Greg's long sigh. "Rowan, you're a good person, an honorable man. That's all you need to be a good dad. You'll be okay. I promise."

Rowan didn't think so. Yeah, sure, he'd get to meet his son or daughter in six months or so, but Jamie's absence would be a huge hole he'd never be able to be fill. But, damn, his kid was going to be a lucky little soul, having her as his mother, with excellent grandparents, a great-grandmother and two awesome uncles.

God, he missed Jamie.

In Nashville, whenever he'd started longing for her, he told himself that in a couple of days, he'd be back at her side, back in her bed. That life would be back to normal soon. But last night had been hell on steroids. He'd paced his large apartment, hating the white walls and the white furniture, feeling like he was locked up in an unpadded cell.

He'd woken up, alone in his bed, and decided that he hated his apartment. He didn't think he could spend another minute in it. His opinion hadn't changed. Tonight he'd either sleep on the couch in his office or book a hotel room. He wasn't going to spend another sleepless night in a pseudo-snowstorm.

"Rowan, are you still there?"

Rowan pulled himself back to the present and gripped the bridge of his nose with his thumb and index finger, trying to squeeze the pain away. He needed to distract himself, and that called for a change of subject.

"We need to meet. I have reams of notes about the design for the eco-development," Rowan told Greg. Then he hesitated, wondering if Greg still intended to work with him. "If you want to back out, now is the time."

Greg took a moment to reply. "I'm gonna pretend you didn't say that, Cowper. And, yeah, let's meet later this week. Why don't you come to our place? We can work and then eat."

He made a face. "I don't know if—"

"Oh, get over yourself, dude," Greg told him. "Jamie is our sister, but you're our friend too. And since you're our niece or nephew's dad, you're now family. I'll text you. Do not wuss out, or I will track you down."

On that threat, Greg disconnected, and Rowan leaned back in his chair once more, shaking his head. Greg and Chas were good people, and he was glad that they weren't choosing sides, that there was space for him in their lives.

He'd made a connection, not only to Jamie but also to her brother and his husband. He hadn't spent much time with her family, but he knew that, had things been different, they could've become his family too.

How could so much have changed in so short a time? What was it about her that just made sense? It was like she'd pushed her hand into his rib cage, grabbed his heart and wouldn't let go. She was beautiful, sure, but he'd known more attractive women. She wasn't perfect. She was stubborn and was as emotionally reserved as he was.

Independent—fiercely so.

But he didn't want perfection. He knew the world was messy. Life had its ups and downs. He wanted a woman who'd had her share of bumps and scrapes, someone who was resilient. He needed a woman in his life who didn't throw up her hands at the first obstacle.

He understood that hearing the baby was viable was a huge shock, an out-of-the-blue thunderbolt, but she hadn't given him a chance to be part of *her* life. Maybe now that she had the baby she so desperately wanted, she didn't need him. She was financially independent, not scared to make her own decisions and she had an excellent support system. What did she need from him? Sex?

She could buy a toy if she wanted to get off.

Screw that. He knew that no machine would come close to matching how he made Jamie feel in bed. He made her squirm and scream, took her to heights he knew were previously unexplored. He got her—in bed and out.

Sure, he wasn't outgoing and couldn't work a crowd like her ex did. He worked too hard, was too ambitious and could only tolerate a few hours at the society events her family attended on a routine basis. But she had a hold on his heart, and he loved her, dammit. He'd never felt this strongly about anyone before—ever—and he knew that, for as long as he lived, she would be the one he wanted to be with. It was that simple...

And that complicated.

He wasn't the type of guy to sit on his ass and accept what was handed to him. He made his luck, and he never admitted defeat. He'd fought for everything he had, established a multimillion dollar business against all the odds.

Jamie wanted to push him away? Well, he could push back too. He could bring his drive and determination to winning her love.

Rowan rubbed his face, feeling edgy and more than a little desperate. He knew what he had to do.

But he didn't have the smallest clue on *how* to accomplish his goal.

After Greg and Chas had ushered her up the staircase, Jamie, beyond exhausted, pulled her drapes closed and climbed back into bed. There was no way she'd sleep. Yet the moment her head hit her pillow, she drifted off and woke up eight hours later, feeling physically refreshed.

Her mind, unfortunately, was still a mess.

After checking the ultrasound photograph—yes, she was pregnant; it hadn't been a dream—she climbed into the shower and washed her hair, trying to process the events of the last twenty-four hours.

She was *pregnant*. The baby intended to stick around, and she was going to be a mom.

She was going to be a *mom*.

No, she was *already* a mom. She was carrying a baby, holding life.

Would her baby have her brown eyes or Rowan's blue? Her hair or his? Somehow, despite using protection and being careful, she and that amazing man had made a baby.

Their little person, determined as hell, had fought to be here. Jamie smiled. She already knew she had a warrior on her hands. And that was okay; she wanted a kid who challenged her and the status quo, a child who would make her a better mother, a better person.

Her child would be like Rowan in that way.

Rowan challenged her, made her better. He encouraged her to step outside her comfort zone; to live a fuller, more interesting life. He'd helped her come to terms with Kaden's death, and she was slowly trying to forgive herself for arguing with him that dreadful day.

Rowan had given her the one thing she thought she'd never have—a child to hold, guide and raise.

But she didn't want to do it on her own or co-parent at a distance. She wanted to wake up with Rowan, talk to him, spend the night making love.

She wanted him to know that she admired the hell out of him for pulling himself out of what had been an incredibly tough childhood to become a successful businessman, using his intelligence and wits.

After Jamie pulled on a pair of beige capri pants and a white T-shirt, she closed her eyes, cursing herself for her knee-jerk reaction yesterday. Love and good, honorable men didn't come along often. What was wrong with her? Instead of talking through the situation and her feelings, instead of trying to find a way forward, she'd made a unilateral decision for both of them, something she wouldn't have accepted if the shoe was on the other foot.

And it was even worse because Rowan had experienced a series of rejections in the past, and she'd added one more to the list.

She couldn't be more ashamed of herself if she tried.

Jamie couldn't look herself in the eye, so she turned away from the mirror and slipped her feet into a pair of sandals. Not only had she rejected him but she'd also spoiled his I'm-going-to-be-a-daddy moment.

Jamie felt overwhelming remorse and regret. She'd ruined a precious memory for him and had cheated him of feeling excited because she'd wanted to control the situation, because she'd been trying to protect herself.

She didn't know if their relationship could be salvaged, if there was any chance of finding their way back to each other. But she could, maybe, make up for yesterday.

She needed him to know she was sorry, and that she loved him. Loved him fully, utterly, with no qualifications.

He owned her heart. It was time he took charge of it.

Rowan knew he should eat, but he couldn't bear the thought. He was dog-tired, but knew he wouldn't sleep. His concentration was shot, so working wasn't an option. He glanced at his watch and saw that it was nearly half past five. He could go for a run. Maybe exercise would blow the cobwebs away.

He looked up when his PA knocked on his door, carrying a brown box and her bag over her shoulder.

She held up the brown box and walked into his office to place it on his desk. "Oh, this just arrived for you," Belle told him. "'Night."

Rowan stared at the plain box, his attention caught by the lack of shipping labels. The box didn't have his name on it, either, and that was weird. Leaning forward, he reached for it, pulled it to him and slowly lifted the lid.

The box was filled with blue and pink tissue paper, and he cocked his head to the side, intrigued. He couldn't remember when he'd last rustled through paper to find a gift. He carefully lifted each piece, folding it before tackling the next sheet. After folding four sheets, he looked into the box to see a tiny white pile of fabric, folded. He picked it up and lifted it to eye level and saw that it was a tiny onesie. He looked at the label—it was for a newborn baby. His heart jumped into his throat. He'd never realized babies could be that small.

Jamie must've sent this, but why? He turned it around, saw the black writing on what he now realized was the front of the onesie…

Hi Daddy,
Mommy told me you are awesome, and that you
are going to be the best dad ever. I can't wait to
meet you!

Rowan felt his eyes burning and his hands shaking, and he bit his bottom lip. There was something else in the box… He lifted out a simple wooden frame and immediately recognized Jamie's positive pregnancy test affixed to the backing underneath the words "You're Promoted!"

He stared down at the box, not sure what it meant, what he was supposed to do. Call her up and thank her? Hotfoot it over to her house, take her in his arms and kiss her until she couldn't breathe? Option number one was sensible, but option two was his favorite.

He tossed his gifts back into the box, pushed on the lid and reached for his phone and car keys. It would take fifteen minutes to reach her house. God, he hoped she was there. If not, he'd head over to Greg's house, then her parents...

"Going somewhere?"

He whirled around at the sound of her voice, and his knees buckled when he saw her standing in the doorway to his office, her shoulder resting against his doorframe. To a stranger, she'd look relaxed and cool, but he could see that her hands were shaking and immediately noticed the apprehension in her eyes.

"You're here," he stated.

She nodded. "Hey."

He waved her inside and tossed his keys and phone down next to the box. Not knowing what to do with his hands—he wanted to reach for her but couldn't—he jammed them into his pants pockets. They stared at each other, and Rowan wished she'd say something, but when she didn't, he nodded at the box. "Thanks. I...um..."

God, how could he explain how touched he was? How a brown box containing two simple gifts filled him with warmth and gratitude? "You didn't have to," he added gruffly.

She sat down in his visitor's chair and perched on the edge. "I really did. I spoiled what should've been a happy announcement. You deserved better than that, and I'm so sorry."

He leaned his butt against his desk, facing her. "Did you mean it? The words on that baby's garment?"

Her lips twitched. "The onesie? Yeah, I meant it. I've never been so sure of anything in my life."

He pushed his hand through his hair, feeling like he

had a golf ball stuck in his throat. "I don't know what to say…"

"Tell me you forgive me for being too much of a coward to tell you yesterday how I feel about you."

Jamie held her breath, watching the emotions fly across his face. For the first time, all his shields were down. She could see his confusion, his shock and the tiny flicker of hope.

"Thank you for our baby, Rowan."

"*Our* baby?" he croaked.

She nodded, suddenly feeling powerful and determined. He was her man. This was their baby and she wasn't leaving here without a) an understanding and b) him.

They were going to be together, raise this child and their other children together, in the same house, sharing their lives. She didn't care if they married or not, but they would be a team, sharing the good and the bad, the ups and the downs of a messy and imperfect life.

"I'm not sure what you want from me, James," Rowan said, his eyes not leaving hers. "I need you to spell it out, in plain language."

Okay, then. She crossed one leg over the other and linked her shaking fingers over her knee. "I am completely, utterly in love with you. I never wanted to be. I fought it, and I am still bone-deep petrified of loving you this much and losing you. But I'd rather be scared and living with you than not having you in my life at all."

He stared at her, his mouth slack with shock. Oh, God, had she gone too far? Had she scared him rigid? Was she asking too much?

She bit her lip before backtracking. "I know it's a lot to take in. And I know you're leery of commitment or being in a relationship, but we *have* been in a relationship these past two months, Row, whether we want to acknowledge it or not. We like each other. We get along well, and the sex is freakin' amazing. If you need some time to get used to the idea—"

"Shut up, James."

She jerked at his low command, confused by the harsh note in his voice.

"You love me?" he asked, his eyes laser-sharp.

She nodded.

He folded his arms, tipped his head to the side and the corners of his mouth lifted. "Okay, then."

Okay, then? What the hell did that mean? She waited for him to continue speaking, and when he didn't, she asked, "That's it? I spill my guts to you and that's your response?"

He slowly shook his head. "No, this is…"

Before she could form another thought, Jamie found herself in his arms, her breasts pushing into his chest, his mouth over hers and his tongue sliding past her teeth. God, she didn't think a man could move so fast or that she could be turned on so quickly. One kiss and she was pulling his shirt out of the waistband of his pants; her hands were on his skin and she was standing on her tiptoes, her mouth fused with his. Rowan groaned, picked her up, and she wound her legs around his hips, rocking against his shaft.

God, she wanted him. Here, now…

Immediately.

Carrying her across the room, Rowan slammed his office door shut, locked it and hit a button next to the door, turning the glass windows dark. Dropping her to her feet, he undid the button to her pants, pushed the fabric down her hips and slid his hand between her legs, causing her to whimper with delight. She opened his belt, undid his pants and pushed her hand inside his underwear, needing to feel him rock-hard in her hand.

When she pulled him free, Rowan picked her up again, rested her back against his office door and pushed inside her, filling her in one sure, hot stroke. Jamie dropped her head back against the door and panted, chasing that sexual high only he could give her.

This wasn't pretty sex, she decided. It was bumpy and fast and hot and sweaty, but it was real and it was theirs—their moment, their life. And when they came together, furious and fast, she knew it was a new start, the birth of a new life.

Minutes later, Rowan rested his head against her forehead and closed his eyes. "Holy crap, sweetheart. That was…intense."

She ran a hand through his hair, held his strong neck in her hand. "If that's going to be your response every time I tell you how I feel, I'll do it all the time."

She couldn't help remembering that she still didn't know how he felt about her. But she wouldn't demand to know. Love not freely given wasn't love at all. She touched his cheek, reached up to gently kiss his mouth. "Are we good?" she asked.

"So good, sweetheart," he told her, resting his cheek against hers. He allowed her to slide down his body and cuddled her close. "No, we are amazing. Let's get cleaned up and then make some plans," he suggested, his big hand stroking her back.

Plans? That sounded like progress.

Dressed again, Rowan handed Jamie a bottle of water and led her over to his leather couch. He pushed her down into the plush cushions before dragging the coffee table sideways and sitting down on it, facing her. He pulled her water bottle out of her grasp, cracked it open and handed it back to her before opening his own bottle and downing half the liquid in one long swallow.

She sipped, her mouth suddenly closing. He looked so serious, like he had a lot on his mind and didn't know where to start. She got it: this was a big deal for him, and she shouldn't rush him. But she was dying here!

"I—"

Rowan shook his head. "My turn to talk."

She wanted to yell at him to start doing just that, but she gathered the little patience she had and tucked her now-bare feet up under her butt.

"I love you, you know. So much."

She looked at him—saw the emotion in his eyes, on his face—and placed her hand on her heart. Such a simple statement but so powerful. And it was all she needed. Just knowing that he loved her meant that nothing was insurmountable. They were a team. Each a half of a whole.

"I'm glad," she replied, just as simply.

He put his water bottle on the coffee table next to him and leaned his forearms on his knees, his eyes on hers. "I didn't want to love you, and I thought I could resist you. I thought I wanted a solitary, shallow life, but you changed all that."

"By getting pregnant?"

He shook his head. "No. I would've fallen for you baby or no baby—I probably was in love with you from the moment we met. I think you are what I need, the one person I was looking for."

Jamie sighed, overcome by a rush of emotion. His love wasn't linked to her carrying his child. That was such a relief because their love was based on who they were to each other.

"I'm so happy to hear that," Jamie told him. "I've been living in a vacuum since Kaden died, but you brought me back, Row. I don't think anyone but you could've done that."

He leaned forward and kissed her softly, gently—an I-can't-wait-for-what-comes-next kiss.

Pulling back, he nodded at the box still sitting on his desk. "Why did you send me those things?"

She smiled. "I felt bad because I spoiled the moment. I told you I was pregnant and immediately insisted you shouldn't get excited because I'd lose the baby. Then, when I found out our baby was healthy, I spoiled that moment too. I hoped the small gifts made up for that, just a little."

He shook his head. "They aren't small to me. Did you mean it?"

She knew exactly what he was asking: Did she mean what was written on the onesie? "Absolutely. You're such a good man, Rowan. I'm proud of what you've done with your life, how you've battled the odds and won. I intend to make damn sure that our kids know how awesome their dad is."

"'Kids'?" Rowan asked, cocking his head. "More than one?"

She grinned. "Oh, hell yes." She tapped her stomach. "This little person is going to need company. Are you okay with that?"

He looked a little bemused and shell-shocked, but he nodded. "Yeah."

She patted his knee, laughing at the hint of fear she saw in his eyes. "After two, we'll consider another. Deal?"

He smiled. "Deal. But only if you marry me."

It was her turn to feel blindsided. "Marriage?" she squeaked. "Seriously?"

"Mmm," he murmured, his eyes full of laughter.

"But you don't *want* to get married."

"I want to marry *you*. I want to call you my wife, be your husband, do this properly."

Well, all right, then. She released her breath and tried to get the world to stop spinning. At best, she'd hoped that Rowan would move in.

"There are benefits to getting married that you haven't thought about," Rowan told her, linking his fingers in hers. "Your mother will never worry about your love life again."

"True enough. But marrying me means taking on my family, Row. I love them and they are a big part of my life."

"I like your family, and I'm already good friends with Greg and Chas. Greg called me yesterday to check up on me. I appreciate that. Luckily, I can afford to let your grandmother fleece me at poker, and your dad can teach me golf." He looked down, scratched his forehead. "I need a family, James. I need you and the family we'll create."

He was right—he did. And she needed him. To love her, to cherish her, to be her lover and her friend, her partner as they tried to win at life.

"Well?" Rowan asked her, the small smile on his face suggesting he already knew her answer. "Will you be my first and last love?"

Her heart sighed, then sighed again as joy slid through her veins. "Absolutely. In this lifetime. And the next."

* * * * *

COMING SOON!

We really hope you enjoyed reading this book. If you're looking for more romance, be sure to head to the shops when new books are available on

Thursday 4th August

To see which titles are coming soon, please visit

millsandboon.co.uk/nextmonth

MILLS & BOON

THE HEART OF ROMANCE

A ROMANCE FOR EVERY READER

MODERN

Prepare to be swept off your feet by sophisticated, sexy and seductive heroes, in some of the world's most glamourous and romantic locations, where power and passion collide.

HISTORICAL

Escape with historical heroes from time gone by. Whether your passion is for wicked Regency Rakes, muscled Vikings or rugged Highlanders, awaken the romance of the past.

MEDICAL

Set your pulse racing with dedicated, delectable doctors in the high-pressure world of medicine, where emotions run high and passion, comfort and love are the best medicine.

True Love

Celebrate true love with tender stories of heartfelt romance, from the rush of falling in love to the joy a new baby can bring, and a focus on the emotional heart of a relationship.

Desire

Indulge in secrets and scandal, intense drama and plenty of sizzling hot action with powerful and passionate heroes who have it all: wealth, status, good looks…everything but the right woman.

HEROES

Experience all the excitement of a gripping thriller, with an intense romance at its heart. Resourceful, true-to-life women and strong, fearless men face danger and desire - a killer combination!

To see which titles are coming soon, please visit

millsandboon.co.uk/nextmonth

LET'S TALK
Romance

For exclusive extracts, competitions
and special offers, find us online:

f facebook.com/millsandboon

🐦 @MillsandBoon

📷 @MillsandBoonUK

Get in touch on 01413 063232

For all the latest titles coming soon, visit
millsandboon.co.uk/nextmonth